FALSE GRITS

The Strange Case of George C. Murfrey the Third

By Tom Berry

To ACW for inspiring me to write the book,
To Carol Adams and Maureen Thomas for their help
And to John Powell who came up with the title

AUTHOR'S NOTE

This book had its beginning as a lark! I would read excerpts of it to my writer's group that met on Sunday afternoons, enthralled with the twitters of mirth and the scowls of disdain as my meager audience enjoyed or endured those readings aloud.

After reflecting upon finishing <u>False Grits,</u> I realized that for us who have deep discernment, this is a book of life, not just to entertain or to bring forth disgust, whichever the case may be, but to enlighten!

It is my hope that those who peruse the pages of <u>False Grits</u> will reach that same conclusion by diving through the often dirty murky waters of life finding that elusive pearl of wisdom hidden beneath.

TABLE OF CONTENTS

Contents

PROLOGUE

Historians report that the Korean Conflict, which began June of 1950, just after graduation, leaving a new crop of high school and college students in the United States wondering what they would do that summer; the answer came with the call up from the draft into the Army. Some wanted to serve and volunteered.

In 1951, after the conflict had seen Seoul, Korea captured twice by the North Koreans and North Korea invaded by UN and South Korean forces, the generals and politicians decided to talk this bloody war over; maybe reach a truce

On October 25, 1951 these generals and politicians met in Kaesong, North Korea, but the discussions were soon changed to an obscure village called Panmunjom; a site both sides could suffer with.

Meanwhile the war raged on.

While the fighting continued up and down hills designated by numbers, but later known by the names the troops gave them, the negotiations went on and on. No one could agree on anything. The negotiating sides could not agree on the size of the table, the number of chairs and where each side would sit.

This took time.

And while fighting men lost their lives, the generals and politicians fought their own battles. These were serious disagreements which tried the very soul of these patient battle hardened negotiators. It came down to who got the real estate known as 'Heartbreak Hill'. UN forces, which included Americans, fought their way up the hill getting their asses shot up as they valiantly took the hill.

Then it was the North Korean's turn to take the lead while climbing up that lethal hill. They had to overcome the rain of bullets poured out from American rifles, machine guns and exploding grenades that came rolling down upon them. The avalanche of destruction did not stop the determined North Koreans, who pushed the Americans off the hill occupying it once more.

This did not sit well with the American officers, who had the unpleasant task of sitting across from the joyous and smug North

Koreans, making no effort to hide it from their usually grim noncommittal faces.

Immediately, the American combat troops were sent word from the negotiating generals to retake that important dirt hill at all cost. They received blistering words from their Commander, General Matthew Ridgeway, who they called "Old Iron Tits' behind his back because he wore two live hand grenades on the front of his uniform which hung down like drooping tits.

Old Iron tits sent the word out: "How in hell can we negotiate a peace treaty if we keep letting those gooks take away our hard fought land? Take that damn hill and keep it!! We negotiate from strength; not weakness. Hold that damn hill!"

After that inspirational message, hold it, they did. At least until the Chinese stuck their yellow noses into it and with the most tinny sounding bugles giving music a bad name, wave after wave of Chinese soldiers died trying to make it up that blood soaked hill as they slipped and slide on their comrades bright red blood.

Still, the heat of battle continued with each side claiming glorious victory.

This numerical location, Hill 851, claimed the dubious distinction of being the most costly in the history of the World

Month after month, at the end of each day, each negotiator would leave the large tent at Panmunjom, in total frustration.

Something had to be done to end this war.

An atom bomb was out of the question; General McArthur had been fired when he insisted on going back into North Korea.

What the Americans needed was some kind of secret weapon that could bring this crazy conflict to termination. Already 55,000 American soldiers had lost their lives and countless others- their body parts. The VA hospitals and the cemeteries were filled to capacity.

The military think tank at the Pentagon was burning the midnight lights in an effort to come up with a solution to the problem.

"How about germ warfare; anthrax for instance?" was Colonel James Bernard's suggestion. This was quickly vetoed.

"It can't be controlled on the battlefield. Our own troops might be wiped out. The American public would never stand for that," commented Major Issac Whipple in his soft high soprano voice.

"Well then, how about poison gas?" was another halfhearted suggestion that never made it out of the canisters?

The mention of poison gas rang a bell. A bright young Lt. Alan Benson whose daddy, Senator Bryce Benson, had just gotten the nineteen year old graduate from Virginia Military Institute posted to the Pentagon instead of the front lines in Korea had an idea he could not contain.

"I remember a soldier who I heard about when I was stationed at Camp Pendleton. Her name was Fannie Mae McBride, but reverently known by the other soldiers as 'Big Fanny'."

The civilian liaison advisor shook his head looking in disbelief at this wet behind the ears shave tail-- like he didn't have all that was coming to him.

He exclaimed loudly, "Who in God's green earth is "Big Fanny'? I can't wait to hear this cockamamie story." He added, "I am sure the President would like to hear it also." He added drily, "He likes a good story. You know it lightens his day."

The Military officers glared at the shave tail and then at the civilian, Peter Poteet, whom they disliked, turning their attention back to a now red faced Second Lieutenant who didn't have enough sense to keep his mouth shut. As the second hand on the wall clock clicked loudly in the stillness, they awaited his reply.

After Major Mike Carlton began tapping the "war table" rather loudly with his unused pencil much like he did when he was once a third grade teacher, young Benson summoned the courage to speak.

Clearing his throat, Benson said, "The story goes like this: Fannie Mae McBride traveled all the way from Leslie, Arkansas aboard a Trailways bus to Fort Sill, Oklahoma to enlist in the United States Army. The recruiter turned her away because she was badly overweight, tipping the scales at 357 pounds. Besides that, the recruiter wrote in his notes, that she had an overwhelming body odor which he noted when he was downwind from her."

Benson paused smiling boyishly.

"A little humor by the recruiter in his notes," he continued. "Well according to the only witness who survived, 'Big Fanny' turned red in the face, then purple and just let out a long lingering 'FART'!"

"Did I hear you right Lieutenant? She passed gas?" asked Colonel Bernard incredulously.

"That's the story I got while I was in Special Forces before being transferred here. I personally interviewed enlistee Donald 'White Cloud' Snodgrass a Cherokee from Talleahquah, Oklahoma. He was the only survivor except for Big Fanny, that is. You probably saw the account in the news recently about the recruiter and two enlistees who died of unknown causes that day."

"Snodgrass only survived because he was in the progress of stepping outside to get some fresh air due to the terrific body odor of Big Fanny. I quote to you in his own words: 'She smelled like she had had nine days of sex without bathing and then had fallen into a septic tank.' end of quote."

Peter Poteet, the civilian, exclaimed excitedly, "Good golly, Miss Molly, I have never heard of such a thing. Go on. Go on!"

The military men turned and glared at Poteet again-- this time with greater hostility.

"Snodgrass reported that she flatter blasted, whatever that means. He estimated it lasted about three minutes. An exaggeration, I am sure, but nevertheless a record." Benson let that sink in.

"Anyhow, when the fumes had cleared, Big Fanny was nowhere to be found. It took the FBI to track her down. They found her in the little town of Leslie, Arkansas on Ira P. Shootinque's pig farm. Being forewarned of her potency, when they found her out in the hog pen shouting, 'Sooeee!' they approached with caution and spoke in soothing tones."

"'Yes indeed, Miss Fannie, it was a mistake', they assured her. 'You can certainly join the Army.' They waved a paper in front of her and said, 'See here. They have already processed your paper work.'"

"They suggested that she bathe so she went down to the creek and jumped in. After she changed clothes, she was transported to the enlistment center in Little Rock where she was sworn in. They even had an oversized uniform ready for her." Benson stopped a few seconds and then said, "Oh yes, the FBI agent in his report jotted down that at the time they had the confrontation in the pig yard, there were 8 to 10 scraggly hound dogs hanging around. As Big Fanny approached them, one yellow dog called Old Lick got up quietly and slinked off with his tail between his legs. The other dogs were not as astute. When she got close to the dogs, they got a whiff of her, running off yelping wildly." Benson who now had the undivided attention of the group, beamed broadly. He said, "There is more. In the words of the FBI agent, 'Even the dogs refused to sniff Big Fanny'"*

He looked over and saw Poteet writing it all down furiously.

"I have copies of the reports," said Benson as he began to pass them out.

"Is there more?" asked Major Whipple exasperateratingly obvious that this subject offended his delicate sensibilities.

"Yes Sir. It's in the reports."

"Well you are quite a story teller so why don't you finish," said Whipple with a sigh." We can read the dry reports later."

"Big Fanny became Private McBride in spite of her overweight problem. Her individual trainers used kerosene soaked cotton balls stuffed in their nostrils and treated her with obsequious respect. Not because she smelled bad even after bathing, but because she was considered a lethal weapon. Her trainers kept gas masks handy and believe you me, they donned them if she as much as let out a squeaker." He pointed to the notes handed out and said, "In the reports, you will note, on one occasion she 'flatter blasted, as on that fateful day in Oklahoma, the alert trainers all making it out of the building safely. They made no beans about leaving Big Fanny alone until the air cleared."

"At the present, Private McBride is undergoing medical testing to see what makes her flatulence so deadly. One of her doctors, a Dr. Alphonse Aholie, a doctor about my age from India wants to do exploratory surgery. He joined our Army to get U.S. citizenship. I understand he is considered a genius."

12

After a short break in which the staff huddled with the exception of Peter Poteet and Lt. Benson, the group took their places at the war table. Colonel James Bernard rose up from his seat and firmly stated, "Well done Lt. Benson. It has been agreed, that you should be transferred back to Special Forces in Washington, D.C. and from there you will take charge of this lethal weapon at once." Bernard spoke slowly, "Do Not Let that Indian doctor do surgery on Private McBride. We have an idea where we can put Private Mc Bride, who wants to serve her country."

The Orders were cut giving Lt. Alan Benson his first real assignment. As soon as he could be ready, both were to be deployed to Korea.

The top secret mission known only by the few was called "Mission Rectum."

The Special Forces knew what they had. All they had to was to contain her. She went through rigorous training which included having to bathe at least five times a day. Experiments were made that lasted several weeks to find a perfume, which matched Fannie's chemistry, satisfactorily cloaking her still lingering odor.

From the scientific department of Redstone Laboratories, one of the scientists had been experimenting with a substance that was to be given cattle which would curtail the amount of methane gas they emitted in to the air. Many learned scientists blamed all that methane gas being passed into the atmosphere to be the cause of global warming. Nothing was said about the contribution humans made. They developed a large purple pill which seemed to work on lab cows.

When Lt. Benson learned of this breakthrough, he ordered a smaller pill which would be given Big Fanny.

It worked.

She was able to control her emissions not posing a danger to her own troops.

After this enormous breakthrough, orders were cut sending Lt. Benson and Private Fannie Mae McBride to Panmunjom, Korea. Benson was given a sealed envelope marked Top Secret which was to be opened upon arrival in Panmunjom.

Prior to leaving for their top secret destination, a final test was given to Private McBride. She was taken off the purple pill and fed a large heaping of red beans and rice. Then she was placed in a room with only a bevy of little animals for companions. She was urged to break wind and await the results.

She did her best, straining at the so called bit.

The test was an immense success.

Not one of her companions survived.

It was mid June 1953 when the deadly duo arrived. Talks were still going on to no avail. Everyone was grim faced and exhausted. Any fears that Benson had that they might settle before Big Fanny had a chance to do her patriotic thing, quickly vanished when he saw his superiors leaving the large tent where the negotiations were taking place, nodding theirs heads in disbelief that the North Koreans could be so petty and hard headed.

The next day, Lt. Benson and his aide showed up to take the place of one of the American negotiators, Colonel Ventura, who had suddenly come down with a virus. This morning the North Koreans refused to discuss a truce unless they were allowed to get the pitcher of water first. The Americans politely asked if they could leave the tent to consider this request.

It was a clear crisp cool spring like day. At the present the canvas flaps on the side of the huge tent were all down. Later after it warmed up they would be rolled up. Only the entrance was open to the tent.

When the American officers got up to leave the tent, Lt. Benson followed; Private McBride being left standing behind like some dumb Do-Do bird.

A wry smile of satisfaction spread across the faces of the North Koreans. One of the North Korean Generals, smiling, turned to the General on his right saying loudly, "Looks like our strategy is working. The Americans lack our patience. I think they are ready to capitulate."

General Hui Pong Jong, who had been educated at U.C.L.A., looked around. Spotting Big Fanny, he said, "Watch what you say. They may have left a spy." He then nodded toward Big Fanny who walked over to the entrance and seemed to be looking at something outside.

Another general in an exuberant mood laughed and said, "Who? That porker! Look at her. She is too stupid to be a spy."

As they all broke out in loud laughter, another General, between laughs, stated, "That is the poorest excuse for a soldier I have ever seen. She is an insult to all of us."

Big Fanny walked from the entrance to the great table facing the Generals with a vacant look, turned around bending over cutting loose with her best flatter-blaster, ever. It lasted a good one and a half minutes, the noxious spray like a fog creeping over the generals before they knew what hit them.

Big Fanny then proudly marched out of the tent stopping only to gently close the entrance door behind her.

Her handler, Lt. Benson, was waiting in front. He asked, "Mission Rectum accomplished?"

"I recken so," said the smiling private who now spit out a plug of chewing tobaccy as if it was something nasty.

The next day, July 10th, another nice day, was still cool, but the wind had picked up blowing any remnants of the polluted air out the now opened side flaps of the tent. Lt. Benson and Private McBride were not present when the Americans took their place at the table. Colonel Ventura, now recovered from his virus, remarked, "We really need to do something about the sewerage system around here. I believe we are downwind from it today."

Another officer drolly said, "That so. I never noticed it before today."

After a thirty minute wait, a North Korean General, they had never seen before walked in stiffly and announced that the terms heretofore proposed by the United Nations were now accepted by the Republic of Korea. The paper work was being drawn up.

That was it. On July 27th the cease fire agreed upon, was signed by all sides. The Conflict ended.

The Lieutenant and his aide flew back to the states.

"If you ain't got no more missions for me, Laytenant Ben-son, I would kinda like to go home." Fannie Mae said.

"Let me see what I can do. I think I can get you into the inactive reserves. That way you won't have to attend those meetings. This reminds me you need to keep taking those purple pills. The Army will send you some every month."

Private Fannie Mae McBride was mustered out of the Army, an unsung heroine, with an Honorable Discharge. Later the Medal of Honor was mailed to her after the President heard all about her part in ending the Korean conflict. The North Korean Generals affected were never seen or heard of again.

Years later, when the Army sent its representative to Leslie, Arkansas to call up Corporal McBride (she had been promoted) for a new secret mission (something to do with a Saddam Huesein); they learned that Fannie Mae McBride had met with an untimely death. She had gone up on Nubbin Ridge to pick flowers when a herd of wild razorback hogs, peculiar to her home state of Arkansas, resented her invasion of their territory. They charged her with their sharp tusks sniffing wildly literally forcing her over the ridge onto the jagged rocks below.

Alan Benson, now Lt. Colonel Benson persuaded Washington to move Big Fanny's body to Arlington Cemetery.

They dug her up and at her second funeral, she received a twenty-one gun salute reserved for heroes. As the Marines decked out in their bright uniforms shouldered their rifles, Lt. Colonel Benson laid a wreath at her headstone. It read: "Private Fannie Mae McBride, Medal of Honor-Korean Conflict".

She was buried next to the Unknown Soldier; a sad ending for such a patriotic soldier whose exploits has been kept secret to this very day!

CHAPTER ONE

The Portent Birth

The sparkling waters of the Gulf of Mexico shine like polished diamonds when the water is calm; a flat rock can almost be skipped to Cat Island four miles south of Gulfport, Mississippi, but all this serenity changes when the wind blows hard causing the waves to mount up into white caps boiling caused by a sudden squall, making sunbathers, soaking up the sun on brightly colored beach towels, run from the blinding, stinging sand whipped up by the angry storm.

The scene of sailboats in bright array racing in regattas; yachts, cabin cruisers and open faced motor boats all going somewhere interrupted by violent clashes of lightning and bomb-like explosions of thunder, head quickly for safety of the yacht harbor.

So it was that this seemingly carefree environment was further challenged when after nine hours of hard labor by his mother, little baby George Cedric Murfrey the Third made his extraordinary entrance into this world with promise to leave a memorable effect on those lives he would touch.

Like the calm gentle sparkling waters that lap the shores of the Mississippi Gulf Coast that can suddenly boil into turmoil, so it was when little baby Murfrey made his extraordinary entrance into the delivery room at Memorial Hospital at Gulfport.

There had been a shortage of nurses when the call came for registered Nurse Mary Ann Cranston to come out of retirement from five years of bliss being persuaded to "help out." She was a wee bit rusty, up in age and it had been many years since she had worked in Maternity. She was nervous! All her reasons for retiring in the first place came crashing back, her wrinkled face showing her worry.

"Doctor Morse!" she called out in a shrill voice, "he is not breathing!" Moments earlier, Nurse Cranston had been handed the still baby while the young handsome dark haired physician turned his immediate attention to the ripe firm breasts of Nurse Beth Allen. After the little fat baby had been pulled out of the cavernous womb of this morbidly obese thirty-five yea old mother, the doctor must have thought his job was over. What was she supposed to do now?

She was new to the delivery room procedures having never worked in one in the past nor with this young doctor since coming out of retirement.

Did he expect her to read his mind?

Dr. Morse was also out of his comfort zone. He generally delivered babies at Garden Park, a private hospital, where competent knowing nurses took over, after he did his skillful part of delivering children. Disturbed by the frantic cries of Nurse Cranston, the arched eyebrows and hungry eyes formerly focused on Beth Allen, quickly snapped over to the source of this unwarranted intrusion.

The loud mouthed nurse had not wiped the baby off, nor had she cleaned out his nose. But Dr. Morse calmly, with suppressed irritation speaking slowly and distinctly through his clenched teeth said, "Nurse just slap him on his fat little ass." Then he added, "And clean him up.!"

"I did! I did!" cried Cranston and for good measure gave this uncooperative new born a good whop, but without success.

"I think you had better come over here doctor, if you don't want a dead baby on your hands," the nurse said in a low determined voice which was almost a growl. Now with an increased worried look on her face, she asked herself. "Why didn't I stay retired?"

Dr. Morse shrugged his young shoulders in exasperation, telling the object of his attention, Nurse Allen, now nervously running her fingers through her bleached blonde hair, "Hold on a minute. I have something important to tell you."

Seeing the obstetrician flash his winning smile, giving Nurse Allen one last ogle, Nurse Cranston hit the panic button and screamed, "Hurry doctor! You better hurry doctor! This child is dying!" Then to emphasize the urgency, she screamed at the top of her coarse voice, "We are going to lose this one!"

All this commotion woke up the baby's mother, still in her stirrups, delivering the afterbirth onto the shiny tiled floor. After the one gigantic

18

push the mother had fallen back into blessed sleep, snoring peacefully again.

"Wha, What?" said Agnes Murfrey whose nine hour ordeal had ended when big baby Murfrey finally slid out of her largemouth womb. Even though her feet were still fastened to the stirrup and the gates to hell wide open, she did not seem to mind, now that the intense pain, racking her body, was gone. She had done her part; now snoring even louder in an effort to drown out the yelling and vociferous screaming taking place. She did not hear the doctor say "Go back to sleep, Agnes!"

Dr. Morse slipped his green surgical mask over his nose and swiftly grabbed the baby from Nurse Cranston, who was just standing there like awkwardly. Then he noticed that the umbilical cord had not been severed. "It's alright," he nervously chuckled trying to act unconcerned. "The life line is still connected."

Against his better judgment, Dr. David Morse had taken on Mrs. Agnes Murfrey as a patient. She was a large repulsive heavy set woman with a big flat nose and bushy eyebrows; unlike his bevy of svelte good looking high class patients who had the money to pay his high fees. It had been a surprise when Agnes came up with his exorbitant fee. She had turned his head when she said, "I came to you Dr. Morse, because I heard you were the best."

Unlike his other patients, who under his stern instructions, kept their weight down during pregnancy, Mrs. Murfrey's weight went up. And where was this lady's husband? She did not list one on her information sheet. Probably never had one!

Morse had his receptionist schedule Agnes' office visits at 3:00 p.m. or later so she would be his last patient of the day. He did not want her seen by the other high class ladies. She was directed to park her long black 1939 LaSalle in the rear of his office and to use the back door to enter the office. No waiting room for Agnes. No. She was put in one of the spare rooms in the back to cool her heels. It never occurred to Dr. Morse that the reason he disliked fat pregnant women was because it required more effort on his part or perhaps because they were unappealing to the eye or maybe because it had been drilled into him in med school that obesity was an unhealthy disease unto itself, nor did it ever occur to Agnes that her obesity was a problem for Dr. Morse or for her husband who suddenly left for parts unknown without explanation,

Somehow, Mrs. Murfrey had heard about the State of Mississippi providing free hospitalization to those birth mothers who qualified.

She qualified.

So MHG the public hospital was chosen and now he had to deal with this incompetent nurse who dared to raise her voice to him. This would not have happened at Garden Park.

There was one consolation. Nurse Beth Allen was a fox! And she was responding to his make-out attention. His keen sense of smell picked up the scent of this sexually excited woman letting him know she was ready.

He had never lost a baby and he was not about to start now. Delivering babies was like serving food in restaurants. One bad meal and the word would get out. This was not going to happen and neither would this blonde bombshell who had fallen into his lap, suffer neglect either. What a body!

He turned his attention to this upstart butterball. While showing this baby who was boss, he would at the same time impress Beth with his skills and prowess.

Another challenge-another victory!

He would not let this baby who probably would never know who his daddy was, get the best of him.

Although his office was constantly filled with young high society ladies with great bodies, some even making a pass at him, Dr. Morse made it a rule never to cross the line. They could expect exaggerated compliments about their pulchritudinous bodies and an inappropriate hug or two. That was as far as it went. It made no difference that a few even professed their love for him.

A lesson was learned when pretty boy ex-doctor Joe Little, gynecologist was caught screwing his patients, consequently sued by irate husbands and finally run out of Gulfport.

Dr. Morse had two rules: No screwing the patients and no fraternization with the employees.

Nailing the young pretty nurses, provided by the hospitals, which seemed to stand in line for his favors, was sufficient unto itself. Word of his prowess had gotten out among the nursing staff in both hospitals and they could not wait to try him on. For some strange reason, during a delivery, his testosterone increased to which the young nurses responded. His sexy smile, a conjugal embrace, revealing his potent readiness, was usually all that was needed.

Today, it was the heaving pear shaped breasts and that minute body scent that told him she was available and ready. Little did Beth know he had been busy during the nine hour ordeal that Agnes Murfrey had been experiencing prior to delivery? This was a record setting day. After securing a private room, in which to rest while waiting for the birth pains to indicate Agnes was ready, the nurses over at MHG literally lined up to knock on his door asking if there was anything they could do to make him more comfortable. Dr. Morse had no desire to perform a caesarian operation on this extremely obese woman with those heavy layers of fat hanging on her, so he waited, enjoying the perks that came his way,

On this memorable day, at Memorial Hospital eight nurses had entered his room and eight left with smiles on their faces while adjusting their uniforms. As soon as the obstacle, baby Murfrey presented, was overcome, it was only fitting that the gorgeous Nurse Allen would be the one to break his record that should hold up for many years to come.

First, he must work his magic. He must get this reluctant piglet to breathe, yell and cry. No doubt the nine hours of hard labor had also taken its toll on the infant. Still in stirrups, the mother had raised the crescendo; snorting and snoring louder than he had ever heard, making it difficult to romance a young maiden with all that cacophony of irritating sounds, but with rising testosterone, he was sure he was up to it.

"Attention everyone!" shouted the doctor over the crescendo like a barker in a circus. "Don't leave yet! Behold, I have a new born baby who doesn't want to cooperate. Well now, I have an answer for that! I will demonstrate a technique that will bring forth the spark of life--a technique that will introduce this cute little fat baby into our world, who has had it so good for nine long months. Now it is time for him to join the rest of us."

With a deftness of a skilled surgeon, he cut the umbilical cord, clamped it off, cradling the baby waltzing in long exaggerated strides over to a long table covered with a sterile sheet, laying little Murfrey on his tummy, quickly moving faster than the eye could see, he back handed the buttocks of the child, while gently pressuring the lower back and mid-section.

His captive audience watched intently.

He looked down to admire the results of his expertise, but to his surprise instead of a yell, scream or loud cry, all he heard was a large whomp, a loud woosh which came from the baby's behind. This was accompanied by a brown cloud of noxious smelling gas encased in a bubble; the bubble popping, quickly hitting him in the face, spreading across the entire delivery room to his audience of two nurses, who sniffing the foul smelling gas, quickly spilled out into the hall, to the dismay of two other nurses at their station, guarding the delivery room from any intruders.

Dr. Morse stood there stunned with a patch of brown stain around the nose area on his surgical mask; a stark reminder of divine intervention.

His patient, Agnes Murfrey awakened, seeing the baby, uttering, "That's my baby."

And little Murfrey, instead of crying, yelling or screaming, just lay there giggling.

Was the smile on baby Murfrey's face real or just a grimace from gas?

Never-the-less, little Murfrey baby was making his mark in the world!

When the two nurses hastily left the delivery room, they hit the double swinging doors so hard that the doors failed to swing back and close, allowing the guests and expectant father's in the waiting room, only fifty feet away, to crane their necks in an effort to see the cause of the nurses' sudden departure as if the devil was after them. Dr. Morse could see Nurse Cranston crouched down trying to avoid observation.

Nurse Beth Allen had fled to the Woman's Room to take stock of her appearance.

"Nurse Cranston! Nurse Cranston," hollowed Dr. Morse loudly. "Git yore self back in here!" He seemed to have lost his polished debonair accent.

"I need yore hep to tie this here umbilical cord!"

Nurse Cranston was in the process of relating the unusual birth happening to the station nurse, but most of her dialogue was about the doctor ogling and hitting on Nurse Allen.

She was saying, "The hospital shouldn't hire these good looking sexy young women as nurses. They are a distraction. This doctor goes too far. I hope God strikes him down for his wicked behavior."

"What did he do?' asked the station nurse.

"It's what he had in mind to do," replied Cranston. "Oh hell, let me see what he wants and get this over with."

The 64 year old, grey haired spinster was a straight laced devout Southern Baptist from Carriere, Mississippi. She did not stand for any hanky-panky, as she called it, unless it was another Baptist doing it. In that case, she reasoned, there was still hope and the influence of the church would correct it.

She straightened up her heavily starched uniform, marching back into the devil's den, finding it as she left it. Mrs. Agnes Murfrey still in stirrups was snoring blissfully. Her enlarged womb was still open, the afterbirth delivered during the crises, still lying on the polished green floor, the baby on the padded table by the wall still covered with blood, but to her relief, very much alive. The doctor was fiddling with the long umbilical cord that was clamped off.

He looked up, glaring at the nurse, who seemed uncertain as to what she should do next.

"Git over here! I need yore help, nurse," Morse said through his lips tightly pressed over pearly teeth, trying to get control of his self.

"Here, hold this runt while I tie off the cord." he said; then seeing the doors wide open and several curious people gathered around looking in, "and first shut those damn doors!"

Jolted by the stern command, nurse Cranston sprang into action: she shut the doors in the onlookers' faces; covering Agnes with a sheet, sponging off the baby without breaking stride. With the child in her arms, she waited for Dr. Morse to perform his famous trademark belly button knot which she had heard through the grape vine; now she was going to get too see it firsthand.

While Dr, Morse was fidgeting with the cord, Cranston got a large whiff of the lingering foul odor. She said, "Just a moment doctor" handing the large baby back to the doctor.

She then went over to the thermostat and kicked the temperature down several degrees and the air conditioner began to clear the air of the cloud of smelly stuff from the room. She went over to a drawer, slipping on a new blue pair of rubber gloves. In another drawer, she got a fresh surgical mask and walked back to the doctor.

"Let me put this new mask on you doctor," she said as she untied the one that had a large brown spot on it in the nose area.

"I ought to write you up for leaving your post and your patients."

"I understand," said Cranston. "And while you are about it, I will write up Nurse Allen who seems to have run off. I certainly did not give her permission. Did you?" When the doctor did not respond, she added' "I hope she is okay. Maybe I had better go look for her, don't you think?"

"Stay right where you are, nurse. After thinking it over, there will be no write-ups. This was an unusual birth to say the least. Let's get this done, clean up both patients, get them to their rooms and I will go find Nurse Allen and deal with her.

"I bet you will'" muttered Cranston under her breath.

"What's that?"

"I said, I bet she is alright."

"Fine. Hand me those shears. I have finished. Baby Murfrey now has a belly button."

Nurse Cranston peered down at the special belly button, she had heard so much about. It was Dr. Morse's secret trademark of which he was proud, as were the children who later in life showed them off. Those were sexy navels displayed proudly by teenage girls. Even other doctors who later treated those special belly button children would remark as they examined them, "I bet I know who delivered you." These signature navels, as he called them, were his permanent mark, on the children he delivered.

But not this time! This belly button was going to be different!

He decided that he was not going to leave his signature button on this urchin who had given him so much trouble. Instead he would tie the "Haines button". This boy was doomed to be a problem and the sooner he got shut of him without the world knowing he had been instrumental in bringing the trouble maker into life, the better.

"I had heard of your belly buttons, doctor, but they were not described to me like this one. Is this a new style? I think I have seen some like it before, but just can't place it," said Nurse Cranston as she wrapped the baby in a blanket.

Dr. Morse ignored her remarks. In truth, he had tied the signature knot of Dr. Evelyn Haines, his onetime partner. The "Haines button" was not as pretty or nice as his. It was more of a figure eight which sometimes instead of being buried in the stomach, it would stick out in an ugly fashion, all knotted up; a terrible sight—like a pigs' tail.

Dr. Morse thought to himself, "Now when this boy grows up, people will think Dr. Haines is responsible for this atrocity."

Oh, how he hated his ex-partner. The break-up between them had not been pleasant. She was a high strung woman with a mean streak. She bullied the whole office including him.

One morning when he came to his office, he found a guard standing at the door blocking his entrance. Since she owned the building, she had merely kicked him out without his files or patients. When he tried to break into the building that night to get his files, he was caught and threatened, that if tried it again, he would surely go to jail.

It was the talk of the Mississippi Gulf Coast.

The matter landed in the Harrison County Chancery Court under the title, MORSE V. HAINES. He had to find another office and in order to get his files, the Court issued an order that his patients had to go to the Haines office and personally request them.

It had been a setback in his practice, but through winning smiles, sensuous hugs and excessive flattery, his female patients returned to him and soon he had them all coming back, plus more.

But he still hated Dr. Evelyn Haines!

This would be a joke on her. This little farting baby would be wearing her trademark button for all time. Anyone asking, who delivered Murfrey and saw that belly button, would say, "Must have been Dr. Evelyn Haines."

Now that he had done his duty, there would not be a follow up. He would have his receptionist make some kind of excuse, referring the mother and child to some other doctor. Maybe he would send her to Dr. Evelyn Haines. Yes, he would send the file over with a note saying he had handled her patient by mistake.

How he would love to be a fly on the wall when that obese woman and her fat baby showed up at Haines' office and see the expression on that bitches' face when she discovered he had copied her inept unattractive trademark belly button onto the boy. What a lark!

And as for Agnes Murfrey whose vagina was so wide that he could not understand why the baby just did not fall out instead of taking nine hours, well, he would leave that intact. He would not put the customary stitches in her to tighten it up for future use.

"Why the next man that has sex with her will have to strap a two by four to his ass to keep from falling in. Maybe with her love life curtailed, Agnes would not give birth to anymore farting babies". He chuckled. "And what pediatrician did he dislike enough to refer little Murfrey?"

This time he laughed heartedly out aloud startling Nurse Cranston.

"I see you are in a better mood, doctor."

"I am. I am. Mrs. Cranston, would you please place Agnes in her room and the baby with the others. I am going in search of Nurse Allen. If I find her, I will send her back here to give you a hand."

"I bet you will," said Cranston as she snapped off her blue surgical gloves. "I just bet you will!"

CHAPTER TWO

The Unusual Child

George Cedric Murfrey was not named after his father, Alfred Aloysis Murfrey, who had taken off for parts unknown two months after he learned of Agnes' pregnancy. George Cedric Murfrey the Third was not named after anyone; it was just some name Agnes thought up. After all, the father gave no reason for his departure. He just left. So with Agnes, it was don't ask and I won't tell.

Little Georgie, as Agnes called him, appeared to be a normal baby. He giggled; had all his fingers and toes and as he progressed, talked normal baby words. He was like a lot of overweight plump American babies causing people to stop when seeing him in his stroller and say, "Oh, what a cute baby."

Changing his dirty diapers or being around when he passed copious amounts of stinking gas, that would gag even a maggot, did not alarm his mother, being a first time mother, with no other babies to compare the rotten stench, who thought this horrible smell was normal.

Finances dictated that she go back to her job at Western Union, a job she had expertly held for over twenty years. Keeping a baby sitter proved difficult. After a few days of changing little Georgie's rotten diapers, the sitter suddenly found a reason to quit or on some occasions just failed to show up, never offering an explanation or excuse.

On top of that, her shotgun house was beginning to exude a foul houseotocis which even she detected when she came home from work in the afternoon. One time when she approached her house after a hard day's work, there was the baby sitter leaning over from the front steps puking her guts up. Agnes hurried inside to see the baby laughing, passing gas and gooing in his cradle. The spinach green diaper Georgie was wearing was half off and half on. The cradle was decorated with dark green feces.

"I am sorry Miss Agnes," the black teenage girl from down the street said as she wiped vomit from her mouth with a cold wash rag furnished by Agnes, "My stomach's gone bad. Must have got hole of some bad turnip greens." When the black girl, Patsy, called in saying she was still nauseated and could hardly hold water, Agnes took little Georgie to Dr. James Shetlemore, pediatrician, who put the baby on a diet of pabulum and skim milk. This only created great hunger in the child, causing him to cry vociferously or "bloody murder" as the neighbors characterized it. Some commented that a "barking dog wasn't as bad as that baby screaming." It was either put Georgie back on solid food or get run out of the neighborhood. Agnes capitulated.

After running out of baby sitters, Agnes tried taking, not so little, Georgie to child care centers. It seems that the adult food diet fed him, was like 'Miracle Grow' for plants. He grew fast; only more sideways, than straight up. After a day or two each child care center would come up with all kinds of reasons for Agnes to come and get Georgie. One center, the Friendly Play Pen, told her to find another center since they had decided to relocate immediately.

When Agnes, could not find a sitter and had run out of child care centers, she packed up Georgie's play pen and took him to her work.

It was not long before the company sent a man down from Jackson to see why suddenly no one was sending telegrams or night letters, anymore. Since Western Union was in the process of setting up shop in K-Mart Stores, the company man recommended they close that hole in the wall office where only one person and a plump baby worked. They offered Agnes a nice retirement pension if she would retire and not try to follow her job to the K-Mart store, which was located about twelve miles north of the Gulfport business district. The offer was too good to refuse; she took it.

This was fine with Agnes who was barely making it trying to pay the exorbitant child care centers and high priced baby sitters, having gotten wise, doubling and even tripling their charges. The bills now presented by Dr. Shettlemore's office had gone through the roof.

Now she was a stay at home mom who could play bridge with her group of friends. But when her players remarked about her having a sewerage problem, she wisely put Georgie in a room at the far end of the shotgun house. She hired a carpenter to cut a hole in the wall at the rear of the house installing a large exhaust fan which she controlled with a switch in the dining/bridge playing room. Then all that was left was to scrub the walls with Pine Sol. This worked so good, that she got in the habit of placing a dab of Pine Sol between her upper lip and nose when changing Georgie's diapers.

Georgie was a bright little boy. It was not hard to potty train him. He quickly learned to climb up on the toilet, sit on his special seat and do his business. Thus, with the exhaust fan running full blast and a few minor adjustments here and there, at home and in public, Agnes Murfrey and her little son, Georgie, passed for normal people. George was a smart, witty and good humored roly-poly child with cherub cheeks. His smiling blue eyes and eternal grin made his first grade teacher want to hug him.

He lived three blocks from East Ward Elementary School, a two story red brick structure which had a huge metal pipe attached to the side which served as a fire escape for grades fourth through sixth located on the second floor. The little school separated two playgrounds: one that ran from Highway 90 on the south facing the beach and Gulf of Mexico running to the school building and the other one was located on the northern side of the school bordered by Second Street. It had a cafeteria that served good wholesome meals. Miss. Jessie, the unmarried principal considered all the students as her own children, often preparing special delights for them; her seafood gumbo was as good as any served on the Gulf Coast.

Due to the liberal way the first graders were allowed to go to the restroom, whenever the need arrived, George had no problems. Although he stunk up the boy's room occasionally, it had an exhaust fan about as efficient as the one at home so no one noticed for long.

When George entered the Second grade, everything changed. Miss. Ester Newman was a stern, tight laced no nonsense martinet. Straight as a board in posture with high collar dresses and a large rolled bun hair-do from the 19th century she made it her job to put an end to the kids constantly getting up out of their seats and going to the bathroom. Each child would have to quietly raise their hand and wait to be recognized. They would then have to explain which function they needed to do: Number one or number two. She vowed to enlarge each child's kidneys by making them wait. Often when she refused to allow a certain child to go to the toilet in spite of protests: "Please Miss. Newman, I gotta go bad," the kid just wet his or her pants.

She would answer, "Wait until Johnny gets back," or "You just went an hour ago so hold it. I will not have you running in and out of my class room."

Many a child had to sit in their seat with soaked pants and urine dripping onto the floor much to that child's extreme embarrassment. This did not bother Miss. Newman, who maintained strict discipline in her class. Get out of line and get a crack across your knuckles with the rap of the ruler.

About that time, corporal punishment had not gone out of vogue in the public schools along the Gulf Coast. Paddling was still practiced. Actually, at this time the offending kid that got paddled could expect a greater punishment when he came home. It wasn't until the schools integrated that the black parents who resented anyone else especially whites abusing their children, that the teachers quit this practice. Some who did not stop this type of punishment, were suspended after the child in question, made out the punishment he had received, to appear worse than it actually was. Others were threatened with great bodily harm if they dared to lay their hands on their lovely child who beat up all the little ones, taking their lunch money. These unruly black kids made no bones about sassing or even threatening a teacher to their surprised faces.

Miss. Newman did not have to worry about any of that yet. Actually it was an honor to be taken behind the wall into the cloak room located on the other side in back of the teacher's desk and get the whipping. Classmate Ed Smallwood and the rest would whoop and holler as if they were in great pain on the verge of getting killed as they jumped forward after each blow until they reached the far end of the cloakroom. It was: "Ouch!" "That hurt", "Oh, please don't hit me no more," "I'll be good". This yelling, as if in terrible pain, satisfied Miss. Newman giving her another great feeling of accomplishment.

30

It was good old fashioned entertainment that broke the monotony of the often dull class room.

On one warm fateful day George held up his pudgy little hand only to be ignored by Miss. Newman. After what seemed to George an eternal wait, he burst out loudly in a shrill voice, "Miss. Newman! May I be excused? I have to go to the bathroom...now!"

All eyes were on George who had broken a cardinal rule. It had been drilled into the class that they were not to speak until recognized and then given permission.

"Now what have I told you over and over George Murfrey?" said the straight laced teacher. With cold glaring dark menacing eyes that frightened George, she continued, "Didn't you understand my rule? You never interrupt and don't you ever speak until I tell you to do so. Do you understand me?"

"Yes, Miss. Newman, but I gotta go. I gotta go real bad," said George as he squirmed in his seat.

"You are going to have to wait little boy. I have been keeping a record of the times you had to go. You went twice this morning and now it is just 1:30. You'll just have to wait."

"I, I, I-do-do-don't-th- think I ca-can-wa-wa-wait, Miss. Newman," pleaded George who stuttered for the first time in his life. "I, I, I tha- think I am ga- going to pa- paa poop in me britches."

The whole class thought this was funny. They twittered and laughed.

Shocked to hear the word, "poop", Miss Newman corrected the little urchin who dared using that dirty word instead of the "number two" she insisted upon. "George Murfrey, You know better than to use that nasty word. Now you will just have to hold it. Another word like that and I will wash your mouth out with lye soap." With that, the teach went on with her talking and chalking at the blackboard.

While Miss. Newman had her back to the class, writing on the blackboard, with screeching sounds George lifted his right leg and got relief by letting go a whopper which was all gas and sounded like someone sat down on a whoopee cushion. This brought giggles, squeals and loud laughter from the class.

31

Ed Smallwood, who sat next to George, leaned over and whispered in his ear, "Do it again."

George, who was still full of gas, obliged him with a squeaker that sounded like a balloon with the stem pinched while letting out air. This one lasted a good thirteen to fourteen seconds.

This day the gas packed a punch, quickly reaching the recesses of the entire room like the spray of a skunk, hovering there like a dark smelly cloud.

And it hovered there.

"Pee-you!" bellowed Ed Smallwood. He was joined by a chorus of "Phew-you" as well as loud giggles from the students holding their noses.

The second grade classes as well as the first and third grades were all on the first floor. On this spring day in the afternoon, the gentle winds from off the Gulf had pushed into the beaches and land mass causing the cooler morning air that had prevailed earlier to retreat inland. Since the windows were opened to let the cool fresh breeze flow in from off the Gulf of Mexico, Ed Smallwood, the leader of the class, simply jumped through one of the open windows and was quickly out onto the South playground; the rest of the class, little squirts, the boys in T-shirts and short pants, the little girls in play suits, merrily following suit. The only ones left in that room with a smelly cloud like fog was a red faced George Murfrey and the thin grey haired teacher with a hair bun frowning severely while trying to hold her breath.

Quickly, she grabbed George by his left ear and marched him out of the room and down the hall to Miss. Jessie's office.

On the second thought, Miss. Jessie, who loved all her "children" was a bleeding heart and probably nothing would be done, Miss. Newman simply sent George home with a note to Agnes telling her not to feed George beans during the school week. It was a good idea, because George's clothing along with everyone else's clothing in the second grade classroom had the awful smell of the outhouse. As soon as she rounded up the rest of the class, they were held in the cafeteria until their mothers came and picked them up.

The next day, notes were sent, phones rang and even some parents came to the school wanting to know how their child had gotten into an overflowing cesspool. They asked, "Did the toilets back up?"

The Principal, Miss. Jessie, who was kept in the dark, had no answer to that or other questions as to when the sewerage system would be fixed. Even passer byes who sniffed the lingering odor asked about it. Soon a committee was formed and the Mayor, Miss Jessie's cousin, was presented with petition to pass a bond issue demanding that the City of Gulfport put in a complete sewerage system, sewerage plant and all. The bond issue passed with little objection and the days of cesspools and septic tanks became a thing of the past.

A mini parent-teacher meeting was held between Miss. Newman and Mrs. Murfrey and it was decided that George would not eat beans during school days either at home or if beans were served in the cafeteria, peanut butter and jelly sandwiches would be George's table faire on those days. Furthermore, in the future all little Georgie had to do when he had the urge to pass some gas was to simply get up quietly and go outside and let it go; the constant Gulf breeze would dissipate the problem.

This carte banc went with George through the twelfth grade. It was known throughout the school system as the "Newman Plan". It was probably Ester Newman's greatest accomplishment as a teacher over shadowing her kidney enlargement plans and many paddling's that warmed many a tiny behind.

CHAPTER THREE

Member of the Eastside Gang

Besides being remembered by his classmates as well as school officials for the second grade fiasco, Little Georgie became known for the strange clothes his mother made him wear, sent to him from his cousins in Virginia who boxed up their discarded clothes they had out grown and mailed them to Mrs. Murfrey. While the kids on the Gulf Coast were wearing short pants, George sported corduroy knickers, and a white silk blouse. Instead of a regular baseball cap, George wore, one with a pointed top and a very short bill. This outfit amused the kids who called him "Georgie Porgie", "Murph" or after the second grade fiasco, "Stinky" depending on their mood.

Actually the clothes looked brand new; the Virginia kids must have refused to wear them. The mothers of his classmates approved of this humpty-dumpty kid with his rosy cheeks and eternal smile and freckled face. He was always polite. As a result he was invited to their birthday parties and was made a member of the "East Side Gang" which consisted of Ed Smallwood, Zach Brown, Joe Edwards and Tom Bradly who lived close by in the neighborhood.

The gang would all go to the movies every Saturday afternoon to the Royal Theatre, which they named the "Royal Roach House" to see their favorite cowboy flick. The place, which served as a large baby-sitting center for smaller children, was a mad house raising the ire of the East Side Gang. There was no way to quiet these rambunctious urchins, so George was sent to sit in their midst where he let would out a loud smelly one. He would then head for the popcorn counter as the kids holding their noses rushed into the lobby. Whenever George cleared the multitudes as they called it, he was congratulated becoming the hero of the day. He was accepted by his peers; made a part of the "gang" and on those good days, a hero. It was a happy time.

The gang was always into something. When they reached the age which made them eligible to join the Boy Scouts, their parents

34

encouraged them to join up. It would give them something to do while learning a skill such as tying knots or starting fires without matches.

Mr. Ted Simkins, who had no boys of his own, just three daughters, took on the position of Scout Master of Troop 603 in the Pine Burr District of South Mississippi. He loved leading boys. Unfortunately, he believed in tough love and was meaner than hell.

The Scoutmaster before him had resigned when he could not handle that fun loving bunch of pranksters. Mr. Simkins vowed to control this wild bunch who failed to take scouting seriously. None had advanced past the rank of Tenderfoot, but he would change all that.

One of his means of correcting those, who failed to heed his rules, was the Belt Line. He would line up the boys who numbered thirty three into two sides and the offender had to run in between the anxious boys of all sizes who had taken their belts off and with the belt doubled up would swat the runner as he tried to dodge the stinging blows that landed from head to toe.

Ed, Joe, Zack, Tom and George sported welts, bruises and even lacerations about the arms, shoulders, back and legs from their turn at the Belt Line.

In the past, it had been fun to be paddled by teachers in the cloakroom; this type of punishment was no laughing matter. The belts not only stung and hurt; they left marks and cuts when some of the scouts swung the wrong end of the belt striking with the belt buckle, all of which had to be hidden from their parents. It wasn't long before it was "get Simkins" time.

One evening after the sun had gone down the opportunity presented itself. Mr. Simkins drove up in a brand new black Oldsmobile and parked it in back of City Hall where their meetings were held. While George and several other Scouts were busy tying knots in preparation for the Camporee to be held in Stone County next week, Joe, Ed, Zack and Tom were outside attaching a whistling car "bomb" to the scoutmaster's new Oldsmobile, which he had failed to lock. Zack had bought the bomb at a fire-works stand, saving it for the right occasion; this was the right occasion.

After closing the hood quietly, the four entered the meeting late again.

Mr. Simkins looked up and in his rasping whiny voice gleefully said, "Boys, you are late. This makes the second time this month. As soon as we finish tying the square knot, we will all fall outside and these four tardy boys will run the gauntlet. Actually, I am tired of your misbehavior; each of you will run it twice."

Ed Smallwood bent over and whispered one word into George's ear, "Now". George lifted his hind end up off the seat and cut loose with a loud machine gun flatter-blaster. He did not hold back; it seemed to go on and on.

Before Simkins could include George in the group to be punished, the entire troop present yelled, hollered and bolted for the door.

All Mr. Simkins could utter was, "Good God!"

Troup 603 had gathered into the dark alley behind the building and waited for their beloved scoutmaster. He did not disappoint them. He staggered out unsteady on his feet. Without saying a word he opened the door to his shiny new car, cranking the engine. All of a sudden the quiet cool air of the night was pierced by a loud shrill whistling noise which erupted from under the hood of his pride and joy.

Simkins pulled the release leaver inside the car and the hood popped up. The boys in the alley now crowded closer to watch Simkin's reaction. Simkins got out of the car, walked to the front, fumbled under the hood until he found the latch and lifted the hood. As he peered in to find the trouble volumes of smoke were pouring out. Just as he leaned over to locate the source, the firecracker portion of the bomb exploded showering him with confetti pieces of paper. This startled the scoutmaster causing him to jump back striking his head on the upper latch at the front of the hood. "That had to hurt," commented Zack the tallest of the gang. This broke the quiet spell and rancorous bodily laughter broke out; little scouts bending over holding their side splitting bellies while some fell to the ground in uncontrolled mirth. Simkins stood there swaying and as the confetti and smoke cleared, he saw the remnants of the bomb connecting two spark plugs, all that was left, were two wires of the exploding device. He reached down, grabbed the wires and snatched them loose. He turned around and threw the wiring apparatus at the feet of Zack.

How did he know that Zack was one of the culprits?

Then he walked around, opened the door to his car, got in and without a word, cranking the car again, throwing the shift lever in reverse, straightening the car up, silently driving away in his new car, the motor now purring like a kitten, never to be seen by the Troop again..

The next week, Troop 603 representing the City of Gulfport, arrived at Camp Ittywamber without a Scoutmaster. Just Zack, Joe, Tom, Ed, George and two others were all that could make it. They now called themselves the "Bunghole Buddies". In spite of Simkins harsh methods, still none had progressed past the rank of Tenderfoot. No Eagle Scouts in 603. Joe Edwards prophetically said, "These are the moments we will cherish forever."

While the boys were excitedly talking about their new adventure, Zack's mother, Ann Brown, who was driving the group in her Dodge minivan, on the way to the Camp grounds, became concerned that they had no Scoutmaster to lead them. She questioned Zack, "Did one of you boys do something to make Mr. Simkins quit? It seems strange that he never called anyone to tell us he was quitting. I tried to get in touch with him, but his phone number has been changed and his number is now unlisted. One of the mothers went to his house several times, but no one ever came to the door."

"No mom", Zack said with the face of innocence, "One of us boys did not do something to make him quit. Actually, the rumor is that that bunch from Long Beach sneaked over and put that whistler under Mr. Simkins hood of his brand new car. We all loved Simkins; didn't we gang?"

"Yeah, Mrs. Brown, they have always been jealous because we go to their dances and take their girls. Isn't that right?" That part was the truth; the Gulfport boys often found out about the dances held at the smaller schools, serving as suburbia to their city, muscling their way in, cutting in on the out manned boys of towns such as Long Beach, Pass Christian and even Bay St. Louis. The kids in these smaller towns learned not to object or they got their eyes blacked. The school kids from Gulfport never messed with, the Biloxians at their dances; their brawling took place at the Biloxi-Gulfport football game where the spectators from both sides clashed, beating up one another, until the rivalry got out of hand, with mothers hitting each other over the head with their large purses, fathers throwing knock out punches at opponents, causing the game to be suspended for several years.

"That's right, Mrs. Brown." They all laughed.

Mrs. Brown looked back at George who was sitting on the back seat squeezed in between the two other kids, not members of the Bunghole Buddies. She said, "George, I know you won't lie to me. Do you know what happened to make Mr. Simkins quit?"

"Mrs. Brown," George said in a high pitched voice, "I can truthfully say that I didn't see who did it. All I know is when we all went outside to admire Mr. Simkins new car, he had a lot of smoke coming out from under the hood of his car. It started whistling and then "boom!' it went off. He never accused us of doing it. That is all I know"

"Thanks George, I knew I could depend on you to give me a straight story." Zack's mother said, "Here is what I am going to do. When we get there, I am going to talk to whoever is in charge and see if they can get someone to take Mr. Simkins' place and supervise you boys."

"Oh mom," said Zack. "You don't have to do that. We are perfectly able to supervise ourselves aren't we gang?"

"Yeah!" said the chorus.

At Camp Ittywamber, true to her word, Ann Brown talked to the head director of the Pine Burr District and he got Sam Young a tall older boy, an Eagle Scout to be their supervisor.

All Sam Young did was to show the boys their designated tent and give them a schedule of the activities. Announcing that he had activities of his own, as he was trying to increase the number of his merit badges that already crowded a large impressive sash draped over his neck and shoulders. Thinking these anxious young Scouts were ambitious, trustworthy and walked old ladies across the street, like he did, he told the boys that he would be back later after he won a merit badge for surviving off the land without bringing any food or water. This would take a while. He told them, "You Scouts look like a self-sufficient bunch of guys. Think you will be alright? I will be back later to check on you. Remember, be prepared. Okay?"

"Sure," they all said. "You can count on us."

After Eagle Scout Young left to go after another merit badge, Joe Edwards said, "Some supervisor he was. Ed, do you think you could supervise us?"

"No problem," said Ed taking charge. "Now get you stuff in that tent and then we will make plans to see if we can impress the judges of this here Camporee!"

"Whoop-de-do!: shouted Tom Bradley as they stowed their gear in the large tent meant to house fifteen boys, leaving some vacant cots, since there were only seven of the thirty-three in their troop who were in attendance.

The campground looked like a miniature Camelot with its rows of tents sporting each troops' colorful flag displayed in front. Hundreds of future leaders of the country were scurrying to and fro in a determined way--much like ants who had found a source of sweets. Scoutmasters and Assistant scoutmasters barked orders to their young men. Some of the troops, such as the Brookhaven kids, even marched in cadence to their tents. Just about every town and hamlet in South Mississippi was represented in this giant meeting

While the boys made themselves comfortable on their cots, Tom Bradly, who had scouted the area, announced that they were not the only ones without a Scoutmaster. "The scouts from Pascagoula are without one also."

Someone asked, "What did they do; blow up the scoutmaster's car?"

Bradly continued, "They call themselves the 'Shithooks'. They are a rough looking bunch. I hope we don't have any trouble from them."

"I think we had better keep an eye on that bunch", said Jack Rester, one of the Scouts who was not a bonafide member of the 'Bunghole Buddies'."

"Aw, they are not so bad," said the new supervisor Ed. "I know a few of them. One of them is Buddy Ray. He is the quarterback on the Pascagoula football team. His dad and my dad go hunting together. They won't bother us if we don't mess with them, but we have to make sure they don't out do us. My dad would never hear the end of it from Mr. Ray on the next hunting trip,"

After getting secure in their tents, it was an impressive array of Boy Scouts who assembled on the parade grounds, all lined up, standing at attention.

Troop 603 looked unimpressive with only seven boys present to represent their area. Eagle Scout, Sam Young had arrived to stand in front of the boys in place of a Scoutmaster. No one seemed to mind except Ed Smallwood, who felt he had been demoted. Tenderfoot George Murfrey proudly stood with his buddies. Overlooked was the fact that his uniform was soaked with sweat and two of his shirt buttons had popped from their button holes exposing his bellybutton, a protruding figure eight knot, sticking out like a curly pig's tail.

After the welcoming speech, the Pledge of Allegiance and the recital of the Boy Scout Oath which no one in Troop 603 knew, the various troops broke up to begin the competition between each other.

Sam Young, the part time supervisor, quickly disappeared after handing a sheet with the list of projects to Joe Edwards. Joe perused the sheet and stated, "Our first project is to build a fire without using matches. We are supposed to start the fire by rubbing two sticks together. It says here that we will be judged by how long it takes to get the fire going and the quality of our fire."

"No problemo," said Tom Bradly, whose family had recently vacationed in Cancun, Mexico where he picked up their language. As a Boy Scout, he came prepared. He quickly pulled out a large powerful magnifying glass from under his shirt and after showing it to his buddies, hiding it just as fast.

Ed, taking charge, ordered, "Zack, give 'Stinky' that stick of dynamite you brought."

Zack handed George a large three inch bright red firecracker with fuse of equal length.

"Stinky see that pile of kindling over there? No one has claimed it for their fire building test. Run over there and plant that cracker under the stuff. Hurry before they show up, but don't let no one see you doing it."

George nonchalantly waddled over to the indicated pile of what looked like debris to him, looked around to see if he was being watched and seeing no eyes on him, slide the large firecracker under the pile.

Mission accomplished; George strolled back to his admiring pals as if on a leisurely walk in the park.

"It's a done deed", said George breathing heavily from the thirty yard round trip.

"Alright, all we have to do is wait", said Ed. "Zack you and Joe get ready to start your fire."

No sooner had Ed given his instructions; there came Troop 407 from Brookhaven marching up in unison. A highly decorated Eagle Scout was calling cadence, shouting, "Hut, two, three, four…" They halted briskly and their leader asked politely if anyone knew where their project was located.

"I think it is over there." Ed Smallwood pointed to the pile of kindling, leaves and twigs where George had planted the Cherry Bomb, serving as a distraction that would allow them to start their fire unnoticed.

"Thank you very, very much', said the leader and with that said, he marched his boys to the designated area. He could be heard yelling, "Fall out!" Troop 603 anxiously watched one of the boys pull out two sticks fastened by a leather cord while another produced a piece of flat wood. On kid was working the two sticks back and forth while another held the flat piece of wood. Soon smoke was pouring from the flat wood then it burst into flames.

While one of the Brookhaven scouts ran over to get an observer, Tom Bradly said, "So that is how you do it. I wondered about that."

"Distraction coming up. Get that magnifying glass ready, Tom," said Ed their leader trying to speak with an authoritative voice.

Just as the Observer was leaning over, admiring the successful fire, all of the Brookhaven bunch crowding around proudly, the fuse of the

41

firecracker lit. Sparks flew and then "boom!" the fire blew up scattering embers, twigs and ash all over the Observer and Troop 407.

While they were knocking red hot embers that were burning small holes in their once neatly starched uniforms, Bradly, with his powerful magnifying glass, had gotten his fire going. While Ed called for an observer, Tom made the magnifying glass disappear.

Troop 603's fire did not blow up, holding first place for a short period until some little kid said he saw George squatting down earlier near Brookhaven's now burned out smoldering hole in the ground.

"It was that fat kid. I saw that fat kid doing something", the squealer tattletale little kid said, pointing to George who suddenly looked very guilty while his buddies assumed the air of innocence.

"Don't say a word", said Ed to George. "They ain't got nothing on you. It's your word against that kid's."

When George refused to confess, maintaining he knew nothing about it, he was ordered to be confined to his tent until further review. The rest of the troop went on to enter the knot tying contest having only to sneak their already tied knots from out of their pockets without being detected.

Later, that afternoon, his buddies came back to the tent, full of laughter and mirth. Zack said, "George, did you hear what happened? You might be in the clear."

"No," answered George almost in tears. He had been busted the first day of the event.

"That rowdy bunch from Pascagoula went one better than us. One of them had apparently put some gasoline on their pile of sticks. When they got it lit, poof! A flame shot up singeing the eye brows of the Observer. Now here's the clincher. They blamed it on that kid who squealed on you. Said they saw him over there by their pile; same as you."

"What happened to them?" asked George, now taking heart.

"Oh, they all got confined to their tent and that kid was sent to his tent crying like a baby. "

They were all laughing their heads off including George who now felt better.

"Stinky, we owe you one", said Ed. "Don't we boys?"

And to show their appreciation, they all gathered around George shaking his hand or patting him on the back. George beamed. Now he knew he was fully accepted by the gang.

Just as the fickle finger of fate had smiled on George, eight hours later, his acceptance as a Bunghole Buddy quickly changed.

Everyone had gone asleep including George who was now being chased by a fifteen foot alligator that had crawled into the tent. The gator lunged at George shaking his cot with it long vicious looking snout. When George started to run, the gator took off after him. It was amazing how fast that gator could travel while swinging its' tail in an effort to knock George's feet out from under him. The powerful jaws of the gator were just inches away when George went into his skunk mode. As he sprayed the gator, then waking up to the shouting and cursing by his former buddies, he realized they were cursing him. His foul smelling gas was probably his best to date. It smelled worse than the waste dumped from a travel trailer while being emptied; Troop 603 resented being blasted out of their blissful sleep by this overwhelming smell; they had a busy day ahead of them and needed their sleep.

The Bunghole Buddies scattered in all directions; not returning until the fumes cleared. George was banned from the tent. They even chased him up a tree. To keep George up the tree, so he could do no more harm, each scout took turns urinating on the tree trunk. The tree, now designated as the "pissing tree", was kept soaked by not only Troop 603 peeing on it, but by neighboring scouts who got pleasure directing their hot yellow streams upon the soaked tree.

It took one of the Officials to lift George from the tree and rescue him from his now turncoat friends. Several hours later, Agnes Murfrey leaving her bridge game, journeying to Camp Ittywamber to pick up her son, took him home.

From that day forward, George was no longer called "Stinky". His new name was "Fart's Murfrey".

CHAPTER FOUR

Disgraced and Cast Out

After the Camporee fiasco, the East Side Gang aka the Bunghole Buddies, avoided George like the plague. He was non persona gratis. He was shunned. He was laughed at. He was the butt of ridicule. He had no friends. The merry bunch of rascals he had tried so hard to please; showed their displeasure. All they could talk about was how he had been exiled to the pissing tree until one of the soft-hearted officials took pity on Farts by rescuing him.

His social life was dead in the water.

No more parties. No more being one of the "In Crowd". No nothing. His face broke out with pimples. He developed rosacea, which replaced his rosy cheeks with a deeper redness much like that of an alcoholic.

He told his mother what had happened at the Boy Scout meeting involving Scoutmaster Simkin's sudden departure and then explained in detail the nightmare at Camp Ittywamber. Agnes had no objections when Georgie told her he wanted to drop out of the Scouts because no one would speak to him.

George was an island. He had no social life, but he wasn't a quitter. He poured himself into his studies. Soon his report card showed all "A's".

But even the sophisticated nerds of the school avoided him; his grades higher than theirs, made them look bad.

George used his small paltry allowance his mother provided to try over the counter remedies for his flatulence problem, but when Gas-X, Beano, D-Bloat, Gaszymine and even home remedies did not work, he asked his mom to get him an appointment with a doctor. She did, but the prescription, the doctor gave him, did not work.

His life was in shambles. He turned to food for solace and grew-heavier.

He heard an underclassman say, "Look at that fat fart." as he wallowed down the hallway bumping into students trying to pass him. He could pass for Humpty-Dumpty. His life was irretrievably, broken and shattered.

Misery loves company so when George was not in class or in the library studying, he would go down to the basement, a poorly lit place with a furnace room furnished with two Lazy Boy recliners Web had appropriated, whiling away the time talking with Web Moran, the school's short bespeckled black middle aged janitor, also on the heavy side. In the winter, it was warm down there with the coal furnace going full blast to heat the radiators in the classrooms. He and Web talked of many things including how unfair life was to both of them. Web's wife had left him for a high yellow jig and it looked like George would never get married much less having a wife desert him. He had never been even out on a date.

To Web's astonishment, George developed his flame thrower technique down in that basement. He would open the furnace door where the red hot coals were baking and shoot his gas into the opening. As he perfected the art of shooting a blue flame, he could shoot one three feet away. There was no smell or after effects once he got the hang of it. Furthermore, he learned the art of avoiding setting his pants on fire or even singing or scorching them. While George was down in Web's quarters, no one had the vaguest idea where he was. Actually, no one cared.

They say that when one door closes, another opens. George's new door opened in the form of a recent student named Durwood Sanderford. Durwood had transferred to Gulfport High from San Luis Obispo, California. Ahead of his time, he sported a ponytail to go with his bleached hair and ear rings. The kids at school wanted nothing to do with him making it inevitable that he and George hooked up as they were both ostracized birds of a feather.

Durwood was everything George was not: He had a cool way with the girls while George was shy. "Woody", as he was nicknamed, was a natural dancer with steps no one had seen before; George had two left feet.

45

Woody liked to teach; George wanted to learn.

Everyone liked to pick on and ridicule George, but Woody demonstrated his black belt karate techniques on a few of the unwise ones; after that no one bothered either boy, fear of Woody's martial arts ability being enough to protect both boys. His defender made sure no one called him by his opprobrious nickname, "Farts".

George was overweight; Woody was slender and muscular. Woody barely got by in school; George excelled.

The two began to complement each other.

Woody had no problem getting a date but did run into difficulty fixing George up in order to double date. Woody drove a baby blue convertible to school.

After they became best friends, it became an unbreakable friendship.

While George's allowance was small, Woody's parents spoiled him. His dad was an engineer at NASA, located in Hancock County, the next county to the west of Gulfport.

Life had taken a complete turnaround.

When Woody's grades climbed to all "C's", his dad approved of George, taking them fishing on their twenty-four foot Boston Whaler. They wade fished around the barrier islands for Speckled Trout and went offshore to the oil rigs for Grouper, Cobia, King Mackerel and Amber Jack.

Thanks to George, Woody learned to gig Flounders. When the tide brought the flat fish into the shallow water, the boys would follow their tracks as the sought after the fish burrowed under the sand. With bright underwater lights they would silently creep up to where they saw two small eyes staring out from the hidden fish, also looking for a meal that may swim by him. George, with a sharp eye, was better at spotting these delicacies. They would gig a few put them on their stringers, bringing them home to be eaten.

"Where did you learn how to track Flounder," asked Woody.

"I really don't know," George said seriously. "It is hard to grow up on the Gulf Coast and not know how to catch fish. Now take those Soft Shell Crabs. I read somewhere that they shed their shells as they grow larger. There is a short passage of time when the shedding crab is vulnerable to other predators, which enjoy eating this delicacy as much as we do. The way we get them is by spotting the discarded shell and also following their tracks."

They walked along the shallow waters barefoot, sometimes until one in the morning. When winter was on its' way, George one afternoon, while the tide was out, took Woody over to the jetty that reached out from the road on the way to the Gulfport Yacht Harbor. There they cleared a large circle of the rocks that were present and used the rocks to surround the circle.

When they finished, George took a paint brush and made a mark. "Now," he said, when winter comes, the Flounder will come in and burrow down to wait for prey. Since we will know they are in this area where we won't snag our hooks on a rock, we can drag our bait slowly across the front of the fish; he then will attack it and we will catch a fish. It is that easy."

Both families enjoyed the bountiful catches the boys brought home from their excursions. It was not long before Woody's father entrusted him with the Whaler. The duo began fishing the local Tournaments. George took first place in the Flounder category and Woody got a trophy for the largest Red Snapper.

George or "Murph" as Woody began calling him, never had a friend like Woody. It no longer bothered him that his former buddies had cut him out of their circle. Once again George was invited to parties by the girls who liked Woody's pony tail; his rippling muscles, his suave talk. In short, they liked Woody and learned to include Murph if they wanted Woody to attend their functions.

After one of the dances at the Community center on the beach three Seabees from the nearby Navy Base jumped Woody, when Woody objected to the use of bad language and despairing remarks about Murph's girth. Woody whipped all three. They wanted to press charges, when the police showed up, but they did not get anywhere with that. The police could not believe that this scrawny little kid could beat up those bigger men.

It wasn't long before Murph introduced Woody to Web, the janitor. The three would sit around in the basement quarters and tell stories and jokes they heard.

"That is a mighty fine friend you got there George." said Web one day.

"I know said George. "He is my best friend and besides you, my only friend."

During the three years that Woody attended Gulfport High, the two boys were inseparable. Seldom did anyone call George, "Farts". During that period, George still had his embarrassing problem, but he had learned to deal with it. When he was full of gas, it had to go somewhere, so George would dispose of it in the furnace in the basement. He also had a special pillow his mother had made for him. The inner stuffing was lined with a charcoal filter. This seemed to capture the smell if George passed it very slowly into the cushion. If anyone asked why he toted this cushion around, he answered, "For medical reasons."

For three years, George had a clean record. No mishaps. Of course the Newman plan was always in effect, but George seldom used it. It was George's private hell which he learned to live with.

They graduated in May from GHS. George graduated tenth in the class, winning a scholarship to Gulf Coast Community College. During the graduation exercises, when George Cedric Murfrey the Third. stepped upon the stage to receive his diploma, amid mild applause, there came a loud voice from the back row of the auditorium uttered by a small heavy set bespeckled black man whom no one recognized as Web Moran since he was fully dressed for the occasion in his Sunday church going clothes. Web yelled out, "That's my boy!"

Those who looked around asked each other, "Can this be Murfrey's father?"

Woody decided to go to the community college with his friend even though his family had the money to send him anywhere in the country. That summer, they got jobs working as carpenter's helpers building houses in a new subdivision. Georges' weight dipped dramatically. He had to get new clothes, which was good since he now went regularly on blind dates, thanks to Woody.

The vehicle of life was running smoothly. They had plenty of money to spend on dates. The fishing was good. Woody was crowned King Fisherman in one of the tournaments. Life was ecstasy.

Then the wheels rolled off!

Nine-eleven happened. In New York City two commercial jets hijacked by terrorists crashed into the Twin Towers sending them into a pile of rubble while another terrorist held airplane took out part of the Pentagon in Washington D.C. Before George could fully comprehend what was going on, Woody joined the United States Air Force.

"Why did you do such a thing?" asked George. "I would have joined with you."

"I just got caught up in it all and wanted to do something for my country," said Woody. "Besides, I didn't think they would take you with all that weight. I don't believe you could pass the physical. Don't worry, I'll stay in touch. I chose the Air Force because it was safer than being a Marine or foot soldier in the Army."

After boot camp, Woody was sent to Iraq. George got a picture of Woody in the open door of a helicopter behind a deadly looking machine gun.

Two months later George got word that Woody had been killed in action by a heat seeking rocket fired from the ground, slamming into Woody's helicopter while on a mission. He even saw the name of Durwood Sanderford, Gulfport, Mississippi listed on the television program, Meet the Press, the following Sunday along with a list of other American boys who gave their lives for their country.

A beautiful part of the life of George Cedric Murfrey had ended!

CHAPTER FIVE

911 Fallout

George should have had a clue that Woody was going to abandon their college plans and join the service. They had entered Gulf Coast Community College in mid-August, had gotten their books and began attending classes. It wasn't long before Woody said in disgust, "This is not for me. I will never make it. I think I will quit."

Startled, George said, "Don't quit. I will help pull you through. Besides they have tutors to help you. Just because they took you out of my classes and set you back is no reason to quit. They know what they are doing; bringing you up to snuff is their job. All those bad grades you made back in California set you back. You are lucky they caught it before we went on to Ole Miss".

"I don't know, Murph. I don't like being put back in the dummy class. You should see all the hayseeds and ignorant blacks they put me with. I know it is not their fault. Those schools they came from didn't give them much of an education. If you think California is a culture shock, come sit in my classroom."

"Just hold on, man. You will make it through. It is only for two years. I have heard that we have some of the best professors in the nation. They retire and come down here and are offered part time jobs. The teaching is in their blood. I have heard we even have a computer professor here who once taught at Cal-Polytech and even wrote programs that are being used this very day in our computers. Right here we have the cream of the crop of college professors."

"I will try Murph, but I can't promise you anything. I never liked school. I may drop out and join the French Foreign Legion," Woody joked.

"For your information, the Foreign Legion was disbanded."

"See how ignorant I am?"

"That is why you should stay in school. Even if you don't go on to a major college, you will still get a better job if you get your associates degree," Murph argued.

All had been for naught. Woody still bolted. He joined the service and died for his country.

Now George had lost his best friend.

"Why! Why!' George would shout and throw things up against the wall of his bedroom.

"Cut that out boy!" his mother would shout back. "It is not the end of the world."

But to George, it was the end of the world. At first he was mad at Woody for dying. Then he was mad at the President for letting, what was now called a phony war, happen. Then he became irate with God for letting this happen. Anger turned into hurt. He could not forgive God for taking his best friend from him. He had never been religious even though his mother had marched him to church each Sunday as a child. His spirit did not match those syrupy do-gooders who spoke to him with honey dripping from their lips seeming always to be joyous and happy, but they probably never lost their best friend.

He and Woody had visited various churches, to meet girls. They would sit in the back of the church and pass notes to the young maidens. Sometimes the notes would be humorous and the group would break out into giggles and uncontrollable laughter. On several occasions an Usher would have to go over and quiet them.

When the teenagers left church, none of them could have told what that day's sermon was about, even if their lives had depended upon it.

But now George blamed God. He was distraught and blamed the Lord for taking away the only real friend he had ever had. What was he to do?

He certainly was not ever going back to church; not even if they did have some good looking Christian girls.

After the hurt and anger came depression and hopelessness.

It showed up in his school work. Where he had once been a top student, he just didn't care anymore. He was just a warm body sitting a desk at the Junior College staring out the window at the birds flittering about or pulling worms out of the ground.

Once more the fickle finger of fate had given him the bird! And it wasn't the proverbial early bird that got the worm either.

He moved to the back of the classroom. Formerly he liked to sit on the front row where he could pay attention without distraction. Now he sat in the back of the room where he could not be seen diddling on his notebook when he wasn't bird watching.

He still made "C's" that semester. A lot of the studies had already been covered in high school; maybe he absorbed a little just sitting there. He did barely enough to keep his scholarship, but he was on thin ice. He was warned that he needed to pull his grades up or lose his scholarship.

Then one day in walked this small thin older guy with a pointed chin, slamming his books down on the desk next to George, loudly under his breath saying, "Damn!"

This got George's attention. He looked up at this small five foot four person, who was obviously older than the other teenage students. He had to be twenty-five or older.

"What are you looking at?" said the narrow face with a deep baritone voice.

"I am looking at a small man who just slammed his books on that desk and woke me up," said George.

The gruff man with the gruff voice gave George a dirty look and then tossed his head back and laughed. He looked at George with kind grey eyes and said, "That's good. Woke you up did I? Say that is good." He stuck out his hand and said, "My name is Hanson. You can call me Mutt."

"I am George Murfrey, said George shaking his hand. "You can call me for dinner."

"Seems as if someone already has."

They both laughed and from then on the vacuum left by Woody's death was filled by an angry Mutt Hanson and that suited George just right.

"Jesus. I have already had these damn courses and here I am in this po-dunk college," said Mutt.

"Why are you here then," asked George who arched his eyebrows in amusement.

"My dear father is punishing me. I was sentenced to the University of Edinburgh in Scotland for two years. They didn't like my style of living and threw me out. I joined the Scottish Brigade, but when I got wounded over in India, they discharged me; so here I am. Actually, those Scots talked a good fight, but we mostly did our fighting in brothels and pubs. I was ordered to charge the Punjabs and with those bag pipes shattering my ear drums, there was nothing else to do but to run away from that terrible ear grating noise, they call music. I got ahead of the battalion and some cranky Punjab who obviously didn't like the music either, shot me with an old rusty rifle.

So to punish me for returning to the states, my father sent me to this God forsaken hick school instead of letting me go to Ole Miss where I wanted to go. He said, 'He didn't want to waste the money. So what is your excuse?"

Ignoring the question George asked, "Are you Doctor Hanson's son?"

"If the high and mighty doctor hasn't disowned me, I have to admit it. That crock of crap can kiss my ass," said Mutt vehemently. He then stood up and said, "Say, you aren't doing anything but sleeping in class; let's cut this class and go get a beer. What do you say?"

"Fine with me," said George who was in one of his bad moods that morning and besides he wanted to hear more about his guy's seemingly colorful life.

Gulf Coast Community College, formerly known as Jeff Davis Junior College, because of its' proximity to the coastal home of Jefferson Davis, the first and only President of the Confederate States of America, was placed between Gulfport and Biloxi, on the Gulfport side of the city line. There were barrooms down the street on either side. Mutt chose a bar on the Biloxi side just outside the western gate of Keesler Air Force Base. It was generally inhabited by Airmen who came to relax, drink a beer, shoot pool or chat with the bar girls that hung out there-especially around pay day.

There were about four airmen in the Pink Poodle Lounge when Mutt and George strolled in. Immediately George recognized the short haircuts and polished black shoes and knew they weren't locals. They grabbed a table and each had a cold Heineken beer.

"My treat," said Mutt as he gave a five dollar bill to the old grey haired waitress, who was also the bartender and owner.

"Keep the change," said Mutt.

One of the airmen made a remark about George calling him a "porker."

Mutt, who had ready guzzled his beer looked at George and said, "You going to take that? That punk called you a porker."

"I've heard it all before. No matter."

"Well it matters to me," said Mutt now standing up--all five feet four of him. He called out, "Hey, punk, just who are you calling a porker?"

Seeing Mutt, who was half his size, the airman answered, "Go figure it out 'Shorty'."

In an instant Mutt was up and in the airman's face. He said, "You don't know me well enough to call me 'Shorty'."

The startled airman pushed Mutt away, but when he shoved Mutt in the chest, Mutt countered with an upper cut to the man's chin. The tall airman was knocked backwards into a wall sliding down it quietly to the floor. George could literally see a little bird above the man's head going, "Tweet-tweet-tweet".

Immediately another airman came bounding over. He said, "You can't do that to my buddy!"

Wham! Without a word, Mutt hit him with the same type uppercut, and this airman a blonde youngster not much older than George also hit the wall and quietly slid down beside his buddy.

"I guess I can," said Mutt. Then turning toward a third airman who was moving his way, Mutt said, "You want some of this?"

This boy, also a teenager, back tracked. He said, "No".

"How about you?" Mutt asked the fourth airman, still at the pool table.

He answered quickly, "No, not me."

The old waitress/bartender/owner came around the bar and pointed at Mutt and then at George and then pointed at the door. She said in a quiet hoarse voice, "It is time to go."

Mutt said, "Let's go Murfrey. Lets' find a more friendly bar." The two walked out from the dark stale beer smelling bar into fresh air, the sunny day blinding them momentarily.

They found a similar lounge down the street and after several beers, Mutt told George, "You are getting a lesson in beer drinking 101. I hope you pass this course. It is essential that every college student pass the course."

George had no intention of passing the course. He merely sipped on his Heineken while Mutt put his away with the gusto of a drunken sailor. Before long, Mutt was in no condition to walk or drive his Camaro sports car. George helped him into his automobile. He knew where Doctor Hanson's large mansion was located on U.S. Highway 90 overlooking the Gulf. When George walked Mutt to the backdoor of the doctor's house, Mutt was now beginning to regain his composure.

"Thanks my new friend. Say whas yore name?"

"George Murfrey."

"I knew that. I knew that. See you around the campus." With that Mutt straightened up the best he could and went into the house.

George knew the area; he had walked it many times on the way to East Ward Elementary School, two blocks away. The doctor's property ran all the way from Beach Boulevard to Second Street, so all he had to do was to walk west along the sidewalk, turn North on Pratt Street cross over the railroad tracks and walk a half block to his small shotgun house. It was a short distance even if he did have to carry his heavy college text books in his back pack.

Although the two cut class frequently to go and matriculate for Beer Drinking 101, they miraculously passed the beer drinking course and college that year. The scholarship committee let George slide for another year, but warned him that he needed to pull his grades up. Mutt was able to pass without cracking a book because he had already had those courses and more at the U of Edinburgh. George was able to speed read and learn enough during exam week to pass with "B's" and "C's".

During the summer months, with his new found friend, the two shot pool at the Palace Pool Hall, one of Mutt's local hang outs, while George introduced Mutt to the wonders of the Gulf of Mexico. Beer in hand, Mutt would trail George along the shallow waters near the beach at night while George tried to teach him how to gig flounders or pickup an occasional Soft Shell Crab. Mutt, in turn, sprang for a deep sea fishing trip on a charter boat.

On that trip Mutt carried a case of Miller Lite on board and generously passed around the chilled beers to the charter boat captain and his crew. When the beer suddenly vanished, although they had just gotten into the Spanish mackerel, Mutt hollered, That's enough. Let's go home."

Mutt did not take Woody's place, but he stuck to George like a true friend and no one had better mess with him or feisty Mutt would strike like a cobra.

Agnes Murfrey did not like Mutt with his surly attitude. He did not even try to pass pleasantries when he was around her. He always seemed to have a "cool one" in his hand.

"George, I don't like your little friend," she complained. "I think he is a bad influence on you. Why don't you find some nice sober friends? This one will get you in trouble. Go to church and meet some nice people there."

"Aw, mom," said George. "He is alright. You just have to get to know him. He has a heart of gold. You know he is Dr. Hanson's son, don't you?"

"I don't want to get to know him and I don't care whose son he is. Look at your grades. You never did that bad before you met him."

"College is a lot harder," said George to his mom who had never made it past the twelfth grade.

"Well, you just have to try harder. If you would stop coming in at all hours of the night maybe your grades would pick up. Don't you have any homework?'

"I did it all at school," lied George.

The Mississippi Gulf Coast has many distractions--mostly in the form of barrooms, lounges and night clubs. Each night Mutt and George were on the prowl trolling for loose women who were also on the prowl. Being half lit and finding a half lit woman on vacation also looking for some fun, was very exciting to George. A lot of them did not seem to mind that he was a fat slob; alcohol does such wondrous things.

On one joyous episode, Mutt had rounded up two willing waitresses out for a night with a devil may care attitude. They all crowded into a curved white leather imitation booth at the Glass Crutch. After a few drinks, everyone was getting amorous. Even George's gorgeous beauty, a tall robust gal from So-So, Mississippi, did not seem to mind that he was slightly overweight, They were smoothing it up hot and heavy. Rachel, caught up in the moment, did not seem to mind when George bravely felt her proud breasts.

But when the slightly overweight lover got up to let out a little excess beer, Mutt, in a mischievous mood, leaned over and told Rachel, "You know, George has a real bad habit?"

"Oh, what's that?" said Rachel casually.

"I hate to be the one who tells you, but I think it is my solemn duty. George just will not wash his hands. I have tried to get him to wash his hands, but you know what he tells me?'

"What?" said Rachel, who was obsessive about cleanliness, wasn't liking what she was hearing.

"He tells me, 'I don't pee on my hands' And you know what else? There is more."

"Now what?"

Mutt leaned over and put his mouth near her ear stating in a righteous tone. "I just found out Dr. Wassaman from the Department of Health is looking for him. George tells me that little rash all over his belly will go away, but I don't know. It would not be right for you to get it too."

Rachel was such a compulsive obsessive person who washed her hands so much that she had dish pan hands with cracked fingers always scrupulously inspecting the silverware, never serving her customers a dirty spoon, knife or fork. Her obsession carried over into her personal life. She never bought bent cans at a grocery store, thinking somehow the contents had gone bad, rejecting any food in which the expiration date was anywhere near expiring, wiping down all canned goods and even packaged groceries with germ killing sanitary wipes..

George came bounding back to the table, in an amorous mood hoping to take up where he left off. When he sat down and attempted to throw his arm around Rachel, she pushed him away and said in a loud harsh voice, "Don't touch me!"

"You are kidding?" said George incredulously.

"Don't even think about touching me, Buster," said the obsessive cleannie.

When Mutt, and his designated girl for the night, broke out with a gut splitting side holding laugh, George looked at his friend suspiciously. He said, "What's going on here. Hanson, I know you had something to do with this."

"I know all about you peeing on your hands and Dr. Wassaman looking for you. No telling what kind of disease you are carrying," Rachel said hurriedly. "Come on Marge, let's leave these dirty creeps."

The two waitresses stood up; brushed the front of their dresses down and left in a haughty manner.

Mutt, who was rolling around in the booth with laughter, didn't seem to mind the loss.

"Okay Mutt, I know you set me up. Let's hear what you told that goofy waitress."

In between chuckles, Mutt had to tell of his brilliant prank, which left George un-amused, vowing to get even.

Mutt had no qualms about spending his dad's money. George, on the other hand, had to nurse the funds he received from the U.S. government under a Pell Grant and his scholarship.

When the two went out nightly, they dined in style. With plenty of excellent restaurants along the coast, Mutt insisted that they sample the gourmet dinners from each one. They dined on T-bone steaks, Lobsters, Crabmeat Alfredo, Broiled Pompano seafood combination dinners as well as other tasty delights, Mutt always grabbing the check.

When the drinks were ordered, Mutt put them on a tab, which was usually astronomical. Finally George, who had recently hit his mother up for a few extra dollars, turned to Mutt and said, "You have been picking up the tab all the time. Today, I am going to treat you. You can order anything on the menu."

"I can't believe it. You have out fumbled me for the bill all those times until I thought your hand was stuck in your pocket or maybe you were playing a game of pocket pool. You say order anything on the menu?"

"That's right," said George. This is my treat."

After finishing the superb meal at Frenchie's Seafood Restaurant, Mutt said, "George since you have been so nice and are catching the bill for the meal, I will provide the after dinner drinks at my father's expense." He laughed. "What do you recommend?"

"I have heard that Drambuie's are a nice after dinner drink," said George who had never tasted one in his life.

Mutt held up his hand with two fingers and said to the waitress, "Two Drambuie's."

The good tasting drinks came in small glasses about the size of a shot glass. Mutt gulped his down in one swallow.

"Aah!" he said, "how about another?"

They had another; then another and soon the waitress announced that they had run completely out of Drambuie's. This did not stop Mutt who was beginning to enjoy himself. He ordered Daiquiri's. They drank Daiquiri's until the waitress announced that they had drunk up all the rum.

"Make them with gin," shouted Mutt who now was feeling no pain.

That night they closed the bar. George paid his tab and Mutt had to produce a credit card to handle a bar tab that was ten times the amount of the price of the meals.

"Don't buy me no more meals, George," said Mutt as he staggered out the door.

Soon after that, Mutt quit going to class altogether. They were rolling them on to victory each night and it got to the point that Mutt could not make it to class on time. Best just to drop out and drop out he did.

George did not dare drop out. His mother monitored his activities and made sure he got up and went to class--hangover or no hangover. Many a time, he had to hang on to this desk as the room whirled around and around. That professor droning on and on did not help any. George just held on for dear life.

But being young, he was fortunate; most of his hangovers didn't last past ten or eleven in the morning. Those morning classes were pure hell.

"Are you alright?" asked a sweet voice coming from the chair, Mutt had recently vacated.

George looked up and saw this humped nose plump girl looking at him with concern.

"I am fine," said George. "Just a little nausea."

"Too much night life, I expect," said the girl dryly.

This remark caused George to take a closer look. It was a friendly face with freckles on her cheeks which were also rosy. Her hair was light brown and the intelligent looking eyes were emerald green, the most beautiful he had ever seen which separated her from all the other overweight girls he had seen on campus. Instead of a bulging pants suit, this one wore a flowery dress.

"How very astute of you, my dear," said George deepening his voice; how did you deduce that?"

"Oh, it was not hard. I bet if I lit a match close to you, you would burst into flames." She added, laughing. "The nose knows."

"You got me there," said George. "And where did you come from. I don't believe I have seen you before."

"Oh, I have been here all along, George Murfrey. From what I have observed, you have been operating under diminished capacity."

George was both annoyed and proud that this saucy girl had noticed him and had even found out his name.

"Well, my dear, you have me at a disadvantage due to my diminished capacity. I don't have the privilege of knowing your name."

"It's Maybellene Modine. You can call me May." She stuck out her soft little hand and George grabbed it with his big mitt.

"Nice to meet you May. Where do you call home?"

Before she could answer, Professor Bartlett addressed the class, "Please open your books to page 339. Today we will read excerpts from Will Shakespeare's Romeo and Juliet..."To be continued," whispered George. "See you after class."

"Okay," May whispered back. "And I promise not to light a match."

"Thank God. You sure had me worried."

CHAPTER SIX

Boy meets girl

It boosted George Murfrey's ego to have a person of the opposite sex notice him, seek him out and even move to the back of the class room to sit by him. It didn't matter that with the humped nose and a body like his, no other boys found May attractive. As a matter of fact, males had found Miss. Modine repulsive and had joked about her ever since she had lost her baby fat. Most men would have argued that she had kept the greater bulk of that commodity.

She had left her seat and had journeyed to the back of the room to sit next to him! That was a plus and inwardly he smiled in satisfaction to himself. So what if she was overweight, definitely not pretty except for those smiling green eyes and over did it a little with the perfume. She was witty, easy to talk to and she was nice. That mattered!

They met after class. Both had two hours until the next class. After having coffee in the break room, they went outside and sat under a large oak tree sharing sandwiches. George had a crunchy peanut butter and jelly sandwich; May brought two tuna fish salad sandwiches. He apologized for his hangover, the remnants, of which was only perspiration, still giving off fumes. He told her that he and his friend Mutt had gone out the night before and had partied a little. She had already seen Mutt and had checked him out.

"Will he be coming back? I mean, will I have to move?" asked May.

"No. I don't think so. Mutt says he has dropped out for the semester. He did not like college much, but in his defense, he had already taken these courses at the University of Edinburgh and, of course, found them boring. Some of the curriculum I, too, have already had at Gulfport High."

He learned that May hailed from Woolmarket, a small country village just north of the college. She owned her own automobile, a used

Buick. She shared an apartment with another girl a half mile down the street from the college on the Gulfport side.

They had a lot in common besides similar physiques. Both had received government aid and were also in college on scholarship. Neither had really ever dated anyone without being fixed up on a blind date. George acted like the man of the world; Mutt had set him up with drunken broads which made him somewhat experienced. In truth both were virgins and hadn't the slightest idea of what a sexual experience was like. Neither one had much money.

"If I can borrow my mother's car, want to do something Saturday night?"

"George, are you asking me out on a date?" May inquired. She always seemed to be amused by his antics.

"I guess I am," said George. He shrugged his shoulders. "You are so easy to talk to; it just seemed natural that we see each other Saturday night; that is if I can borrow my mother's car."

"You won't have to, George. I have a car. We can go in mine, if you put some gas in it."

As George was getting out of his last class, Mutt showed up.

"How was it today? I just got up and I have already worked up a thirst. What do you say we head over to Little Jacks and grab a cool one?" said Mutt in his deep scratchy voice.

"Alright by me, but I want to go home early tonight. No heavy drinking. I need to be home by ten. I have already been threatened with immolation by a girl in my class."

"No kidding? How is that?"

"She said she would strike a match and burn off the fumes. I was impressed. She even moved from the front of the room and took your vacant seat." George gave Mutt a wry self-satisfied smile then said, "I have a date with her for Saturday night. She is going to pick me up in her car."

"Say, I guess you have been learning something from your old buddy. You certainly had me fooled with all those strike outs. That was pretty fast work. This girl have a name?"

"Yeah, she has a name. I don't just ask no-name females out. Her name is Maybellene; says, she remembers you."

"Maybellene. Maybellene. I am afraid I can't place her. What does she look like?"

"Oh, she has brown hair and the prettiest green emerald eyes you have ever seen and a smile...her smile will wilt you down," said George.

"Still can't place her."

"She is built like me."

"What?"

"She is kinda heavy like me."

"Oh, I think I know the one. It is not that big ole fat girl with the humped nose is it?"

"That's the one," laughed George.

"My, my, that girl needs an extreme makeover." Mutt hesitated and then added, "Maybe she can cook."

"It's a date, for God's sake. It is not like I am going to marry her."

"Famous last words. I can fix you up with something better than that.

"That's the trouble, Mutt. The ones you fix me up with; think they are better than me."

"And they are George. They are."

They both laughed.

The nightly carousing and heavy drinking continued as he and his friend Mutt rolled them on to Victory. But not so much for George who alternated with what he called dates with his new found friend, May Modine.

He found out that May's life had been no bed of roses. Her mother died suddenly when she was five and her father who was unable to raise a young girl, was persuaded to let her aunts divide the responsibility between them. At age eleven, May got a job in a locally owned dress shop where she worked after school. All the way through high school, she worked at various jobs such as five and dime stores and even an insurance company where she had to quit when her boss almost raped her. That was when she let herself go. She gained weight and found that this repulsed those instant lovers who had only one thing in mind.

When she graduated from high school, she left Woolmarket and moved into an apartment.

May was proud of the fact that she was independent and had no patience for complainers. Being fat and on the repulsive side did not bother her, since she had no time for romance. It was not in the cards. George was different. He came across as being harmless. His idea of a big date consisted of trips to the movies and a large carton of popcorn. They were both classified by the "in crowd" as being outcasts. One of the students at the junior college even drew a cartoon which depicted a fat girl and an exaggerated fat boy coming out of the woods saying to the girl, "It was a nice try Miss. M, anyway." It was obvious that the two were too obese to perform intercourse. The cartoon drew a lot of laughter among the student body when the cartoon was published in the school newsletter.

Drawn together, they actually enjoyed each other's company.

On their inexpensive dates, they would sit on the seawall overlooking the Gulf of Mexico, talking or in their bare feet, take walks along the water's line. George even brought out his Floundering gear; they could be seen at night from U.S. Highway 90, with a bright light on a pole, walking in the shallow water, searching for the flat fish burrowed in the sand with only the two eyes showing.

Agnes Murfrey liked May. She was a steadying influence over her son who had gone off the deep end after his friend Woody was killed in action. Agnes had no use for Mutt, who was always blowing his horn in his flashy sports car, bringing George home intoxicated at all hours of the night.

Agnes loosened the purse strings, giving George money to finance his dates with May. She bought George a nicer set of clothes and even had May over to eat some of those Flounders the two had caught. The Flounders, his mother's favorite, stuffed with crab meat and Italian bread crumbs proved to be delicious.

"I would like to have that recipe, Mrs. 'M.'" said May while eating a slice of Pecan pie topped with Vanilla ice cream.

"No problem, May. Do you play bridge?"

"No, Mam. I have never had the time, but I think I could learn. That is when I get the time. I work part time and go to college except, of course, when I am with George," said May as she laid her pudgy hand on his arm.

"I wish you could use your influence and get him to stop running around with that Mutt Hanson," said Agnes Murfrey. "He will never take the place of your deceased friend, Durwood. As my mother used to say, 'That man is False Grits'. He is not the real item. No true friend would lead you astray like that. Get yourself another friend."

"Aw, Maw," said George. "Mutt is alright."

"Mrs. M., said May with a puzzled expression on her face. "I am not familiar with that expression—False Grits. What does that mean?"

"Whenever grits is cooked the right way, it is thick and tasty. If you get a plate of something runny that won't stay on your fork; well, that is false grits. It has no substance and almost impossible to eat. You know kinda like trying to eat a bowl of soup with a fork."

George was getting it from both sides. The next time he saw his friend Mutt point blank asked, "You still seeing that fat broad? You need to spread yourself around. Remember there is safety in numbers."

"We are just friends," assured George. "I can talk to her. She doesn't just talk about herself like some of those other girls I met. I like her. Besides we have something in common," said George smiling.

"I know--two roly-polies."

"Wrong! She has a gas problem just like me."

"No!" screamed Mutt. "The next thing you will be telling me: you two make music together."

"Listen. Last night she let out a big one. I mean a big one. It smelled just like red beans and rice. It was so thick I could taste it."

"Great balls of fire," said Mutt holding his nose. "That should be enough to quit dating her."

"What are you talking about? I love the taste of red beans and rice."

"Oh, I get it, Farts," said Mutt with emphasis on the nickname. "You are putting me on. Say you are putting me on. I don't know if I can handle this. It was bad enough last night that you filled my car with

66

your stinking gas, that even I, with my shot olfactory nerves, could smell it!"

"Okay, I am putting you on. But you did not have to stop the car right on Highway 90 and jump out with the door open and start waving your arms like you were getting rid of the gas. It actually embarrassed me seeing those cars passing by, the passengers staring and laughing."

The next afternoon, after getting out of his last class, Mutt, who always showed up like clockwork, did not appear. George had to catch the city bus to get home.

"I got busted for D.U. I." explained Mutt. "They made me stay in jail overnight before they let me out on bond. My father found out that I dropped out of college. He kicked me out of the house and cut off my allowance."

"Where are you living now?"

"I moved into the Will's Hotel on 25th Avenue. Its' a cheap hotel; I will find a nice apartment when I get on my feet. I still have my car and my credit card, but who knows how long that will last. I may be on foot. They said I registered point two on the drunk meter. I usually don't drink before picking you up. Hope I did not put you out ole pal."

"That's alright. Maybe, May and I can pick you up if you lose your car."

"No need for that. The city bus runs right by my door; all I have to do is to walk to the corner to catch it."

"That is kind of harsh, isn't it? Just kicked you out?"

"This has been going on a long time. Ever since my dad insisted that I go to college in Scotland. To piss him off, I got kicked out, joining the Scottish Brigade. He did not like that. After being wounded in India, I got out after serving two years. We just don't see eye to eye."

"Yeah," said Mutt with a wry smile. "That Punjab who shot me did me a favor; I got discharged with a small pension. I also get money from the trust fund, my mother left me when she died, but my dad doles it out like it was his. I sure would like to get another trustee."

"Maybe everything happens for the best," said George. "I haven't said anything, but my stomach has really been hurting me lately and I am filled with really bad smelling gas, which you commented about."

"I think I am going to lose my scholarship and the Pell Grant. With May's help, I am trying to pull my grades up, but it may be too late. Math has got me down. I have an "F" going into my exams."

"Things are tough all over," commented Mutt thinking of his own troubles.

That night, George was in such pain, his mother had to drive him to the Emergency Room at the Memorial Hospital at Gulfport. He thought it was his appendix, but the pain was on the wrong side. They diagnosed it as extreme gas pains and gave him some pills and a liquid to take telling him to consult his physician.

Agnes took him to Dr. Alfred Broussard, Family Practitioner. The doctor ordered G.I. series. The results came back and the doctor diagnosed his problem as having a prolapse and acute diverticulitis. While George was getting the word from his doctor about his malady, he was unable to control the sudden swelling, brought on by the stress, of his belly. The gas had to go somewhere.

To the consternation of Dr. Broussard, George said, "See, Dr. Broussard. I have just demonstrated my problem,"

As the office filled up with the pernicious foul smelling gas like no other the doctor had ever sniffed, he told George to please leave and go home; that he would be in touch. Unfortunately, when George opened the door, the trail of gas followed him into the waiting room. Those sick patents cleared out quickly-- some were cured and some became sicker. The receptionist, after throwing up in the ladies room, later quit, saying the job was too much for her.

Dr. Broussard had Stanley Steamer clean his rugs, hired a painter to paint his walls and hired a new receptionist. He called Agnes about his bill and the bills for the tests ordered at the hospital.

"Dr. Broussard, I never dreamed those bills would be so high. I will have to pay them on time. All I have is a small pension from Western Union where I used to work and Social Security from George's father. You said you needed more tests. Frankly, I cannot afford them."

"Have you thought about getting George on Social Security Disability Benefits? He has the worst case of diverticulitis I have ever seen. In my opinion it is permanent and he is definitely unemployable.

68

Tell you what Mrs. Murfrey; I will help you fill out the paperwork. No need to bring your son in. I will send in my medical report and that should do the trick."

"Oh thank you Dr. Broussard. Can you get him on Medicaid?"

"Don't thank me, Mrs. Murfrey. Your son's claim is legitimate; just one more thing-please don't bring George back to my office. He really stank up the place. When I went home, my wife took one sniff and would not let me in the front door. She made me go around to the back door, take off all my clothes, and throw them in the garbage can before she would let me in. There I was standing at the back porch naked as a Jaybird. She made me bathe before she would have anything to do with me. Just do that for me and I promise, I will get George his disability benefits."

Getting George Cedric Murfrey declared totally disabled, was not that easy. George had never held a job. He would have to draw on his father's Social Security. Fortunately, Mr. Aloyisus Murfrey had pulled in a high salary as a welder, before hitting the road, and had continued to work somewhere out west.

But that did not matter. What mattered was that Social Security was not about to give George a monthly check on Dr. Broussard's say-so. They ordered their own tests, but when their own doctor reviewed the medical reports of Dr. Broussard as well as the hospital reports, he nixed further testing and agreed with Dr. Broussard. From the reports, he understood perfectly about the incident in Broussard's office; he wasn't about to let that happen to him and his office.

Even then Social Security hired a vocational expert, who in his opinion, stated that Mr. Murfrey could still work George was capable of pasting buttons on women's blouses or could be a paper clip bender.

Agnes hired Attorney Roswell Jones to appeal the denial. The hearing was held in Hattiesburg, Mississippi before Judge Wayne Collins, a retired Circuit Court Judge from Mobile, Alabama. Attorney Jones asked the Social Security expert if where there was a job within a hundred miles for a button pastier or for a paper clip bender. When the vocation expert said there were none, Judge Collins went on to review the report that told of the gaseomyletitis episode in DR. Broussard's office and concluded that it would be impossible for other workers to work near George without some kind of gas mask.

After a brief conference with the attorneys, Judge Collins concluded that all parties agreed that no demonstration by the Claimant would be necessary.

The Judge banged his gavel and said, "Disability granted!" This meant that George would receive the sum of $587.00 per month as long as he was disabled. The Judge, who had observed George like a Chicken Hawk, added, "I want it in the record that I observed that Mr. Murfrey was clearly grimacing in pain as he clutched this stomach throughout the hearing.

Now Farts Murfrey and Mutt Hanson, were equals financially. Mutt received $204.00 monthly from his pension the Scottish Brigades gave him for getting shot up in India and $400.00 per month allowance from his mother's trust fund whenever his father loosened the purse strings.

The night life was out. No sleazy women hanging on their arms which Mutt habitually picked up. That was over and out!

His car having been taken away, now Mutt either had to catch the bus or walk to town.

The fall out continued. George did not make good enough grades to move on to a major college. He graduated second from the bottom from Gulf Coast Community College with an Associates' Degree.

Maybellene graduated Suma Cum Laude and was offered a job as a loan officer at Friendly Finance Company. She took it.

Occasionally, George was allowed to borrow his mother's car if he had a date with May. Other times, May would furnish the transportation.

Now that Farts was declared totally disabled by Social Security, he took it to heart. A job was out of the question; no sense looking for one. He and Mutt were constantly seen walking around town, gesturing with their hands vividly, while arguing about world politics. They continued their debates while dining at Joe-Bob's Diner or at a drug store that sold noon day meals. Then they attended matinee movies at the Gulf Theater, but their favorite hang-out was the Palace Pool Hall.

CHAPTER SEVEN

The Palace Pool Hall

The Palace Pool Hall was situated across from the L&N Railroad station, a historic dilapidated station from the nineteenth century. If one walked to it, the pool hall was about four blocks north of the Ship Harbor and two blocks west of Twenty-Fifth Avenue, the main thoroughfare in Gulfport. Many considered the pool hall, an eye sore, due to the derelicts and undesirables who came and went. Except for patrons who hung out at the pool hall and a few passengers who waited for a train, there wasn't much traffic in the area. South of the pool hall were closed and boarded up businesses. The area east of these businesses, including the pool hall, was bordered by an alley where they kept the garbage cans and received deliveries. Being partly secluded, not very many persons, who weren't part of the defined customers, ever ventured in to shoot pool.

In their present state of affairs, Farts Murfrey and Mutt Hanson fell into the designated categories for those pool hall patrons; in fact they became regulars.

Inside, the establishment, was a large dark room lighted only by the shielded light bulbs that hung over eight worn and beat up pool tables. The wooden bar, with its' many cigarette burns, scars and discolorations, was 'L" shaped running almost the length of the room. The bar was lit by various beer signs; one which would blink on for a few minutes and then turn itself off. The, only other source of light, a blinding light, came when someone opened the door to come in or exit during the day. Anyone walking by the establishment would get a whiff of stale beer, pine sol, urine and cigarette smoke. Spittoons were placed strategically around the room; they were never emptied.

It was a hot day in July. Mutt and Farts had gone to the matinee at the Gulf Theater showing once more and again, "For a Few Dollars More" starring Clint Eastwood. After the movie, they decided to walk over to the Palace and shoot a game or two of eight ball.

Due to the heat, the huge exhaust fan, in back of the room, was turned off so that the air conditioner could keep the customers cool.

The intermittent neon Budweiser sign plus heavy clouds of cigarette smoke made the old daytime customers appear as ghouls sitting at the bar. Later, after getting off work, the bar would fill up to capacity, with hustlers, pool sharks, duffers, learners and drinkers. When the pool tables were full, others would drink a beer and wait for someone to finish. Players could be heard shouting, "Rack 'em up" to Tony the retarded rack boy.

Beer was the beverage of choice for the red necks, alcoholics, near-do wells and locals who frequented the establishment. Sometimes higher class businessmen or maybe a tourist wandered into the confines. The bar kept a bottle of Old Stag whiskey, if they wanted liquor. Usually after one drink, their curiosity would be satisfied, the amazed on-lookers sliding off their bar stools, hitting the door with great speed.

Mutt Hanson and Fart's Murfrey were well known at the Palace. Both were considered duffers. If one made a spectacular shot, he could be heard saying, "I had rather be lucky than good!"

Each eight foot pool table had six wide pockets that allowed the occasional "lucky" shot.

On this fateful afternoon they made their way to the last pool table which was located at the end of the room where in the wall was the extra-large exhaust fan that normally sucked out the cigarette smoke, the stale beer and the urine smell that came from the Men's room located to the right, behind the far end of the bar.

When Fart's was present the exhaust fan would suck out the occasional blossoms that were emitted by him when he became excited, a fan much like the one installed in his home.

That fateful day, all the tables were in use. The two derelict icons of Gulfport stood at the bar sucking on a Bud Lite watching an excited and loud bunch of teenagers trying to play pool on their designated table. The teenagers were obviously learning the game. Lined up on the table were five or six quarters which indicated that they would be using the torn and ripped table for quite a while.

When table four became available, Farts and Mutt were forced to use that one, if they were going to play pool. They were on their fourth game of eight ball and fifth Bud Lite; Farts had gotten lucky; Mutt scratched while trying to sink the eight ball making Fart's the winner.

"Rack boy!" Fart's yelled in his high voice that came out when he was excited. "Rack em up tight this time, Tony," said Fart's.

Farts leaned back, putting all his weight on the pool stick to get a good break hitting the cue ball with such force that after striking the triangle of balls, his once white cue ball went flying off the table.

What made this break so unusual was not the fact that he broke from an angle instead of hitting the balls straight on: That happened often when Fart's broke. On that particular break, balls blasted by the cue ball, went every which way like a herd of stampeding cattle. One of the balls, the eight ball, which had spent a lot of its life in the spittoon that was conveniently located, flew off the table. On table three, Big Jake Bannister, the meanest man in the room, was in the process of putting away the nine-ball for one hundred dollars. He had leaned over and was in the process of making the shot when the errant spit covered eight ball catapulted from table four, flew over striking him in the pit of his back. Bright green in contrast to the other pool tables, designated number three table, which had recently been recovered, did not stay that way long. Jake's pool stick missed his cue ball and dug into the new cloth making a long furrow down the pool table. Furthermore, the eight ball, when it struck Jake in the thoracic section of his back continued rolling up until it struck him in the back of his head. The eight ball bounced off the table on to the floor, rolling toward the front door.

Not only did the 6'6" tall, 275 pound truck driver from Lizana, Mississippi, miss his one hundred dollar shot, but the furrow in the table ran about three feet exposing the dark grey slate. The sign on the wall in front of Jake's table caught his attention momentarily. It stated plainly in large letters: "Torn pool table--$15.00 per inch. Jake could not count that high, but he knew it was bad.

Not only did he lose the hundred dollar bet, but he would owe over $400.00 for the damage to a pool table that would be out of operation until it could be recovered.

"Yeah," he thought to himself. "I will just owe it instead of beating them out of it."

As the shock wore off, there was laughter from the drunks at the bar including Toothless Tom who giggled in a loud shrill voice thinking it was extremely funny.

Big Jake did not think it a bit funny. When the crowd saw Jake's rage building, they ducked their heads, the cackling suddenly ceasing.

There was not probably a single ball in the Palace that had not been soaked in the tobacco juices found in those spittoons; no one had ever seen them emptied. There was a legend passed down from drunk to drunk that one of the former derelict patrons, Jim Burrows, was down in his luck and took the bet of $10.00 that he would take a drink from one of the spittoons. The story goes that Jim lifted the spittoon and began to drink and drink without stopping. Those watching yelled, "Stop. Stop! You won the bet!'

But Jim kept on drinking the contents, until the spittoon was empty. When asked why he did not stop, the now $10.00 richer bum simply replied, as he wiped the brown-green substance from his mouth, "I couldn't stop. It was all in one piece."

Jake wore a white body shirt which was his pride and joy because it showed off his large muscular ham hocks, he call arms. When he turned his back to the bar, the row of drunks saw the yellowish brown spot where the eight ball had struck him in the middle of his back, the stains leaving a dotted trail, where the ball had rolled up his back.

"Bulls eye!" Toothless Tom cackled in a high loud voice. No one contained their laughter this time. Everyone, sensing that this was to be a historic moment, stopped what they were doing and focused their attention on the developing incident.

Big Jake turned, focusing his attention on Fart's Murfrey, who was trying not to join in the mirth, but was unable to contain himself, his rolls of fat shaking up and down as he laughed shrilly.

Jake, who never liked a fat boy, shook with anger, his muscles rippling through out his body, his jaw grimly set.

"You rotten son of a bitch! You miserable fat bastard!" he shouted in a deep harsh loud voice. "You! You made me miss my shot. Can't you keep your balls on the table?"

Jake looked straight at this round face whose cheeks showed the result of too much drinking, now reddening further from embarrassment. This poor excuse of a human even held his pool stick like some girl with two fingers.

Like a ping pong match, the watchful eyes, of the patrons, clearly enjoying the altercation, swung their attention toward Farts.

Failing to recognize extreme danger, Farts said in a high pitched voice, "My balls are not on the table. They are right here." Then he grabbed his crotch.

"What was that?" snarled Jake. "What was that you said?"

Farts glanced at the ripped pool table and back into the feral animal eyes which were blazing, immediately knowing he was in deep shit. Sweat popped up on his forehead. He frantically looked for an escape route.

There was none.

At the rate this behemoth was approaching him, he had no chance. Fart's 350 pounds of fat was no match for Jakes 275 pounds of hard muscle. He just stood there like a scared rabbi, eyes blinking. On the front of Jake's shirt were specks of fish scales and fish blood which told him Jake had been fishing earlier that day. In a scabbard on Jakes belt was a large blue bone handle Bowie knife with which Jake probably killed sharks as well as people who knocked their pool balls into his back.

When Farts did not cut and run, Jake came to an abrupt stop. He paused for a moment. The whole place was quiet except for the hum of the air conditioner and a beer box that had kicked on. Thick smoke hung under the pool table lights giving the scene a macabre effect. For a moment time was frozen.

Everyone shifted their attention back to Jake. Maybe the quiet stillness was what made him stop and pause. Jake trying to get some calm back said, "I asked you a question, you fat fart."

"Big Jake," answered Farts in a higher octane voice. "I was trying to be funny--you know lighten things up. When I said my balls were not on the table, I didn't mean nothing by it."

Mutt Hanson stepped in between Farts and Big Jake and looked up at the towering giant. He said in his deep baritone gruff voice, "He didn't mean nothing by it, so why don't you go back to your pool game?"

Bartenders worth their salt can sense a problem before it gets out of hand. Edward "Slim" Flourisant, the bartender with twenty-eight years under his bar tending belt, had been enjoying the confrontation, but now he knew he could lose his job if the pool hall was demolished. In his mind he pictured Big Jake throwing pool tables around like sacks of cotton trying to get to Farts and then breaking every crooked pool stick in the house over Farts' fat head and anyone else who happened to get in the way or foolish enough to try to stop the melee once it started.

Slim threw down the dirty bar towel he was using to polish a beer mug, hurrying around the bar in an effort to stop the fight that was building up like a Gulf squall.

Still looking for a way out, Farts started backing toward the same wall that his cue ball had bounced off earlier, while, Big Jake tossed Mutt aside like the flick of a fly.

Slim was not going to make it in time; the crowd of patrons blocked his way. They did not want to miss the slaughter that was about to take place.

As Slim finally made it through the crowd of spectators, he saw Big Jake holding Fart's by the neck, with super human strength lifting Farts' off the floor, his feet dangling. The other arm was drawn back with a balled up fist cocked like a pile driver on the other end. He was about to deliver the coup de gras.

"Stop!" commanded Slim.

What seemed like an eternity in which time was frozen again, the action stopped; the deadly blow never came.

Instead, there came a "woosh-flappy-flappy-flap" that sounded like the humongous proverbial whoopee cushion being sat upon. It lasted the fifteen proverbial seconds that Farts was good for.

The enveloping smell was horrendous.

As soon as the fog struck Jake, he loosened his grip dropping Farts to the floor like a large hot potato. Instinctively, Jake turned and began to push through the crowd to the door. He could hear Toothless Tom yell, "Come back and fight you coward!" Now, Big Jake was the one looking for an escape route. He bulled his way through the unmoving crowd pushing and knocking them out of the way like pins in a bowling alley, reaching the curb out in front of the Palace, taking a deep breath of fresh air, then threw up the cheap green Falstaff beer he had consumed earlier in copious amounts which gushed out like water from a fire hose then falling to his knees.

As Jake puked up his guts in now what became dry heaves, he was joined by drunken customers who formed a line at the curb on their knees, also, as they barfed loudly. People passing by in their automobiles had never seen the like. It looked like Muslims, who instead of saying their prayers to Allah, were throwing up everything they held in their stomachs. Then Toothless Tom staggered out blinded by the bright light from a sun going down, tripping and falling onto Jake's back with enough force to tip him over into the gutter streaming with vomit. Others were literally crawling slowly out of the pool hall like insects that had been sprayed with pesticide, slowly dying.

Only Mutt, Farts and Slim, the bartender remained in the vacated pool hall. Like the captain of a ship going down, Slim did his last duty. He pointed to the door with one out stretched arm that sported a long tobacco stained bony finger and croaked, "Get out!"

"Well, I never!" protested a recovering Farts who was now triumphant.

Mutt, whose damaged olfactory nerves somehow had built up immunity to Farts' gasses, said in his deep voice, "Come on. Let's get out of this crazy place. It stinks in here."

He grabbed Farts by the arm, propelling him out of the door, where the former patrons were retching loudly, then crawling and falling over, trying to get off the hot pavement. Now the sun was sinking fast; street lights were blinking as the vapor lights tried to fire up. Moths were already striking those lights that now stayed lighted sending the insects plummeting down to the street, some landing in the expelled beer pretzels, peanuts, pickled eggs and pigs feet, the gourmet fare hitherto fore served in the Palace, all now flowing in the gutter like a small yellowish stream.

As Mutt and Farts stepped over prone bodies, they could hear the giant exhaust fan of the place start chugging to clear the inside pollution. They had no idea that turning the exhaust fan on was Slim's last duty before he collapsed onto the filthy concrete floor. Calmly leaving the scene the two miscreants walked around the corner toward Twenty-Fifth Avenue. Big Jake, still down, rose up, tossing Toothless Tom off his broad eight ball stained back, uttering wildly, "Get off me, you drunken fool!"

With that, he slowly straightened up, staggered to his "dualie" white Chevie pick-up truck pulling off behind the traffic jam of other former customers who were trying to make their get-a-way.

Jake turned the corner in the big truck to the left, heading toward Twenty-Fifth Avenue which would take him out of Gulfport onto his home in Lizana up Highway 49. He spied Mutt and Farts, who looked like they were on a stroll through the park, without a care in the world. He threw on his brakes bringing the heavy pick-up to a grinding stop, but when he heard the sirens, seeing the flashing blue lights heading his way, he thought the better of continuing the altercation, now flooring the large white truck, leaving only a black cloud of diesel exhaust from his truck.

Because of the traffic jam by the departing vehicles, the squad car was unable to make the turn in order to park in front of the Palace. They parked on Thirteenth Street a half blocks away, walking around the corner the rest of the way. Seeing about fifteen drunken men and one woman crawling around the sidewalk as well as the erratic driving of the departing vehicles, one of the Officers pulled out his radio and called for back-up. This was a first for them.

While one officer called headquarters, Officer Frank Baldwin yelled, "Tell them to bring emergency vehicles and enough transportation for fifteen or twenty people." He added. "Tell them it looks like a disaster hit here!"

When Officer Baldwin approached the wide open front door, there was a young man propped up next to it, mumbling incoherently. The other bodies were slowly getting up, ambling off, as if they were the walking dead, the crime scene vanishing before his very eyes. They acted like they did not hear him, when he yelled for them to stop! He later explained this phenomenon to his chief. "They acted like a bunch of Zombie's; like my orders did not penetrate their brains."

Officer Baldwin got his next shock, when he stepped into poorly lit pool hall. It was quiet like a tomb. And to go with the eerie feeling that set the hairs on the back of his neck climbing, was a body lying on the filthy floor. On closer inspection, it was Slim Flourisant, the bartender. He knelt and placed his fingers on Slim's neck. There was a faint pulse.

He detected the odor of rotten eggs; on second thought, he wrote in his report, "it must have been the toilets over flowing." The earlier pungent skunk-like gas had been sucked out by the exhaust fan and all that remained was the residual cloying odor that clung to the walls, the pool tables, the wooden bar, the Juke Box and Slim.

What attracted Baldwin to the lit up juke box, programmed to play a record every thirty minutes, if no one fed it with dollar bills or quarters, all of a sudden, the mechanism within the juke box began to whirl as the tub holding the records spun, an arm reaching over picking up a record, then dropping a it down onto the turntable, another arm containing a needle landing on a preselected record, the juke box blaring out, "Matilda! I cried and cried for you. That was the only thing I knew to do...."

This wailing song of the singer, who had lost Matilda, was out done by the wailing of the Mobile Medic square shaped ambulance that had pulled up in front of the entrance. Baldwin rushed out the door to see his partner, Officer Ben Joseph collaring ole Toothless Tom, who was jabbering something incomprehensible. He had a knot on his forehead the size of a fifty cent piece All the officers could make out from the jabbering was something about a "Big Jake, that done this," pointing to the large bump on his head.

"In here!" screamed Baldwin who was also pointing, not at the toothless one, but inside the pool hall. "And hurry! There is a man dying in there."

The mobile medics rushed in with a stretcher, checked Slim's vital signs and placed him on a rolling gurney while another medic fastened a mask to his face and began giving Slim a dose of pure oxygen. They grabbed the end of the gurney, pushing, him to the ambulance, sliding him into the back, slamming the door and within seconds the meat wagon took off, wailing it low ear piercing sound as it faded into the distance, while the juke box inside having finished with "Matilda" went back into its silent mode.

The oxygen did the trick. By the time the wagon arrived at the Memorial Hospital at Gulfport, or MHG as it was called, Slim had regained consciousness, was sitting up, the medics holding their noses from the foul smell that clung to his clothes.

Since MHG was only about two miles from the pool hall, the ambulance made it to the Emergency Room Entrance within five minutes. They made Slim lay back down on a gurney, rolling him quickly into a private room, leaving him there as they slammed the door behind them upon their rapid exit.

Slim seemed to be alright when the E.R. doctor came in to examine him. He wrote on his prescription pad and handed to the nurse standing by. It read: "Discharge this Pt at once and order a taxi to take him home." The other E. R. patients, victims of car wrecks, knife fights and a busted appendix protested vociferously about the rotten smell of the outhouse that seeped from under the door where Slim was housed. A nurse quickly sprayed an air freshener which masked the odor. She then went outside and handed the half used canister to the cab driver, who had just driven up.

"Here, you will need this!" she said to the confused driver. He did not stay confused long after Slim was walked out to the cab and propelled into the back seat by two attendants. The driver made use of the freshener by spraying down Slim before driving off.

Only Toothless Tom was arrested by the cops that day, the rest having taken advantage of the distraction with Slim and his crises.

"They fled and managed to get away." the police report stated. Toothless Tom was hosed down before being given an orange jump suit and placed in a nice air conditioned cell with clean air.

   The officers, wanted to leave the doors to the pool hall open for the night: They told the Assistant Chief on duty that there was no danger of anyone going in there to rob the place, but the acting chief nixed that idea. He could not fathom how the smell could be that bad. Everything was left on including the lights and the juke box which continued to loudly play, "Matilda, I cried and cried for you..." every thirty minutes, all through the night, up until the daytime barman came to work the next morning. He took one sniff, covering his nose with his handkerchief, went over to the junction box throwing the main switch cutting everything off, departing with great speed.

CHAPTER EIGHT

Murfrey closes pool hall

The entire town of Gulfport was in a stir over the closing of the Palace Pool Hall. The patrons, who included the all-day drinkers, the pool hustlers, the laborers, stopping to play a friendly game or to shoot the bull over a cool one as well as Mutt and Farts, who called the place home, were all out on the street

Like a chain reaction, everyone was affected.

The all-day drinkers could no longer sit and drink their way into a stupor and not be bothered as they mumbled incoherently.

The pool sharks took their business to Larson's Billiard Hall on Pass Road, but Larson ran a tight pool hall; he made sure his customers were not fleeced by the hustlers. His clean spotless place was illuminated by numerous overhead fluorescent lights in which even motorists passing by, could see through the picture glass windows from their vehicles. The atmosphere was all wrong; it was not conducive to underhanded sharks out to make a buck at the victim's expense.

The daily camaraderie, between the hard working blue collar boys, came to a halt. It was a ritual for them to stop every afternoon at the Palace; drink a few brews, shoot a few games of pool before going home to the demands of an angry wife and the sassy brats who were in constant turmoil. A few beers helped them get over the rigors of the job caused by an irate foreman after the usual screw-ups or perhaps the serious threats from some job bully, much like Big Jake. The fact that their hands and fingernails were dirty, their clothes caked with grime and sweat only made them more attractive to the bar molls who hung out at the Palace, trading dirty jokes and lewd suggestions with them.

The all-day drinkers migrated over to Johnnys' Bar, a tavern located across from the Hancock Bank in the heart of the business district. Johnny already had his hands full containing his own customers, keeping them from offending the businessmen, women and children and policemen who passed by his place regularly, having had

82

numerous complaints about the loud profanity and obscene language and guffaws over dirty jokes that occasionally filtered out from his bar on to the street.

The all-day drinkers from the Palace brought with them, new challenges for Johnny Bertonelli. One harmless drunk, one-eyed Joe, became confused, wandered out of the bar onto the corner of Twenty-Fifth Avenue and 13th Street, unzipped his already stained britches, letting loose a steady stream of yellow urine that astonished men, women, and children passing by. "It was like a cow pissing on a flat rock" was the way, one astute observer described it.

In Belgium on the streets of Brussels, a father once got separated from his very young son becoming frantic. When he found the boy, much to his relief, the boy was standing on the corner taking a leak. The father, so grateful, he erected a monument of the boy pissing, like a water fall, on the spot where he found him. This had become a must for tourists to go see the "Mannequin Piss".

There was no statute erected for one-eyed Joe. Instead he was barred from returning while Johnny rounded up the other day drinking drunks, woke them from their mumbling bliss and threw them bodily into the street with a warning: "...and stay out!"

The confused drinkers ambled down the street to Stavos Candy shop where they sold candy to the kids in the front part of the store and alcoholic beverages in the rear. Their customers were mostly business men who needed a snort now and then, during the day in order to endure their irate bosses who stayed on their backs about errors being made plus a drink or two before going home to their angry wives and their snotty nose, sassy mouth urchins with their unbelievable expensive demands.

The hair, on the back of Rau Stavos' neck, stood up when he saw a band of red faced vagrants heading for his door. He had been sweeping up scattered M&M chocolate covered candies, spilled by a bawling child who wanted a replacement and not getting it. Leading the way was one-eyed Joe, who had had an accident due to the rude treatment he had received earlier at Johnny's Bar. The front, of his soiled khaki pants was soaked and his fly was still unzipped. Rau dropped his broom and ran to the door just in time to turn the knob to lock it. He quickly grabbed the sign on the door that said "Open" and flipped it around to "Closed".

After trying the door handle to no avail, one-eyed Joe stuck his one eye up to the glass door and peered in. He could see the bawling little boy who has dropped his candy as well as other customers who were looking at him beating furiously on the door.

"Open up in there! I can see you. You are not fooling me. Open up!"

Joe was joined by five or six other daytime ghosts, who needed to be hidden by dark bar rooms; not exposed to direct sunlight. It was frightening to the young crying boy who stuck his head into his mother's front legs.

Rau held fast and one by one the defeated bunch wandered off totally confused.

They were now displaced persons.

It was the beginning of a new era in the City of Gulfport. The Palace Pool Hall customers fanned out in an effort to duplicate what they once had. Some went to Biloxi, which had several pool halls of the Palace caliber, but the Biloxians who never liked Gulfportians, resented the invasion and inflicted black eyes, busted lips and bloody noses on them to demonstrate their dislike. Out in rural Harrison County these refugees could expect worse; they were known to use baseball bats.

The word was out!

The displaced refugees blamed Big Jake Bannister. He had better not show his face around Gulfport. Even the police were alerted to pick him up on sight. They had an APB out on him.

Mutt Hanson, displaced by his father, and now by the closing of the Palace Pool Hall, had no place to go. He did not fit in at Larson's Billiards. It was not conducive to his type of drinking and pool shooting. He tried Bogie's Lounge in the Best Western Motel on the beach. It was dark the way he liked it and had a few high class ghostly phantoms, who drank all day replacing beer, with sipping scotch. He gave it a try, but when he got loaded and began talking loudly in his harsh gruff voice, several sissy boys, who pranced around glad handing everyone, except him, while carrying a Tom Collins or Pina Colida in their hands, objected strenuously to him.

There was nothing left for Mutt to do but to silence his critics by a punch up the side of their egg sucking heads. When he was thrown out, the police were outside waiting for him, taking him to the grey bar hotel. After he sobered up, he was corralled with other drunks and taken before the ugly talking judge, he knew quite well, and was given sixty days in the county jail.

Mutt did not mind being sentenced to a work detail painting curbs a bright yellow, being quite good at it. He hated the lectures from the Judge, who was a drinking buddy of his father, about how he was wasting his life. Somehow his matriculation at the U. of Edinburgh always came up.

Farts Murfrey, also had his problems: With Mutt in jail, he was in a quandary as what to do during the day until his girlfriend got off work. His mother was enjoying the fruits of her retirement from Western Union; her routine not including George, meeting each day with her lady friends to play some duplicate bridge.

George hated it, when "the crew", as they called themselves, came to his house to play. They all talked at once and never seemed to listen to each other. Such distorted conversation drove him bonkers. He would leave, when his mother would let him drive her vintage gangster mobile, a black, 1939 La Salle probably once owned by Al Capone or one of his co-conspirators.

Ordinarily, his routine was to sleep until noon, watch Judge Judy on TV and after 5:00 p.m. he would hook up with "Patty Cakes", as Mutt called her, and they would find something to do such as walking along the beach barefoot or just sitting on the seawall discussing world events.

May leaned toward the Republican viewpoint, because her boss was a staunch Republican; George took the Democrat side after he heard that the Democrats were responsible for making it possible for him to collect Social Security disability benefits. They disagreed, but never fought. After a long day of work, May was simply too tired to fight about anything.

85

Whenever her roommate was away, May would smuggle George into her apartment, where they innocently watched television.

Most of all George missed his friend Mutt. On one bright sunny day, he walked up town on the chance he would see his friend painting curbs. Sure enough, halfway down the street just north of Johnny's Bar on Twenty-Fifth Avenue, he saw Mutt, paint brush in hand dripping bright yellow paint on the sidewalk while greeting him.

"How is it going?" asked Farts, leaning up against a building, trying to look inconspicuous.

"I am alright," said Mutt. "That sorry assed judge gave me ninety days, suspended thirty and told me not to come back or the next time it would be double." Mutt put his dripping paintbrush down on the curb, straightened up, lit a cigarette, puffed on it three times and threw it into the gutter.

"That ass hole told me, if I did not stop taking up his time, he would run my skinny ass out of Gulfport. Those were his very words!" He looked at Farts with a twinkle in his eye.

"I told him, if it wasn't for people like me, he would have to work for a living. He did not take that too kindly. I had to stand there and listen to his monologue for ten more minutes about how he knew my family and what a disgrace, I was. How my dad, the great doctor had given me a superb education in Scotland and maybe I should have stayed there."

"I tell you, I would have liked to have tried his honor on, but those two thugs in uniform were just itching for a chance to jump me, so like the gentleman I was, I held my peace."

"You did right," commented Farts from the wall he was leaning on. "Can't you apologize and tell the Judge you have learned your lesson and won't do it again. Maybe he will cut your time seeing as how you are doing such a great job painting curbs."

"Been there and done that, but thanks for the complement on my expertise as a curb painter. No other jail bird can hold a paint brush to me."

"I sure miss the Palace. Have you heard when they will open again?" asked Farts.

Mutt bent over, picked up his dripping paint brush and made several swipes at the curb. He said, "I dunno. Talk around town is to keep it closed forever. I heard some of the high muckety-muck businessmen have petitioned that Senator from Pascagoula to run a bill through Congress and get the Coast some kind of urban renewal. Their plan is to change the face of the whole Gulf Coast. You know --remove all the eye sores. On the list beside the Palace Pool Hall are Mary's Drive Inn, Katie's Cafe and Pud's Liquor Store. Tear those down and there goes our watering holes and sobering up cafes. All this because of one magnificent blast from your blow-hole," he guffawed.

"Speaking of a blast I am bored. "Can you still shoot those blue flames?"

"Are there cows in Mendenhall?" said Farts. You gotta light?"

Mutt stood up and produced a long wooden match from his shirt pocket. He then approached Farts from the side.

"Let's see." he said.

As Farts bent over with his large derriere facing 25th avenue, Mutt lit the match by flicking the head of the match with his thumb nail. Farts was leaning with both hands against the concrete wall of the building in order to get full stabilization. He cut loose with his best effort of the day. As the full load of gas was forced out, Mutt threw the lighted match and stepped back quickly.

A bright blue flame about twelve inches in diameter and three feet long shot out like a miniature flame thrower.

While Mutt was standing to the side safely in amazement, a brown Ford Explorer was passing the area headed north on 25th avenue. Watching from the passenger side was little Jimmy Jenkins who had his nose pressed against the door window.

"Mama, Mama!"

"What is it, Jimmy?"

"Mama, I just saw a big fat man shoot out a big blue flame from out of his big fat ass!" exclaimed little Jimmy.

"Now boy! What did I tell you about lying and what have I told you about calling people fat asses. Your father has got to quit talking like that around you. And furthermore, young man, you quit making up stuff like that. You hear?" said his mother who was itching to haul over and swat this small copy of his dad.

"But mama, I know what I saw!"

"Jimmy!"

"Yes mama, but I saw what I saw." Jimmy turned his head and started a long sulk; which he was very good at.

Mary Thomas, who was a waitress in the Palace Café (no relation to the pool hall) almost directly across the street, witnessed the brief blue flame. Excitedly, she called the Gulfport Police station telling the dispatcher of the unusual incident.

The manager of Firestone's had just paid his bill for a cup of coffee at the same cafe and was trying to jay walk back to his store when he, also briefly saw, what he reported to be a broken gas main, shooting out a blue flame.

This really got the dispatcher's attention.

"Car 54. Check out reports of a broken gas main that just occurred south of the Firestone Store. Ten-four?"

"Ten-four. We are on it." Car 54, was heading south about a half mile north of the incident in front of the Catholic Church. The responding officers swung into action. With blazing blue lights flashing and a grating horn blasting at intervals, traffic quickly cleared in front of them as they sped to the scene.

"Uh, oh!" said Mutt. "Here come the gendarmes".

"See you later,' said Farts as he quickly squeezed into a four foot space between Firestones and another brick building. The space allowed Farts to waddle to an alley located behind the buildings. He took a left turn and hoofed it down another street toward home. The patrol car had to make a U-turn at the traffic light on 13th Street, drive past Johnny's Bar on the corner in order to pull up in front of Firestones located just south of the L&N railroad tracks.

The two cops jumped out and ran over to Mutt, who was busy slapping bright yellow paint on the curb and singing in his best baritone voice, "Make the world go away. Get it off of my shoulders."

"What's going on here?" questioned the tall skinny cop.

"Nuthin' occifer," replied Mutt in his best imitation of a dumb hick.

"We got a report that a gas main blew up shooting out flames. You know anything about that?" said the fat accompanying officer.

"Naw, I ain't seen dat sire." said Mutt disrespectfully. "And I'se been hear de hole time."

"We got another report," said the skinny one. "From the waitress across the street at the Palace Cafe, who said she saw a fat man with a flame thrower shooting out blue flames. Know anything about that?"

"Naw. Ain't seen nuttin like dat neither. Say, was that fat man you described as fat as dis occifer?" pointing to the heavier policeman with his paint brush.

"Don't get smart with us, Hanson. I recognize you now. You get smart with us and we will take you straight to jail and tell them you gave us trouble. They will throw you in the hole and forget you were there," said the fat officer clearly not liking the insult.

"Yeah, it will be my pleasure," said the other officer.

"Well I ain't seen no flame thrower around hear," said Mutt in a high pitched voice as he stood up with his paint brush dripping yellow paint into the gutter. If they were going to drag him to jail, they would have yellow faces when he got through with them.

"Okay, then," said the heavy set officer eyeing the quivering paint brush, fully loaded. "We are going to check on this incident. You wait right here."

"Occifer, I ain't going no whar. I'se gonna stay right hear and paint this here cerb, just like the Judge Cardell done tole me to. Judge Cardell was insistent about getting dis here cerb painted. Take me away from dis cerb an you will have de Judge to answer to."

Abruptly, in a huff, the officers turned and marched to the Firestone Store where the manager, Eric Blake, could not say he saw a fat man or woman near the area where he had seen the blue flame. All he could say was "It was a big blue flame. I can tell you that."

"Can you better describe the flame you saw?"

"It was a very large flame; four or five feet in length. It reminded me of the flame from an exploding gas line. Again, I did not see any fat person there. There was this convict in orange uniform, who was painting the curb. Why don't you go ask him?"

"We did, but you know how those people are. We could not get any sense out of him."

The two officers jay-walked across the street, strolling into the Palace Cafe to interview the waitress, but she was of little help. All she could describe was a big long flame like from a flame thrower looking like it came from a big fat person at the scene. Her brief view of the incident was blocked by a SUV traveling north. After it passed, she did not see the flame or the fat person again, but thought it was her duty to call it into the police department. No one else in the Palace Cafe saw anything out of the ordinary and probably would not have said so if they had.

In their written report, the officers concluded that it must have been a "back fire" from an automobile. They could find no other source or other witnesses to the purported incident to support any other conclusion.

After that mind stretching episode, the officers decided they needed a break. They cruised down to the Waffle House on U.S. Highway 90, each getting a cup of coffee. The heavy set officer got a jelly filled donut. As they were sitting at the counter, the fat officer said, between bites," That Hanson didn't fool me a bit. He was hiding something. I don't guess we will get the truth out of him. Do you?"

"Doesn't Hanson run around with a fat guy named Murfrey? I think I have seen those two walking around town."

"I believe he does. But if Murfrey was there, how did he disappear so fast? I don't think he could disappear like that," said the officer snapping his fingers.

They both sipped their coffee and cogitated on the matter awhile.

Finally, the skinny one, Bill Blanco of Hispanic descent, said, "Wasn't Hanson and Murfrey at the Palace Pool Hall the other day, when the fight broke out and the sewerage over flowed? I hear they caused it."

"Yeah, it comes back to me now. We never got no proof. No one would talk and the ones who did were a bunch of stupid drunks who didn't know shit from Shinola. I remember Murfrey now." I would like to pop that fat turd up side of his fat head with my billy-stick. No offense intended to you Joe. That Murfrey always has that possum eating crap grin on his rosy red face."

"No offense taken," said Joe Parent. "Don't worry. We will get our chance. Wherever Hanson goes, he causes trouble and where you find Hanson, usually you will find Murfrey."

"Say," said Officer Blanco. "I have been thinking. May be we should have searched that Hanson. They make cigarette lighters that throw out a big flame."

"I don't know no lighter that throws out a flame as big as the one those witnesses described. Do you?"

"No, but you know how witnesses enhance things."

"They sure do. You know we got an APB out on Big Jake Bannister for fighting, destroying property and fleeing the scene. When we catch up to him, I feel we will get to the bottom of what happened at the Palace."

"How come they shut it down? The sign said, 'For Renovations'. What is there to renovate?"

"You did not hear? The officers, who were the first to arrive, after the fight, did not find anyone inside except Slim, the bartender. He was on the floor unconscious. They said the stink was like nothing they had ever smelled. They said they had smelled dead men whose corpses had rotted for forty days and their smell wasn't as bad as the smell in the Palace Pool Hall. Both lost their dinner. According to them, the only cure for that place is to tear it down or if they could get approval, burn it to the ground.

"Sounds far-fetched to me," said Joe Parent. "At least when the Palace was open, we knew where the derelicts, deadbeats, drunks, hustlers, pool sharks, goons and crooks were located. Now they are scattered all over the place."

Getting up from the stool, Officer Blanco threw a dime tip on the counter. He said, "Lets' take a cruise around town and see if we can spot Big Jake's pick-em-up truck or some of those other undesirables you just listed."

"Good idea," Officer Parent agreed.

Big Jake was not found. One of his hobbies, when not busting heads in pool halls, or skinning sharks, was listening to his police scanner. When he heard his name mentioned that the police were still looking for him, he decided to avoid the City of Gulfport and shoot some pool in the out skirt villages known as Kiln or Delisle.

There was a tavern called "Little Lil's" at the crossroads in the county that had a pool table. It had been over a year since he had been barred from the premises for beating up two pool players who had whipped him playing nine ball. Accusing them of hustling him, Jake had broken the only two straight pool sticks over the heads of the two offenders. The two injured players had been regular customers who fed the juke box and spent a lot of money at the dive.

Jake hoped that all had been forgotten by now or maybe it was under new management. But as luck would have it, Big Jake was not going to play pool that day.

Leaving his wooden frame house in Lizana, that could use a paint job with its white paint peeling off the exterior, he stopped off at Manson's Quick Stop to get a pack of Marlboros. Bud light was on sale. "Might as well get a six pack to drink on the way to Lils," he reasoned. That way he would not have to pay the higher bar prices to get a buzz on; he could drink his six pack on the way and have his buzz when he got there. While Jake was at the far end of the Quick Stop looking into the cooler for his beer, in walked none other than George Cedric Murfrey, AKA Farts.

Since Farts' mother was having an uproarious bridge party, after he arrived home from seeing his buddy, Mutt painting curbs, he knew he would never be able to stay in that house. He did not want to be seen in Gulfport or surrounding areas including Biloxi, where he might get his ass kicked, so after getting permission to borrow his mother's car, he agreed to have the car back by 5:30 p.m. that day.

It was then 2:30 p.m. and all Georgie intended to do was to drive up Highway 49 to Saucier and get an Icee; then turn around and come back. Maybe he would stop at the Super Walmart in North Gulfport.

Somehow, he missed the store in Saucier, so he turned west and found himself in the little village called Lizana. Seeing Manson's Quick

Stop, he decided to get his Icee there. As he walked into the converted wooden frame shotgun house much about the size of George's house, he saw that it had been converted to a small grocery store.

He did not see Big Jake, who was in the back by the beer coolers trying to decide whether to buy Bud Lights or to try a new beer called "Big Mouth", which came in a quart bottle. It had a wide mouth on a squat bottle brewed in New Orleans. It only cost seventy-nine cents a quart.

While Jake was trying to make up his mind, Murfrey asked the petite blond cashier about the Icee and was told that the Icee machine was "Broke Down".

"How about a Yoohoo? Do you have any Yoohoo?" he asked sweetly.

"Right down that aisle next to the beer coolers, you will find the Yoohoos with the cold drinks, said the blond, Miss. Bettye Younger, pointing in the general direction.

Just as Jake had decided the Big Mouth was the better bargain and was taking a long swig from the bottle, Farts started down the aisle in search of the Yoohoo.

Jake felt the effects of the cheap beer almost immediately. "Wow! What did they put in that brew?" said Jake aloud to himself. As he was taking a longer swig from the quart bottle, he glanced over to his right and saw the object of his present troubles standing there at another cooler, retrieving a Yoohoo from the box. It was that fat piece of crap from the pool hall. That porker had gotten away with knocking a filthy eight ball into his back and making him miss his money shot not to speak of causing him to tear the cloth of the pool table; his subsequent banishment really pissing him off.

This had to be Jake's lucky day. He could not believe his eyes. Now this fat farting machine had fallen into his big grimy hands? It had to be providence.

They both fixed eyes on each other.

Jake had fire in his eyes; Farts had fear in his! Again he was like a rabbit frozen in place by a reptile, there was that moment before Farts swiftly took off heading down the aisle nearest him which contained

93

canned goods, candy bars and motor oil. In an effort to head him off, Jake chose the next aisle which carried bread, Little Debbie cakes, Moon Pies and other delicacies.

He sat the bottle of Big Mouth on the floor and headed down a parallel aisle in big strides with a determination that Farts would not get away from his wrath this time!

In a panic, Farts careened into the goods on the aisle next to him sending cans of spinach, corn and hominy grits flying and crashing in all directions, trying desperately to reach the end of his aisle before Big Jake headed him off.

But Farts clumsiness slowed him down; as he reached the end of his aisle; Big Jake was already standing there like a big angry giant!

"You will not get away from me this time!" screamed Jake. He was now four feet from the frightened Farts Murfrey, already sweating around his brow with flickering eyes of sheer fear.

And Farts did what he always did when scared. He farted!

"Oh, no you don't. Not this time, you filthy, nasty stinking piece of filth," belched Jake with Big Mouth foam on his lips.

"Not his time! I am going to see that you never do that again!"

Holding his breath, Jake unsheathed his Bowie knife pushing it quickly into Fart's belly, parting layers and layers of fat as it entered. When he jerked out the large knife, there came a noise like a balloon being deflated. SSSSSh!

"Ut, oh," said Farts.

Jake quickly sheathed his knife while passing a startled cashier who had seen it all on the big curved mirror hanging from the ceiling, throwing a five dollar bill on the counter, saying as he rushed out of the door, "Keep the change."

About that time, Jake brushed by Mr. and Mrs. Killegrew, who were entering the store to get some eggs, milk and bread. The Killegrews' took one sniff, turned around and staggered back out down the steps in a daze. Bettye, who had taken in a quantity of the bad smelling air, made her way to the door as if in slow motion, went down the steps chucking up the contents of her stomach, which consisted of

Fritos, a Baby Ruth, a Pepsi and an ice cream bar, consumed earlier at Manson's expense.

She was still bent over losing her Fritos, when Deputy Sheriff Branch, on his way home, passed Jakes' truck leaving the area at a high rate of speed. He then saw Bettye puking and heaving. The Killegrews', his neighbors, were leaning up against their vehicle, trembling, shaking and holding on for dear life. As the deputy was pulling into the parking lot, out came Farts Murfrey holding his stomach as he stepped through the doorway, rolling down the steps bowling Bettye over, both stretching out on the black asphalt parking area.

The two lay there without moving until two Mobile Medic ambulances that had been called in arriving about the same time. Bettye Young was whisked away and taken to MHG where she was admitted in spite of her smell of vomit mixed with the stink of defecation, surrounding her like a shroud.

The vehicle carrying Farts Murfrey was halted at the Emergency Room entrance, the driver being told to wait as they were "full up".

Somehow, the hospital had gotten word that the passenger was none other than Geroge Murfrey, known by them for shutting down the Palace Pool Hall after rendering their former patient, Edward Flourisant, the bartender, unconscious. Personnel did not want their hospital to receive the same treatment as the Palace Pool Hall; that is they didn't want the hospital stunk up necessitating closure for renovations.

David Stark, the MHG administrator, alerted about the impending situation, was springing into action; his staff manning the computers to see if there was some other hospital that might accommodate Murfrey; now with a bottle of plasma hooked up to him, out in the Mobile Medic ambulance, blocking the entrance. .

Dr. McIntire, the E.R. doctor was sent out to examine Murfrey to see how bad the wound was. Much to his surprise, he found very little bleeding. "As a matter of fact," he said. "It looked like the wound had closed itself up." After putting in five butterfly clips, holding his nose, he added. "This will hold him until someone else gets him. I won't be responsible for sending him home, if he needed further treatment."

FALSE GRITS

CHAPTER NINE

Baltimore General Hospital

David Starks, a five foot tall man with a forty-five inch girth himself, did not want that fat Murfrey fellow in his hospital, a hospital ill equipped to handle his type of case. There was only one answer: Find another hospital willing to take him. Under his orders, his staff was "Googling" and "Yahooing" with pertinent information to other hospitals throughout the land.

"Exclude all those within a three hundred mile radius," commanded Starks. "The further away the better." He didn't want any kick-backs, retaliation or law suits. "And let them know what they are getting," added the administrator.

Starks knew what they had. He had gotten a full report of the happening at the Palace Pool Hall. Several of the hospital attendants were among those shooting pool there on that fateful day. They had reported it to Starks after he got wind of the event while the attendants were scuttle-butting at the hospital coffee shop.

The Governor of the State of Mississippi, running for re-election, made one of the planks of his platform, a promise to protect hospitals and doctors from high verdicts in malpractice law suits. Starks knew the governor on a first name basis. In anticipation that his busy staff would find a hospital crazy enough to take Murfrey, he got the Governor on the phone.

After explaining the problem, the Governor said, "If you can get a hospital to take him, I will make our medi-vac helicopter available to fly him to that destination. As a matter of fact one of our copters is now on the Coast at Keesler Air Force Base in Biloxi. I will have that copter fueled and ready to go. All you have to do is transport Mr. Murfrey to the air field; they will do the rest."

By the time Starks had hung up the phone, Mrs. Jo Ann Maybe, head computer clerk, announced that they had a "winner".

"The winner is the old Baltimore General Hospital in Baltimore, Maryland. As a matter of fact, I talked to Dr. Alphonse Aholie who is Head of Poisonous Gases Department. He wants to treat Mr. Murfrey personally. Dr. Aholie is world renown in his expertise and treatment of such cases. He even said that he thinks he can get his department to take care of the expense of flying Mr. Murfrey to Baltimore, the hospital footing the bill for treatment." She looked at the head honcho of MHG in a quizzical manner and asked, "David, just who do we have out there in the Mobile Medic ambulance. Why is he so important?"

"You don't want to know, replied Starks. "But I will tell you this: One of our attendants, Mark Wimper, was shooting pool in the Palace Pool Hall a couple of days ago. He claims Murfrey cut lose with a gas attack which lasted over one minute and created an odor so rotten and bad that the pool hall had to be closed down. They could not get the smell off the walls and he tells me that the smell from cigarettes, stale beer and urine was obliterated."

"Frankly, I cannot take the chance of anything like that happening to our hospital. We had one of the victims, Eddie Flourisant, who we admitted briefly to our emergency room. He was lucky that they gave him oxygen or we would have been stuck with him as well a smell that was like an overflowing septic tank. If you ever had a septic tank overflow, you would know what I mean. Our Poodle wandered down the street and got in to one, but that is another story." Starks' face became scrunched in response to the mental picture of his little white toy poodle covered with browns smelly feces from the house down the street.

Within minutes, Dr. McIntire reported that the patient was well enough to make the trip; that he had given the patient an injection; that should make him comfortable throughout his trip.

The waiting Mobile Medics opened all windows of the box looking ambulance and fixed the back doors to stay partially open in order to have adequate ventilation. They used up a bottle of air freshener on the way to Keesler AFB and were glad to find the medie-vac helicopter waiting for them with the pilot and co-pilot already in place.

The pilot, Lt. Juan Gonzales told Ben Strong, one of the medics that Strong was elected to make the trip to Baltimore. He wanted to know if Murfrey was dangerous or had a life threatening disease.

"All I know," said Strong, who climbed into the helicopter, "is that this guy is accused of closing down the Palace Pool Hall several days ago: Something to do with a fight there and over flowing toilets. Now up in Lizana, he got himself stabbed. He is sedated and I don't think he will be any trouble. He does stink, but I think we got that under control. We sprayed him down real good with Fabreze." He pointed to a new bottle of air freshener which he had pilfered from the ambulance.

"I don' think there will be any trouble, but if there is, why don't we just land and throw him out." Ben began to cackle at his joke and laughed so loud that he had to pull up his pants and take up a hitch in his belt.

Lt Gonzales did not look too happy about transporting the passenger now, belly up on a gurney, snoring very loudly. The noise of the helicopter would drown that out, however.

It was a good night for flying. Clear all the way; stars twinkling brightly and they could see the light of the passing cities shining below. It was an uneventful trip. They were able to land at the hospital on top of the roof, a space pad provided for helicopters after following the hospital's transponder beacon to the area. Still sleeping peacefully, George Cedric Murfrey was unloaded and taken to his room.

When George opened his eyes the next morning, he was looking at a little short brown skinned be-speckled man wearing a surgical mask. It quickly came back to him, the horror of being stabbed in the belly by Big Jake at the Quick Stop in Lizana. He remembered he had been in the process of purchasing a Yoohoo. His throat was parched. He really needed a Yoohoo!

"Yoohoo," he said with a hoarse whisper.

"And yoo hoo to you, too," said the short squat physician who seemed to be looking his quarry over.

"Let me introduce myself. I am Dr. Alphonse Aholie, Chief Surgeon of the Poisonous Gas Department. Do you know where you are?"

George lifted his head and looked around. It was a small room with lime green painted walls. He was in a white enamel iron bed like those he had seen in World War I movies or maybe insane asylums. There was a sink with a small mirror on one wall to his left; on the other side was a worn out leather chair in which the doctor stood behind with his hands on the back.

"Gulfport Memorial?" he croaked.

"No! You are in Baltimore, Maryland at the Baltimore General Hospital. You were flown here last night. Are you hurting anywhere?

Pointing to his stomach George said, "Just here, where I got stabbed. Has my mother been notified? I am not in any trouble am I?"

"All in good time, no, you are not in any trouble that I know of. Why do you ask that my boy? Just take it easy. I will have the nurse give you a shot to ease the pain. You are in good hands. Don't worry about a thing."

George noticed the masked doctor was dark skinned, speaking with an accent.

"How long do I have to stay here? I don't feel that bad."

"We want to run a few tests and then, we will see. Are you hungry?'

Yes, sir. I could eat a pot of beans."

Patting George on the shoulder, the doctor said, "We will see that you get fed after the tests. Can I get you anything else?"

"Where is the TV? I have visited the hospital before and I know the room is supposed to have a television. Can you get me one, doctor?"

The kindly old doctor who looked to be in his sixties or seventies said, "Well my boy, we will see what we can do. Just be a patient, patient." Catching his own joke, Dr. Aholie let out a whoop that startled Murfrey. He then stood on his toes and gave Murfrey a thump on his big belly.

"Ouch!" said Murfrey.

"Did that hurt?"

"Kinda. I am kinda sore there where Big Jake stuck me with his fishing knife."

About that time, a tall nurse, wearing a heavily starched white uniform and a funny looking hat, came into the room with a tray. She hooked it to the side of his bed. The tray contained a bowl of good smelling broth and a glass of what looked like grape juice.

"There my boy, you just eat and relax and I will be in to check on you later. Before I leave, I need to ask you one question. Did you ever know or hear about a Fanny Mae McBride from Leslie, Arkansas?"

"No. Who is she? I could ask my mother. Can I call her?"

"All in good time my boy, all in good time." The doctor and the nurse headed out of the room. Nurse Jane Bates had never seen Dr. Aholie so joyful. He was actually humming to himself.

Within minutes, Murfrey had drained the bowl of broth along with the grape juice and before he could call out for more, two nurses came into the room pushing a cart with instruments on it. The food tray was removed. One nurse held his right hand while the other had his left. The one on his left took a small rubber hose and wrapped it around his upper arm. She then tapped the center of his inner arm. Meanwhile the other nurse had grabbed his index finger and had jabbed a sharp blade into it.

"Ouch! Why did you do that," asked George anxiously. She paid him no attention, but collected a small amount of blood into a glass vial.

The other nurse holding a long silver needle connected to a larger vial with a plunger said, "Just hold still. I am going to draw a little blood."

She plunged the long needle into his arm and immediately blood ran into the tube as the nurse backed off on the plunger.

While this was being done, the other nurse was sticking a thermometer into his mouth telling him to be quiet.

Now the other nurse was listening to his heart with a stethoscope. The nurse on his right now had slipped a cuff over his right arm and was taking his pulse and blood pressure.

All this was done so fast that Murfrey was speechless; which was good since he had a thermometer in his mouth. When the nurses finished, one thrust a small bottle into his hand and said, "Now we play, 'Pee in the bottle'. I will be back in a little while to get it."

Both nurses laughing, turned out the light to his room, wheeling the cart from the room leaving Murfrey alone and in the dark except for a dim night light.

He called out, "Hey, wait! I want to call my mother...and I am still hungry."

Ignored, Murfrey would have none of this. He slid out of bed, found the light switch and padded over to a metal desk type cabinet. On top, was a pitcher of water and two glasses. He opened the door to the bottom half of the cabinet and found some slippers, which he put on. He didn't find a robe, but did find the bathroom.

Going to the door, he stuck his head out into the gloomy long hallway. The walls were grey and the floor tiles another color of grey. Only dim lights lighted the hall. It was so quiet, that a pin would be heard if it hit the floor. He noticed the cold draft which came in on his open gown from the rear.

"Hey! Anyone! I am still hungry. When do we eat around here!" he shouted. Murfrey was still shouting when a large nurse with short grey hair walked silently down the hallway in her white shoes that made no noise.

"Mr. Murfrey, get back in bed. You are recovering from a serious injury. You have no business being out of bed. If you like, I will get you some ice cream, but you will have to get back in bed and stay quiet."

Murfrey recognized authority when he saw it. He said, "Yes mam. I would like some ice cream--vanilla." He padded back to his wrought iron bed and waited.

True to her word, Nurse Andrea James, came back with a small cup of vanilla ice cream and a small wooden paddle for a spoon.

Without a smile, she said, "Mr. Murfrey, try to get some sleep. Tomorrow is a big day. You are scheduled for a lot of tests. Then we will see if you can eat solid food. If you have trouble sleeping, I will give you something to help you sleep."

"Thanks," said Murfrey as the dove into the ice cream.

Nurse James reached down under his bed and came up with a cord with a button attached to it. She handed it to him. "Push this button if you have trouble sleeping." she said without smiling and was gone.

Murfrey finished the ice cream by licking the cardboard top and cup. Sleep came easy to him, but at 3:00 a.m. two men in white shirts and trousers came in handing him a pill and a glass of water. One said. "This is to help you sleep."

"I was sleeping," said Murfrey. It took an hour before he went back to sleep.

The next day came two hours later.

"Rise and shine, Murfrey," said a deep voice. With one eye open, Murfrey saw that it came from one of the men in white who had awakened him just hours earlier to give him the sleeping pill.

"Whaat?" said Murfrey who was still groggy from the successful pill. "What do you want?"

"Time to do some testing," said the second male in white. He was a husky little man who pushed a wheel chair up to the bed.

"Let me alone. I wanna sleep," said Murfrey pulling the skimpy pillow over his head.

"Not today, you don't," said the one with the deep voice. He noticed two hairy arms reaching out and grabbing him. With ease he was dragged out of his bed.

"Watch out. You are hurting me."

"Sorry. Now get into the wheel chair," said gruffy with the hairy arms.

"We are going for a ride, so get in and hold on," said the one holding the arms on the back of the wheel chair.

This accomplished, Murfrey was hurriedly pushed along the corridor to an elevator.

"Where are we going?" asked Murfrey who was collecting his senses.

The gruffy one interjected his idea of humor, by saying, "We are going up to get you a kitty cat scan. Yesterday, we ran out of Kitties. Hah. Hah!" he laughed. "When we finish, we are going to get some more of your blood. Then it is breakfast time. After breakfast, it is to the x-ray department for more pictures. Believe me it is going to be a fun filled morning."

"I can hardly wait," came a voice from Murfrey which he hardly recognized as his own. He was beginning to wake up.

When they came to the Imaging Department, there were two females in white starched uniforms and a male also clad in white waiting for him.

A pretty brunette stepped forward. "Are you George Cedric Murfrey?" she asked.

"That's me," said George still trying to clear the cob webs from this unrealistic dream.

"Good," she said. She wrote something down on her metal tablet. "Would you like to stand up or lay down for this test? We have both kinds of the latest cat scans in this hospital."

George was still tired. "Let me take it lying down. This won't hurt will it?"

"No," she laughed. "It is a bit noisy, but it won't hurt."

They placed him on a padded board and were about to slide him into this tunnel.

"One more thing," the male nurse added. "You must be perfectly still or we will have to do it over. Do you understand?"

"Y Yes. I understand," said George who was getting nervous and becoming very wide awake. Having never been stabbed before, he was not aware just what tests were necessary, having no choice but to go along with the treatment.

"Good. It won't last long. We just want to take a few pictures. It is going to make a lot of noise, so don't be alarmed. Okay?"

"Okay."

Into the tunnel, they slid him. A switch was thrown and the most god-awful clanking and rumbling noises he had ever heard began, sounding like a cement truck with sticks of iron being thrown around. Sheer terror went through him. This was worse than the fear he had, when Big Jake stabbed him at the Quick Stop. He froze, which was just what they wanted. His pucker string tightened; no gas escaped. Finally the clanging stopped and out he came from the tunnel.

"Do you think it could have been a little louder. Next time I want to do it standing up," said a red faced George, almost in tears.

"Looks like you are going to get your wish," said the male nurse. "We were supposed to do it with contrast. Sorry, but we missed that, on your orders. Shouldn't be too bad. Besides you are a veteran now."

The third nurse, a dark haired heavy set one, almost as round as Murfrey, said, "That is my department." She grabbed his left arm and examined it. "Looks like someone has already been here." She wheeled an IV bag on a stand around to his right side, palpitating his right arm with solid blows from two fingers and then ramming a long needle into his arm.

This hurt. Murfrey was about to come off his pad, but in anticipation, the available staff held him down, The black haired plump nurse placed a strip of adhesive tape across the tube joining the needle in his arm.

"Now don't move sweetie or you will jerk it out. You don't want me to have to do this over again, now do you?" She sounded nice, but with conviction.

"No," said Murfrey.

After the contents went into his arm, he was placed in the stand-up CAT scan. When that was finished, it was back to the wheel chair and another wild ride. This time, it was back to his room for breakfast. Cold oatmeal and warm grape juice awaited him. He cleaned his plate.

Two new attendants were anxiously waiting for him as he chewed his last bit of oatmeal. Then it was back in the wheel chair.

"I need a cup of coffee,' said Murfrey.

"Later. After these tests, maybe," said the shorter stocky attendant who raced the wheelchair along the hallway while picking up speed.

Another session of giving blood, why all the blood work? Murfrey could not understand it.

He had his hearing tested; his eyes tested. He finally produced urine and the bottle was whisked away. Then it was down to the basement for pulmonary tests.

This test was not a blur like the others. One which Murfrey, as well as the old woman with brown bulging bloodshot eyes and big snarly lips, would not soon forget. The woman of average height wanted him to blow into a tube. She looked as if she could use a doctor herself. Her face was a dull grey like the complexion of a dead person.. Nurse Smothers had several other patients blowing in tubes. Namely, two old men and a middle aged woman sat at a long table blowing into their tubes, respectively. Urged on by Smothers, they were blowing hard and then coughing up oysters. Never had Murfrey seen such hawking, coughing and spitting in unison.

The nurse would pass down and pat each hawker on the back and say, "Very good, Mr. Tisdale. That's nice Miss. Beacham. Spit it out Mr. Edwards. Blow harder. Blow harder! That's it. All right-em-good. Now spit it out."

When she got to George, who was watching the spectacle in amazement, she said, "What's the matter with you Mr. Murfrey. Blow into that tube!"

Murfrey blew, but no oysters came up.

"Well it looks like Mr. Murfrey is not going to donate. Come over here Mr. Murfrey. Lets' test your lungs." She led George over to another tube which was hooked up to a slender glass tube that had a small ball inside it with a scale marked on the side.

"I want you to blow hard and keep that ball up as high and as long as you can. You had better not disappoint me."

Murfrey took a deep breath. He did not want to disappoint the good nurse this time. He expanded his lungs to the maximum.

With a mighty exhale, the ball lifted up. It hit the top with such force that it shattered the glass letting the little ball escape, rolling quickly off the table onto the polished light green floor and under another table, hitting the legs like in a pinball machine.

"What the hail!" exclaimed Nurse Smothers. "You broke my spirometer. You! You broke it! You broke my Spirometer! Out! Get out of my lab.!" Murfrey just sat there amazed. The little red ball that rolled across the floor reminded him of the eight ball that had left the pool table at the Palace, made its way to the front door as if to escape. That other incident seemed so long ago.

As when he got nervous, Murfrey began to nervously giggle.

She pointed at him with a crooked finger that looked as if it had been broken at one time in her storied life. "I mean you fat boy. This is not funny. Orderlies! Orderlies! Come get this man. The test is over!"

"Did I pass the test?" asked Murfrey.

Almost immediately, the two attendants appeared with the wheelchair.

"Get this smart ass out of my lab! Now!"

One of the attendants remarked, "Looks like you passed that test with flying colors. Ain't nothing wrong with your lungs."

With the test being cut short, George was able to return to his room just as his lunch was arriving. The dried-up stringy chicken over rice and peas and a mixture of broccoli was still warm. Apricots were the desert.

"Now this is more like it," said Murfrey as he scoffed up the meager meal.

Before the day ended, Murfrey would have been tested for his heart, lungs, eyes, ears, brain, stamina and even his stomach which showed fast healing. He had had cat scans that took pictures of all areas of his body and x-rays in other places.

The only test left was to run a small camera up his rectum and get pictures from the inside. These were left for the following morning. That afternoon he was scheduled to see a shrink.

Dr. Aholie fully expected to have the results of all tests on his desk before noon the next day. He had plans for Mr. Murfrey the following afternoon.

CHAPTER TEN

The Skunk-man

Doctor Alphonse Khristma Aholie was pushing seventy-five years of age. At one time in his early life, it looked like he would achieve greatness. That was back in the nineteen fifties when in the U.S, Army he briefly had Private Fanny Mae McBride under his care. He just knew that she was some kind of rare mutation-a throw back in evolution. She could issue a deadly spray from her rectum that baffled science-but not him. If only he could have done exploratory surgery on that freak of nature, he could have proven his theory. Alas, the army had other plans, leaving his precious theory hanging out there in the wind.

Would he ever get another chance?

Now some fifty plus years later, all he accomplished, in that time period, was to design a fine cut hemorrhoid operation for the Army, which was used by all the services as well as the Veterans Hospitals. Two small cuts in the rectum and the hemorrhoids dried up. With this method, he was able to operate on as many as thirty patients with piles a day. His proud record, in a day, was the grand total of thirty-two.

But this accomplishment did not get him the notoriety he dreamed of. Instead, he was known as the "hemorrhoid doctor". Behind his back, they called him the "Ass-hole" doctor.

Where did all the years go?

Dr. Aholie did get one research article published in the American Journal of Medicine entitled, The Effect of Methane Gas Emitted by Humans and Cows on the World Population. United States Senator, Bryce Benson took this treatise seriously. Unfortunately his peers in Congress did not recognize this threat to humanity. It was blocked in the United States Senate, when the Senator tried to get funds for a follow up study. At that time, the government was on a frugal kick as they tried to reduce the never ending deficit.

One feather in the doctor's surgery cap: He had risen to Department Head of Poisonous Gases. But this was in the run down, once abandoned Baltimore General Hospital which the U.S. Government took over, pretty much giving him a free hand. No longer did the U.S. Army have complete jurisdiction over him. Only the Pentagon endeavored to control him and he did not think they watched him very closely. Left alone to experiment, operating on hopeless patients, he felt he had a free hand to do as he pleased at BGH.

It was the Army that had snatched Private McBride out from under his scalpel, but that wasn't going to happen a second time.

The Hindu gods of fate had smiled on him. It took them a long time, but out of the blue, George Cedric Murfrey had fallen in to his capable expert surgical hands; at last he could prove his theory. This time he would present the medical world with hard cold documented proof.

He would prove that every so often, nature screwed up. He would once and for all prove that a human could be born with a set of sacs in the rectum just as a skunk. If he was correct, this patient, George C. Murfrey, had a set of those telltale nipples on each side of his anus, like a skunk. Those nipples, from which a secretion was delivered through glands, would be the proof enough.

Tomorrow, he would have his proof. Tomorrow, he would operate on Mr. Murfrey who got into barroom fights and fights in quick stops where he got himself stabbed by some redneck, as the inconsequential lower class humans often did. But he would give Mr. Murfrey his fame and justify his having taken up space on the earth.

Tomorrow!

He could hardly wait. All the tests had been done except for the last one. Murfrey would get an enema to clean him out and then the small camera would be inserted up the rectum to take pictures that justified going into the area for a specimen, which after being preserved in formaldehyde, would grace the top of his desk.

The next morning, Dr. Aholie sat at his desk waiting for the results of the tests. As they filtered in, he saw that George was an extremely healthy young man in spite of his obesity. Everything checked out. The urine test showed a normal person with no chemical elements that were of any help. Maybe he should have had the urine of a skunk tested, but he did not have time to get a hold of a skunk and make him pee. This windfall did not give him the time to be completely prepared. He could not hold Murfrey here forever, while they found a skunk and besides, word would get out the way it always does, and it would be Fanny Mae McBride snatched from him all over again. They might even check out his past experiments on patients suffering from various respiratory and lung diseases who had died quickly on the operation table.

The results of these comprehensive tests done on Murfrey were delivered into the eager hands of Dr. Aholie.

"Damn!" he uttered out loud. "Why couldn't the test done on Murfrey show any of the chemical components that make up the oily secretion that were sprayed by a skunk? Oh, well. Nothing ever comes easy."

He reasoned further as he looked over the history Dr. Iskara Meanie, the in house Psychologist had taken from a brief session with Murfrey. Meanie said Murfrey was too doped up to carry out any real psychological tests. The shrink was able to scan the numerous reports and documents that came with Mr. Murfrey from the Memorial Hospital at Gulfport. He saw where the classmates in the second grade called him "Skunkie", a degrading nickname that affected the boy's psyche. Maybe, they knew. Out of the mouths of babes...and all that. Even back in grammar school Murfrey had sprayed his stinking secretion which caused part of the school to be evacuated wherein people passing by complained about the smell of sewerage overflow. Mere methane gas would not linger like that. It fit the skunk theory where the spray from skunks lingered for several days as it spread out over the countryside.

There was no other answer. All other explanations had been systematically excluded.

This man had to be a freak of nature. He had to have the glands of a skunk and today, he would prove it!

He had done his homework, researching the anatomy of a skunk, applying differential difference reasoning in his diagnosis. The study of the secretion sprayed by a skunk had often been fraught with errors. Shameful errors! Bad testing! The phenomena associated with this supposedly defenseless animal was its protection from predators, by its potent spray.

Reading Murfrey's history, he saw a change in the potency of Murfrey's spray as he grew older. Maybe, he had not evolved yet the way Fannie Mae McBride did in ability to actually kill, with her deadly gas, but Murfrey could not be far behind. Furthermore, almost each time, Murfrey had sprayed he was being threatened, wasn't he?

What had been so astonishing was how faulty the so-called scientific testing had been in determining what actual chemical compounds did make up the skunk's spray. First, they thought it was a sulphur compound. Next, it was chlorine dioxide. No, they argued, it was croyl mercapton. Then it was a combination of isopentyl mercapton and methyl croyl disulfide.

Those scientists were all wrong. The last word was that the chemical composition of skunk's spray was either butenylemthyl disulfide or butenyl propyldisulfide, chemical words not easily understood even by this brilliant doctor from India. So how would anyone hope to compare Murfrey's chemical composition of his spray to that of the skunk? Like medicine, it was not an exact science. Besides, the meager lab at BGH did not have the facilities to analyze the chemical compounds found in Murfrey's stool. Sending the sample off to a competent laboratory would take months to get the results. The stingy government would probably veto the expenditure anyway.

The fact remained that the spray of the skunk brought on violent retching, sickness and even a runny nose could be compared to those victims at the Palace Pool Hall and especially one Eddie Flourisant, the bartender. To Dr. Aholie, it was all the same.

He sat at his desk thumbing through the test results, the psychological profile, and the history. He became more convinced that he was on the right track; he just knew he was right.

He could hardly wait. Maybe he would get a break with the spy ware, nicknamed the Bullet, stuck up Murfrey's ass, taking pictures; maybe, just maybe those nipples would be there.

He closed his eyes and made a cathedral with his hand resting on his polished walnut desk. In deep thought he could picture it now. His colleagues would be in the operating room awaiting his arrival. He would scrub up. Don his mask and surgical cap, then the gown. If the pictures taken by the tiny camera did not reveal nipples inside Murfrey's anus, he would solve that piece of the puzzle with the deft skill of his scalpel. Oh, yes, better wear a special mask in this case. Just in case this man with skunk glands decided to let loose his oily spray capable of reaching over a mile, closing down businesses, rendering his victims with violent sickness. What about the staff assisting him? Shouldn't they wear the special gas mask?

Well, let them get a whiff. Their imminent sickness would only further verify his indisputable findings.

He came out of his revelry long enough to call down to supply to send up a gas mask like the type used in industry when they sprayed toxic chemicals. He wanted it ASAP!

As he sat there, he realized there was one minor problem: Mr. Murfrey had no knowledge he was to be operated on, much less an exploratory operation that could cost him his life.

No matter.

Besides who was watching; who really gave a damn what happened to this derelict? No one missed the other derelicts he had experimented on, but they were too far gone when he got them. At least no one questioned his surgical abilities.

Yet, there would be no consent form in his file, because he had not given his consent. It would be all over before the fat bastard knew what happened. If he woke up, all he would know was that he had a sore ass hole. When he was told that he was now famous and given a percentage of the scientific awards, the soreness would quickly disappear.

Who was it who said, "The ends justified the means?" Was it Zarathusa who spoke?

Besides Dr. Rance Phillips, that dumb ass, assisting in the operation, was so stupid, he would not suspect a thing. It was operate now and ask questions later.

The wake-up call came at five-thirty that morning. First, before Murfrey could get his eyes open and focus clearly, a nurse rammed home a large needle filled with some kind of stuff that made all his fears go away.

It did not bother him when two new attendants grabbed him. One was black and the other a big white man. Or was it a white man and a black? One never could tell.

"Come on. Get into the wheel chair. This is your day. We gotta get you prepped and ready for your operation." That voice seemed to come from the black attendant, but Murfrey couldn't be sure of that either.

"What operation? He asked groggily. He thought this was a dream.

Someone far away laughed at his question. "Never mind about that, just you wait until Dr. Aholie gets a hole of you. We done seen your chart and paper work. It seems you enjoy spraying your fellowman with your filthy septic tank gas. The good doctor is going to tear you a new ass hole." The man in the nightmare laughed his hollow laugh.

The other attendant said, "When you leave here, that is if you leave here, you are going to have a brand new asshole."

"No one told me about an operation," said George meekly. "You have the wrong person."

"Yo name is George C. Murfrey ain't it? No we don't got the wrong person, do we Mac?"

"No Mr. Murfrey, if that is your real name, we have the right person," said Mac.

"They should have told me," said Murfrey. "They should have told me," he whined. "Besides, I did not sign a consent form. Don't I have to sign a consent form?"

As they pushed George down the hall, the black attendant said, "They don't have to get your consent here, fool!" He chuckled. "Not when Aholie gets you, he don't need your consent. Not in this place."

The white attendant, a movie buff, said in his best Mexican imitation, "Consent form. Consent form! We don't need no stinking consent form." They all laughed; even Murfrey.

They were moving down the hall at break-neck speed. "Slow down. Slow down," said the helpless George C. Murfrey.

"Can't slow down," said the black one out of breath. "We be already behind schedule and the doctor, he like to be on time."

They wheeled him into the prep room and after standing George up, walked him over onto a cold white plastic table. An elderly nurse was ready with a bottle of liquid which she poured onto his genitals while the attendants held the squirming unwilling Murfrey down on the table.

Out came a straight razor in the hands of the ugliest woman, he had ever seen; she even had Nurse Smothers beat. A vision, out of Halloween night, it was. This hospital had to have a collection of the worst looking nurses on earth, like from the cast of a horror movie. Where on earth did they get them?

"Don't squirm or I'll cut your dick off." said the ugly H'aint. She had a harsh crackly voice that went with her scary scrootched up, wrinkled face and fierce piercing eyes.

The white attendant holding him down warned in his best imitation of Humphrey Bogart voice, "If you move, I will do more than let that nurse slice your prick off." Bogart then reached over and squeezed his nuts real hard to make his point. George screamed!

Enjoying his movie role, the one white one, then looked over the table to his helper and said, "Hey, Paulie. Remember, that last guy who would not lay still?"

"Yeah, it was that black dude. I remember. When Nurse Croath severed it, I wrapped it up in a newspaper and took it home to show my wife who was always saying she wished I had a bigger one. "

"What did she do when she saw that one?" asked Mac.

"First she fainted. Then, when she came to, she yelled at me, "You killed Henry! You killed Henry!"

"Say. That's a good one. You didn't kill Henry, did you?"

"Naw, I never could catch the dirty little bugger. But when I do it will be Bob's your uncle after that; no more Henry. Know what I mean?"

By now, Nurse Croath had severed all the hair follicles around George's privates.

"Heh. Heh," she laughed in her witches' voice. "That was a good one." She wiped the lathered razor on a fresh towel. "No trophy here, Boys. Look at that teeny weenie."

In self-defense, George's privates had gone into hiding--even his sore nuts. The nurse knew her business; there were no nicks.

While the two attendants were rolling Murfrey down to the next stop, they were whooping it up; enjoying their work.

"You bunch of cretins," George muttered under his drug induced nightmare.

Down to the elevator and up two floors the jocularity continued until they rolled Murfrey into the room where there were a dozen filled beds on wheels. These were wounded soldiers and marines who were transferred over from Walter Reed Hospital due to an over flow of the wounded from Iraq. The beds were lined up like airplanes awaiting take-off on a runway. Above them was an electronic bulletin board that gave the scheduled time each veteran would receive his operation. George C. Murfrey's name was seventh on the list showing exploratory surgery. Doctors Aholie and Phillips were listed as the operating doctors.

Each bed had a bottle fastened to it wherein the patient was being given an IV.

George was helped from his wheel chair by his now serious attendants who could not have been more concerned and polite. He was placed in bed seven, an IV placed in his left arm.

Still out of it, George vaguely heard the attendants arguing that George should go first as Dr. Aholie did not like to wait.

He heard: "This is Johnson. He is only here to get an amputation. Can't you put Murfrey ahead of him?"

The nurse running the show grabbed Murfrey's chart, perusing it carefully.

She said, after going over the paperwork in her metal tablet, "Well the good doctor will have to wait. Mr. Murfrey was ordered to have his rectum scoped. Get those attendants back here."

A few minutes later, Paulie, the black attendant and Max, the white, showed up with the ubiquitous wheel chair. They were not at all happy. In fact, they were grim faced after being chewed out by the head nurse, snatching the needle and tube from George's arm, designed to put him under for the operation.

"Sorry Murfrey, we missed the best part," Max said. "I dare any normal person to decipher Aholie's chicken scratching that passes for handwriting. And that was dirty, for that old hen of a nurse, to blame us for the mistake. Someone should have printed it out. Ain't that right Paulie?"

"Damn right," said Paulie. "Murfrey, or 'skunkie' or 'farts' whatever your name is, you have caused us enough trouble. You better not cause us any more trouble. Don't even blink your eyes."

But Murfrey did cause more trouble. When they arrived at the lab where Murfrey was to have his picture taken --up his rectum, it was discovered that no one had given Murfrey an enema to clean him out.

"I am not going to stick my, new state of the art, camera up that fat boy's ass with all that crap still inside him. You need to take him to the Prep department and get it done. Then bring him back."

At this time George was snoring softly; the small amount of sedative he had received intravenously had put him to sleep. So with his head hanging to one side, his mouth drooling saliva intermittently, he was brought in for the enema.

Meanwhile, Dr. Aholie, who had checked with the surgical waiting room, finding his patient, had been taken away, called the testing department where the protoscope was to take place.

Nurse Helga Schmidt another unpleasant looking nurse, picked up the phone on the first ring. "Well what is it now?" she bellowed.

"Nurse, this is Dr. Aholie," he said in a melodious voice, which doctors learn in med school.

"Well, what is it doctor, A-holie?" with emphasis on 'holie'. We have all these wounded soldiers shipped in from Iraq and I am busy. So spill it."

"I just called to see what the hold-up is on patient, George C. Murfrey. Would you check on that please? Everything is on hold in surgery, if you know what I mean."

"I know doctor. Don't let no monkey spoil the show." She brought up Murfrey's name on the computer and said, "Looks like Murfrey is getting an enema as we speak. Hold on. I will transfer you so you can get it first-hand."

Before the doctor could object, he could hear the phone dialing the prep department. "This is Nurse Vilonia. May I help you?" said a syrupy voice at the other end.

"Uh, this is Dr. Alphonse Aholie," he said still in his calm soothing voice.

"Yes, Doctor Alholie, how may I be of service?"

"I need to know the progress being made with George Murfrey. I understand that you have him."

He heard nurse Vilonia shouting in the back ground, "Do we have a patient named Murfrey?" A few seconds later she said, "Yes, doctor, we have him. If you hang on I will go see what progress is being made." She laid the phone down leaving it on speaker phone. Dr. Aholie could hear her addressing the attendants and nurses who were working on Murfrey.

"Dr. Aholie is on the line and he wants to know your progress," Vilonia shouted.

"You tell the good doctor that we are knee deep in shit. This is no easy job. The smell is awful. Each of has had to leave the room to change the charcoal filters in our masks. I have had to change mine three times already. Tell him we are almost through."

Another voice sounded off, "Tell him we have evacuated about forty-five to fifty pounds of this filth. Every one of us has thrown up at least once."

Another voice, a female, piped in, "Tell him not to send any more patients like this one or we will quit. Ask him if he is a friend or an enema?"

There was a chorus of uncontrolled laughter. It sounded like they were having a party down there.

When they were through with the comments, one said, "Yeah, let him come down here in this cesspool. Doesn't he know dirty work takes time? When we are through with this patient, he will be as clean as a whistle."

"I would never blow on that whistle!" Laughter again.

"Whew! Tell him he needs to come down and sniff for himself."

Nurse Vilonia returned to the phone and said sweetly, "Doctor, they are just finishing up. It seems there was a lot of fecal matter and...."

"I heard, Nurse," he screamed. "I want a list of everyone participating in that enema and an accurate weight of the recovery matter." He slammed the phone down.

It seems that neither waiting nor humor was the doctor's forte'.

Couldn't anything go right in this cock-eyed hospital? His patience was wearing thin!

Murfrey who was knocked out on drugs slept through it all. But it was not an easy sleep. He dreamed he was back in the second grade. Miss. Newman was fussing at him for stinking up the neighborhood, her included. She had tried to mask the odor with strong perfume, but Miss. Jessie, the Principal has sent the teacher home with instructions not to come back until she rid herself of that awful odor. While the enema was being performed, Murfrey could smell it just like yesterday.

Dr. Aholie sat in his office tapping his fingers on his large walnut desk. Normally, everyone in the hospital was afraid of him. Why was today different?

Could that bunch of incompetent odd balls have been affected by Murfrey's skunk powers? The only person he was afraid of, who took no crap off him, was that Head Nurse Schmidt. Sometimes he wished he was back in Pashaw, India, his home village, where he would be a big fish in a little pond. It had been a long road up until now and he was becoming more impatient by the minute.

The phone rang. Good news. The tiny camera was up Murfrey's fat ass and pictures were being taken and put on DVD. A copy of the disk would be sent up pronto for his viewing. Yes, there were no obstructions. Mr. Murfrey's passage way was as clean as a whistle.

"It won't be long now," he thought. One thing, he could never understand, was the Army's interference with his operating on Fannie Mae McBride fifty years ago. Nothing had changed; he was rash and impatient then. He wanted to put her to sleep; do an autopsy on her where he was sure to find skunk glands and those skunk nipples in her rectum. He had learned of the testing that was done in Alabama on a bunch of Negros. They were subjected to various amounts of poison gas and of course, they all died. This dark page in American history had been kept a secret, but he was privy to all those records as head of poisonous gases. Why was the case of Fannie McBride any different? Those blacks were expendable. Even George Murfrey was expendable if it came down to it.

While he was tapping away with his fingers, the DVD containing the tiny camera's findings was brought up and placed in his DVD player.

He watched with close intent interest.

Nothing!

He rewound it and put it on slow speed.

Still nothing! No nipples like those of a skunk. It was a clean healthy rectum and colon. He would have to go in. Maybe further up Murfrey's colon, he would find those nipples and glands that had to be there; maybe they were hiding.

The operation was on. His heart began to flutter.

Dr. Aholie took his good time washing up. He wanted to savor every moment. His assisting nurse helped him with his cap and then his starched white lab coat which he wore to set him apart from the rest. Actually his staff thought he looked like some crazy professor from a scary movie.

His assisting doctor, Dr. Phillips, had already scrubbed up and was there with the rest of the surgery team, including the Anesthetists standing by.

The star of the show, George Cedric Murfrey, lay prone on the operating table, without a care in the world. He was still dreaming and snoring away.

"Turn him over and let's get on with it," commanded Dr. Aholie soon to be known formerly a hemorrhoid doctor, but thankful he had had so much experience operating on rectums.

Dr. Rance Phillips, who was standing by to assist, handed Aholie the thick file on Murfrey.

"You better look at this," said Dr. Phillips.

Dr. Aholie took the file and glanced through it quickly. "So? I have seen it. In fact I have studied it. Let's get on with it. Give me my gas mask and scapula please."

The nurse placed the scapula in his hand and was reaching for the unusual looking gas mask with round breathing vents on each side/.

"Hold it! Hold it! You can't operate doctor," said Dr. Phillips. He was a young doctor in his forties with blond hair and clear blue eyes. He had a firm jaw which Dr. Aholie was looking at right now since Phillips was a head taller than he was.

"And why Not?' said Doctor Aholie indignantly.

"The tests show, for one thing, that there are no tits inside this man's rectum. That was your theory wasn't it?" Dr. Phillips said gesturing with his hands. "There is nothing to operate on. Nothing! Why operate on this man now. It is a useless operation."

"Useless! Useless! Who are you to tell me it is useless?" he screamed. "I make the decisions here. Stand back. I am going in. Just because the camera missed those nipples, not tits by the way, does not mean they are not there. Useless! Useless, you say! You, are the only useless thing in here doctor."

"If you can't be of help, then take your useless self and leave my operating room. I have had enough of your interference."

"I have no doubt about what I will find. It is like operating on a gallbladder where the tests did not show gall stones, but the patient had all the symptoms. We knew those stones were there, so we operated and behold, there they were. Remember that operation? You assisted me."

"Shall we begin? You will see I am right in this case also."

Dr. Phillips stepped forward placing himself between Murfrey and Doctor Aholie. He said, "The Hippocratic Oath commands us to do no harm. Have you forgotten that? This is not a gallbladder operation. I have been to the medical journals and researched as far back as the sixteen hundreds on the subject. There are no tests to support you on this. All we have is a history of this man who on occasion passed some foul smelling gas. I also, have read the file on Fannie McBride. There is no resemblance to those symptoms. This man's gas has not killed a soul. And now that he has evacuated some fifty pounds of feces, he is, in all probability, cured."

"Has he passed any poisonous gas in the past or since he has been here? The answer is no! You have nothing doctor. Nothing!"

"Are you through Doctor Phillips? I will not listen to any more of your insubordination. I am chief surgeon here. You are merely an assistant."

Dr. Aholie lifted his head to let his bloodshot eyes bore into Dr. Phillip's clear baby blues and said, "Let me be perfectly clear on this. I am going to operate on this man and I am going to show that I am right and you are wrong. Nothing is going to stop me; not even you. Either assist me or get out. I will operate without you. And when the operation is over, I am going to write you up and this hospital will no longer employ you."

CHAPTER ELEVEN

Escape from BGH

Little did Dr. Alphonse Aholie know that when the administrator of the Baltimore General Hospital hired Dr. Rance Phillips one of Dr. Phillips duties was to keep an eye on Aholie.

The administrator, Alfred Clark, told Dr. Phillips, "Dr. Aholie is a brilliant surgeon. His two cut hemorrhoid technique, which he developed, was a stroke of genius. It saved the hospital and government a great deal of money; it meant that no longer would this once extremely painful operation take several hours to complete; it meant that the doctor could operate on as many as twenty patients a day. Healing begins instantly and the swollen hemorrhoids began to heal right away as they dried up. And the patients liked it too. Costly convalescence, which took up needed space, has been saved."

"But back to Aholie, like a lot of geniuses, he tends to go off the deep end. Besides learning his skills, one of your other duties will be my watchdog. Part of your job, besides assisting him, will be to make sure he doesn't do anything that will get us sued by some hot shot malpractice attorney. Think you can handle it?"

"No problem," said Dr. Phillips. "How far can I go?"

"You have carte Blanc," said Admistrator Clark.

After that condition had been imposed on Dr. Phillips, he had watched whatever Dr. Aholie did, like a super spy. He closely reviewed each and every file on each and every patient they operated on. Although there had been highly suspicious operations performed by Dr. Aholie where the patient did not survive, this particular case was different.

Today was the most egregious example of the loose cannon he had been watching. It was a deep end, alright in more ways than one.

Forgetting the gas mask, with scapula in hand Dr. Aholie did an end around quickly and before Dr. Phillips knew what was happening the deft hand moved to make its incision.

Before Aholie could slice into Murfrey's exposed rectum with the razor sharp knife, he felt a tight grip on his arm.

What was this? Did Phillips dare to grab a surgeon who was in the motion of making a cut?

When Dr. Aholie realized, that Dr. Phillips had grabbed him, his blood began to boil, veins standing out on his forehead, heavy haired eye brows arching, bloodshot eyes bulging, flashing with hatred.

"Get your hands off me! You incompetent jerk," he screamed. He jerked his arm loose from the vise grip jerk that held him. As he stood there glaring at Phillips, for a moment it appeared that he was going to make a few incisions on Dr. Phillips.

This was unpardonable. It was verboten.

It was an unwritten stead-fast law, that no one ever touches the body of a surgeon after he had spent fifteen to thirty minutes scrubbing up.

Dr. Aholie turned to his assisting nurse; dropped the scalpel into her hand and calmly said, "Now I will have to scrub up all over again. Nurse please call security. I want this man removed. After he is gone, I will continue my scheduled operation." He turned, looked at Dr. Phillips intently and with emphasis said, "Goodbye Phillips."

"I don't think so Dr. Aholie. If you had looked through this file thoroughly, you would have noticed that there is no consent to operate signed by the patient. If you operate and are sued, I will so testify. It is you, who will be eliminated from this hospital, not me. This is wrong and you know it."

"The consent form must have been misfiled. I am sure he signed it," Aholie lied.

"No doctor! I have monitored this patient from day one. I talked to the two attendants, Paulie Jones and Maximillan Athernon. They both verified that they picked up Mr. Murfrey this morning. Mr. Murfrey, when he was told that he was to be operated on, objected strongly and he even brought up the fact that he had not signed a consent form. Would you like me to summon Mr. Jones and Mr. Athernon?"

"Not necessary. That throws a different light on the subject." He turned to his nurse while fidgeting with his cloth mask and announced,

"The operation is cancelled for today. Take the patient back to his room. I will reschedule after we get rid of the technicalities." He then ripped his surgical gloves from his hands with a pop, snatched his cap from his head and threw them both on a table. He then took off, the still pressed white lab coat, and let it drop to the floor and quietly walked out leaving the highly starched lab coat standing by itself.

Once more, George Cedric Murfrey had dodged the bullet, or in this case, a very sharp scalpel.

Again, the two attendants, Paulie and Max, were summoned to pick up Mr. Murfrey and return him to his room. They silently and glumly pushed him through the hallway; this time on a gurney with a sheet covering this small mountain stretched out snoring and snorting.

Perhaps it was the harangue that had just taken place that registered in his sub-conscious, but instead of snoring and sleeping peacefully, Murfrey was now snorting in fits and at times snoring so loudly and making primeval grunts and screams that it sounded like some wild animal on the loose. As he was being wheeled past the other patients' rooms, it disturbed those inhabitants so much, that they too, let out awful howls which brought the nurses running from their station. The nurses were ready to make a quick escape; if it turned out that indeed a wild beast was somehow roaming the hallway.

"It's alright, ladies," said Paulie laughing. He was now regaining his warped sense of humor. "It's just Mr. Murfrey in 403. It was a no go, today. Aholie and Phillips got into it and cancelled the operation. From what I heard, we missed a good one."

One of the nurses said, "We heard." Pointing at the snorting Murfrey, she asked, "What's his condition? Did Dr. Aholie or Dr. Phillips send any instructions?"

"Nope," said Max who stopped to talk to the inquisitive nurses. "I guess we will just let him sleep it off."

"That sounds good. Come on back boys when you get him tucked away in bed. I have another patient to transfer to X-rays. It's old Bill McIhenry."

"Ain't ole wild Bill died yet?" asked Paulie grinning.

"Not yet, so get your bee-hinds back here on the double before he does expire."

There is nothing like a little hospital mirth to lighten the human tensions, especially in that hospital which was a throw-back in time.

It was after 6:30 in the afternoon before George awoke. He came out of it confused and thirsty. With his hands he felt around to check his privates. They were still intact, but he was as smooth as a baby's butt. The spot on his belly, where Big Jake had stabbed him, itched. The butterfly clips that had been attached to the wound had been removed. Now he recalled with a shudder just where he was.

Since he had been at BGH, he had been in and out of touch with reality due to drug inducement.

The last thing he remembered was being wheeled to the operating room, but he could not remember why. It flashed before him: the horror of being told to lay still or have his penis sliced off, someone grabbing him by the balls that still ached.

. Then there were so many tests. Now, it came to him that he had seen this runt psychologist who interrogated him about his life as a child and how exhausted he had been when the interrogation ended. He remembered the x-rays, the cat-scans, the drawing of blood and being probed from both ends.

It popped into his mind that a camera had been run up his butt and when he hollered, it brought no sympathy from the perpetrators. One had even told him while finding his vociferous complaints, humorous, "Quit your bitching. I don't feel a thing."

He shuddered as he thought about the desperate situation he was in. He had never been allowed to make his phone call. As he rested in bed, bits and pieces of the past twenty-four hours popped into his head. Were they real?

Had he dreamed it, when Doctor Aholie told him that he had nipples up his ass and that was the reason for his gaseous problems? He dismissed that recollection as being too absurd--too bizarre. But it stuck in his mind that this doctor had smiled and said he was going to cure him. The operation was to cut out those nipples. He, remembered, protesting that he had not consented.

125

As best he could, he squirmed and turned over stretching to reach for his bung hole. When he found it, it was kind of sore, but still unscathed. He smiled. He did not have a new one.

What had happened? Perhaps, he would never know.

Why was he back in this bleak dingy pale green room with only the white enameled iron bed, a porcelain sink, a grey metal cabinet and one dilapidated old chair?

Again he probed his body with his fingers and came up with the itching scar from the knife wound and then where his pubic hairs had been, it was as smooth as a baby's behind.

He pondered. What kind of hospital was this that shaved away your manly hairs? Maybe this was some kind of a new psychological treatment dreamed up that he had not yet heard of.

At any rate, George did not want to go through this experience again; he had to get out of here; but how?

He slid off the side of his bed, his feet finding the two cloth slippers placed there by some thoughtful soul to keep his feet off the cold polished floor. He straightened up; swayed a little as he cleared his head, and awkwardly he wobbled to the door and tried the handle. It was not locked.

Walking to the nurse's station, he saw three nurses in a huddle. Two older nurses were telling a pretty black haired young nurse about the earlier argument between the two doctors and about the botched operation.

He saw one of the older nurses hand the young one a metal clipboard. She said, "Here have a look for yourself."

The young one took the file and sat down. She read it with great interest. Suddenly she exclaimed, "My God! Sweet Jesus!"

Then one of the older nurses looked over and saw George slowly making it down the hall.

"Mr. Murfrey, what are you doing out of your room? You know you are not supposed to be down here."

"I am hungry. Actually, I am starved." George had not eaten since the night before and the clock on the wall showed it was 6:41 p.m.

"You missed your supper. They served at five. You were sleeping so well, they would not leave your tray. How about some ice cream? The kitchen is closed. We are going off duty in ten minutes. Maybe Anna can find you something. The older nurse nodded toward the pretty young nurse standing there staring at him. She was a small nurse as nurses go. About five two, George reckoned. She had black hair tucked under her old fashioned nurse's cap and a set of large brown eyes. The way she smiled at him let him know that this was a friend.

"What kind of a hospital is this? I need a real meal!" said George, who was raising his voice in frustration.

"Now don't you get horsey with us, Mr.Murfrey. We are not the cause of your problem. Be nice and we will see what we can scrape up. Meanwhile, do you want the ice cream?"

George shook his head in defeat, "yes" and ambled back to his room. In a few minutes, he got a small cup of vanilla with the small wooden paddle for a spoon. This was the same kind of ice cream served at kiddie parties and in the cafeteria at school many years ago.

George saw that his server was the young pretty nurse they called Anna.

"Would someone please tell me what is going on?" George asked in a high pitched voice.

Anna smiled and said, "You poor boy. You have been through it huh? I see you are from Gulfport, Mississippi. I am from Lucedale, Mississippi. I will get you some peanut butter and graham crackers. The dining room has closed. I will be back after they have gone off duty in just a little while. Okay?"

"Okay," said George who perked up. "Maybe you can spare another cup of ice cream. I like strawberry."

About an hour later after George had consumed a whole box of graham crackers along with a jar of peanut butter and strawberry ice cream. Anna Wilkins returned to room 403 to find George staring at the ceiling.

"Hi," said the nurse with a smile.

"Hi. I was just doing some thinking. I don't know why I am here. For a while, I thought I was here for my stab wound, but I did not get any treatment for it. It looks like it has just healed on its' own. Do you know why I am here? Did I dream that I was to be operated on for passing gas?"

"You poor man," Anna said with sympathy. "I have seen your chart. You have been through so much. This is basically a research wing of the hospital. Right now we are treating a few wounded, who were shipped in from Iraq. They are in the other wing. Usually we get the terminally ill who have nothing to lose. Oops! I can't believe I said that. Anyway, I was surprised when I saw you the other night. You were not like the other patients."

"Honey, your file says they were going to cut you open to find your skunk glands that make you spray a poisonous gas. Didn't you know that?"

"Why I never heard tell of such a thing. I don't know why you are up here in Baltimore anyway."

"Baltimore? You mean Baltimore, Maryland. I vaguely remember something about Baltimore, but I thought it was a dream. I have been dreaming a lot. I don't know what is real anymore!" said George who was beginning to get excited.

"You did not know that?" Anna thought for a minute. "That explains it all. I don't know what is going on here, but I would sure like to find out. Dr. Aholie is an old doctor. He hardly ever operates, except on terminal patients. Dr. Phillips, Dr. White, and Dr. Haas do most of the other operations. You know what? We Mississippians need to stick together."

"Can you get me out of here? I never agreed to be here. I never signed anything. No consent." George pleaded almost in tears.

"Do you have someone who can come pick you up?"

"Not in Baltimore. I don't have any clothes. Do you know where they put my clothes?" he asked, choking up.

"I will look around. If I can't find any, you are about the size of my daddy. If I can't find yours, I get some of his. I will see what I can do. Do you know someone who you can call to come and get you?"

George brightened up. He replied, "You bet I do! My mother, my girlfriend, and my buddy. They don't even know where I am. Can you help me?"

Anna went back to the nurses' station and returned with a thin red cell phone clutched in her hand.

"Even a criminal is entitled to one phone call," she said. She handed the phone to George.

"I don't think it would be wise to call out on the hospital phones. Use my cell phone. Don't worry about the cost; I have a lot of unused minutes, so it is free." She smiled and said, "Feel better now?"

"Thanks. I used to shoot pool with a guy from Lucedale," said George a matter of factly.

"What's his name?"

"Vernon King."

Anna shook her head and lost her smile. "Yes, I know him. He was several grades ahead of me at Lucedale High. He was always in trouble."

"Sounds like Vernon. He lost his temper at the pool hall and whipped an old man with a pool stick. They arrested him. I don't know what happened to 'ole Vernon. He was a pretty good pool player as far as I can remember."

"Go ahead and make your calls. I have to make my rounds and check on the patients. I will see about your clothes."

George started dialing. He got lucky. Mutt happened to be in his room and was called downstairs to the pay phone in a small lobby.

"Hey Mutt," George said. "Am I glad to get you. I thought you might be in jail."

"They put this ankle bracelet on me and kicked me out. I still have to report each day and work off my sentence. Where in the hell are you? Your mother and May both are worried sick about you. Someone said they thought Big Jake stabbed you, but I called all the hospitals on the coast and they did not have you."

"Listen, Mutt, I am in a lot of trouble. Jake did stab me and they shipped me up here at a hospital in Baltimore, Maryland," he said excitedly. "They are trying to do a lot of strange things to me. I need to make my escape. I have someone who will help me. Can you come and get me?"

"Baltimore!" Mutt exclaimed. "You know I can't drive. They took my license from me. The next time I drive and drink, they are going to send me to Parchman Farm for three years. Look, I tell you what. Your girlfriend May has been worrying me sick about you. I will call her. She should be off work and at home about now. If she can take off from her job, we will come and get you. Call me back in fifteen minutes."

George called his mother next, but got a busy signal. He tried Mutt and Mutt answered on the first ring.

"Look, George, I did get May on the phone. She is leaving right now to come pick me up. As soon as she gets here, we are hitting the Interstate and will come on up there in her Buick. If we drive through the night, we should be there early tomorrow morning. We will drive all night. Tell us where we can meet you. How did you get to Baltimore? No, you can tell me after we get there. I am going out front of the hotel and wait for May after you tell me where to meet you."

"Meet me at the main Greyhound Bus station in Baltimore, Maryland. I am in the Baltimore General Hospital, but won't be here for long. I have someone who will help me get out of this place. Just look for me at the bus station; I will be there."

A little later, Anna returned to George's room.

"I did find your shoes and socks. I have some clothes coming since I could not find your clothes. I hope my Dad's clothes will fit you. I found your wallet and your Mickey Mouse watch. There was twelve dollars in it. You will need some more money. Twelve dollars is not enough." Anna handed him a bunch of dollar bills; it was fifty dollars. She said, "You can pay me back when you get back to Mississippi. We Mississippians need to stick together."

"Thanks. I got in touch with my buddy and he and my girlfriend are on their way. They should be here tomorrow morning sometime. Thanks for the money and the clothes. I will never forget this. As soon as the clothes arrive, I will dress and go."

"You need to stay here until I make my early morning rounds. Then I can report you missing when I check on you at 6:00 a.m."

George asked, "How many patients do you have on this floor?"

"Five. Not including you. Why do you ask?"

"I will tell you in a minute. Is there anyone on the floor, where they took me to be operated on?"

"Not until 4:30 or 5:00 in the morning, maybe later. Are you up to something?"

"Maybe," said George smugly.

"I don't want to know, but whatever it is, would serve them right." "Besides," she thought, "What can this man do besides turning over a few chairs or breaking some vials?"

Later after they arrived, George tried on the clothes. Anna had brought him. The pants were a little short, but there were no complaints. His shoes that had been located were a blessing. The shirt furnished was a size two extra-large covered with flowers. No wonder her dad had given it away. It made him look like a tourist and that was alright.

What really made his heart soar was the thought that his pal, Mutt, and his girlfriend, Maybellene, were on the way to pick him up. Everything was in place; all he had to do was to wait.

Drugs are not easy to shake off. George had been sedated from the time he left Gulfport and throughout his stay at BGH. Now he was coming out of the twilight zone. He was still groggy. Anna had him wait in his room, after taking a shower; soon he was fast asleep snoring away, but fully dressed. She was to awaken him at four in the morning.

Right on the dot, Anna shook him out of his deep sleep. He thanked her; even gave her a big hug and quietly left the ward. He took the stairs up to the fifth floor--the fatal operating room where they cut open peoples assholes.

George knew what he wanted to do. He just did not know if he could muster up. Did he have it? Could he call upon his reserves and do it at will?

George strained with all his strength and, much to his surprise he squeezed out a stinker that was one of his best. It even surpassed the bomb he dropped at the Palace Pool Hall. The cloying oily stream, of the most rotten gas ever emitted from a human, was turned loose. The off and on effort lasted only 45 seconds, but the effects would last for days, even weeks.

Before the cloud of stinky stuff could catch up with him, George quickly left the room closing the door behind him.

Anna had drawn a map to be used for his departure. It proved accurate. She had even provided an employee I.D. tag. No one challenged him as he slipped out the side entrance used by employees. He looked at his identification tag; today he was Joe Blount.

Outside, he nervously flagged a cab. The driver a brown man with a Pakistani accent did not seem to notice. After directing the driver to take him to the Greyhound Bus station, George sat back and took in the scenery of skyscrapers. Even at that time in the morning with the city waking up, it took fifteen minutes to get to his destination. Darkness was fading as the sun struggled to displace early morning clouds from off the Atlantic. He was charged ten dollars for the ride and gave the driver a five dollar tip.

Now, the city was bustling. He did not plan to return to Baltimore any time soon, so to kill time, he walked around looking in store windows. What amazed him, were the sales that were going on back in Gulfport, Mississippi were all happening here in Baltimore. He found an open coffee shop and treated himself to the "Big Breakfast." It contained a six ounce steak, hash browns, three eggs and a stack of pancakes. The waitress kept the coffee coming and George began to feel like a man. It was a good feeling; he was free! But for how long?

The air was still cool from the night, fresh and invigorating. The sky was turning from pink and black to a blue. The dark stretching clouds had given way to marshmallow puffs. Never did George feel so good to be alive, but the nightmare he had been through still tugged at his memory. With a new lease on life, he strolled into the bus station.

People were milling around and the station was filling up with passengers who also had high expectations. In the restroom, the all-nighters were using the sinks to wash up. They were taking mini baths, as others who just wanted to wash their hands, waited.

All George had to do was to wait.

CHAPTER TWELVE

Rescued and returned to Gulfport

At ten forty that morning, May Modine and Mutt Hanson walked into the Baltimore Greyhound bus station. They almost ran into George, emerging from the men's room, where he had been using a stall as a hiding place whenever he saw a cop enter the station. Periodically a policeman would come into the station, survey the crowd as if he was looking for someone in particular. If they were looking for him, George was not taking any chances. He would wait in the stall listening to other men relieve themselves of their bodily wastes. It was ironic that he had to listen to the men farting and endure their feeble attempts to produce a real smelly.

He would wait until he thought the coast was clear and then come out to watch the parade of people entering and leaving the station. Had his gift to the BGH been discovered? Had his absence without permission been noticed? The stall in the men's room proved to be his safe haven.

He could not know that there was complete pandemonium back at Baltimore General. Nor could he know that nurse Anna Wilkins had clocked out with a headache minutes before all hell broke loose.

First, the employees, who entered the fifth floor to set up for the day, were hit full force by the stench from the squeaky bomb, dropped earlier. They took two steps inside and quickly retreated. After waiting over five minutes for the elevator, they abandoned that idea and made for the stairs. As they hurried downward, they were met by fourth floor employees, who had a similar thought. This combined group met those trying to escape from the third floor and by the time they reached the lobby, a stampede was taking place.

The air conditioning system, pulling the noxious gas and smell from the fifth floor was contaminating the other floors, through its duct work.

133

All of the elevators were being used to move patients, who were not ambulatory. As the fleeing employees came out of the stairways, they were met with personnel handing out gas masks and sent back to floors upstairs to help with the evacuation. For the time being patients and equipment were being taken over to the newly built right wing which had its' own heating and air conditioning system, unaffected except for the odor carried into the wing by the stinking patients being moved as well as those moving them.

While the stunned patients from the left wing were being settled in, the employees with gas masks were sent to retrieve documents, oxygen machines, drugs instruments, bed pans, carts, monitors, wheel chairs and gurneys. Other hospitals, in the area, were contacted to take special patients with special needs.

Like a Chinese fire drill, a whole wing of a hospital was being closed down in an erratic way. The employees without gas masks, who tried to help, began to retch and upchuck their breakfasts and any remaining bile. Some fainted or became so weak, that they had to be hospitalized themselves. One three hundred pound man, who had had his hip replaced the day before, after getting a whiff of the terrible smelling stench, somehow climbed over the railing on his bed in a screaming panic, hitting the floor, tearing out his stitches, a large pool of blood spreading across the floor. While he lay there bleeding, the nurses who could not lift the man searched for security personnel to help them. Finally after twenty minutes of horrified painful screaming, four husky men were able to place the man on a mobile bed and take him to intensive care in the right wing, already crowded to its limit.

Those employees, who had just gotten off duty prior to the disaster, were called back to help deal with the overwhelming load which included more patients and employees alike collapsing from the sickening gas that had invaded the left wing.

Dr. Alphone Aholie did not have an operation that morning; he elected to stay home due to the fact he was suffering from extreme depression. Once again fate had dealt him a terrible blow. Murfrey had been literally snatched from his surgical hands. The discovery, that would have made him famous, had been thwarted. He was trying to regroup over his third cup of brandied coffee, when the phone call came in informing him of the catastrophe.

His first impulse was to ask the caller, "What about George Murfrey? What did they do with him?"

"Doctor, it will take a while to locate each patient. Right now they were all moved to the right wing in a hurry. Some are being transferred to other hospitals. I will try and locate the nurses and doctor on duty to see if they know where they put him. I am sure he is alright. He is not listed among those injured in the move. He is bound to show up."

"What's your name nurse?" demanded Aholie. "I want that man found and I want him found now. Do you understand?"

"My name is Angelina Brownlee and we are doing the best we can. We are doing all we are capable of doing, I assure you. You must understand that a whole wing of the hospital was contaminated. We are fortunate that no one has died. You would have to be here to understand how bad things are," said the anxious nurse.

"I am coming right down there and when I get there I expect you will be able to inform me of Mr. Murfrey's whereabouts," screamed Aholie in a high pitched voice as he slammed the phone down on the receiver with a crash. He then took the whole phone apparatus and threw it up against the wall of his living room. The phone disintegrated as it punched a large hole through the dry wall exterior. This was just too much! It was bad enough to put up with the incompetent personnel at the hospital, but now this!

Thirty minutes later, after dodging ambulances that were going to and from the hospital as well as other official responders such as police vehicles, fire trucks and government investigators, Dr. Aholie found a parking place and hurriedly trotted up to the Emergency entrance. It was the continuance of his ill-fated luck that the first person he collided into was Dr. Rance Phillips, his newest nemesis.

"You! You! You are the cause of all this!" screamed Dr. Aholie in a breaking high cracking voice, almost incomprehensible.

"What in the world are you talking about? Are you having a breakdown, doctor?" asked Dr. Phillips with a puzzled look.

"I know that George Cedric Murfrey had something to do with this. Don't ask how I know. I just know it. You should not have stopped me from operating. We wouldn't be having this disaster." Dr. Phillips had to step back from the spit being sprayed from this lunatic.

Doctor Aholie continued, "Murfrey's a skunk. A skunk do you hear. Find him and let me operate. I can prove it. Get that skunk over here now. We have got to operate!"

"Calm down doctor. You are attracting attention."

"Calm down! Calm down! I can't calm down! I have got to operate!" shouted Aholie even louder. "Get the hell out of my way." He gave Dr. Phillips a shove and made his way to the main desk. Still screaming and spitting, he got up into the face of the nurse in charge.

"Have you located Murfrey yet? Well, have you?"

The nurse looked at this disheveled man, heavy eyebrows arching over fierce blood shot eyes a heavy smell of liquor on his breath, not looking like a doctor at all; he could have passed for one of the alcoholic patients.

"Just who are you sir?" asked the nurse.

"I am Doctor Alphonse Kristna Aholie from the vacated left wing. I called down and told you to find this patient. I need to operate on him immediately. He has skunk glands. Only I know it. Nobody will listen to me."

"Are you telling me this Murfrey fellow is half skunk and half human?"

"If you put it that way; you are wasting time. Find him. I have to operate. We cannot waste another minute."

"Just a minute, sir," said the nurse. She turned her head, cupped her hand over her phone and said in a low voice, "Find security. I have a man up here who says he is a doctor, but he isn't acting rationally. I am afraid he will hurt himself or someone else. He claims his patient is half skunk and half man. He wants to operate on him if he finds him. Hurry!"

"Well," shouted the doctor. "Did you find him? I have got to operate on this man before he shuts down this section of the hospital.

This man is dangerous." Dr. Aholie was practically in tears with exasperation.

"Sir, I have someone coming who will help you find him."

Dr. Aholie could tell from the body language of the nurse that she was not telling the truth. He said, "No you are not. Nobody wants to help. I will find him myself."

As Dr. Aholie turned to leave, Dr. Phillips, who had been standing behind him, listening to the conversation, grabbed the doctors' arm. He said, "Why don't you wait until your help arrives?"

This time Dr. Aholie turned and with one powerful punch decked Dr. Phillips, who was sent sprawling across the floor much to the dismay of the desk nurse landing at the feet of the crowd of onlookers who had gathered.

Dr. Aholie took several steps to proceed further into the hospital when the two security guards arrived. "Stop!" shouted one.

Aholie increased his speed in an effort to get away, but a flying tackle by one of the guards took him down.

"Take him into that room and hold him," said Dr. Phillips, now back on his feet, pointing to the file room. "I will get something to calm him down and be right back."

As Dr. Aholie was scuffling with the security guards, he shouted, "Help! Help! Let me go. I have an operation to do. I have to remove skunk glands from a patient!"

A few minutes later, Dr. Phillips arrived with a hypodermic needle and syringe, injecting the liquid into Aholie's neck. The outraged doctor slumped immediately. His last words, determined to the end, were, "I have to operate. I have to operate now. Please let me operate."

Thirty minutes later, while the unconscious doctor was being strapped to a gurney and loaded on an ambulance waiting to take him to a local mental institution, George Murfrey and his two rescuers were leaving the city limits of Baltimore.

George, hyped up, was explaining his ordeal as best he could.

"Most of the time," explained George. "I must have been under heavy sedation. It was like a great mist went over me. I remember getting stabbed by Big Jake and then I went into shock and...."

Mutt was snoring and May had her head up against the passengers' window. She too, was out like a light. The rescuers had driven all night to get there. Now after back tracking on highway I-95, back through Washington, D.C., they let George take over the driving. Traffic was heavy so all George had to do was to go with the flow which moved in a steady not too fast fashion.

Anna had been a blessing. She had located his wallet that contained his driver's license as well as the keys to his mother's house and to her 1939 La Salle automobile. He was driving that gangster looking car the day he was stabbed. Was it still parked outside that Quick Stop where he was stabbed? She was going to be plenty mad.

Although George had only about six hours sleep that last night at BGH, he had practically emptied a pot of coffee for breakfast and with nervous energy, he was not the least bit sleepy. All he wanted to do was to put as many miles as he could away from Baltimore.

He stayed on I-95 through Washington D.C. and at times with horns blaring at him, because of his uncertainty crossing the great city; he slowly made it through, entering the State of Virginia.

By mid-afternoon, just outside Richmond, George pulled into a McDonalds for a pit stop and more coffee. They left Mutt in the car still sleeping. May took over the driving while Mutt and George set up a duet with their snoring.

After driving through Richmond, May left I-95 and transferred to I-85 which would take them as far as Montgomery, Alabama before another change.

Finally, after traveling through North Carolina and part of South Carolina, as the sun set in the west, May pulled into another McDonalds and they filled up on milk shakes, French fries and burgers. Further down the road was the Candlelight Inn. Whipping the Buick Le Sabre into the entrance and with her credit card she got a room with double queen sized beds. Without taking off their clothes, May and George climbed into one bed and Mutt the other. On the way into Gastonia, South Carolina, Mutt had persuaded May to stop at a liquor store where he purchased three bottles of Thunderbird wine.

They were over tired; the way one gets when exhausted. Thus, while Mutt celebrated drinking his cheap wine, George and May watched television.

To George's horror there was a news broadcast about the evacuation of BGH. It showed complete pandemonium as people with gas masks scurried around while those without the masks bent over vomiting their guts out. Ambulances with flashing lights were pulling in and out of the premises. Even a helicopter landed on the grounds to evacuate wounded soldiers back to Walter Reed Hospital in Washington.

"Wasn't that the hospital that had you?" asked Mutt, who had taken the wine bottle from his lips to stare at the scene that showed people on stretchers being loaded on Mobile Medic vehicles. The newscaster stated that an amateur photographer had used his cell phone camera to capture those fleeing the left wing. In the clip, were nurses in stiff white uniforms, attendants, assistants, and doctors, ambulatory patients with bandaged heads, some with arms in slings and others on crutches or using canes. All were literally pouring out of the left wing like wasps that had been attacked. Police and security had donned gas masks and were sealing off the wing.

"No one knows what caused the noxious gas that has enveloped the whole left wing, but it is believed that there was a break in a sewerage line beneath the hospital that let loose the dangerous fumes in the form of methane gas. Care has been taken that no one lighted a match as there was fear of a fire."

The announcer droned on, "Fortunately, no one was seriously injured, but as you can see this old hospital could not take care of the overflow of patients from the left wing and many had to be placed in outlining hospitals."

"On the lighter side," the announcer said. "A Dr. Kristna Aholie, who obviously breathed in too much of the gas; had to be sedated when he insisted that the cause of the catastrophe was a patient of his who was half skunk and half man, emitting into the left wing dangerous gas like a skunk."

The announcer then held up a drawing of a man with a pointed chin, beady eyes and black wavy hair that had a white stripe down the middle.

The announcer stated, "Here is a sketch by police artist, Fred Roberts, which portrays what the 'skunk man' probably looked like. If you see this man, do not provoke him, or he will turn around, lift his tail and when he does that, you had better run. You know what is coming next." The newscaster and his co-anchors all broke out into loud laughter, the sports announcer made like he was falling out of his chair with side splitting amusement.

The news announcer looked down at the sportsman who was stealing the show, and commented, "It was not that funny."

The station then broke for a commercial.

Mutt Hanson, eye witness to the Palace Pool Hall incident, knew what Fart's Murfrey could do. He turned to George with a sardonic smile and in his deep voice asked, "Farts were you responsible for that fiasco? That's the hospital you were in. I knew it. It looks too much like your handiwork."

Farts' jaw tightened. He said, "They had it coming to them. They were going to cut me open whether I liked it or not."

"I don't blame you. I just wonder why May and I are not affected."

About that time, May Modine, who was gaseous, joined in with a loud flatter blaster of her own."

Farts laughed. "I better not try to match her. I don't want to push it."

"She has you beat," said Mutt.

"That is because I am tired and used up. Be warned. There is always tomorrow."

May started laughing. Then Farts joined in. And then Mutt began to give a loud "he-haw". It was contagious. All tension was broken. The trio laughed and laughed. Tears rolled down Mutt's face. Mutt gasped, "Lets' stop and get some rest."

"Okay by me," said Farts. Then after a pause, he laughed even harder in his tenor voice.

May, whose sides began to ache from the mirth chuckled, "We had better stop. They are going to throw us out."

Mutt answered, "I have been thrown out of better motels."

"I bet you have," said Farts. The laughter which had subsided reached a higher crescendo.

This was a typical motel built in the 1950's. The walls were thin and paneled in sheets of imitation walnut. The beds had been upgraded since then, but the green shag pile carpets were still the same except for wear. It came with a small refrigerator and a microwave of the same vintage.

The manager, who did not want to lose any patrons, finally, after thirty minutes of complaints, called their room. He said, "This is the manager. We have had numerous complaints about too much noise coming out of your room. Can you hold it down?"

"Yes sir." said May. "Sorry." She hung up the phone and explained, "That was the manager and he wants us to hold it down. Haw, haw, haw. Can we hold it down?" She fell back on the bed in uncontrolled laughter.

"With me and May in this rickety bed I believe we can hold it down, I don't think we will need you Mutt," said Farts wiping his eyes. "Say what were we laughing about anyway?"

"Hell if I know, said Mutt taking another swig out of his wine bottle. "But I will tell you one thing: I haven't laughed this hard since I was a boy. Have you Farts? Have you May?"

"Me neither."

"Not me either," said May. She took the TV clicker turning off the television while   Mutt switched off the lights and soon the only objectionable noise was the deep snoring coming from Mutt and the high pitched snorts Farts was making. This the other residents could stand.

The traveling trio, were up early, becoming quickly glued to the news on the television. The closure of the left wing of the Baltimore General Hospital became national news due to the "skunk man" being on the loose. The sketch of the skunk man was shown on Good Morning America, The Today Show, The Early Show, CNN, and Fox. The newspapers carried the sketch with the caption: "Have you seen this person? Beware." The National Inquirer planned a full report that included sightings of the Skunk Man over the years. He was as hard to find as the Loch Ness monster, or Sasquatch. It was the joke of the land. The sketch artist rushed to copyright the portrait and name. He immediately entered into a contract to have the sketch emblazoned on T-shirts with the caption stating, "I survived the Skunk Man's fumes at Baltimore General." Sightings of people who resembled the sketch were reported, some even calling 911 in a panic.

When May, Mutt and Farts arrived in Gulfport, they were well aware of the coverage of the Skunk Man even on the radio. No one seemed to take it seriously. They were not surprised when they picked up a copy of The Sun Herald, the Gulf Coast's daily newspaper; it even had a write up and the sketch. The Times Picayune of New Orleans went into even more detail, but did not correct the rumor that the skunk man had been the cause of BGH's left wing being shut down. It mentioned that the BGH was an old out dated hospital and that the government was thinking of tearing the whole structure down instead of repairing the damage.

It was no surprise, when the late shows such as the Jay Leno Show, David Letterman Show and Conan O'Brien, all had a joke about it. Leno said that the skunk man was really a U.S. Senator. Letterman joked that he was the brother-in-law of his band leader, Paul. O'Brien stated that the skunk man had returned to New Jersey where he could easily blend into the population without being recognized.

Back at home, Farts was trying to blend in and get back to normal living.

May warned: "George you have got to pull in your horns. I know there is a lot of good in you. From what you told me, the Baltimore General did you no harm. It looks like the work of that crazy doctor and from what has been on the news that man seems to have gone down in disgrace. No one takes him seriously."

"You have got to get your life back. You need to think about the future. If you are still grieving over your lost friend Woody, it won't do you any good."

"You could have gotten in serious trouble in Baltimore. Lucky for you, they haven't tried to tie you in with the closing of the hospital. This time, you really did it big," she said. She laid her pudgy hand on his. "The very idea, that one man passing gas could create such a catastrophe is beyond belief. That is in your favor," she added thoughtfully.

"Unless, they found out about my closing the Palace Pool Hall," commented Farts. "Hey, I hear the Palace is reopening next week. That's the good news."

"So what's the bad news?" asked May.

"The bad news is that I will certainly be banned from there: Mutt also."

"I can't say I am sorry," said May. "But wasn't it Big Jake's fault? He is the one who started it and later stabbed you. Is he in jail? If not, he ought to be."

"Mutt tells me that he was arrested and was trying to make bond. I hope they keep him"

"You need to find another form of amusement, like going to Church with me. Where is Mutt? I haven't seen him around since we got back."

"Mutt has a drinking problem. He was drunk when we hit Gulfport after drinking all that Thunderbird wine."

"Yeah, that's right. I really got tired of his hollering over and over, 'What's the word: Thunderbird. What's the price? A piece of ice', said May smiling.

"Like a broken record," George added. "But, to answer your question, he didn't bother to put his ankle bracelet back on when he got back and the next day he continued his marathon drinking. They picked him up at Johnny's Bar which somehow was back in business, drunk as a real skunk and gave him more time. It seems that he got into a peeing contest with a bunch of other drunks out in front of the Bar, which incidentally is now permanently closed down. He says the men's restroom, stunk so bad, he preferred the street. He says he won the contest; the mothers with their children weren't happy. This time he is serving day for day at the Harrison County jail. No more painting curbs for him."

May frowned. "What a wasted life. I heard his father, Dr. Hanson, disowned him. Is it true that he went to the University of Edinburgh?"

"Yep, and he also served in the Scotish Brigrade; got shot in India, and now gets a pension. He is a good loyal friend. Not much he would not do for me. Besides you, he is my only other friend. Go figure. I wish there was something I could do for him. He really went the distance for me coming to Baltimore, literally."

CHAPTER THIRTEEN

FBI investigates

The fact that Dr. Alphonse Kristna Aholie had been disgraced, discredited and the butt of jokes at the BGH as well as all over Baltimore, did not daunt or deter the doctor's belief that George C. Murfrey did in fact have skunk's glands plus the complete apparatus to spray his awful gas or had definitely been the culprit who was responsible for shutting down the left wing of the hospital.

After Dr. Aholie was released from the psycho ward and suspended from the hospital, it was left up to Dr. Iskara Meanie, in house psychologist, if or when he would be allowed to come back to his job.

Aholie had resignedly accepted these terms: He could play possum and pretend that he had dropped his passionate belief that Murfrey was part skunk. He convinced the psychologist that he had put this out of his obsessive mind; he was reinstated and given a small office in the right wing of BGH while the government decided whether to spend its precious money to repair the old hospital or just tear it down.

He did not plan to give up, but he would move very slowly and cautiously in his endeavor to prove to the world that Murfrey was endowed with skunk glands through evolution. He vowed never to be branded a crackpot again.

His attack came from a different angle. During the Korean conflict, as a doctor in the Army, he had developed contacts in the Pentagon, who had a hand in drawing up the plans, putting Private Fannie Mae McBride in the armistice meetings with the North Korean generals, ultimately ending the war.

After he heard of "Big Fanny's" untimely death, he called his contact to get permission to dig up Private McBride so that he could do an autopsy which would surely prove that she indeed had the glands of a skunk, enabling her to render her victims helpless and/or eventual death.

145

The contact, Adjutant General John Patton, followed up the request but turned him down.

"Kristna," he said. "I have checked out your request and there are two reasons why it must be denied.

"What are they?" demanded an inpatient Dr. Aholie, who was tired of being blocked at every turn. "I am tired of being blockaded. This could be a great discovery for our country's defense."

"The first reason is…," drawled the adjutant who had not lost his southern accent. "Because Fannie Mae McBride was never embalmed back in the country in Arkansas, they just declared her dead, put her in a pine box and buried her in a family cemetery. By now the body has probably decomposed so that all that is left is bones."

"I would like to see that for myself,' retorted Aholie. "Sometimes the body will mummify on its own with all organs still intact. All I would need is a day or two to check it out."

"Kristna, I knew you would probably say that. Here is the second reason: Washington found out she had died and was buried in Arkansas and since she was a Medal of Honor recipient, playing a major part of bringing the Korean War to an end, they dug her up and if you want to visit her, she is now re-buried right next to one of the Unknown Soldiers in Arlington Cemetery."

"There is no way we are going to disturb her again in front of the whole world. This was a secret mission she was involved in and it will remain a secret. You go digging up a body in Arlington and the press will start their own digging and the outcome would be disastrous. No sir. This discussion is over. Go elsewhere with your theory. Come back when you have a better request."

Now Dr. Aholie, after all those years, was back with his better request.

After filling John Patton in on the details about George Cedric Murfrey, plus the findings that there was no evidence of methane gas or any sewerage overflow at BGH, it had to be Murfrey who caused it.

"Sounds like you may have something worth looking into, Kristna. If I had not been a part of the Fannie Mae McBride project, I probably would not pay any attention to this theory," drawled John Paton. "Tell

146

you what I will do. I will have the F.B.I. and Homeland Security look into it." He started to hang up and said, "I'll get back to you."

"Wait. Don't hang up. It seems Murfrey has disappeared. No one knows where he went. He has been misplaced, so hurry."

"Like I told you Kristna, we will see what we can do."

Indeed John Patton did file a written request for Homeland Security to check out George Cedric Murfrey the Third and to let him know their findings.

This investigative request was passed on to the F.B.I. chief in charge at the Baltimore office. Ed Amsler, the head man, took a look at the two page request which contained the history of the BGH disaster plus Dr. Alphonse Kristna Aholie's information and after recognizing that he was the first class nut being involved in the request, simply placed the paperwork under his already overcrowded, overburdened stack of investigative requests. Since this request was not critical, it would have to wait.

Under the "tickler system" set up in the office, the file was pulled in two weeks and under the rules, it needed a written review by the chief.

Amsler looked at the request again. He did not want to bother his local agents with this request, so he passed the buck to the office in Jackson, Mississippi. They were to do a check up on George Cedric Murfrey the Third, a resident of Gulfport. After he was found then they were to check him out thoroughly for any "terrorist activities".

Getting into the mood, Amsler changed his mind, dispatching one agent in Baltimore to collect any evidence of a chemical used to poison the air at BGH. He put a note in the file that he believed DR. Aholie's theory to be pure hog wash, but since there was a possibility that a chemical may have been used to make everyone sick from an awful smelling gas, it needed to be looked into. "It could be some insidious use of a chemical being tested by either a terrorist, a prankster or someone who had a grudge against the hospital." he added to his remarks in the file.

The Baltimore local agent, Ted Brunson, was a hotshot. He wanted to impress his superiors. He had been given an investigation to be covered by him single handedly, which normally called on three or more agents. Within three days he filed his report which had statements from Dr. Alphonse Kristna Aholie, Dr. Rance Phillips, Head Nurse Helga Schmidt, Nurse Angelina Brown, Attendants Paulie Jones and Maxmillian Atherton.

From the interviews by Brunson, he concluded, in his report, that George Cedric Murfrey had been railroaded into an operation based on a theory by Dr. Aholie that Murfrey was the "skunk man". Since the operation was without Murfrey's consent, the operation was scrubbed. This would give Murfrey a grudge.

There were several others mentioned who could have had a grudge against BGH. There was Alan Simsky who had been refused admittance for the tenth time. It appeared that Simsky would show up at the hospital with severe complaints of stomach pains which after numerous tests, nothing would be found, he would be released from the hospital, He had vowed to get even, when refused admittance the last time.

Billy Booty, another disgruntled person, had been removed by security for hanging around and propositioning the nurses. He vowed to sue for the rude treatment he had received, but had not done so.

Nurse Frances McIlain was fired recently for stealing drugs. She had been seen sneaking around the hospital several days before the incident.

All the persons of interest had been checked out by agent Brunson with the exception of George Murfrey who had disappeared during the fiasco, probably slipping away when there was subsequent placement of many patients to other hospitals; none of the participating hospitals had any record of ever receiving Murfrey.

Brunson's report was placed in Amsler's growing file, the file not being reviewed again until two weeks later.

Chief Amsler, a small balding man with a bulldog face, a copy of J. Edgar Hoover, noted that the file contained no positive findings of any chemical used to pollute the air at BGH. There was no residue of any kind. There were, of course, new clear traceless chemicals which had been developed that could not be discovered unless tests were conducted

148

at the time they were put in place. So far, there was no evidence to suggest such a chemical was used.

Meanwhile, all the nurses who had come in contact with Murfrey were screened. One nurse, Anna Wilkins, admitted loaning Murfrey fifty dollars and letting him use her cell phone to him to make a call. Three calls were dialed to the Mississippi Gulf Coast of which two calls were traced to the Wills Hotel in Gulfport, Mississippi. The desk clerk at the Wills Hotel, an obvious old man, did not recall any calls from Baltimore, Maryland. The first call had lasted five minutes and the second call had lasted two minutes.

Further follow up with Dr. Rance Phillips revealed that Dr. Aholie had obviously become obsessed with the idea that Murfrey was the "skunk man" and had to be sedated and sent to a mental hospital for tests. The agent was given a copy of Murfrey's file which did not show any tests to confirm that Murfrey deserved to be operated upon. One of the head nurses from the prep department, nurse Vilonia, verified the record that stated Murfrey was given an enema which netted about fifty pounds of feces prior to his being sent up to the fifth floor for the operation. Dr. Phillips concluded, "That Murfrey having been cleaned out thoroughly could not have produced the amount of gas that had shut down the left wing of the hospital." He added by way of information, that this was a world record. No other enema had produced so much feces and he was thinking about listing this feat in the Guinness Book of Records.

Nurse Angelina Brownley, the nurse on the main desk during the evacuation of the left wing stated that Dr. Aholie came to her desk delirious, screaming about the 'skunk man" and an aborted operation.

Fred Roberts, the sketch artist, who drew the depiction of what the skunk man looked like, admitted it was his own rendition and that he had never heard of, seen or met George Murfrey.

Nurse Veda Smothers, Head of the Pulmonary Department, expressed strong feelings about George Murfrey. He had apparently broken a Spirometer used to test lung strength. She said he blew on the instrument so hard that it disintegrated. In her words: "That fat bastard just blew the instrument to pieces. I hope you throw the book at him."

The other nurses interviewed all agreed that Murfrey was no bother as he had been sedated most of the time and never said anything except, "I am hungry."

The two attendants Paulie and Maximillan, stated: "That when they told Mr. Murfrey he was being operated on, Mr. Murfrey became very upset stating he did not consent to the operation nor did he sign a consent form. Mr. Murfrey, they said, never made any threats of any kind after he was told of the operation or at any other time while they observed him. As for the broken Spirometer, after it broke, Murfrey asked if he passed the test.

After further reviewing the file, chief agent, Amsler, concluded that perhaps George Murfrey was a victim of circumstances, but the file would remain open until reports of the investigation ordered in Mississippi were received and had reached his desk. No arrests or charges were being considered.

Gulfport agent, Randle Ross, handled the investigation of George C. Murfrey on the Mississippi Gulf Coast. His first duty was to check with the local authorities to see if George had a record. He was clean, but his running mate, Mutt Hanson, had numerous misdemeanors ranging from fighting to public drunk. Ross was directed to interview Jacob Bannister, AKA Big Jake. He refused to talk with the agent unless his attorney was present since he was now charged with the stabbing of Murfrey. His attorney, Henry Bland, did not allow any questions about the stabbing in Lizana, but let Jake answer other questions. Jake seemed to know a lot about George Murfrey. He described in detail, in his own slanted version, the incident at the Palace Pool Hall. He really embellished the power of Murfrey's fart that evacuated the pool hall and the sickness that followed. He knew about Mutt Hanson, May Modine and where Murfrey lived.

Next, the agent interviewed Edward "Slim" Flourisant, the bartender who admitted that Murfrey's farts were stinkers, but doubted that it caused all the damage detailed by Jacob Bannister

Next, Maybelline Modine, age twenty-four, who was a loan specialist at the Friendly Finance Company, admitted knowledge of George's ability to pass gas, but down played it as harmless. She stated that she had been around him when he passed gas, but had never noticed anything unusual about the smell or its punch. She said, "I do it too. Everyone does it." She did admit that she and Mutt Hanson did travel to Baltimore to pick up George Murfrey at the Greyhound Bus station, and had brought him back to Gulfport. She said that Murfrey related that a "mad" doctor had tried to operate on him without his permission.

When Agent Ross attempted to interview Mrs. Agnes Murfrey, the mother of George Murfrey, she refused to talk stating that she did not know anything. Upon arriving at the shotgun type house where the suspect and his mother resided, the agent noticed that at one end of the house there was a super large exhaust fan, the kind paint and body shops use to suck out paint fumes. He concluded that this was the area where the suspect slept. He did not smell anything unusual inside the property, but did detect an odor of Pine Sol and Febreze. She did state, as the agent was leaving, that her son was a "good boy".

Agent Ross was not the go-getter like the young agent in Baltimore, having been in the field for many years; this one did not smell right, figuratively or literally. He did a thorough background check on George Cedric Murfrey the Third aka "Farts" Murfrey. His search went back in time to the East Ward Elementary School; upon finding the Second grade teacher, Miss. Newman, who, even though in her failing years, remembered George Murfrey. She remembered one episode and smiled when she told Ross of the "Newman plan". "George had a gas problem", she said. "No more, no less."

He interviewed Officer Edwin Smallwood of the Gulfport Police department, now a detective. He brought the agent up to date through the years as a Boy Scout and gave his opinion of the pool hall episode: "Farts Murfrey really has bad gas. Not everyone is affected by it, but if you have a delicate stomach, it can make you gag. I don't believe he was capable of closing down a hospital, however," Smallwood said while laughing out aloud.

Agent Randle Ross was unconvinced that Murfrey's gas problem could cause such a calamity; said so in his report. He could, if ordered, place a surveillance camera on the telephone pole across the street over-looking the Murfrey residence and even a bug could be planted in the old LaSalle automobile, which Murfrey drove on occasion. If Murfrey was a terrorist, he would have to have access to chemicals of some kind. At the present time, there was not enough evidence to get a search warrant from the U.S. Magistrate.

When Chief agent Ed Amsler received Ross's report, he ordered the surveillance camera placed on the telephone pole across the street, a bug in the family automobile and a bug for the residence telephone. They would watch the activities of Mr. Murfrey closely.

Amsler wished that Ross had not interviewed the mother, the girlfriend and the friend. He was afraid they would tip off Murfrey, making it harder to get him to show his hand. But the F.B.I. is a patient agency and they would wait and watch. If indeed Murfrey was their man, he would do something in due time; that is unless he was a "sleeper" who could show up years later when they least expected it.

He would keep Homeland Security up to date on the investigation, but he would not give any credence to the idea put forth by that crackpot Dr. Alphone Aholie that George Murfrey was the "skunk man".

In the spirit of his hound dog sniffing out this perpetrator, he would put more agents on the trail of tracking the suspects escape from Baltimore, Maryland to Gulfport, Mississippi. There would be no stops on the way that he would not know about. While he was about that, he would order that a GPS tracking device be placed in the LaSalle vehicle as well as Maybellene Modine's Buick LaSabre.

Several weeks passed and his agents had come through again. Maybellene Modine had used her credit card for the journey. It was fairly easy to follow their trip and know where they filled up with gas, where they ate and where they slept on the night the trio returned.

The agents came up with no concrete evidence except that the three all stayed at the Candlelight Inn in Gastonia, South Carolina where they partied most of the night. The three of them stayed in the same room drinking and raising hell. The manager told of the complaints and the finding of an empty bottle of Thunderbird wine the next day. The room had been cleaned the next morning and although samples of dust and anything else the agent could seize were tested, there was no evidence of any noteworthy chemicals. In fact, there was nothing.

If these suspects were terrorists, they had been well programmed. Their cover was well protected. Time would tell. All Uncle Sam's agency had to do was to wait.

CHAPTER FOURTEEN

Death in Walmart

While Ed Amsler was waiting for George "Farts" Murfrey to screw up; Farts would have to mess up on his own without any help from his pal, Mutt Hanson, now in the county jail. Farts had tried to visit him, but the jail had rules about non-kinfolk visiting; they weren't allowed.

Even though the pool hall had reopened, what was the use of trying to get his ban lifted? He had no one to shoot pool with and he did not fit in with the all-day drunks, even if he had been inclined; after all, he still had to watch his back in case he ran into Big Jake Bannister with his big Bowie knife. Even though he had gotten away from the Baltimore General Hospital scot free, there still lingered in the back of his mind the fear of someone figuring it out that it was he who had caused the left wing to be shut down; perhaps it was his conscience speaking.

Farts was idle and idle minds need something to do.

The nights were alright. He and his gal, were now becoming great friends, and more. They saw each other every night and on weekends. It was those days during the week that caused him to invent things to do.

It seemed that his mother was either cleaning house, washing dishes or clothes. When she wasn't doing those chores, she was playing Bridge with her friends. They had all become proficient in the game and now they were playing tournaments. Agnes Murfrey had gotten her name in the Sun Herald as a second place winner along with her partner, Betsy Brumfield. Now in mornings or whenever a tournament or even friendly games were being played, Agnes and Betsy got together and worked on their signals so that they were on the same page whenever one of them bid. They got so they could read each other's minds, facial expression and cards. It seemed that Betsy was always over at the house. Georgie stayed back in his bedroom.

His gas problem had actually increased after the enema, courtesy of BGH, cleaning him out. It seemed no matter what he ate, it turned to gas. Consequently the large fan's switch was continually flipped on by his mother. She had to close the door to his room or see all lightweight goods such as newspapers, paper plates and light clothes being swept out through Georgie's room into the large fan that created a wind tunnel.

It could be heard chugging away, but in spite of the noise the fan made, Georgie was dropping large bombs in his room.

Tat-ta-tat-tat-tat-tat-tat went Georgie's efforts like a machine gun. Then it would be a loud flatter-blaster. Agnes could swear it shook the foundations. Then later, it was ka-pow! George could be heard laughing at his feat. He had gained back the weight lost at BGH. When he moved around laughing and saying loudly, "That was a good one!" his three hundred fifty pounds of jolly shook the house further. But when George was heard farting the Star Spangled Banner, which startled Betsy Brumfield, that was too much. No one could practice playing bridge under those circumstances.

"Doesn't he have some place to go?" Betsy asked trying to be nice about it.

"Yes," said Agnes. This will never do." After she turned off the large fan, she knocked loudly on Georgie's door and shouted, "Georgie come out here. I need to talk to you."

"What is he doing in there?" asked Betsy. "Now it sounds like he has mastered 'Dixie'."

"George Murfrey! You come out here! Now!"

"In a minute mom. I have to change my shorts; I think I did something in them." He cut loose with a long squeezer that lasted thirty seconds. "There! That feels better," he said. "I won't be long."

Agnes Murfrey quickly reached up from her chair and flipped the convenient switch and the large fan ran until his mother figured the air had cleared.

"Betsy Brumfield is here and my bridge group is coming over in about twenty minutes so don't take too long. I am going to let you borrow my car." She backed away from the door, turned to Betsy and said in a low voice, "Against my better judgment. The last time he borrowed it, the police towed it in and I had to bail it out from the pound. It cost me one hundred five dollars."

155

Agnes yelled," I want you to go to Walmart and buy some groceries and something for your diarrhea."

Hearing the latest offer of a Walmart trip, as well as using his mother's car meant an afternoon away from the jibber-jabbering of the bridge ladies who never ceased from the time they arrived, until they got into their vehicles and left. They must have had some language of their own, for Georgie could never decipher any of it.

"Okay, mom," he called breathless through the door. He was throwing on clothes with great haste. "I'll be out in a minute." Then talking to himself, he said, "It must have been my rendition of Dixie that got her. This has got to be my lucky day." He laughed. All those weeks since he had been back, this was the first time, Agnes had let him use her car.

The door opened and out stepped Georgie wearing a pair of blue jeans big enough to stuff a small boy in each side of the pants, his Saints' football sweatshirt with the logo, "Who Dat Gonna Beat Dem Saints!" on it, barely covering his famous Haines naval, the figure eight knot protruding noticeably, when he raised his arms; it looked like the pigtail from the rear end of a small hog.

"I'll need some money, Mom. Its three days before the postman runs with my Social Security check. I have got the shorts."

"That's not all you've got," said Betsy Brumfield to herself.

"Here, take this twenty and a ten and buy some bread, crackers and two pounds of cheese," said his mother. Better make it sour dough bread and that hoop cheese, you like so much."

"Keep the change, but don't you ask me for any more money and there had better not be no more mishaps. I don't want my car towed again, and for heaven's sake, don't pass any gas in my car. Keep the windows rolled down, if you get the urge. Oh, yes, buy something for your loose bowels. Not that pink stuff; get that Imodium Plus. It will dry you up. Now get boy, before my other guests arrive."

George spied a bowl of mixed nuts on one of the card tables and helped himself to a fistful. Then he saw on the other table, cakes and finger sandwiches, and moved to get his large paws on those delicacies.

As he was stuffing the nuts in one of his pockets, his mother seeing the decimation of the nut bowl, quickly moved to block him.

"No you don't. These are for my card players. If you are hungry, go to Burger King and get a whopper. Now git!"

As Georgie stumbled down the steps, he reached in his pocket and brought out some peanuts, pecans, almonds and cashews and threw them into his eager mouth.

A carload of bridge players pulled into the yard. Mrs. Sally Smoltz rolled her window down and called, "Hi, Georgie. How ya doing?"

"I am fine Miss. Sally."

"What a dreadful man," said Beatrice Moody, a very stern woman who never slumped in her chair. She was the driver of the group.

"I know," said Sally the group hypocrite. "I don't know how Agnes stands it. He is always hanging around. You would think he would get a job wouldn't you?"

Abigail Bowden piped up from the backseat, "I hear he is disabled. He gets a disability check from the government." Abigail invariably disagreed with whatever was said.

"Foo," said Beatrice, who never worked a day in her life, "A person can work if they want to. My cousin Ralph has a bad back, but he goes out and picks up pecans with one of those 'grabbers'. You know, so he won't have to bend over and hurt his back some more. Well let's not concern ourselves over Agnes's problems. Look, here comes Bertha Barnhill with her gang. She has that Freddie Burr with them. I would not want to have her as my partner. I can't understand why we even let her play."

"Or that she even wants to play; she is so dumb," added Sally Smoltz.

"I hear she is gay," piped in Abigail from the back seat.

"Shh! They might hear you, said Beatrice. "You don't know that for a fact, now do you?"

"No, I don't know for a fact, but she wears a butch haircut, dresses like a man and hugs me and rubs her tits on my back while I am trying to play bridge and I don't like it."

About that time, the door opened to the shotgun house and out stepped Agnes. "Come on in ladies," she said in a shrill voice. "Lets' play some bridge."

Eagerly, the two vehicles unloaded the two sets of women all jabbering at once.

George, who had been sitting behind the wheel of his mother's black 1939 LaSalle, the only worthwhile gift left behind by his father, he had never known, shook his head as the flock of hens rushed up the steps to start their bridge game. He would have liked to have stopped by the Wills Hotel, an old run down hotel that catered to old single men, some ladies of the night, out of work laborers and transients, but his sidekick, Mutt, was now residing at the "Grey Bar Hotel" courtesy of the City of Gulfport. It had cost Mutt when he took off his ankle bracelet in order to make the trip to Baltimore.

Had the City cut off its nose to spite its face? Mutt was their only good curb painter. Those other winos could not paint a straight line if they wanted to. They were more apt to stray from their job in search of a bottle of vino. At least Mutt took pride in his work.

Today George would have to go it alone. His girlfriend, May, was at work and he didn't dare go by there after her boss had run him off; he had a rule that no boyfriends or spouses were allowed to hang around the premises. Instead, George would pass by her work place slowly blowing his horn.

After World War II, the City of Gulfport grew in the only direction available: North. Walmart built its super store ten miles from the business district where Mutt painted curbs. It was a nice sunny day in the area. The calm waters of the Gulf were being transformed into one to two foot waves as the warm southerly winds flowed in over the land. The Gulf air was always clean and fresh with a hint of salt.

Twenty-fifth avenue turned into U.S. Highway 49 as George cruised toward his destination. He pulled into the massive parking lot of the Walmart store, driving up and down rows of parked cars in search of a spot close to the door as short walks tired him out, bringing about a profusion of perspiration that left him wringing wet by the time he entered the store.

He got lucky. He found a place within fifty feet from the front door. It was a handicapped spot, but he had a plastic blue card, he stuck in his front window that proclaimed that he was indeed handicapped; it had been no trouble getting his doctor to mail him a note to give to the authorities in order to procure it.

He smiled to himself as he put the blue card in the widow. After he had won his disability case before a judge at the Social Security hearing, he had compared notes with the other disabled men who hung out at the Palace Pool Hall. One bragged how he had taken a hammer and had beat on his hands causing them to swell prior to the hearing. At the hearing, he told the judge, while showing him his hands, "How can I be an auto mechanic with these hands?"

Another crony explained his devious method, "I got in the backyard and strained my back real good while trying to pick up the rear end of my pick-em-up truck. I was bent over and could barely walk into the room. The judge let me stand during the hearing after my lawyer helped me out of the chair.

In both of those cases, the judge said, "I can see there is no way you will be able to work. Disability granted."

Others got their disability from smoking having been diagnosed with chronic COPD. The claimants, who used alcoholism as an excuse, had a tougher time getting their disability, unless their liver or heart was giving out, the criteria being they did not have long to live.

But no one could top George Murfrey nor could they duplicate his acute and permanent gaseousmylitis. The Social Security judge did not want any demonstrative evidence in his case.

One of George's favorite past times was to enter Walmart or K-Mart and go up and down various aisles, dropping a little noxious gas blossom. He would quickly leave the aisle and then watch from a distance as a shopper would travel down it to find an article. After several steps and a good whiff of the substance, that shopper would make a terrible face, hurriedly leaving the aisle from the direction he or she had entered. It was great sport to watch the different reactions. Some even cursed loudly.

His plan today was to play his game of "Fart and See".

159

This particular Walmart store had two entrances: one to gain access to the grocery section and the other for regular department goods where shopper could find clothing, hunting and fishing supplies, paint, hardware, televisions, toys and automotive goods. Both sets of doors faced west with the doors for grocery shoppers being north of the other set of doors. At the rear of the store was a McDonalds where one could eat hamburgers without leaving the store. This appealed to George, who had gotten no sustenance from the handful of mixed nuts he had pilfered earlier. He would forgo the trip to Burger King, settling for a Big Mac, instead.

When he exited the LaSalle, he made a bee line through the doors past the grocery section and to McDonalds located at the rear of the store.

After waiting in line for a few minutes, he ordered two Big Macs, large fries, and a large coke. This smaller version of a McDonalds did not make milkshakes or he would have opted for one.

He polished off the hamburgers, fries and coke, burped loudly and sat there to survey the area. Suddenly he was hit with the urgency to evacuate his bowels. The rest rooms were close by, also being at the back of the store.

As he entered the men's room, an old man was wiping his hands on a pull out paper towel. The elderly man left; George had the room to himself. He did his business and felt much better. He had let loose a small amount of gas, but hoped he would still be able to play his little game. As he was in the process of washing his hands, a middle aged man entered. The man stopped cold and exclaimed loudly, "Good God! What a stench! Why can't those low-lifes do their business at home?" The man left hurriedly, heading toward the front of the store. George, did not want to be identified as the perpetrator-low life, so he quickly left and ducked between the row of luggage and comforters. Sure enough, after the outraged man had gone about fifty more feet, he wheeled around with a face that could stop a charging bull and eyeballed the restroom door in hope of seeing just who the author of that awful smelly was.

George surreptitiously looked around the corner of his aisle, seeing the angry man just standing there staring at the door to the men's room waiting to see what kind of low life emerged. Finally, natures call getting the best of the upset man, he quickly walked toward the other restrooms located in the front of the store.

Farts Murfrey enjoyed traveling down each aisle pretending to search for merchandise. When he would get to the middle of an aisle with no other person on it, he would cut loose with one of his bad smelling bombs that lingered until the air conditioning sucked it away. The fun was taking up a position where he could watch the results. It really was quite amusing to see someone amble down the aisle, get a whiff and watch their very fast departure, forgetting all about buying anything on that particular aisle.

Today, as he strolled through home furnishings and on to office and school supplies, he strained to let out some gas, but nothing happened. "Must have depleted my stock in the restroom." he mused.

Undaunted, he continued walking down various aisles. He explored men's clothing, then the camera and television department and on to fishing and hunting with little luck.

He was out of gas!

Killing time, he made his way to the paint section, the plumbing area and automotive aisles. He could not summon even a squeaker.

He headed back to the rear of the store and over to shoes and boots. From there he went to sewing materials. He spotted the arts and crafts area which composed about three aisles. No one seemed to be in that portion of the store.

But, it was in the middle aisle of the ladies' lingerie aisle where Farts ultimately stopped, really straining to pass a little of his foul smelling obnoxious gas. To his surprise, the walking must have loosened him up for just as he let out a very loud tra-rat-ta-tat, it went unheard, due to the overhead speakers calling out loudly, "Will Mr. Boyce Harvey please come to customer service; your party is waiting."

Knowing that this was no ordinary squeaker, but more like the bomb he dropped in Baltimore at BGH, he quickly vacated the aisle and stopped at the automotive aisle which ran perpendicular to the lingerie aisle he had just left.

As he turned around, he saw a middle aged lady toting a large green purse which matched her chartreuse pants suit.

Suddenly, as she approached the contaminated area, she stopped. Then she reared back, began to quiver and jerk in spasms violently, falling to her knees and throwing up. Betsy Matthews had eaten spaghetti at lunch and it came gushing out like a dam had burst.

Farts watched in amazement as spaghetti in six to eight lengths flew out hitting the shelves wrapping around braziers, slips and panties.

As she heaved, he stood there petrified. She stopped puking, clutched her chest on the left side and slowly collapsed onto the floor.

Quickly over the loud speakers came an urgent voice: "Code red on aisle nineteen. We need a clean-up on aisle nineteen."

No sooner had the message been broadcast, within thirty seconds two young men in Walmart garb rushed down the aisle. One had a bucket and the other a mop. They were later identified as Tim Rucket and Alfred Hoda.

Farts remained frozen, watching without moving.

The two men dropped the bucket and mop respectively and rushed to the aid of the woman lying perfectly still on the polished vinyl floor. Tim seeing the vomit on the floor lost his dinner, retching violently. Alfred backed away, slipped in some vomit, fell; then turning around began to crawl on his hands and knees toward the end of the aisle. It was in slow motion that Tim Rucket crumpled at the feet of Mrs. Matthews. Alfred tried to get up and fell. He too, began to retch and throw up.

The smell that was in the form of a small cloud began to spread from the area. Many of the customers in the vicinity described it as an overflow of raw sewerage. They dropped all notions of shopping, instinctively rushing to leave the store. The vapors followed them as they passed other customers. This set off approximately one hundred fifty men, women and children, clerks, cashiers, stock boys and department managers all who stampeded in an effort to get out of the store. Those who got in the way or didn't move fast enough were trampled. The loud speakers blared again stating in a nice calm voice that there was an emergency; would everyone please walk slowly to the front of the store and go outside.

This seemed to inspire greater effort from the stampeders. As more people ran toward the front doors, the now loud voice from the loud speaker shouted, "Don't panic!"

Someone who had seen Mrs. Matthews and the two Walmart employees lying still on the floor, cried out, "Its' a terrorist attack! The store is going to blow."

The now shrill voice from above called down through the speakers, "Calm down! Quit running! Stop pushing! Woman and children first! There is no reason to panic. Calm down everyone Calm do...." The announcer caught some of the stench that had risen to the observation booth above and left his post in mid-sentence.

The air conditioners became overloaded, causing the electricity to fail. Overhead fluorescent lights went out leaving the store in semi-darkness. There was only the daylight from outside the front doors to show the way. Later a movie buff described the scene similar to the mob leaving the movie theater when the "Blob" attacked it.

When the lights went out, another type of blob, Farts Murfrey, came out of his trance. He followed suit. It was time to take his mother's LaSalle home.

Like a dream, Farts could not believe what he had seen. The lady in the chartreuse pant suit was prone on the floor with two employees accompanying her. They were as still as corpses. He could not see them breathing. The only thing moving around them were strings of spaghetti moving as they dangled from the shelves nearby.

As Farts ran through the store with the other stampeders, he said to himself, "I didn't do that. There has got to be some other explanation. I have dropped more farts in that particular store than you could shake an air freshener at and no one ever fell to the floor before. There has to be some other explanation."

He heard a loud crash from over the grocery side of the store. Shelves were being knocked over and cans and bottles crashing to the floor, as people in horror, ran or were pushed into them violently. Then crash after crash followed as the domino effect happened. Women screamed blood curdling screams. Someone hollered, "Help! Help!"

In front of Murfrey, someone yelled, "Get the hell out of my way!"

It was not pretty. Farts began to panic also. He saw people in front trampled and people in back urging him on; he could not stop if he wanted to. He just went with the flow. When he got the chance, he detoured around the trampled bodies and found himself in the jewelry department. He heard the wailing sirens of Mobile Medic rescuers heading to the store. The front was now visible. Those, who could, were getting into their automobiles and trucks and speeding off. He angled over to the north side of the store and saw, except for those being trampled, most customers had left the store.

He could see his mother's black gangster automobile, the 1939 LaSalle just outside the front doors. There were plenty of parking spaces available now. It was waiting for him. It sat there by itself, all alone. All he could think of was to get in that car, hit the ignition and speed off just like everyone else was doing.

Not very far from the LaSalle, the television crew from WLOX, came to a halt and were setting up. He could see Karla, the pretty young blonde reporter, interviewing one of the persons who had managed to get out of the store. As he came out of the front door into the bright sunlight, he heard the person being interviewed say the word, "Terrorist".

Mobile Medics with their bags and equipment were rushing past him to go into the store. He was amazed at the speed they had gotten there. He reached into his pocket, grabbing the car keys while dodging the medics.

As he was within twenty-five feet from the La Salle, someone yelled, "Stop!

Stop that man!"

He looked around and saw the store manager and a heavy set man, he had never seen before, pointing at him. The heavy set man shouted, "That's him. That's the terrorist. I saw him on the store monitor. It's him! Stop him somebody. Don't let him get away!"

Murfrey's heart went into his throat. What was this man saying? He had better get out of there while the getting was good. He began to trot with his huge belly bouncing up and down. He almost made it to his vehicle when he was rudely grabbed from behind, thrown to the tarmac and with his hands wrenched backward violently he was handcuffed.

A short fat cop, almost as obese as George, yanked him up and paraded him before the television camera which honed in on his sweating face. The manager and his accuser edged in order to get their faces on camera also. Where there had been a sparse amount of people, suddenly a crowd formed around them.

"That's him officer. That's the terrorist, who tried to blow up the store. I saw it! I saw the whole thing from upstairs while I was watching for shoplifters on my monitor."

Murfrey, while nodding his head in disagreement, heard a loud voice from the crowd that had formed, "They've got the dirty terrorist. He tried to blow up the store!"

"He has already killed a bunch of people! Lets' get him!"

Murfrey fainted.

When he blinked in from his twilight zone, he was being dragged by a policeman on each side and literally catapulted into a black and white patrol car. Murfrey was trying to rise up from his seat when he saw angry faces, ugly men, and not so pretty women running along the side of the slow moving squad car, beating on the door windows with fists and their purchases in Walmart bags. One of the officers hit a button that gave out a "barump-barump" loud strident sound. When this did not stop those younger men from running along the side of the car, the officer in the passenger seat spoke into a microphone and loudly told the crowd to stand back or they would go to jail.

The efficient crew from WLOX trained their camera on George's panic stricken face. When he saw the lens of the camera staring him right in his eyes, he slid down and wedged himself between the back seat and floor board. He had never been as frightened in his whole miserable life.

165

CHAPTER FIFTEEN

Murfrey arrested

The two officers, who herded George into the police station, knew how to handle a terrorist such as George Murfrey, having just returned from the F.B.I. Academy in Washington D.C.; they had the certificates to prove it. They had been taught that you could not go by appearances. Even that nice looking grandmother may have a bomb strapped under her out dated dress. They were not about to be fooled by this rosy cheeked fat man who moaned in sheer terror. He could be a sleeper in disguise.

One of the tactics they learned was how to take down a terrorist in less than three minutes. Their chemical spray canisters, filled with Mace, were replaced by Tasers. If this man just twitched like he was going to give them trouble, he would be tasered. There was so much they had learned, that they hoped most of it could be used on Murfrey before they forgot all that stuff.

On the way to the police headquarters, Murfrey was unable to get back up from off the floor. He was wedged in tightly. When the car door opened, it was not easy to drag him from the car. The heavy set officer, dubbed by Murfrey as Jeckel, attempted to grab him by the shoulders and when that didn't work, he said to his partner, "Come around to the other side and grab his feet."

The other officer, a thin lanky man with a sharp nose and protruding Adam's apple said, "Don't you kick me or I'll knock the shit out of you."

George complained, "I was just trying to help you. The cuffs are biting into my wrists and my arms hurt. I think my shoulder is wrenched."

Unable to get a good grip on the terrorist, the fat officer went around to the front seat, leaning over he grabbed George by his belt, lifting him while hoisting him, moving him a foot or two. Leaving George half hanging out of the door head first, the two officers were able to drag him out of the car, letting him slide to the pavement face down. George stayed in that position while the officers, who were now breathing quite heavily in spite of their terrorist training, caught their breath.

George dubbed the skinny officer, who was panting heavily, as Heckle. He wore a sardonic grin like a scarecrow along with his uniform that hung on him loosely.

"This concrete is hot," complained George.

"Shut up, said Jeckel whose reddened face showed disgust. His Aqua Velva after shave was pouring from his pores. The other officer shouted, "Git up!

"I can't, said George.

The fat cop was about to give George a little encouragement, accorded terrorists, by kicking him in his side, but noticed that he had an audience, so they tried to standing George up, without success. Several other policemen, who had come outside to watch, came over, gave them a hand and after fastening leg irons on George, he was propelled into the air conditioned headquarters.

He was not booked in. Instead, he was hustled to a small room to be interviewed. At the academy, they had learned to interview; not to interrogate. Of course, they were one and the same; it just sounded more humane. At least the jurors, who never wanted to believe a confession could be coerced, would believe what was said during an interview.

Once inside the small grey room with a beat up grey metal desk and three grey metal chairs, the officers could practice what they had learned. All those films they had eagerly watched, when the terrorists at Guantanamo Bay were being "interviewed", could now be used. They did not have a huge tank filled with water to use the water boarding technique, but they could use the other techniques until they could talk the chief into getting one, or maybe just sticking his head in a commode and flushing it a few times would suffice.

George was thrown into a chair under a single naked light bulb which dangled from the ceiling. He noticed that the desk he faced was all beat up and scarred; soon he would find out how it got that way.

It was not standard procedure for two uniformed policemen to conduct an interview. They had skilled detectives for that. But at the present, there were no detectives available. So instead of guarding the prisoner, the two cops decided to loosen up this suspected terrorist; after all they were the ones who cuffed him. They should get the credit.

They were kind enough to take off the handcuffs, leaving the leg irons on. George was able to read their names while they made up their minds as to how the interview would go. The tall lanky one was Carvin and the short squatty one was Waddel.

After a few moments of silence the interview started with a bang. Officer Waddel took his night stick and slammed it down on the beaten and battered desk.

"Just who are you?" shouted officer Carvin in his raspy voice.

"I am George Cedric Murfrey the Third, sir," said George in a high pitched voice. George never used the "Third" part, but hoped the officers would be impressed with the title. They were not.

Actually this answer must have infuriated the officer who now shouted, "Don't give us that crap. We want to know who you really are. Let me warn you. You don't want to play with us. Now tell us who you are and where did you come from."

Before George could answer, there was a knock on the door. Officer Waddel waddled over to it and another officer stuck his head in and whispered something to Waddel. They both looked at Murfrey with deep frowns. George squirmed in his chair. They were whispering about him and it wasn't good.

After an eternal silence, Waddel spoke," Now you have done it. Besides being a terrorist and wrecking Walmart, with your poison gas, the lady, Mrs. Betsy Matthews, just died. Now you will be charged with her murder as well as being a terrorist." Waddel gritted his teeth, rolling his lips back, speaking through them, face contorting, said, "I'd like to take you apart and see what makes you tick."

Murfrey drew back as Waddell tried to reach across the battered desk. He was going to give this murderer a good knock up beside his head. His protruding belly kept the blow from ever landing. But this didn't stop Waddell. He came around the desk and with an open hand slapped Murfrey across his ear. He literally rang Murfrey's bell. Besides the ringing of the bell, George also saw an array of stars.

"Now suppose you tell us what chemical you used to kill that lady. You cooperate with us and we will go easy on you," said the skinny one, Carvin. "If you don't cooperate, well you saw how bad my partner, Waddell, hates terrorists and murderers." Carvin, who had a longer reach, leaned across the desk and put his face within inches from Murfrey's nose. George could smell as well as see the chewing tobacco stains around his teeth and corners or his mouth.

"I didn't kill anybody," said Murfrey who mumbled uncertainly; maybe, he did kill that lady.

"What!" shouted Carvin. "Speak up!"

"I said, I didn't kill nobody and I ain't no terrorist."

Officer Waddell added a new dent to the metal desk with his night stick. He pointed that instrument of destruction at Murfrey and said, "You better tell us and tell us now! We are getting tired of you saying you had nothing to do with what happened at Walmart. Do you think we are stupid? They have you on video. You were on aisle nineteen just before Miss. Betsy came down that aisle. We have you on video looking from aisle sixteen to see if your chemicals worked. We know you did it and you know you did it!"

George could not believe his ears. How could those officers get that information that fast?

Carvin, was back across the desk in Georges' face. He looked into George's eyes with his cold brown eyes and said smoothly as his harsh voice would let him, "Why don't you tell us how you did it?"

"I didn't do anything," protested Murfrey.

"You hear that, Frank? You hear that? This fat punk says; 'I didn't do anything,'" said Carvin imitating George in a high pitched mocking voice.

Waddell hoisted his fat butt up on the end of the desk and in a serious tone said, "We know better. George. Can I call you George? Now if you want a break, you had better come clean and tell us all about it. We can clear this up right now. The detectives are on their way right as we speak and they won't be as nice as Officer Carvin and I."

169

"That's right," said Carvin, who was leaning into George's face again spraying tobacco juice. "And don't forget those two Walmart employees, you poisoned. One is in intensive care and we don't know about the other one. Should that one in intensive care die, there will be no hope for you, if you don't let us help you."

George was actually too scared to speak. He just sat there and shivered.

Waddell waddled back around the desk, stopped and said, "Admit you are a terrorist and we might let you go. I will speak to the D.A., and I will put in a good word for you--say how you cooperated."

"You would let me go?" asked George as he perked up. Maybe they would let him go. If they would let him go, he would admit to killing Kennedy.

"That's right," assured Carvin. "Tell us and you can go. Are you a terrorist?"

"I guess I am," answered George feebly.

"Speak up," rasped Carvin. "Say, I am a terrorist."

"And that you let loose a chemical in Walmart," added Waddell who had moved back closer and was butting in.

"I--I let loose...What was that you wanted me to say so I could go home?"

"Tell us you used a chemical and what it was. You will feel better. Hurry before those detectives come barging in here."

As if on cue, the door flew open and in stepped Detective Ed Smallwood.

"What's going on here?" demanded the detective. He did not appear happy.

"Detective, this terrorist was just confessing. If you would just give us another minute, we will crack this case," said Carvin who now looked guiltier than Murfrey.

"So you are getting a confession, are you," said Smallwood. "I don't suppose you thought to read him his rights, did you?" The dumb look on both of the amateur detectives answered that question.

"Okay boys, I will take over."

"But detective," protested Waddell who did not want to leave.

"Get out! You boys don't know what you are doing," said the detective getting angry. He looked over and saw his old schoolmate, Farts Murfrey. "Is this your terrorist?" he laughed.

"It sure is and he confessed or was confessing. If you will just give us another minute" said Waddell who was still not willing to move his huge bulk off the metal desk and out of the room.

"Your so called confession is no good if you did not read him his rights. Too bad you did not know that. A little learning is a dangerous thing."

"We were getting to that," said Carvin who reached into his pocket and pulled out his packet of Red Bull and popped a plug into his mouth.

"I bet you were," said Smallwood. "You junior detectives know who this boy is?" Smallwood started laughing.

"Yeah," said Waddell who began to sully up. He did not like the way the detective talked to them--like they were stupid. What did he know? He did not see what had happened at Walmart. There he was laughing, while one woman had died, and maybe two more on their way. The callous bastard. How he hated those pompous detectives especially those who laughed at him. And he did not like those D.A.'s either, who threw out their cases after all their hard work. Just let the prisoners go. Those dogs gave law enforcement a bad name by turning those guilty bastards loose. But most of all, he hated those high and mighty Judges, soft on crime, who reprimanded him in open court in front of everyone.

"Don't you ever come into this court again with your loose testimony," the Judge had warned. The good part, however, had been when the Judge then turned to the District Attorney and said, "Don't you ever bring another case like this to my court."

What had gotten Waddell really off on this Judge was when the Judge turned to the Defendant, apologizing before letting him go. But that wasn't all. Later the D.A. chewed him out. On top of that, this very detective, Smallwood, criticized him, also.

"Well do you know who he is?" asked Smallwood once more.

"He is a terrorist and that is all I need to know. That is who he is and he just admitted it. Didn't he, Carvin?"

171

"Sure is," said Carvin as he spit the wad of tobacco into the trash can in the corner, making, a "kay-plunk" sound as it hit home

"This boy is no terrorist. This is Farts Murfrey, a local boy who has lived here in Gulfport all his life. I went to school with him. He is harmless."

"Hey, Farts, remember that time you gassed the Scoutmaster?"

George who came out of his trance-like shock when he saw Ed Smallwood come to his rescue, giggled nervously. Somehow, after all that he had been through lately, he felt guilty about what happened at Walmart and was ready to admit it. If only he could turn back the clock to the days when he was a Boy Scout. Gassing the scout meeting while his buddies placed a bomb in the scout master's car was one of his greatest moments. He had been accepted back then; praised as a hero.

Smallwood turned back to the two cops and asked. "Did you even bother to book him in?" Their stunned silence answered that question. "Okay, Farts you can go. Do you need a ride?"

Farts nodded in the negative. He wasn't sure he heard right. He could actually leave this house of horrors. He looked at his newly found buddy from long ago quizzically.

"That's right. I said you could go. Now go before these keystone cops start in on you again."

That was all George needed to hear. He bolted out the door, passing the desk sergeant near the entrance quickly going down the steps; then turning around he went back to get his wallet and money they had taken from him..

Carvin and Waddell, looking amazed, started to leave the room.

"Stay!" commanded Smallwood like they were dogs.

The two officers slunk back and settled into the metal chairs. They knew what to expect: Another reprimand was coming. They hoped they would not be written up and have the reprimand put into their files. It would be pulled when promotions came out. It was so unfair. Such was the life of a policeman.

The interview had taken place at the satellite police station about one and a half miles north of Walmart and ten miles north of the central business district of Gulfport. Farts had been frisked for weapons when arrested having had his thirty dollars and some change taken from him. Fortunately, the possessions had been handed to the desk sergeant, who had not filed the stuff, so George was able to pick it up. All he had to was to sign a sheet saying he got all his possessions back and leave.

"Is it all there?" asked the matronly looking woman who served as desk sergeant as well as dispatcher.

George was in a hurry to get out of there. He said, "It looks like it is all there."

"Count it,"

"Yes sir. I mean yes mam," said George. He counted it and checked the items. "It is all there. Can I go?"

"You may go, Mr. Murfrey. I hope we don't see you back here."

That was all the encouragement Murfrey needed. He quickly scooped up the bills, change, wallet, car keys and pocket knife. As he stuffed it all in his pocket, the loose change hit the floor and he had to chase down a quarter and two nickels.

When he stood up and turned around to leave, he bumped into the two men who had identified him in the parking lot of Walmart. The middle aged man in the brown suit was the store manager. He had seen him there on many occasions. The other man, the big one, was the one who said he had seen George on the monitor. Both stopped dead in their tracks and gave him the once over. As George was striding toward the door, he heard the manager ask the desk sergeant, "You are not letting that man go are you?"

"He has been cleared to go," replied the sergeant.

"We will see about that," said the manager. "Let me speak to the detective in charge."

George knew what this was all about. He flung open the door to the station, literally running down the steps as fast as it was possible. All that was in his mind now, was to put as much distance between him and the station. As he stumbled trying to walk briskly down Highway 49 along the side of the road, he pondered over what had happened. He had not murdered anyone, yet they had accused him of murder.

And what was a terrorist? He didn't even know what it took to be called a terrorist. He was accused of that also.

What if they changed their minds? He shuddered and tried to pick up his pace, stumbling, almost losing his balance.

After a block of hurrying, he realized that the heat was stifling. His throat was parched. Sweat began to drip from his forehead. He mopped this face with his handkerchief. His once rosy cheeks blended in with the rest of his reddened face. He almost wished he was back in the station where he shivered from the cold, but he plodded on block after block.

The shoulder of the road was hazardous. Pieces of large truck tires blocked his way at times as well as broken glass and other debris. At other times he had to walk on the grass to get around the trash. He picked up cockle-burr stickers on his socks and trousers. He stumbled like a vagabond, but did not stop. In this area of North Gulfport, was a black community which was divided by Highway 49. Cars passed him at high speed as he wobbled panting and sweating profusely.

Up ahead, he could see a small group of black men loitering. One was leaning with his back up against a pink building. Several others were crowded around him and laughing.

"Don't these people ever work?" thought George ironically.

He noticed they were all young men probably in their teens or twenties.

George quickened his pace. His throat was dry, his shirt wringing wet with sweat.

The group suddenly stopped laughing and turned to look this fat man passing in front of them.

The tall light skinned one who had been leaning up against the wall straightened up and yelled, "Hey man, you got a light?"

George ignored him and kept walking.

"Hey fat boy, I am talking to you. I need a light." Slim was angling toward George.

This got George's attention. "I don't smoke and if I did, I would always carry a match or a lighter."

"Hey mothar. What did you say? Hey! Slow down. I am talking to you. What's your hurry?"

George turned his head to see the tall slim man approaching him on the double. His buddies also ceased standing around and were now trailing Slim. It was a small parade behind George.

George stumbled once more, arms flapping to keep from falling, head down almost losing his balance as he scooted forward like a large bowling ball with wings, which was caused by this shoulder of the road with a lot of debris covering it, then tripping over a piece of tire that had peeled off a vehicle some time ago. Up ahead there were beer cans, broken bottles and small rocks threatening to finish the threat. Stopping, he bent over out of breath, clutching his chest.

When he straightened up, he saw that the foursome had gathered all around him. One had bleached his hair which was now orange. Another was wearing expensive Nike shoes and a gold chain around his neck, sporting dreadlocks. The smallest one was twirling a chrome plated chain.

"Man, you alright?" the one with the orange hair asked.

"I am alright," gasped George. He could see he was surrounded.

"What you doing, man? You out for a stroll?" dreadlocks asked.

The short one said as he twirled his two foot chain. "He out for his Sunday stroll; only it's not Sunday." This brought some haw-haws from the group who examined George like he was some kind of fat bug.

The tall light colored one George, dubbed as Slim, looked George in the eye and seriously said, "Hey man, how about lending us ten dollars?"

He was blocking George's path. No longer needing a light, he added, "We need a loan. We be broke."

George was dripping from sweat. He mopped his face and said, "Men, I am broke too. I just got turned loose up the road from the police station and I am trying to"--he sucked in some air--"yeah, I am trying to put some distance between them and me."

"Who-eee," said dreadlocks. "What they have you for?"

"Murder and terrorist."

"Who they say you killed? You don't look like no killer to me," said orange hair.

"They are blaming me for three deaths at Walmart, but I didn't do it. Look I need to keep going, if you don't mind."

"Hey, I just saw that on TV. You the dude in that police car. Yeah, I saw you. They say you was a suspect. My moma just got back from there and she say they run everyone out of the store and put yellow tape around the front doors."

"Hey man, you need a place to hide? We can hide you out. No police will find you," said dreadlocks, who had a kind heart.

"Thank you anyway, but they let me go. You know; not enough evidence to hold me. I'll be okay." They parted and George began to stroll off with the group following. Cars were whizzing by. An occasional vehicle would blow the horn as it passed. A Chevy Nova passed loaded with teenagers who shouted, "Get off the road you fat pig." There were arms sticking out the rolled down windows. All were shooting George the bird.

The group caught up with George. "Walmart ain't never shut down for no reason. You musta done something," said orange head.

"Come on man, what'd you do?" asked the runt with the chain. He had stopped twirling the chain.

"I didn't do anything. They just picked on me because I was on the next aisle from the one where this woman dropped dead. Look fellows, I have got to be going before they change their minds."

The tall one dubbed Slim looked down the road and saw a familiar black Crown Victoria Ford with its fishing pole antenna pulled back and it was coming their way.

"Uh, oh. Looks like they done changed their minds. Guess we better be off." Quickly they disappeared, vanishing in seconds.

The black Ford slowed down pulling to a stop where George was standing.

"Get in. No sense standing out there in the heat, Farts. You want to get a heat stroke," said Ed Smallwood, his child hood pal and newest best friend, now that he had rescued George.

"Thanks," said George as he entered the air conditioned vehicle. It smelled of leather. The radio was cackling interspersed with static about some drunk at newly reopened Johnny's Bar once again becoming rowdy and trying to pick a fight,

George catching his breath, sucking up the cold air coming out of a vent on the dash, said, "I don't think I could have walked another twenty feet. You are not going to take me back there are you?"

"Now, why would I do that? Farts, I know you didn't kill anyone. You may pass some foul stinking gas, but other than stinking up the place, it is not deadly. Those two jokers, Waddell and Carvin were playing junior detectives. When we get the results from the autopsy on that woman, I bet it will show she died from natural causes or some pre-existing problem."

"I will warn you, though. They are not going to let it go. Short of manipulating or planting evidence, they could succeed in arresting you again. So you need to look out for those two. I have had dealings with them before; I will have to hand it to them, they are creative."

"You think they might arrest me again?"

"Well Farts, I would not be surprised. You need to get a good lawyer."

"Ed, you are playing with me. Right?"

"No Farts, I am serious. After you left, the manager of Walmart and the man who monitors the camera looking for shoplifters said they passed you on the way into the station. They were extremely irate about me letting you go. That man who had been on the overhead monitor at Walmart wanted us to drag you back. I took their statements telling them we had to wait for the autopsy report to come in before making an arrest. You are the only suspect; showing you all over television as the terrorist, did not help. I will be getting a lot flack over you, my friend. Say where can I drop you?"

"My mother's car is just up here at Walmart."

They pulled into the parking lot, now empty; the 1939 LaSalle having been towed away once more.

"I guess you can drop me at my mothers' house. I can get my girlfriend to take me to the pound and bail out the car again. My mother won't be very happy about that."

Ed reached over and turned down the air conditioner in the car. The windows were beginning to fog up and he had to run the windshield wipers to clear off the front windows.

"God, how I hate this high humidity! Whatever you do Farts, don't go back to Walmart. Go to K-Mart, but stay away from Walmart. Don't even go to the one in Biloxi."

"I got you," said George. "I always did like K-Mart."

Detective Smallwood pulled the black Ford into the shell drive way which ran along the side of the slender house. He noticed that at one end of the house there was a large fan set in the wall. At the present time the long louvers were closed indicating that it was not running.

"Say how is your mother?" Smallwood asked. "Remember the time she came to get you at the Pine Belt Camporee after they kicked you out. What was that for? Oh, yes. I remember. They accused you of blowing up that camp fire."

"All I did was to plant a firecracker, Zack Brown gave me. I never told on anyone."

"Farts, that and the reason I didn't believe you capable of doing what they accused you, is why I turned you lose, today. We owed you one. Now we are even. Look, pal. Let me give you some good advice. Don't go letting out those stink bombs of yours in public anymore. Go down to the seawall and let the whirlwind deal with them if you get the urge. No sense feeding the firestorm about to start up. I will be seeing you."

Detective Smallwood backed out of the driveway and scratched off.

CHAPTER SIXTEEN

Murfrey indicted and jailed

After the Walmart fiasco, George began to pull in his horns, hanging around the house not going anywhere. No one saw him in public, but everyone on the Gulf Coast saw him over and over on television. There was much controversy as to whether he should have been held in jail or turned loose. All those public figures, who loved to see themselves on the boob-tube, had something to say. Conflict and controversy kept the news media going. The District Attorney came on television assuring the public that his office was looking into the matter; those responsible would be brought to justice. The bald headed manager from Walmart was unhappy that Murfrey had been released. Although guarded in his comments, he added that he did not think, as far as George Murfrey was concerned, he, Mr. Murfrey was not out of it yet. In his opinion, an arrest could be imminent. The television station kept the ball rolling as long as they could, but other news soon pushed this unsolved crime off the news. Life went on--except for George who mostly stayed in his room like a mouse. When he wasn't close to home, he would walk down to the beach which was only several blocks from his home, taking a bag of bread with him, feeding the squawking seagulls. This seemed to give him peace, but Farts had that inner feeling that things were not right.

The hammer was about to drop. Dread of the unknown kept him awake at all hours of the night. The business up in Baltimore had weakened his resolve that he had in no way caused that lady's death. Maybe he did have powers to poison the air and render sickness and death. All he could do now was to pull in his horns and go low key. It was not funny anymore; no one was laughing.

His friend, Smallwood, had told him to get a lawyer, but a good one would cost mucho dineros. That was a joke. Where was he going to get that kind of money? So it was "wait and see."

The Great State of Mississippi was waiting until the next grand jury met before taking action. In Mississippi, the D.A. can by-pass the usual arrest, the bond hearing and the preliminary hearing, by taking a case directly to the grand jury. That procedure seemed to fit this case.

At a preliminary hearing, the State had to prove probable cause. Sometimes the Judge would go off the deep end and refuse to bind the prisoner over to the grand jury. This would make it harder to get a grand jury to indict. Further, in a high profile case such as the Walmart death and its temporary closing, the press and television reporters would have a field day.

This was not a case for heavy publicity. In the Great State of Mississippi, what happens in the Grand Jury room stays in the Grand Jury room. It is one sided; only the State's witnesses testify, without any cross examination from the defendants' attorney, who would not be allowed into the Grand Jury room. Furthermore, there would be no court reporter present to take down the testimony; no transcript to trip up a witness, who was not fully schooled at that time prior to his appearance before the inquisitive Grand Jury, as to how she or he should testify. On the other hand, at a preliminary hearing, the Defendant could have a court reporter present taking down testimony which could be used later to impeach the unschooled witness.

The autopsy report had come back on Mrs. Betsy Matthews. It showed that she died of a heart attack. Her arteries were clogged and she suffered from various embolisms. She was a walking time bomb. The two Walmart employees had recovered. One, had gone back home to Escanaba, Michigan; the D.A.'s office was having trouble contacting him. It would probably become necessary to send someone from the D.A.'s office up to Michigan to try to persuade him to return for the trial. The other employee, Alfred Hoda, was a local boy, but after being interviewed, the District Attorney came to the conclusion that this dumb cluck would mess up his testimony as well a free lunch.

Marcel Beekman, was a ruthless District Attorney. He was a local boy from Lizana, Mississippi which is just up the road from Gulfport in a rural area of Harrison County. He had admired the rural Baptist preachers who held revivals in his area as a boy. He patterned his arguments after these preachers and the court rooms were packed with people who loved to hear him speak. He had a face like a shark. His prominent nose fit his pointed jaw. His eyes, when they would bore into a witness, seemed to pierce into the inner soul. It was his ability to make the most innocent person on earth look absolutely guilty; he lost very few cases.

One of the reasons he lost so few cases, was not only his skill in trying cases, but he had the power to select only the best and easy cases. This was a skill in itself; knowing what cases were dogs and when to avoid them.

The case against George Cedric Murfrey was a dog in Beekman's opinion.

The cause of death was shaky. Fortunately, the Pathologist leaned heavily for the State. He hated criminals and was usually the best witness in a murder case. He could be counted on to sway the jury with his charts and gestures in open court. Defense attorneys hated him; they called him "Dr. Death". The pathology report stated that the cause of death was due to a poisonous substance set forth in the air at Walmart. That was the culprit; Mrs. Matthews had been able to cope with her infirmity until a mysterious poisonous gas killed her. In Mississippi, it was no defense that the person killed was weaker than the normal person. The killer did not have the right to demand a strong healthy person; the jury would be so instructed.

It sounded good. The local doctor at Gulfport Memorial Hospital quickly patterned his opinion to match that of the pathologist.

They had no material evidence of a chemical substance used. None could be found. This meant the State would have to rely on experts that they could count on. Of, course, the defense would probably have one of their own, but the State with more money to spend, could have two or three of them, all saying the same thing.

Beekman had a report on George Murfrey. He lived across the railroad tracks two blocks from Soria City, a black community. In other words, many people considered George as trash living on the wrong side of the tracks. And more to the point, he had no financial resources to hire some hot shot lawyer. Murfrey would have to rely on a Public

Defender who probably was carrying a load of over seventy criminal cases and could not devote the time needed for this case.

One recent Public Defender had filed a motion in court saying that under federal guidelines, seventy cases or more were too much for a Public Defender to represent his clients in a fair and just manner. The district attorney laughed out aloud when the Judge solemnly asked the lawyer if he thought he could not do a proper job with that case load. When the attorney answered in the negative, the Judge banged his gavel and said, "You are fired. We will get a lawyer who says he can do the job!"

By going straight to the grand jury, there would be no publicity, until the indictment came out. Trial would be set and the D.A. would do all he could to block the press and television from reporting anything except what he gave them in the form of press releases. With his skills, he should be able to pull off this dog case and send George Murfrey to the gallows!

All that stuff about Murfrey being released after the initial arrest and the arresting officers reprimanded, would be declared superfluous and excluded from trial by the Judge.

The fact that George Murfrey was a local boy, well known in the vicinity, could not be kept out of the news media. There would be a lot of discussion around Gulfport about this rosy cheeked fat man who paled around with another icon: Dr. Fred Hanson's son, Mutt Hanson. To the populace, they were two harmless individuals who were seen in various cafes drinking coffee or just walking around town in animated discussion about politics, their hands flying up and down in heated animation. To the local people of Gulfport, they were just two laughable derelicts who looked innocent. Fortunately for the D.A., the jury could be picked from other areas of the county. Add those faithful jurors who somehow were on the jury list at every term, whom Beekman knew he could count on, along with those from outside Gulfport, left him feeling, he could get a jury who did not know of Murfrey plus a few who despised a fat man on questionable disability who did not work, but was physically able to frequent those dens of iniquity---pool halls.

Beekman would count on Jacob Bannister, AKA "Big Jake" to inform the jurors of George's activities in the pool halls. Although he had stabbed Murfrey, his case would be presented to the same grand jury that would indict George Murfrey. This was a stroke of genius as well as good luck. In the grand jury room, he would tell the grand jurors that Bannister had stabbed Murfrey in self-defense; that it was necessary that his case of Aggravated assault be presented for their consideration. Furthermore, Jacob Bannister had cooperated with the authorities in the Murfrey case, having been present when the Palace Pool Hall experienced the same poisonous gas that hit Walmart. In the case of the pool hall incident, Bannister had personally seen Murfrey at close range reach into his pocket, pull out a packet of something that appeared to be a yellowish substance then later within seconds, poisonous gas came from the area of Murfrey causing evacuation of the pool hall. The fact that the same kind of incident as in the pool hall within a short period of time happened, involving the same person, namely, George Murfrey, would be allowed at the murder trial. Furthermore, his eye witness in the pool hall caper, Bannister, who claimed self-defense, had to stab George later to save himself.

Eddie Flourisant, aka "Slim" would be allowed to testify that he was exposed to the gas, was taken to the hospital; that a very profitable business in Gulfport had to be closed down because of the stench Murfrey caused.

This would be tied in with the videos taken by Walmart monitoring shoplifters which showed Murfrey on aisle nineteen, where Betsy Matthews died. He could be seen reaching and putting something on the shelf. The camera would be frozen to show Murfrey's hand reaching and withdrawing from the shelf. Betsy's violent death as she retched and collapsed on the floor was a beauty. The two Walmart employees falling to the floor would be icing on the cake as they heroically went to the assistance of Betsy. Next, the film would show George Murfrey hanging around the scene of the crime watching his victim die and never lifting a finger to help. It was cold blooded murder!

As Marcel Beekman, although considering this a circumstantial evidence case, began to believe it was not such a dog after all. Maybe his first instinct was wrong this time.

The interview of Big Jake Bannister by the district attorney's own investigators had paid off. Brian "Bum" Ketch, a big burley bald headed man with arms the size of most people's legs, had persuaded many recalcitrant a witness to tell the truth. He had been a deputy sheriff in Cochise County, Texas and knew the methods. His partner, Ted "Tadpole" Mann admired Bum and followed his dubious lead. Together they encouraged Big Jake to come out with the "truth".

"We already know how the incident at the Palace Pool Hall happened, so why don't you tell us the truth," said Bum Ketch.

"You know how it happened? So why do you need me to tell you?" smarted off Jake with his attitude.

"Let us put it this way," said Tadpole, whose nickname matched his physique. He was able to conjure up a sincere face when needed. "We know that Murfrey had in his possession some kind of a chemical substance that he set off at the Palace. You were there and witnessed the unbearable smell that made a lot of people sick, including Slim, the bartender. So why don't you tell us that?"

"He had some kind of gas, alright," smirked Jake. "Is that what you want to hear?"

Bum Ketch grabbed Jake by the arm with a grip Jake had never felt before. "We just want you to tell us the truth that you saw this Murfrey set off some kind of chemical. You were there. You had to have seen it. And you being the true citizen you are, and knowing Murfrey was a danger to society as well as to yourself, when he confronted you again, you had to stab him in self-defense. Why you should get a medal instead of being charged with aggravated assault. Now, isn't that the way it happened?"

Tadpole chimed in, "That's right isn't it Jake. You tell us the truth and we will tell the D.A. you cooperated and I promise you, no I can't promise you, but I will say in my opinion, the D.A. will see that it was self-defense. Maybe instead of being indicted, you will become the star witness in putting Murfrey away for life or maybe worse. How would you like that?"

Jake, who had been slumping in his chair, straightened up. He said, "The way you said it, is the way it happened."

Jacob Bannister was charged that he had willfully, maliciously and feloniously stabbed George Cedric Murfrey, but because he became a witness for the State against Murfrey, he was granted immunity as long as he testified to the "truth" at trial.

When the Harrison County grand jury handed down its indictments in the June term, there were ninety-seven new cases among which was a multi-count indictment charging George Cedric Murfrey with one count of Capital Murder and one count of terrorism act. Also in the paperwork was an indictment charging Jacob Bannister with Aggravated Assault. Bannister, who gave a sworn statement that George Murfrey did indeed produce a packet of a yellow powder which he set off at the pool hall causing a poisonous gas to be released, would be granted immunity from prosecution provided he so testified at Murfrey's trial. He was told, "We do this all the time."

Bannister, who was already in jail at the time the indictments were handed down, was released without bond on his own recognizance with instructions not to get in any trouble or he would remain in jail until Murfrey's trial. "You are free to go at this time," were sweet words to Big Jake, hitting the jail house door, whooping it up with shouts of joy as he bounded down the steps to freedom.

After the indictments were processed through the Clerk's office, the District Attorney's office received the copy of the indictment against Georg Cedric Murfrey. This time, the D.A.'s office would serve personally the warrant for George Murfrey's arrest.

Beekman had his staff assembled including his two trustworthy investigators, Brian "Bum" Ketch and Ted "Tadpole" Mann. He told them, "No sense kidding ourselves, this will be a difficult case. It is purely circumstantial and --well--the circumstances are not that strong,

"Sir, I think it is strong. Why do you say that?" asked Ted Mann the tadpole.

185

"Jurors don't like circumstantial evidence. This boy is a local kid. Everyone likes him. There will be lots of sympathy for him. We will handle this case correctly from the git-go. That is why I took this case straight to the grand jury. I did not want any publicity. I didn't want any reporters nosing around trying to find evidence that Murfrey is innocent or showing up the weaknesses of this case before trial. Beekman paused and looked the group straight in the eyes so that they would get his message. He said sternly, "I do not want any pre-trial publicity! If you all understand nod your heads." Everyone nodded assent.

"Okay," he said. "Lets' go low key on this one. No interviews. Lets' get the jury picked and get a conviction. Remember no publicity. Keep it low key. Now Bum, you and Tadpole get a few deputies and quietly go out and arrest Murfrey. When he is in jail, I will issue the statement for the press to print. That's the way we will handle it."

At the same time the arrest warrant was to be served, the investigators armed with a search warrant went to Murfrey's home on East Railroad Street. When the law men knocked on the door, Mrs. Agnes Murfrey was entertaining her weekly bridge players. Upon the investigators and deputies gaining entrance, the bridge group left, scattering like chickens being attacked in the chicken yard.

Every nook and cranny was searched for George Cedric Murfrey, as well as for the chemical substances in question. Neither was found; the only substances found were bottles of Gas-X. DeBloat, Gut Check, Beano and Imodium Plus. These items were seized. Maybe they had been mixed and cooked to create the poisonous substance sought. After all innocent Ammonia and Sudafed were used to make Chrystal Meth, so maybe a chemist could figure out how these items could be used to create a poisonous gas.

Agnes Murfrey was asked where her son was hiding; she said that Georgie had left the house with a loaf of stale bread, walking to the beach to feed the sea gulls. The team of investigators and deputies left hurriedly in two unmarked cars, speeding off to find and arrest this dangerous terrorist and murderer.

They spotted George sitting on the seawall approximately a quarter of a block east of the street entering the Gulfport yacht harbor. He was about three hundred yards north of the muddy waters of the Mississippi Sound often mistaken for the Gulf of Mexico. In between the sea wall and the water was the pristine white sand beach which was twenty-seven miles in length, said to be the longest man made sand beach in the world.

George was just sitting there throwing scraps of bread into the air while about one hundred squawking sea gulls were cawing and cackling, swooping and fighting over the bread crusts. Tourists passing by on U.S. Highway 90 slowed to gawk and film the episode with their digital camcorders to take back home for others to see.

The two vehicles with the lawmen jumped the curb, cruising down slowly toward George on a grassy area. Meanwhile, the breeze from across the Gulf had picked up making it harder for George to get the bread up to the swarming sea gulls. He was seen throwing the crust of bread into the air; one sea gull grabbing it, sweeping low just a few feet from George's head and then making an airplane type turn heading out over the water with about ten to fifteen other sea gulls trailing, screeching and screaming in an effort to catch the bird with the piece of bread so that they could snatch the prize. While this was going on, George would throw another piece of bread upward, repeating the scene by another flock of hungry birds. Tourists from Indiana, Georgia, Louisiana and Alabama were fascinated by the melee. They either stopped or slowed down in order to film the event.

The din of the screeching and cackling birds was so loud that George did not notice the unmarked vehicles stopped some eighty feet from him. He was fully enjoying nature at its' finest as it took his mind off his troubles.

Investigator Bum Ketch had jumped out first and was leading the way. "Maybe we should wait and let him finish feeding the birds," shouted one of the deputies following.

Bum shouted back, "Do you think those birds will attack us?' They did not have sea gulls over in Cochise County, Texas where he came from.

187

Another deputy shouted, "One will just peck your eyes out; then the whole bunch will attack." The deputies looked at one another and grinned. They were having fun at Bum Ketch's expense.

As they closed in, about twenty feet from their quarry, George threw a whole slice of bread into the air. This time three sea gulls vied for the prize. They each got a piece of the slice and tore it into three sections, flying off in separate directions. The other birds, not so lucky, dove and followed in an effort to get a mouthful. They set up such a loud series of screeching and cackling that it could be heard by the spectators slowly passing by, filming the event.

Sea gulls will attack a human when that person threatens to interfere with its feeding. While Bum Ketch moved closer to make the arrest, George threw another piece of bread in the air and at least twenty or thirty birds not only attacked the bread, but swooped down on the officers; some dived and flew closed to their ears while others dropped their bombs on the men. Splat, splat went the white droppings showering the investigators and deputies, alike, with the white stuff that also had a black center. One bird in particular took an intense disliking to Bum, who was nearest to his food source. With a loud screech, it dove at Bum like a fighter plane strafing a target; its target being Bum's right ear. Another followed, dropping its liquid bomb on Bum's forehead, as he was looking up to catch sight of the one that had attacked his ear.

Bum panicked, drawing his weapon with the pearl handle, like a fast draw cowboy, quickly sighting the large sea gull, pulling the trigger. "Boom! Boom! Boom!" He fired three times. One of the bullets, from his 357 magnum revolver, hit the target blowing the bird into thousands of pieces. Feathers and pieces of bird guts and blood flew everywhere showering down upon the group of men including George, the flock of startled sea gulls in the area, frantically flying off in all directions.

George, shocked by the loud shattering gun shots turned toward the group of men advancing and exclaimed, "Why did you shoot Oswald? He was the nicest and biggest of the bunch! You should be ashamed."

188

"Get down," shouted Bum, who pointed his gun directly into George's face with one hand while wiping bird crap from his face with the other. "You are under arrest. Get on the ground." He had a fierce look on his face. He had already killed one adversary and would not hesitate to use his weapon again if George resisted.

George immediately let loose with a flatter-blaster, but it was to no avail as the Gulf breeze simply blew the polluted air away carrying the foul smelling cloud into North Gulfport whose citizens later complained about the need to abolish septic tanks used there.

George dropped to the ground onto his belly in sheer terror. This was his first time to look down into the barrel of a gun held by a wild man with huge eyebrows, fierce eyes bulging, white and black bird crap smeared across his face like that of a painted savage.

The, tourists, who had been moving slowly in their vehicles while filming with their camcorders, cell phone cameras and digital cameras, abruptly stopped their automobiles in order to get better shots of the event. Thinking that the officers who had their weapons drawn were arresting George for feeding the birds, they shouted, "Let him go. All he did was to feed the birds. Let that man go!"

A large middle aged woman visiting the coast for the first time, turning to the now small group of tourists, who had exited their autos said, "How horrible. Did you see that man shoot that sea gull? This is a terrible place. I told you, Henry, that the Mississippi Gulf Coast was a wild unsafe place. We should have gone to Florida."

One of the deputies, unholstered his automatic pistol. He was decorated with splotches of white do-do. He rudely shouted, "Get back in your cars and get moving. Everything is under control."

The lady who had just said disparaging things about the Mississippi Gulf Coast just stood there and glared at the deputy with her hands on her hips. This drew the deputy's ire. "Lady get back into your car or I will place you under arrest for interfering with the arrest of a felon. Tell your husband to drive off or he will go to jail with you."

"Well I never," said the woman as she stood there.

"Come on," Mildred, lets' get out of here. That man means business. No telling what he will do," said Henry. "I am going to write the Governor and the Chamber of Commerce about this outrage!"

Slowly the backed up cars moved with the cameras rolling and snapping and people's jaws dropping as they captured George Murfrey on DVD, being hauled up roughly and thrown recklessly into a black vehicle which now had its blue lights located in its grill, flashing brightly.

Even a freelance reporter from the Sun Herald, passing by, got in on the action. He snapped a beautiful shot of George Murfrey in sheer terror, being shoved angrily into the police vehicle. Giving George the bum's rush was Bum Ketch with bird crap smeared over his face with such a fierce look that would knock a bird out of the sky. The photo, which appeared on the front page of the newspaper in color, was a beauty.

The tourists could not wait to get back to their motels and download their DVD camcorders onto the internet to appear on Facebook, and You Tube. Several editions of the scene along with sounds that had taken place were e-mailed to WLOX, the local television station. WLBT the station in Jackson, the state's capitol, also got copies as well as WWL in New Orleans and WKRG in Mobile. George Murfrey had once again made national news. The television stations across the land could hardly wait to run the clip of the sea gull being blasted. The SPCA national leader was interviewed, vowing to see if Federal laws were violated, and if so, the perpetrator would be prosecuted. There was quite an uproar over the arrest and the bad publicity that the Mississippi Gulf Coast received. No one was happy.

The District Attorney was the unhappiest of them all. Investigator Bum Ketch was called on the carpet to explain this publicity disaster. When Bum entered, Beekman was sitting in his padded executive chair with its high back facing the investigator. Bum wasn't sure there was anyone in the chair until suddenly the chair wheeled around exposing the soul piercing eyes of Marcel Beekman boring directly into his sunken hazel eyes, over shadowed by his excessive bushy eyebrows.

Bum Ketch was a huge mass of muscle whose prowess intimidated many a man, but the long stare he received, turned him into a mass of putty. He waited for the shoe to drop; the wait was not long.

"Shakespeare wrote," said Beekman. "'The thing we feared the most has come to pass.' I picked you to make the arrest, because I wanted it to be low key." Beekman raised his voice. "And what did I get? I got news coverage you could not buy with a million dollars! What were you thinking? Shooting sea gulls in front of God, tourists and the world?" The high back chair turned and Bum again faced the high back.

"Sir, you would have had to have been there to understand," explained Bum speaking to the back of the chair from his rehearsed answer. "The suspect, Murfrey, must have been tipped off. He was throwing something into the air that made about three hundred birds go crazy. He was just sitting there waiting for us. All of a sudden just as we approached to make the arrest, the birds swooped in for an attack on us. Sir, let me tell you. It was bedlam. It was so loud; I could not hear myself think." Bum took a brief breath gasping for air. When there was no response from the back of the chair, he continued, "I shouted, 'You are under arrest,' but the suspect kept throwing, what we learned later to be bread crusts into the air. This was to aggravate the birds, which it did. The birds attacked us and bombarded us with this white looking crap that got all over us. I have never seen anything like it." Bum paused; "It was a form of resisting arrest".

"Go on," said the D.A. who had swiveled back to face him with a scowl, those blazing eyes fixed on his.

"There was only one way to complete the arrest and protect us at the same time and that was to fire a shot into the air to scare those vicious birds off and it accomplished what I intended. Unfortunately, one got into the way and went down. That bird had just tried to tear my left ear off. If I had not nailed him, he probably would have circled around and have been successful the next time. Or even worse, those birds would have gone for our eyes."

Bum smiled proudly to himself. That was a pretty good explanation. "So you see sir, I fired in self-defense and it worked. The

191

birds scattered. As I said, unfortunately one of the birds got into the way of one of my warning shots."

"What! Repeat that last part," said Beekman.

"Unfortunately, one of the bullets struck a bird. It was not intentional," he lied.

"That is your story?"

"That is what happened, Sir."

Beekman, who spent over an hour reviewing every video of the event available, let it ride.

"Well I guess that is as good an explanation as any," he said. "The cat is out of the bag, so to speak. The good news as far as you are concerned is that you are going on vacation. The bad news is that you are suspended without pay for two weeks."

Bum, facing the high back of the high back chair again, slowly got up and left the office, red faced with anger. He was indignant over the harsh punishment. His story was so good; he had begun to believe it. Under his breath, he muttered, "That red neck bastard."

After Bum hit the door, the D.A. said to himself, "That arrogant S.O.B. Does he think I believed that pile of crap? As soon as this case is over, I am going to ship his ass back to Texas."

CHAPTER SEVENTEEN

Tried for murder and terrorism

To get to the courtroom where the trial was to take place, the District Attorney had only to walk across the hall. The sheriff and his bailiff's had to walk a little farther, since their offices were located down the hall at the other end of the building. The prisoners in their orange jump suits were herded into a small holding cell behind the courtroom. Among nineteen other prisoners was George Murfrey in his bulging jump suit with sleeves and pants rolled up. Even though Murfey's case held the spotlight with the news media, his business would have to wait until the other prisoners were attended to. This was for psychological reasons, since the potential jurors seated in the audience were given the chance to watch justice in action while the other criminals did the right thing by pleading guilty, taking their punishment for their horrendous actions against society.

Meanwhile, Joseph Ainsworth, Murfrey's Public Defender, had found a parking place two blocks away from the courthouse, dragging his large briefcase on wheels through the gloomy rain, falling in copious amounts. As he appeared downstairs dripping wet, he had to go through a search of his person and his brief case before being allowed on the elevator to go upstairs where court would be held. In order to go to the back of the courtroom to see his client, Little Joe, as he was known, had to identify himself to an unknown voice that came out of a tiny speaker in the wall and then state his business. He was then buzzed through and allowed to go to the holding cell, locked and guarded by a bailiff. He was told that they could not bring Murfrey out of the cell due to the fact all available conference rooms were taken and further, they did not have the manpower to post a guard in front of the door, while Little Joe conversed with his client. However, Joe could go inside the cell and speak to his client where all could hear, including sneering unbalanced dregs on society in the form of prisoners.

Little Joe's interview with his client was brief.

"Today, the court will take up my motions filed in your case. You will not have to do anything, but sit there and listen. I will give you a ball point pen and a sheet of paper. If you have any ideas or anything to say, write it on the sheet," shouted the small attorney through the bars to his client.

Little Joe had filed some forty five motions which were copied from the Public Defender's Manual, he had received at one of the required seminars held and funded by the State. They were called "canned" motions and the court did not take them seriously having disposed of such in many former cases. They ranged from challenging the constitutionality of the death penalty to quashing the indictment. The fact that all jurors who opposed the death penalty were summarily dismissed, leaving only those who would vote death if given the chance, was attacked in a motion without success.

The only motion, the court gave any thought to, was the one to change the venue. An array of potential jurors were called to the witness stand and questioned about newspaper accounts of the arrest and the television clips of the sea gull shooting. Each and every one, who testified, stated it would have no bearing on their verdict; that they paid no attention to it. They all said that they could render a fair trial. One or two told the court that they were not pleased with the shooting of the bird, but understood that this had nothing whatsoever to do with the issue of murder and terrorism.

All forty-five pretrial motions were disposed of in less than an hour.

The defense was granted two motions. One covered the expense to hire two experts. One of the experts would testify about the merits such as the cause of death and the chemical substance used; the other expert would testify about mitigating circumstances on the death penalty phase, in anticipation of George being convicted. Public Defender Ainsworth informed the court that he already had Dr. Donald Cumberland of the Cleveland Clinic out of Ohio lined up as his trial expert and Dr. Mary Francis Ethridge of the Ethridge Psychology Clinic the other expert in case of conviction in connection with the death penalty phase of the trial.

All Discovery was to be completed prior to trial. Trial was set for August 15th. When attorney Ainsworth complained about the short amount of time in which to prepare for trial, he was told to file a motion if he didn't like it.

"Since this is a Capital Murder case as well as a terrorism case," said the white haired Judge Graham with a kindly countenance, "I am going to appoint Attorney Nancy Grace Best to assist you. Any objections?"

"No your Honor."

Nancy Grace who was standing by in the courtroom, came forward and stood with Little Joe. She was a petite Public Defender whose expertise was cooking pecan pralines of which the Judge was a constant recipient. Judge Graham loved those pralines, looking forward to being supplied with them during trial. He also looked forward to seeing this pretty young lady with nice legs whom he could ogle along with any of the pretty female jurors that stepped forth to do their civic duty.

The Judge said, "There being no objections to the appointment of Nancy Grace and there being no other business before this court, the court will break for lunch. Bailiff, take the prisoner back to the detention center. See you in three weeks, Mr. Murfrey."

"Not if I see you first Judge," said George who was surprised himself over his flippant remark. It just slipped out.

"What's that?" said Judge Graham who had been in the process of leaving the bench with his black robe flowing like bat wings.

"Just a little humor, Judge," said George with a reddened face. He did not think the judge could hear that well.

The Judge's kindly face turned to sheer hatred. "There will be no humor in this Court. Do you understand?" he shouted startling the spectators in their tracks in the process of leaving the courtroom.

"Yes, sir," gulped George.

"No humor," the judge repeated.

Before George could get into any more trouble, the Bailiff grabbing George, swinging his arms around to his back, cuffed him. He was given a little shove. With the leg irons already in place and a chain fastening them to his hand cuffs, the push caused George to stumble. In order to walk and shuffle, he had to bend forward stoop shouldered. He looked like some ape. As he was led out of the courtroom, the television cameras caught George in his ape walk. The newspaper reporter also got a good shot of this fat bloated ape being led by his keeper. This picture appeared on the front page in color in the Sun Herald.

The headline was: "JUDGE RULES NO HUMOR IN MY COURT."

The story underneath the headline stated, "Today, accused of murder and terrorism at the Walmart Store in Gulfport, George Cedric Murfrey, appeared in The Harrison County Circuit Court in Gulfport before Judge Magnus Peabody Graham. The Judge threw out over forty motions filed by Public defender, Joseph Ainsworth. During the hearing, Judge Graham, adamantly told the Defendant, who had tried to make light of the charges, that there would be no attempts at humor in his courtroom; that the charges of Capital Murder and Terroristic Act were serious matters.

District Attorney, Marcel Beekman had stated that he was asking for the death penalty in this case since the combination of Murder and Terroristic Act enabled a charge of Capital Murder. During the hearing when Judge Graham solemnly made his ruling on no humor, the audience in the crowded courtroom began to laugh when some unidentified spectator shouted, "You tell 'em Judge!"

The Judge threatened to clear the courtroom if there were any more outbursts. One of the bailiffs seized one man and took him back into the Judge's chambers. It was learned that Amos Beavers of Pass Christian was charged with public drunkenness after being taken into custody for making the loud remark. The Bailiff, Perry Carlton, stated that Judge Graham simply was not going to have his courtroom turned into a carnival affair."

It took two days to pick the jury. The jury panel selected consisted of eight women and four men with two good looking female alternates. The Judge had called the attorneys up to the bench and told them, "Those twelve jurors look pretty healthy to me. Let's put those two beauties on as alternates so I will have something nice to look at during trial. That is besides you, Nancy Grace."

196

The breakdown of the female jurors were five white women who looked like they hated mankind, three black Aunt Jemima types who could care less if that white boy burned and four men, all Caucasians ranging from a young plumber to a middle aged barber.

Little Joe, being black, figured he could relate to those of his own race. But not to be out done, the Assistant District Attorney backing Beekman up in the case was a tall good looking dark black man, Jack Hines who had never lost a case since being hired.

It had always been the policy of the local trial attorneys to allow any out of town experts to testify out of turn so that he would not have to sit around with the meter running on his hourly expenses. Little Joe was hoping that his out of town expert, Dr. Donald Cumberland from the Cleveland Clinic, would happen to appear during the prosecution's part of the case so that he could interrupt the flow of thought. Dr. Cumberland had assured Little Joe, that it was a farce, that Murfrey could not have opened a packet of chemicals, placing them on the shelf or if the jury believed the State's theory about the chemical packet, that the fumes from the imaginary chemicals could not have caused or contributed to the death of Betsy Matthews. The expert, in his opinion, was prepared to state that this was just a happenstance; that Mrs. Matthews had chosen that moment to have a massive heart attack, then dying.

On the other hand, The State of Mississippi had hired experts who would say the opposite. One expert, Dr. Ben Burney of Dallas, Texas had it all figured out. He would testify that new chemical substances being used in Russia and other countries, which left no residue, could kill a person instantly. All Mrs. Matthews would have to do was to come into contact with the deadly fumes. The other two men who collapsed had not gotten the strong dose of the chemical as it dissipated. The fact that George Murfrey had stayed to watch Mrs. Matthews die was an enigma which he had studied over in foreign countries where the perpetrator always stayed to watch his victim die.

The other State's expert was a local behaviorist expert from the Lyon's Laboratory in Ocean Springs, Mississippi. Dr. Spiro Lyons would agree with Dr. Burney that indeed, George Murfrey was a terrorist.

All the information as to testimony of the experts was provided each side due to the fact that Mississippi had full discovery rules. With each side having all the information to be presented in open court, there was to be no trial by ambush.

In essence the D.A. got around those rules by coming up with last minute newly discovered witnesses, who would be allowed to testify, provided the defense was given thirty minutes to interview that witness. It was hard to conduct an interview with the bailiff pounding on the door telling the defense that the Judge says, "Hurry Up!"

Another trick the prosecution used was the enhancement by it's expert witnesses which went outside the written reports provided under the *Rules of Evidence,* to the defense. The pathologist, Dr. Death, was notorious for elaborating further than what was contained in his reports. The Judge usually allowed this to go on saying, "Overruled. You can cover that on cross-examination."

Then there would be that devastating rebuttal witness who was left off the State's list of witnesses. Under the rules he could refute any evidence offered by the defense

Finally, any errors, mistakes or violations by the Court itself, were only corrected by the trial court itself when there was a Blue Moon. Otherwise, any error made by the trial court was left up to the Appelate Court to correct. Fat chance on that! Little Joe Ainsworth, a veteran of many whippings at the hands of the best ambitious Assistant District Attorneys, money could recruit, was well aware of all those pit falls. He had taken the time to count the number of reversals in criminal cases rendered the year before and found only one. That one was a case of blatant perjury, the lower court had ignored. No other cases appealed by Public Defenders had been reversed the year before by the Mississippi Supreme Court.

Little Joe knew that this case had to be won at trial in the lower court even with the playing field slanted for the prosecution, or not at all.

Of course, in the U.S. of A. and in Mississippi, George Murfrey was presumed to be innocent until proven to be guilty beyond a reasonable doubt. Jurors quickly discounted the presumption of innocence as a loftily phrase. Many felt the accused would not be there if he was innocent. Reasonable doubt was never defined by the court in its instructions. Jurors were left to their own definition; usually discarded when their emotions prevailed in deciding guilt or innocence.

Little Joe and Nancy Grace had decided not to ask for a Special Venire, but elected to settle for the ordinary jury panel. In an ordinary jury panel to select from, the jurors usually didn't know what cases were on the docket for trial. In a Special Venire, the summons were sent out two weeks in advance, giving jurors plenty of time to find out about the case, forming their opinions prior to trial.

All potential jurors who opposed the death penalty were excused summarily. Those who knew George Murfrey, Maybellene Modine or Mutt Hanson went next. What was left were those jurors who said they had not heard about the case and those who had read about it or seen television reports saying they could lay that aside and render a fair and impartial verdict. They all promised to keep an open mind until all the evidence was in and the Judge had given them the instructions of the law they were required to follow.

Surveys showed that sixty-five per cent of the jurors made up their minds after opening statements and eighty per cent formed an opinion prior to the conclusion of the trial.

On opening statement, the prosecution stated emphatically that they would prove beyond a reasonable doubt that George Cedric Murfrey did willfully, feloniously and with malice aforethought kill and murder Betsy Matthews and did perform an act of terrorism in doing so. Beekman stated that at the conclusion of the trial, he was going to ask for the death penalty.

Each time Beekman thundered about the vicious taking of the life of Betsy Matthews, George would wince. All eyes were trained on that guilty no good fat bastard in the form of a heartless devil.

"I am already convicted," he thought to himself. When Nancy Grace Best made her opening statement on his behalf, his innocent look reappeared. The Court then said, "Call your first witness, Mr. Beekman.

The first witness was an irate Kenneth Rushton, Manager at Walmart. He was a squat round bald headed man with glasses. Dressed in a grey silk suit that obviously did not come from Walmart, he testified that he did not see the incident happen, but had reviewed the video. Because the video had not been offered, after objection by Little Joe, he was not allowed to testify about what was on it. The jurors, who were anxious to learn about those videos, gave Little Joe a dirty look, crossed their arms in disapproval. He was able to state that a Code Red alert was given, which meant there was a slip and fall by a customer; two employees, Tim Rucket and Al Hoda were sent to the area to assist the fallen lady, block it off and clean up the mess. He testified further that the two men dispatched had mysteriously also fallen, but had survived death. He further testified that he witnessed the exodus from his store and it wasn't pretty. His store was shut down six hours while the police investigated the cause of the incident. The store was later declared safe and while shoppers were readmitted, his employees had restocked the shelves, making it safe again for the public. Yes, he had learned that Betsy Matthews, the fallen lady was pronounced dead on arrival at Garden Park Hospital, the nearest hospital.

Huey Doolie, one of the security personnel on duty testified that security had been called to the area to help evacuate the store. At the time he did not know what had happened, but later learned that one, George Murfrey, the defendant, had left some chemicals behind on a shelf, letting loose some kind of a poison gas.

"Objection!" shouted Little Joe, making lawyer noises, demonstrating his trial skills. Actually, this was what Beekman wanted him to do. It would make the jurors wait a little longer before they could get that evidence, sure to come. It was his way of highlighting the incident and making it look like the defense was impeding the case.

"Sustained!" shouted an indignant Judge. He did not like the D.A.'s trick.

"Ask the Court to instruct the jury to disregard the remarks about the chemical substance."

By the Court: The jury will disregard the remarks that the Defendant left chemicals on the shelf where one died and two others

200

were injured. I assume that proof will come later. Is that right Mr. Beekman?"

By Beekman: "Yes, your honor. It sure will."

The testimony continued. Disregarding the officer's testimony about the chemical substance was like throwing a skunk into the jury box and telling them to ignore the smell. The security officer, Doolie, testified that he and other employees sealed the area off; that he called Mobile Medic and the Police. Yes, he had seen the video of the whole incident and could identify a man hanging around at the scene.

Q: "Can you identify that man in this courtroom?"

A: "Yes, sir."

Q: "Could you point him out?"

A: "It is that fat man sitting between his attorneys with a plaid sport coat on."

He stuck out what looked to George, a long bony finger which seemed to reach right up to his face. George squirmed and sunk down, lowering his fat body into his seat as best he could. The jurors audibly gasped.

On cross examination, Doolie admitted that he did not see George Murfrey actually place any chemicals on the shelf of aisle nineteen. He admitted as far as he knew, no residue of any chemicals was found on the shelf or in the area. He blurted out that this was for the experts; that the video showed Murfrey reaching for the shelf.

This time the objection of the defense was overruled

By the Court: "Objection overruled. Mr. Doolie can testify as to what he saw. He is on cross examination. Move on."

There were several frowns from the jury directed toward Murfrey and his obstructive attorneys. After Doolie stepped down from the witness stand, the court broke for lunch.

Another security officer, Manley Hass, a tall black man with a serious intelligent face, testified that upon arriving at the scene, which Doolie had cordoned off, that there was this awful odor which smelled like ten day old rotten eggs. He took one sniff and had to back away. At that time he noticed a heavy set man (pointing to the defendant) hanging around staring in the direction of aisle nineteen while everyone else was leaving the area as fast as they could. He testified that he had a gas mask in his locker which had been provided by Civil Defense for just such occasions; that during the time the customers were clearing out of the store, he went and got it. He was the one who turned on the extra air conditioning and ventilation system, but when the load was too much for the system; a main breaker switch popped, causing all the lights to go out. He stayed around to assist the Mobile Medics, who were very efficient; that when the injured were removed, he got the air conditioning system going, clearing the air.

The next witness, Billy Barnes, was the watcher employee who manned the monitor looking for shoplifters. He was on duty at the time and had personally seen George Murfrey go to aisle nineteen, putting something on the shelf about half way down the aisle. He saw George depart quickly; then George was seen watching Mrs. Betsy Matthews walk down aisle nineteen. Murfrey was on aisle sixteen. He was asked to step down and with a pointer he testified from a schematic drawing of the store, just where all this occurred. He marked the shelf in question where George put the stuff with an "X". He drew a circle and put an "x" in the middle where Mrs. Matthews collapsed. Then he marked the place where the two employees who collapsed, had fallen to the floor designated as "E1" and "E2". Through this witness, the marked drawing and the video in question were finally marked into evidence over objection by the defense.

Nearing the end of the work day, the court recessed until eight the next morning, excusing the jurors. The court then took up the oral motion stated by the defense why the video should not be allowed into evidence. While the Public Defenders listed case after case in support of their motion to exclude the video, the court took the time to read over the Instructions both sides had submitted. This would save time after the trial ended. After the Public Defenders sat down, the court, without looking up in a low voice said, "Overruled. The video will be admitted and shown to the jury. If there is nothing else, we will resume tomorrow morning. Everyone be on time. The jurors don't like to be kept waiting in the jury room. Court adjourned." Like a bat, the Judge left the bench with his flowing black robes, but this time George, who was in deep shock stayed silent.

Day two of testimony began early the next morning. The jurors and George Murfrey were startled by the sight of several large video monitors facing them. They seemed to be everywhere. Two of the largest monitors faced the jury at each end of the jury box. The prosecution had one facing their table; the defense had a smaller one facing their table and the Judge had one in front of him.

The video was first played in its' entirety. This was the first time George seen the video and himself on it. Although his attorneys had received a copy of the video during discovery, there was no device to show it to Murfrey in the conference room at the jail.

It showed the defendant walking around slowly from aisle to aisle and at last turning down an empty aisle deemed nineteen. He walked to the middle and appeared to be looking at articles and items on the shelf. This shelf contained women's lingerie according to the monitor watcher, Barnes, who paused the video, while testifying that all that was on that shelf were skimpy bikini ladies' panties and sexy braziers. At that time the jury turned to get a good look at George; maybe he was a sex maniac on top of being a terrorist.

The video resumed, paused again, showing George reaching for something. Barnes commented that it appeared to him that something was being placed on the shelf; that nothing was removed to be taken for purchase.

When the video was returned to normal speed, George was seen leaving the area faster than he had come into it. Just as George cleared the area, Betsy Matthews appeared, approaching the area where George had just hastily departed. The jury watching in awe as Mrs. Matthews looked like she had run into a brick wall. She stopped; threw up what was described by Barnes as spaghetti and as he zoomed in closer, the strands of undigested spaghetti were seen flying out of the victim's mouth, wrapping themselves around various items on the shelves on both sides of the aisle. As her dinner streamed out like a flood, Mrs. Matthews collapsed onto the highly polished floor, jerking like a person having a seizure, literally dying before their eyes.

At the far end of the aisle, from which George had entered earlier, he was seen peering around watching the action, not moving off, until minutes later, as the two employees, responding to Code Red, came hurrying in with a mop and bucket.

As those two rescuers also hit an invisible barrier, they too, crumpled to the floor, vomiting, jerking, laying still as if dead, all the while, George Murfrey could now be seen, at aisle sixteen, frozen in place; just watching.

Next, the security Officer, Doolie arrived, placing a tape barrier closing off the aisle, holding his nose, as he left. Security officer Manley Hass is then seen approaching the scene and then leaving. Later he is seen returning wearing a gas mask. By this time the lights had gone out and George Murfrey was no longer in the area. Manley leaves briefly; later the lights come back on and the spaghetti is seen waving from the shelves again. Mobile medics are seen scooping up the three persons, rolling them out on gurneys. The one identified as Hoda is seen stirring, lifting his head in an attempt to look around. Rucket was not moving; neither was Mrs.Matthews.

The jury watched in silence as the monitor was enlarged by Barnes to show more of the store as the panicked customers pushed and shoved each other. Then after several elder women fell to the floor, they were trampled by people being shoved from behind. George is identified as being in the chaotic group doing the pushing and shoving while being herded toward the front door. As more medics arrive to render aid to the women and children who were trampled, George is seen hurriedly leaving the store from the jewelry section. Over in the grocery area, the domino effect is taking place as someone had caused one of the shelves to fall over striking another heavily laden shelf causing it to fall and so on. As the video ended abruptly, the lights in the court were turned back on. When George looked up, he saw twelve jurors and two pretty alternates glaring at him with hatred accorded a murderer and terrorist..

The prosecution had more. They had subpoenaed the video taken by the WLOX crew who had been just blocks away filming an automobile accident on Interstate Ten. Fortitutiously, they were able to arrive at Walmart about the time the Gulfport police arrived in a black and white police car, its siren piercing ears, a loud horn screeching in spurts. Billy Barnes who had been watching for shoplifters above the shopping area is seen with the Assistant Manager being interviewed by Karla Matheny, the news reporter, when they turn the camera on George Murfrey coming out of the store waddling toward a black sinister looking 1939 LaSalle automobile.

The TV video had sound, but on objection of the defense, the part about Barnes shouting, "That's the man. Stop him!" was edited out. It was ruled too prejudicial.

The rest of the video showed George being apprehended, cuffed and placed in the police car. The police car is shown slowly moving as the mob followed in an effort to grab George and tear that terrorist to shreds. No reason was given by the court as to why that portion wasn't also cut from the video.

Both videos, lasting only about twenty-one minutes, seemed like an eternity to George Murfrey.

The Judge called a recess and George was escorted to a conference room where his two defenders awaited him.

George had no sooner entered the room when he began wringing his hands and saying, "Oh, I am sunk. I don't have a chance. They might as well kill me now." He went over to the wall and began banging his head against the light oak paneled wall which had a hollow space on the other side making a booming noise as George banged away.

The Bailiff, who had escorted George to the room, standing outside the door so that he did not escape, saw George banging his head before the door was closed and was startled by the loud noise.

"I have never seen anything like this," he said to anyone who wanted to hear.

George continued, "Did you see how they looked at me. They hate me. They have already convicted me. What am I going to do?" His voice had become shrill as he looked over at Little Joe and Nancy Grace pleadingly.

Little Joe quietly closed the door. Nancy Grace said, "The first thing to do is to shut up! We have work to do and we don't have much time to do it before we go back in there." Her voice was rising from the strain of the trial.

"Mr. Murfrey, said Little Joe calmly. "You have nothing to worry about. Let us do the worrying. That is what we are paid to do." Joe seemed so unconcerned.

"You tell me not to worry. That is easy for you to do. It is my ass they are going to fry. That D.A. wants to kill me!" Tears began to flow down George's rosy cheeks; he was back to wringing his hands.

Little Joe got up out of his chair, walking over to where George was gesturing with his hands, putting his hands on George's shoulder, leaning down, whispering into George's ear, speaking softly, "I said you have nothing to worry about. The worst that can happen is a hung jury; a mistrial."

George wiped his eyes. "Why do you say that--just words," said George tearfully.

Joe put his mouth even closer to George's ear, whispering again, "Juror number eight, Jasmine Booze is my aunt's cousin. Juror number eleven, Mabel Johnson goes to my church and goes shopping with my mother. I have represented Mabel's son by her first husband and got him out of a burglary charge. I know these two women. I would stake my life that they won't let me down."

"Isn't that illegal?" asked George who was calming down.

"Shh. Lower your voice. There is a deputy outside the door with big ears. You can believe your ass, the D.A. has his ringers, he is sure of also. So sit down and lets' see how we are going to attack that video. We can't use what you said, that all you did, was to fart. It stretches the imagination too far, that someone could pass gas, causing a store as big as Walmart to evacuate."

One thing in your favor, all they have is a theory, that you had a chemical substance, you planted. They can't prove it."

"But that is what I did. I just farted. It is a game I play; I call it "Fart and See". I go down an aisle, let out some gas then I watch those who come down it later running out of the aisle like the house is on fire; it is really quite funny. Didn't you say that lady had a heart attack?"

"That is true," said Little Joe. "And I plan to emphasize that before the jury."

They marched back into the courtroom with an air of confidence.

The Judge looked over at Billy Barnes, who had taken his seat in the witness stand once more. Mr. Barnes, you are still under oath." He turned to Little Joe and said, "Little Joe, are you ready for cross examination?"

"I am your Honor." Joe then lit into Barnes.

Q: Sir, you testified that Mr. Murfrey had a packet of chemicals which he placed on this shelf." Joe had the video in the spot where George had reached for the shelf. He handed Barnes the pointer.

"I cannot see any packet. Maybe my eyes are no good. Would you please point out that packet to the jury. I don't believe they can see it either."

When Barnes hesitated, not moving the pointer, Joe raised his voice and said, Well, Mr. Barnes. We are waiting. What is the matter? The truth is there is no packet of chemicals in this video is there?"

A: No."

Q: I didn't hear you. Speak louder."

A: "No!"

Q: I wonder why you would come down here and say such a thing. Who did you discuss your testimony with before you got on this stand, swearing to tell the truth?"

A: "Mr. Barber."

Q: "Mr. Frank Barber, one of the assistant district attorneys? He told you to say that?"

A: "Yes." Barnes hung his head.

It was evident that Judge Graham was not pleased with that testimony. The jurors now glared at the witness.

"Judge, I move to strike all testimony by this witness about seeing Mr. Murfrey place a packet of chemicals on the shelf on aisle nineteen."

By the court: "Motion granted. All testimony by Billy Barnes that he saw a packet of chemicals being placed on the shelf on the aisle in question is here by stricken. The jury is instructed to disregard that testimony."

"Judge," said the prosecutor. "I think you should also instruct the jury that we don't need testimony of an actual sighting by a witness of the defendant putting a packet of chemicals on that shelf. This man ran from the scene after reaching up there; then Mrs. Matthews died; two employees were also injured. And what is the defendant doing? He is just standing there to see if his chemicals worked!"

By the court: Mr. Beekman save your argument for the close of the case at which time I will instruct the jury as to the law they should follow."

"Thank you Judge," said Mr. Beekman. He turned and smiled at the jury as if he had won the skirmish.

"That is all I have for this witness, Judge," said Little Joe sarcastically. I hope the state's next witness can give us some cold hard facts.

By the court: That is enough, Little Joe. Mr. Barnes you can step down."

Day three of the trial began with the testimony from the coroner who pronounced, Betsy Matthew dead from causes to be determined. He deferred to the forensic pathologist who did the autopsy. The coroner, who had been elected to the office, because no one else wanted the job, was really unqualified. He would not answer any questions other than Mrs. Matthews had died at Walmart deferring all other questions as to specific causation to Dr. Igor Dath, the forensic pathologist from New Orleans.

Little Joe on cross examination drew laughter from the jury and audience when he acted exasperated and asked, "In other words, all you are going to tell us as coroner is that Mrs. Matthews' cause of death is that she stopped breathing?"

Coroner: "I can't even tell you that."

Mr. Ainsworth: No further questions.

Since the nearest forensic pathologist was seventy miles away in New Orleans, the State of Mississippi used him in their criminal cases. Nicknamed Dr. Death, the criminal attorneys in New Orleans feared him with cause. He had a ninety-nine per cent rate of conviction. To say that he leaned toward the State in his testimony would be an understatement. He was an experienced veteran of many court battles and had put many a criminal defense attorney in his place.

To qualify as an expert, Dr. Dath testified that he had served in the U.S. Army; trained as an expert in the field of poisonous gases, their signs and effects on humans. Over objection of Nancy Grace Best, Dr. Dath was accepted as an expert in the field of poisonous gases.

Mr. Beekman: Dr. Dath, based on your training as an expert in the field of poisonous gases, the history you received in this case and the autopsy you performed, do you have an opinion based on reasonable medical probability as to the cause of death in this case?"

Dr. Dath: "Yes, I do."

Mr. Beekman: "What is it Doctor."

Dr. Dath: "Based on my training dealing with poisonous gases and its effect on servicemen plus the fact that I performed hundreds of autopsies on persons who had died from poison gas; further after studying the history in this case which included watching the video furnished by Walmart of Mrs. Betsy Matthews actually dying, and lastly based on the autopsy, I personally performed on the decedent, I reached an opinion based on reasonable medical probability that Betsy Matthews died from a poisonous substance of unknown chemical composition."

Mr. Beekman: "Would you elaborate on your findings, if you please, doctor."

Dr. Dath: "Yes, sir. In this case the video was most helpful. In my study of actual cases of persons dying from poison gas, they invariably stopped dead in their tracks upon inhaling the gas and then prior to dying, they vomited and went into seizure until death released them from that horrible experience. In this present case, we see those very symptoms. Mrs. Matthews stops suddenly after obviously inhaling the gas; then she vomits the contents of her lunch; after that you can see her jerking from a seizure in her death throes. It is a classic case."

Mr. Beekman: Doctor, you mentioned that this was a horrible experience for Mrs. Matthews. Can you tell the jury whether Mrs. Matthews suffered prior to death?"

Dr. Dath: "Yes. The pain she suffered, even for the short time was excruciating and extremely painful." He nodded his head and added, "It was one of the most terrible deaths I have ever seen; I am sorry the jury had to see it."

Mr. Beekman: "Doctor, based on your knowledge of poisonous gases, do you have a scientific opinion about this type of gas used?"

Dr. Dath: "I have kept abreast of the newest poisonous gases that are now available. Most of them have come out of Russia. They are odorless, invisible and cannot be detected after they are administered. Mrs. Matthews must have come in contact with one of the new ones."

Mr. Beekman: "Doctor, having seen the video, do you have an opinion as to how this gas, which killed Betsy Matthews, was administered?"

Dr. Dath: "The video shows only one person in the vicinity who could have administered the poisonous gas and that was the Defendant." (Pointing to George C. Murfrey)

There was a hush in the courtroom as the jury swung their attention from the pathologist to George who had once again, the look of a guilty person.

Mr. Beekman: "That's all doctor. Your witness."

Little Joe knew the tactic Beekman was using. The tactic was to just furnish the jury with the framework and then when on cross examination, let this highly skilled pathologist, who hated defense attorneys, explain and explain until the defense attorney was sorry he ever tried to cross examine the doctor.

Mr.Ainsworth: "How are you Dr. Dath? As you already know I'm Joseph Ainsworth, Mr. Murfrey's attorney. You do remember me from our interview last week don't you?"

A: "I remember you."

Q: "I noticed that you did not tell the jury in your testimony on direct about Mrs. Matthew's heart condition. Do you remember us discussing that condition last week?"

A: "To answer you first question, I wasn't asked about the heart condition and yes, I remember you touching on that subject."

Q: "In your autopsy didn't you find that the arteries going to the heart of Mrs. Matthews were ninety per cent blocked?"

A: "Yes."

210

Q: "And didn't you find two embolisms in her arteries?"

A: "Yes."

Q: "Wouldn't you agree, apart from the cause of death, you have just given your opinion, Mrs. Matthews with her blocked arteries and embolisms, was a very sick lady and a high candidate for a heart attack?"

A: "I don't know what you mean 'high candidate'. She seemed to be leading a normal life. She was doing what women like to do and that is out shopping in Walmart."

Q: "You didn't even consider that she may have had a heart attack and that could be the cause of death, did you?"

A: "I considered it, but based on my experience in these type cases and my findings, I ruled out the heart attack."

Q: "But isn't it true, the symptoms of a heart attack are similar to those seen on the video?"

A: "Some of them. But of course the other factors such as the odor, your client being in the area, seen placing something on the shelf and then seen watching his handiwork, weighs heavily on causation."

By Mr. Ainsworth: Objection, you Honor. Move to strike the part about Mr. Murfrey watching his handiwork.

By the Court: Overruled. You opened the door on cross examination. Move on.

Q: "No one found any chemical substance on that shelf, did they?"

A: "No, but like I said before, there are substances that are virtually undetectable after they are used."

Q: Now doctor you put a lot of weight on the fact that George Murfrey was in the area and by the way, the court has already ruled that the video does not show George placing anything on the shelf in question. My question is could not someone else have placed the disappearing substance on the shelf prior to George getting there?"

A: "That is possible, but based on your clients' actions, it is improbable. What is this man doing looking at ladies' lingerie anyway?"

Q: "In studying the history you said you reviewed, did you not know he had a girlfriend?"

A: "That man has a girlfriend? Well, no. Now that is hard to believe."

Q: "Also, doctor, did you ever consider that if a packet of a chemical substance was placed on the shelf, how did it get there? I mean it had to be in some kind of container, didn't it?"

A: "Yes, but Mr. Murfrey could have palmed it and thrown it away during the mob panic that ensued."

Q: "There is no video that shows that happening is there?"

A: "No, but that doesn't mean it didn't happen."

Q: "And it doesn't mean it did."

By the Court: "Don't argue with the witness."

Q: "Doctor, are you familiar with Dr. Donald Cumberland?"

A: "No. Not that I can recall. Who is he?"

Q: "You say that you are an expert on poisonous gases, right?"

A: "Right."

Q: "Then what is the name of the new type of poisonous gas that leaves no signature such as residue."

A: "I am not familiar with the name at this time."

Q: "Well then doctor, the last time you went to a seminar on poisonous gases was when?"

A: "I go to so many every year, that, I cannot say without consulting my calendar."

Q: "Would you have gone to one here in New Orleans during the past year?"

A: "I cannot remember. Probably did, but I would probably have to consult my calendar."

Q: "Well, doctor, if you had attended the recent one held in New Orleans, you would have met Dr. Donald Cumberland who was in charge of the seminar and the main speaker."

A: "I guess I missed that one."

Q: "No further questions. You are excused."

By the Court: "Ladies and gentlemen of the jury, you will get a break this afternoon. The court has some maters to take up and I am going to excuse you until tomorrow morning. Remember do not discuss this case with anyone including yourselves. See you tomorrow."

Actually the State's expert Dr. Benjamin Burney had had his flight delayed and would not be able to have his expert rehearsed and ready. The court was inclined to be lenient.

CHAPTER EIGHTEEN

The D.A. outsmarted

Court was set to start the next morning at eight. The jury was in the jury room and the defendant and his attorneys waited in their designated room, a small twelve by fifteen cubicle with a table and four chairs. The district attorney asked for more time to talk to his expert and got it. Beekman was not happy with the way the examination of Dr. Dath ended. Some of the jurors might get the idea that the pathologist was hedging a little on his expertise and they would be right. Dr. Burney was the real thing, but he wanted to make sure that he was not tripped up. The extra time in preparation would pay off.

After the one hour wait, the jury was called in. On the witness stand, smiling directly at the jurors, was a six foot seven kindly looking man with a full head of salt and pepper hair. He looked up at the Judge and said, "Judge Graham, I am truly sorry I was not able to be here yesterday, but first my flight was delayed three hours; then I was re-routed; that airplane developing engine trouble. Maybe the bus would have been quicker."

Judge Graham smiled and said, "That is alright Dr. Burney. We are glad to have you. Please proceed."

After spending fifteen minutes having Dr. Burney recite his extensive Curriculum Vitae, he was accepted as an expert in the field of poisonous gases. Beekman asked him if he had reviewed all the statements, medical reports, autopsy report, transcripts, and the video tapes offered and accepted into evidence in the case.

"Indeed I have," replied Dr. Burney who never took his smiling eyes off the jurors.

Q: "After reviewing all the reports and evidence as well as the videos in this case, have you formed an opinion based on reasonable scientific certainty as to the cause of death of Betsy Matthews who died at the Walmart Store in Gulfport?"

A: "I have. Betsy Matthews died as a result of having breathed a poisonous gas."

Q: "Can you elaborate for the jury, Dr. Burney?"

A: "A poisonous gas that attacked the lungs and respiratory system and then paralyzed the nervous system of Mrs.Matthews then brought about death almost immediately."

Q: "Can you identify this poisonous gas?"

A: "This gas is so new that it has not been classified with a chemical name. It is only listed as gas X-2. It was brought into this country by Russian agents. It is difficult to detect; the chemical compound only known by the Russians. At the present we do not have an antidote. It is highly classified by the Department of Defense, so that is all I can tell you about the drug in this case without breaching national security."

Dr. Burney placed in front of him three photos of Betsy Matthews which had been taken of her while going through rigor mortis. They were not pretty. Her jaw had a death grin. As he explained the horrific facial expression, he compared them with other cases where the victims had died from the same poison.

Q: "Now, doctor, have you reviewed the information provided you from an incident which took place at the Palace Pool hall last year?"

A: "I have and it is my opinion that the same poisonous gas was activated in the pool hall as in Walmart. Only the pool hall dosage was not as powerful and no one was injured or at least died. I understand that it produced a terrible smell. In order to disguise the poison, several other chemicals were mixed in with the undetectable substance to cause the cesspool like smell."

"Further, as I understand it, we do have a witness who actually saw the defendant with a packet of a yellow powdery substance just prior to the time the gas was allowed to escape into the pool hall. As I said, fortunately everyone got out fairly safely with the exception of the bartender who was later treated at the hospital and released."

Q: "Dr. Burney, do you have an explanation why the defendant who was in the vicinity on both occasions, was not injured?"

A: "Yes. There had to be delay factor which took several minutes for the chemicals to react which gave him time to leave the scene without injury. As I explained, the mixture at the pool hall was much weaker. It must have been a test or dress rehearsal. Also, after the defendant was later stabbed by one of the customers from the pool hall incident, the defendant was transported to Baltimore, Maryland and treated at Baltimore General Hospital—a hospital that treats patients for symptoms of poisonous gases, I might add. A similar incident took place where half the hospital was shut down. There were no witnesses at the hospital in Baltimore."

By Mr. Ainsworth: "Your honor, I have a motion and an objection to be made outside the hearing of the jury. This is something we have already covered by the court."

By the Court: "Take the jury to the jury room."

After the jury left the room, the Judge said, "I know what you are going to say, Little Joe, but go ahead and get it into the record."

"Your Honor, the defense filed a Motion in Liminie and the court granted it, instructing the prosecution that they could not bring up anything about the incident in Baltimore. Now against the court's orders, this witness has brought it up. As he stated there were no witnesses and no injuries. There was no evidence as to what caused it. To allow this witness to testify about it, as he has done, is to fly in the face of this court and make a mockery of your ruling. We object strongly and hereby move for a mistrial."

Marcel Beekman, district attorney, stood up and stated, "Judge, as you know my expert was delayed in getting here. I tried to brief him on everything not to say, but somehow, this got overlooked. We apologize to the court, but I do not think it will affect the outcome of this trial."

By the Court: Mr. Ainsworth, you objection is sustained. Your Motion for Mistrial is overruled. The court agrees with Mr. Beekman that it does not go so far as to affect the outcome of this trial. I will, however, instruct the jury to disregard that part of the testimony and it will be stricken from the record. Okay, do we have anything else?

By both attorneys: No, your honor.

With the jury back in the courtroom; the court having instructed them to disregard any testimony pertaining to any events that took place in Baltimore, the direct examination of the prosecution's expert, continued.

Q: "Dr. Burney, are you telling this jury that in your scientific opinion that there is a man who is responsible for setting off this chemical compound as you have described and if so, is he present in the courtroom."

A: "Yes, that is what I am saying. He is indeed in this court room and is sitting right over there between his attorneys. (pointing to George Murfrey) I recognize that man as the one in the video and from the statement of Jacob Bannister, who was an eye witness to the pool hall incident."

By Mr. Beekman: "Your witness."

Little Joe got up from his table, walking over to the jury box resting his arm on the railing, never taking his eyes off the jurors. He then wheeled and faced the expert.

Q: "Dr. Burney, your opinions are based on the truth and accuracy of the evidence and statements furnished you are they not?"

A: "Yes, of course. I was not present, but I did have the benefit of the videos furnished me in support of the other reports and statements."

Q: "And doctor, if any of the statements and evidence was false or incorrect, would that cause you to change your opinion?"

A: It depends on how important the evidence was which I reviewed in forming my opinion.

Q: "Your read the statement of eye witness, Jacob Bannister did you not?"

A: "Yes."

Q: "Would you like to review that statement again?"

A: "No, that will not be necessary. Mr. Bannister, I believe is the only eye witness in the case and through his description of the packet of chemicals which he saw in the defendant' hand prior setting off the poison gas in the pool hall, fell right in line with my being able to form the opinion, that I just gave in court. Of course, I did rely heavily on the truth and accuracy of all the documents, statements and evidence given me before I reached my opinion."

Q: "Thank you, doctor for being candid with me. In you curriculum vitae, which you recited before being recognized as an expert in terroristic methods, I noticed that you have consulted and helped the Army to develop anti-terrorist tactics. Is that correct?"

A: "Yes, it is."

Q: "Isn't one of the terrorist tactics, used, is to place a bomb hidden in a location and then monitor it. When the target comes into the area, activate it?"

A: "Yes, that is true. Often the bomb or other destructive material is detonated by dialing a cell phone from someone viewing the area."

Q: "In the present case, could not the compound you described have been set off by a third party watching from a distance?"

By Mr. Beekman: "Objection! He is badgering the witness."

By the Court: "Overruled."

This was both a tactic and a signal used by Beekman of which Little Joe was well aware. The objection was to interfere with the defense attorney's train of thought and also by using the key words "badgering the witness", Dr. Burney was being warned that a crucial part of his testimony was being put in a trap. Beware!

A: "Yes, anything is possible. I even considered that possibility, but ruled it out since we do have an eye witness who actually saw the defendant pull out a packet which he described having a yellowish powder which was set off prior to polluting the air in the pool hall.

Q: "You are talking about Jacob Bannister who has not testified."

A: "That's right."

Q: "And it weighed heavily in naming George Murfrey as the man responsible for the death at Walmart, right?"

A: "Yes, of course. His statement leaves out any doubt as to culpability for that death and the injury to the two employees."

Q: "Any reasonable doubt?"

A: "Any reasonable doubt."

By Mr. Ainsworth: "No further questions."

Prosecutor Beekman decided to call Jacob Bannister as his last witness and then rest. He had other minor witnesses, even another expert, Lyons from Ocean Springs, but he would hold these witnesses for rebuttal. He could tell the jury wanted to hear from this eye witness.

Jacob Bannister strolled into the court room. He stopping momentarily, giving George a long dirty look--a look of sheer disgust, as if he was a filthy pig. He then jauntily climbed into the witness chair, smiled at the jury and then focused on the district attorney.

Q: "Tell us your name please."

A: "Jacob Bannister, but my friends call me Big Jake."

Q: "Where do you live?"

A: "Lizana, Mississippi."

Q: "What is your occupation?"

A: "I drive a truck for a living."

Q: "Do you know the defendant, George Murfrey?"

A: "I know him as Farts Murfrey."

Q: "How do you know him?"

A: "He and this other guy would hang out at the Palace Pool Hall all the time. I would see him there, when after a hard day's work, I would stop by to drink a beer and shoot a little pool."

Q: "On March 17th did you see Mr. Murfrey at the pool hall and if you did, just tell us in your own words if anything unusual happened."

A: "While I was playing a game of nine ball, Mr. Murfrey knocked a pool ball off his table, striking me in the small of my back; I still have aches and pains from the injury. When I protested he took out a small packet and shook this yellow powder. In seconds the place filled up with this terrible sickening gas smell. It was like some kind of a bomb.

Q: "You saw this clearly?"

A: "Yes sir. I was standing just about four feet from him looking right at him."

Q: "Who were you shooting pool with?"

A: "I was shooting pool with Mopey Glassman."

Q: "Is that James Glassman?"

A: "Yeah, I always called him Mopey, because he kind of mopes around." (Laughter)

Q: "Then what happened?"

A: "After Farts set off the bomb, me and Mopey, we hightailed it out of there. The smell was unbearable. Didn't no one have to tell me to go. No sir."

Q: "After that incident at the pool hall in which Murfrey set off some poisonous gas, did you run into him again?"

A: "Yes. I was at the Quick Stop in Lizana getting a beer out of the cooler; when I looked up Murfrey was there. I don't know how he found me. But I tell you, after what happened in the pool hall, I was scared for my life."

Q: "What happened at the Quick Stop?"

A: "Like I told you, I had reached for a bottle of beer, and when I turned around, there he was there glaring at me. He ran his hand in his pocket just like at the pool hall to get some more of that yellow powder. I knew what he was going to do. No one had to tell me. So I took out my fishing knife and poked him in the stomach with the knife. That stopped him and I was able to get away."

Q: "Now Jacob, I want you to think carefully. Did you actually see Mr. George Murfrey pull out a packet of yellow powder and activate it."

A: "Not the second time at the Quick Stop. He did not get no chance, but at the pool hall I saw him pull this packet out. It had yellow power in it and he shook it. Then poof! A cloud of this poisonous gas filled the room. I would swear on my mother's grave to that."

By Mr. Beekman: "Thank you Jacob. Your witness: Mr. Ainsworth."

Big Jake leered at this little diminutive black lawyer who stood before him. He could hardly wait until Little Joe, as he was called, examined him. He had been prepped and he was ready. The assistant district attorneys had showed him how to answer and make this runt of a smart assed lawyer wish he had never asked him the first question. He was anxious and ready. Like a wild animal ready to pounce and destroy,

Big Jake confidently waited for his prey to begin. Oh, how he hated that high pitched voice that came out of Little Joes' mouth.

Q: "Mr. Bannister, are you the one they call Big Jake at the pool hall?"

A: "I have already testified to that. What of it?"

Q: "How tall are you?"

A: "What has that got to do with it?"

By the Court: "Just answer the question."

A: "I am six foot five."

Q: "How long was this packet, you say Murfrey pulled out of his pocket?"

A: "I dunno. Maybe six inches; I didn't measure it."

Q: "How wide was it?"

A: "About three inches."

Q: "And you say it had yellow powder in it?"

A: "Yeah, that is right."

Q: "The six by three inch packet of powder was enclosed in a clear wrapping?

A: "That's the way it was and let me tell you this. That man over there; your client, made no bones about showing it either."

Jake pointed directly at George; his face had a grimace of hate. The sketch artist in court quickly drew the long arm connected to Big Jake pointing at George, enhancing the facial features, which showed disgust and hatred. This was the best subject the artist had portrayed. It would be pictured on WLOX TV at six o'clock news.

Q: "There were about twenty-one people in the Palace Pool hall that afternoon including you. That included also, Slim the bartender, your pal Mopey, Farts Murfrey and his pal Mutt Hanson . Isn't that true?"

A: "I did not count them."

Q: "How long did Mr. Murfrey hold this three by six inch packet in full view, before he caused the powder to vaporize?"

A: "I would say about five to ten seconds. It was easy for me to see what he was doing. I know what I saw. Don't try and trick me."

Q: "Mr. Bannister, can you tell this jury what the vapor looked like?"

A: "I dunno. It was a big cloud."

Q: "You don't know? You don't know. You saw it!"

By Mr. Beekman: "Objection. He is badgering the witness."

By the Court: "Overruled."

A: "It was about this big." (Witness gesturing with is hands)

Q: "Let the record show that the witness made a distance with his hands and arms about five feet. So, Big Jake, there was a cloud of at least five feet. Right?"

A: "Yeah, that's right."

Big Jake had been primed to go into the actual pool game and all those details; here this lawyer was avoiding the subject. He was itching to tell about how Murfrey was a bum always hanging out at the pool hall with his drunken buddy Mutt Hanson who spent most of his time in jail. It was not going according to script and it made him uneasy.

Q: "How come no one else saw this epic cloud but you?"

A: "They probably did. You will have to ask them that."

Q: "I did."

Little Joe inched closer to Jake. He had a sheet of paper with all the names of the patrons in the place and started reading them off. "I asked Harold Barnes; he didn't see it. I asked Art Sanders; he did not see it. I even asked your pal Mopey, who you say mopes around also known as James Glassman and he didn't see it."

A: "Maybe he did, I didn't ask him."

Q: "I have Mr. Glassman standing right outside the courtroom and he is prepared to come in and testify that he never saw a cloud of vapor or of any kind. Not one person saw it and not one person there saw a six by three inch packet of chemicals in George Murfrey's hand; not even Slim Flourisant the bartender who keeps an eye on things. Again I ask you Mr. Bannister, how is it that out of all those people in the pool hall whose eyes were on you and George Murfrey after his pool ball hit you in the back, never saw anything of the kind?"

A: "Look Mr. Ainsworth, all I know is what I saw; not what someone else saw."

Q: "The truth of the matter is there never was a three by six inch packet; no yellow powder and no cloud. All that happened was that Farts, as you called him, passed some smelly gas and you know it!"

A: "That is a lie. That's a lie! I know what I saw and I smelled it too."

Q: "You know Angie Wilkins."

A: "Yeah, she is my woman."

A: "Do you remember talking to her on May twenty-first at her house at about 2:55 p.m.? Let me help you. This was the day they let you out of jail for stabbing George Murfrey with your Bowie knife. You told her at that time place and date that an investigator called Bum Ketch and another, Tad Mann made up the story about the packet and the yellow powder and told you to tell it like that and they would make the aggravated assault charges go away?"

A: "No. No. No. That is not right. It is her word against mine."

By Mr. Ainsworth: "Bailiff would you bring Angie Wilkins into the court room and while you are about it, also bring in Mopie."

As the two were escorted into the court room, the jury gasped. Bannister was becoming unraveled.

A: "I don't remember saying that, but if I did, I was just trying to impress Angie."

Q: "Big Jake did you see Bum Ketch on television shooting that sea gull out of the sky at the time George Murfrey was taken into custody?"

A: "What if I did. Judge, do I have to answer that?"

By the Court: "You are on cross examination. Answer it."

A: "Okay, I did see it."

Q: "And you know that as a result of that incident, your investigator Bum Ketch was suspended, don't you?"

A: "Yeah, I heard that he was."

Q: "Well it seems that Bum was not too happy about getting suspended. I have got him outside that court room door also. Would you like me to call him in so that he can get this straight about your made up story. Let me warn you Mister Bannister, you could be charged with perjury. You could go back to jail if you don't set this straight before I call Bum in here. Bum has assured me that he is not going to stick his neck out and lie for you. So what is it going to be?"

A: "Okay, okay, I admit it. I told those investigators what they wanted to hear. I never saw no packet. I never saw no powder and I never saw no cloud. All Farts did that afternoon was to let out a real loud fart that lasted a long time and it stunk so bad, that I just left in a hurry."

Q: "And you, who were already mad from being struck in the back, which made you even angrier; isn't that right?"

A: "Yeah, I was mad."

Q: "And that's why when you saw George at the Quick Stop, you stabbed him, right?"

A: "I refuse to answer that question on the grounds that it may incriminate me."

Jake hung his head and mumbled the last answer.

Little Joe stated loudly, "No further questions."

Judge Graham looked down at Big Jake who was starting to get off the hot seat--thoroughly defeated. "Hold it!" said the Judge. "Bailiff, come get Mr. Bannister and put him in the holding cell. This court is recessed until tomorrow morning." Then to another Bailiff, "Take the jury back to the Motel and see that they get a real good meal for supper."

After the jury left the courtroom, Little Joe made a motion to dismiss the case. The court overruled the motion stating the state had made out a prima facie case.

"Little Joe," Judge Graham asked with a winkle in his eye, "Did you really have Bum Ketch out in the hallway waiting to be called?"

"Not really, your honor," said Joe with a wry smile.

"Mr. Beekman, looks like he got you there. I suggest you bring Mr. Bannister before the grand jury on a charge of perjury to go with his aggravated assault charge."

"I will see to it Judge," said Beekman.

The next morning in front of a stunned jury, Judge Graham announced to the jury that the State had rested its case and now it was the defense's turn.

"Mr. Ainsworth, Call your first witness."

224

District Attorney Marcel Beekman rose from his seat and walked around his table to face the Judge. He said, "First, the State of Mississippi moves that the case against George Cedric Murfrey be hereby dismissed and all charges dropped. In support of that motion, the parties have reached a settlement which we feel is best for all concerned. As part of the agreement, the Defendant, George C. Murfrey has agreed to enter the U.S, Army." Beekman looked over at George who was looking down at a pencil he was doodling with it on a piece of paper.

"Judge, why the Army wants him, is beyond me. They have even waived his overweight problem which is plain to see."

The courtroom broke out in relief laughter. It had been a grueling trial and now it was over. Somehow, humor that had been forbidden had crept into the courtroom.

"Order!" cried the Bailiff. Then with Joseph Ainsworth on one side and Nancy Grace Best on the other, George stood up at their urging. For the occasion, George had squeezed into a tight blue suit, red tie and white shirt.

Judge Graham looked over at George and smiled, "Are you in agreement with this settlement and Motion to Dismiss?"

"We are your Honor," said Little Joe who had to clear his throat.

"Mr. Murfrey, have your Attorneys explained fully the settlement agreement and the consequences of the Motion to Dismiss? It means that you have not been completely exonerated, because, the jury, has not found you not guilty; it also means that you will join the Army and become the property of the United States government for at least four years. Is that your understanding?"

George, choking up, gulped as he pulled the knot of his necktie over and said excitedly in a high voice, "Yes, Judge, I understand and agree to all the terms."

"Very well, the court finds that the Motion to Dismiss and the Settlement Agreement incorporated therein, is well taken and is hereby granted. The jury is excused. This case was tried real well by both sides. The court thanks you for your service."

CHAPTER NINETEEN

Trial ends with deal

The next day, the Sun Herald, the local newspaper, ran a headline which stated: **MURDER TRIAL ENDS IN DEAL**.

It was shown in Court that Mrs. Betsy Matthews had blocked arteries to the heart as well as two embolisms. Defense Atorney Joseph Ainsworth stated that he had proof that Mrs. Matthews died of a massive heart attack. District Attorney Marcel Beekman said that it was his duty to try these cases in order to protect society. He also stated that he could not for the life of him understand why the U.S. Army took such an interest in the case, but they wanted to recruit Murfrey and that was the deal. Murfrey will be sworn in to the Army later this week.

It was noticed that during the trial, that a Colonel Benson was present and that he was instrumental in bringing the two sides together for the settlement agreement.

The settlement left a lot of unanswered questions such as the cause of death, and was there ever any poisonous gas let loose in Walmart. If not, how is explained that over one hundred people stampeded out of the store? What caused that? Perhaps, with the trial ending so abruptly, we will never know,"

What the people of the Mississippi Gulf Coast did not know was how the deal was struck between the State and the Defendant Murfrey. After court had adjourned, the day before, Lt. Colonel Alan Benson along with two aides, approached prosecutor Beekman and asked for a conference.

He asked that the defendant and his two attorneys be present.

They gathered in the "war room" which was also the conference room where Beekman had held his meeting with his staff ordering them to go low key in the case. When the puzzled defense attorneys with their client were seated, Colonel Benson stood up and said, "I have been in attendance of the trial these past few days and it looks to me that there is a fifty-fifty chance of conviction or acquittal." He turned to Beekman and continued, "Especially after that last witness of yours messed up." Beekman frowned.

Then he turned and faced George Murfrey and his attorneys. He added, "There being a fifty-fifty chance, Mr. Murfrey, there is no telling what the jury will do. If you are convicted, they may even give you the death penalty"

George shuddered.

"Or at best prison. I have been instructed by the Pentagon to make this offer. George Murfrey has no criminal record and that makes him eligible to join the Army. We will take him, if the district attorney drops all charges and the defendant agrees to join the Army. Do you need some time to think about it?"

Beekman nodded his head. He said, "I don't. We would be happy to get rid of this case. Frankly, I would hate to see this nice local boy get the death penalty, when he could serve his country, instead."

The Colonel looked at George and said, "How about you George? I know this is sudden, but the Army is not so bad. You get paid, are served three healthy meals a day, get skilled training, get to go to a lot of places you never dreamed of going to. So what do you think?"

George cleared his throat and replied, "Could I talk to my Mom, my girlfriend and my buddy, Mutt?"

They found another room for George to confer with Agnes, his mother, who was present for the trial along with May Modine. Mutt

Hanson, was brought over from the county jail in his jump suit, which had printed on it: "Trustee, HCDC." Murfrey's attorneys were also present, pushing for the deal. Mutt Hanson, spoke up, "What about me, George? You can't just run off and join the army and leave me. I do have a little experience in combat with the Scottish Brigade, the fiercest fighting group of men the world has ever seen. See, if they can take me with you, while they are in a good mood."

Agnes Murfrey and May Modine were all for the deal so George filed back into the conference room. George said, "What about my weight? Are you sure the army will take me?"

Benson replied, "We are prepared to waive the overweight restriction. Do you agree to join if we do?"

George smiled and said, "I will join if my pal and good buddy, Mutt Hanson is allowed to join up with me."

Colonel Benson turned to the recruiting sergeant with him and said, "How about it Sergeant, can the Army make room for one more?"

"Yes Colonel. We have the buddy system which allows friends to join together I have checked on Mr. Hanson's record. He has nineteen misdemeanor convictions, mostly for public drunkenness. If Mr. Murfrey's attorney can get these convictions purged, we can make a place for him."

Nancy Grace Best, who had done little during the trial, except make a bunch of Pecan pralines for the Judge and a few for the D.A., spoke up. "I have a lot of experience getting criminal records expunged. I think the City of Gulfport will be glad to have the army take Mr. Hanson off their hands. It might even do him some good," she smiled at Mutt. She got up to leave the room, turned to face the group. "I will get started on this right away," she said and then left.

"How about me?" said a sweet voice that had been silent during the negotiations? Everyone turned to see who the voice belonged to;

It belonged to Maybellene Modine.

"How about me, George?" she said more strongly this time. "You can't just run off into the army and leave me. If they can take Mutt, then make them take me."

George looked at her sweet innocent face. "Well what about it, Colonel? Is there another space for May? I want that to be part of the deal. If she can join with us, then you have got your deal."

Colonel Benson, who looked old enough to be their grandfather, shook his head. "This is a whacky world and today it just got wackier. Are you sure you know what you are doing, Miss. Modine?" the Colonel asked.

"As long as I can get a trainer just like you promised George and Mutt and can be on the buddy system. I have heard that on the buddy system; that we will be within sixty miles during our enlistment."

Colonel Benson who had plans how to use George Murfrey in the war effort, agreed to the terms. The recruiting Sergeant later said to the other enlisted aide who had been present, "Damn, that is one ugly woman, all this fuss about recruiting Murfrey. That hump-nosed woman could scare the robes off those rag heads."

Lt. Colonel Alan Benson had to agree with the Recruiter's observation of Murfrey's girlfriend, Maybellene Modine as one "ugly woman", but Murfrey who bordered on being morbidly obese in spite of his innocent blue eyes was no prize specimen of God's creation and how would the Army handle Mutt Hanson, cocky and explosive, especially when he had a few "cool ones" under his belt?

Was this motley cast of three misfits worth it?

The United State Army would soon find out!

FALSE GRITS

BOOK TWO

BAD GAS

PROLOGUE

Murfrey and friends recruited

"Colonel, are you sure about your decision to recruit this man, George Murfrey? I will have to give my report to the President."

"Yes, I am sure Peter; you have the FBI file; Murfrey has no police record other than that one incident. I will admit that when he is wronged, he does react, said Lt. Colonel Benson.

"He is not Big Fanny, although he does have a big fanny," said Peter Poteet laughing. At the moment not taking his position seriously as liaison between the President of the United States and the Pentagon continuing, "And what about the baggage he is bringing with him?"

"Are you talking about his two unusual friends he is bringing with him under the Buddy System?"

"That too! No, I am speaking of fact that you literally used your clout down there in Gulfport, Mississippi to snatch George Murfrey right out of a Capital Murder and Terrorism trial to recruit him for your Special Forces. That is what I am talking about. I am just not so sure about this decision of the U.S. Army to recruit a would-be murderer or an alleged terrorist."

His face turning red, Colonel Benson raising his voice said, "You are forgetting that the Army welcomed Fannie Mae McBride, after she wiped out a recruiter and several recruits when she was refused admission into the army, then admitted her with open arms into the Army during the Korean war and that you personally okayed her being put in Special Forces under my command and how she served our nation honorably in that time of crisis. You have seen the FBI file on Murfrey and know that was a bogus charge when he passed gas in Walmart. That woman died from a heart attack. Murfrey had done that many times in Walmart and even K-Mart with harming anyone except to stink up an aisle."

"Maybe so. Maybe so," repeated the old white haired man who had served under President Truman during that war and many more presidents since then as chief liaison officer. His present president would probably okay this mission with open arms if it meant the country could benefit in the present war against al Qaida and the Taliban in Iraq and Afghanistan. "We have been together a long time since the Korean war. Maybe you can pull this one off too. I guess I have become a little more conservative over the years. I will have to express my doubts in this case, but Alan I will sanction it."

"You know it is ironic that on the one hand you claim Murfrey never murdered or killed anyone with his gas problem; yet you expect to use him in Special Forces for that very purpose."

"Are you overlooking the incident at Baltimore General Hospital that occurred when he was a patient?"

"No, I agree with Chief Ed Amsler of the FBI in his assessment that your boy was responsible for shutting down the left wing of that hospital, but there were no fatalities."

"You are right, but the records show that he is getting there; getting more potent through evolution. Doctor Aholie of the poisonous gases department believes he has the glands of a skunk. So far there is no real explanation for these phenomena of nature. I feel we will be able to use him—only time will tell."

"What have you got to say about those two misfits he is bringing with him into the army? How did that happen?" said Poteeet changing the subject.

"It was part of the deal to get Murfrey to join up. What do you mean-- 'Misfits'?"

"I mean the army is getting one of the ugliest women in the world, if not the ugliest. And that little character, Hanson, is a drunkard and a belligerent fighter with a record as long as your arm to prove it; what about them? None of them are army material as far as I can see."

"Miss Modine is a sweet charming young lady. She cannot help it if she is obese and homely. I promised her that she would get a personal trainer and by the way Murfrey is getting one too. As for Hanson, his long misdemeanor record that consisted of fighting, public drunkenness and disturbing the peace; that record has been expunged. The only place that record exists is in the FBI files and I have ordered that file sealed.

Should Hanson resort to his old ways, we will just have to kick him out of the army with an undesirable discharge. Rest assured; I will monitor those recruits closely."

"You had better! And I will be monitoring you and how you handle them."

Standing up, indicating that the secret meeting was over, Peter Poteet shook the Colonel's hand. "Good seeing you again Alan. It has been much too long; let's do lunch sometime soon," said Poteet,

"Thanks for your half-hearted blessing Peter. How it will end only God knows."

"May God save the U.S. Army and this United States," said Peter Poteet under his breath.

CHAPTER TWENTY

They're in the Army now

The silver-blue Buick LeSabre, a slightly used automobile, May Modine's prized possession, blew down Interstate highway sixty five headed toward Columbus, Georgia via Montgomery, Alabama, driven by a determined serious May, her eyes glued on the concrete super slab as they crossed the longest high rise bridge George Murfrey had ever seen unless one counted the bridge from Mandeville, Louisiana across Lake Pontchartrain into New Orleans, as a boy, which was beyond his remembrance.

At that moment all that was on George's mind was that he had to go real bad; not number one; not number two: it was Number Three!

Deftly his pudgy fingers found the silver lever mounted on the door rest passenger side pushing it backward rolling down the window, then pushing himself upward twisting his body and bending his head on the headliner while he pulled his trousers, size four extra-large, down exposing his bare ass now filling the open space where the window had occupied, creating a closure stopping the loud rushing air which had awakened the third passenger located in the back seat, one Mutt Hanson.

"Barrumph!" Pause. "Barrumph!" came a new noise that broke the sealed silence from Murfrey's large kabossis stuck in the window as he discharged a large quantity of the pressurized gas that had collected; the object of his discomfort. Fortunately this occurrence was not in a populated area so no one was harmed by the smelly gas; that is unless counted were the flock of sea gulls below who flew into the gaseous cloud under the bridge, causing them to become disorientated falling into the wet lands below over which they had been cruising looking for unsuspecting fish; some of them crashing into the bridge while other piled into the salty water with a force that broke their necks..

"Hey was that a good one?" said George cheerfully fastening his belt and zipping up his pants.

235

"One of your best, George," said May sweetly. "But please don't do that when we reach Montgomery. You don't need any more trouble with the law."

"Farts, you woke me out if a sound sleep; damn you," said Mutt rubbing his eyes, leaning forward from the back seat. "I was having such a nice peaceful dream. This petite blonde, the kind I like, was caressing my body; her hands running all over me and ..."

"Spare us the details," interrupted May. "It was only a dream."

"I know, but it seemed so real" said Mutt lying back down on the back seat, grabbing his travel pillow to rest his head.

Springing back up, hunching forward between May and George, he said in his deep voice, "Crap! I can't sleep now. Where are we anyway? How much further is Montgomery?"

"We just passed a sign pointing to Atmore," replied May. "So I'd say about a hundred miles."

"Well step on it May!" said George in his high octane voice. "I just noticed a three legged turtle coming up fast tying to bite one of our rear tires."

"Not funny Georgie," answered May still serious. "You are not going to get me to break the speed limit and get a ticket."

"Yeah 'Georgie'," said Mutt with emphasis on "'Georgie'. Please don't quit your day job if you ever had one. Say Murfrey, come to think of it, I never thanked you for pulling off that stunt not only getting me released from jail, but having my record expunged. I was getting tired of wearing that grey trustee's jump suit every day; it just did not become me."

"Not to speak of Georgie getting himself out of a possible murder conviction," commented May.

"Twas really nothing, my dear," said George blowing on his fingers to his right hand and shaking them. "They never had a case against me or we wouldn't be on our way to Fort Benning to fight for our country."

"How soon we do forget. How soon we do forget," said Mutt nodding his head. "The last time I heard they had plans to build a scaffold in which to hang your fat ass in front of that rickety court house for all to witness. Say May, pray tell, what do you get out of all this? All I can see is that you enlisted in the Army with us. Why would anyone do that when you didn't have to?"

"Mutt you wouldn't understand. One of us had to be patriotic, besides I was getting tired of working at Friendly Finance going nowhere. I get to travel and under the Buddy System, I will get to check on you and Georgie."

"Good luck on that, May. Look you two idiots; if either of you think this is going to be a picnic, just wait until we get to Fort Benning. I know; I have been there."

"Oh, no! Do we have to hear about how you fought the Punjabs in India again?" groaned George loudly. He had been out of jail for four days, formerly accused of murder and now that he was away from Gulfport, Mississippi, he was shaking off the shroud of a possible death sentence from a conviction, returning to this old smart aleck self. He had already deep sixed the fears he once had that the D.A. could get his conviction sending him to the gas chambers or wherever they went to be put to death.

Upon dismissing all charges and expunging Mutt's record, the trio had been taken immediately to the recruiter's office by a deputy sheriff and sworn in. It was an unusual procedure since none of them received physicals which had been waived by the Army with a promise that Murfrey and Modine would get physical trainers and Hanson could sweat out his alcoholic body in the hot sunny hills of Georgia during basic training.

The army had serious plans for Murfrey assigning him to Special Forces under his deliverer, Lt. Colonel Alan Benson. The other two were just surplusage under the deal that had been struck with approval of the Harrison County Circuit Court. They received orders to report to Fort Benning, Georgia in four days. Travel vouchers were furnished, but Mutt being the experienced veteran, said, "If we take the train, there will be some soldiers there waiting for us and they will escort us to the base right away. The Orders say we don't need to report until midnight."

May offered to drive her Buick LeSabre; that way, they figured they would have transportation whenever they needed it.

When they reached Phenix City, Alabama which was on the outskirts of Columbus, Georgia, they told May to drop them off there and for her to go ahead and report in. She had argued with them and lost. They wanted one last fling of freedom; she wanted to get settled. It would be like a bachelor party for the groom who was giving up his freedom. "Bull," said May to Mutt. "You just want to get some alcohol in you. Okay, go ahead, but mark my word, you will be sorry."

As soon as she drove off, the skies opened up and buckets of rain came pouring down. They refused to let this dampen their spirits. "Drink and be merry, for tomorrow we may be in the army," said Mutt joyfully.

They started with a T-bone steak dinner and had a few brews. The evening flew by quickly made up mostly of drinking beer, chatting with other soldiers and flirting with bar maids. About ten p.m. they started to run short of money, so they hailed a cab, and after settling on a price with the cab driver, were driven to the proper area where they were to report.

They were ushered into a small wooden building, already crowded with other recruits who had the same idea. When they gave their Orders to the Sergeant who processed them, he exclaimed, "Where in the blazes did the army find you two derelicts? What is this Mutt and fatso Jeff?"

"No, it is Mutt and George," said Mutt in his deep voice.

"I see," said the Sergeant busting out laughing. "Well boys, on behalf of the United States of America indivisible in this case and for which it stands, the army hereby welcomes you." He was still laughing when the Corporal took charge of them and directed that they go with him. George noticed that the Corporal had on camouflage rain gear and that it was very wet.

They followed the Corporal through a door to the rear of the building into a cleared area where about twenty other men were standing at attention in their civilian clothing.

It was a rainy night in Georgia and they were all soaking wet.

"Fall in!" shouted the Corporal. "Get over there on the end. Yes, you. Are you deaf fat boy?" He led George to the end of the front row, parking him there as the rain went through his suit into his skin.

"You: pint size. You stand in back of Miss. Piggy," the corporal told Mutt. "Now come to attention. Don't run off; I will be back with some more of America's finest."

"What's going on, Mutt?" asked George in a not so cheerful voice.

"I think we just joined the army. I forgot how they treated recruits. Sorry. Just abide by it. It has to get better."

"When?" asked George shivering.

"In about three months; best I can remember."

Another army type came marching out briskly. The rain did not seem to bother him.

"Alright men," he called out. "Left face! For you, who don't know what that means, turn left. Good! Now we are going to march a little. Forward, march!" Indicating with a gesture toward new recruit Murfrey the Sergeant shouted, "Stick out your arms fat boy so we can know if you are Marching or rolling!"

With every man, including Murfrey, swearing under his breath, they marched. And they marched. It seemed like hours before they stopped to rest. They had gone several miles when the Sergeant yelled, "Fall Out." The men knew what that meant. They ran for cover under a nearby structure to take refuge from the pouring rain.

While they were resting, the Sergeant said, "Who among you fine gentlemen has ever had military training?" George pointed to Mutt, who had been taught to never volunteer for anything.

"How much training have you had son? Boy Scouts doesn't count."

"I served two years in the Scottish Brigade and fought in India," Mutt blurted out boastfully.

"Good, you are now a Corporal and will continue to be a Corporal until you mess up. Have the men fall out for some more marching, Corporal Hanson!"

Mutt began the "hup, two three" as the men tried to march.

"Corporal, maybe the men will march better, if you let them sing a song. Do you know any marching songs?"

Mutt started them off with "Roll out the Barrel." When they finished, the Sergeant said, "Very good. Do you know any more marching songs?"

"Only dirty ones, Sir."

"Let's have it."

So Mutt broke out with," Nellie wore a new dress; it was very thin. She asked me how I liked it; I answered with a grin—Wait til the sun shines Nellie…."The singing seemed to make the future soldiers forget the elements and fatigue as they marched through the night. They were the first to march into the mess hall. After eating a hearty breakfast of scrambled eggs, sausage, hash browns, pancakes and S.O.S. (white gravy with a mixture of ground beef) which they poured over a biscuit, they relaxed.

While George was sopping up the last of the S.O.S., the Sergeant came up to him and asked, "Are you George Cedric Murfrey?"

George thought, "What have I done now?" but said, "I confess it is me--at least what is left of me."

George was tired. He was depressed. After marching all night in wet clothes, all he wanted to do was to find a flat place and lie down. He was too tired to even smart off which he would have liked to do.

"Come with me," commanded the Sergeant. "Get your bag with your things."

George turned to Mutt, "Guess you heard?" he said in a low voice.

"Better you than me," said Mutt who also thought something was wrong.

George walked out of the mess hall, picking up his blue athletic bag which had been brought there along with the recruits' other bags, sticking his head inside the mess hall, he said to Mutt, "See you later."

"Not if I see you first," replied Mutt who now felt better after the alcohol he had drunk had dissipated.

George climbed into a jeep indicated to him, throwing the blue bag in the back. He looked at another Sergeant who slammed the gas pedal to the metal and the jeep went screeching off.

"I hope you are taking me to a bed; I have had it," said George.

"The Colonel wants to see you," was all the tight lipped Sergeant had to say. A few blocks later, the jeep came to an abrupt stop in front of another army building much like the first one he had reported to.

"Leave the bag," said the Sergeant as Murfrey reached for it. "Follow me."

They climbed the wooden steps and entered the building. George followed the Sergeant as they went past a pretty female Corporal at a desk.

After knocking on the door facing them, he heard, "Come in."

The sergeant saluted the Lt. Colonel briskly. He said, "Sir, I have recruit George C. Murfrey here as commanded."

"Fine," said the Colonel returning the salute. Looking at Murfrey, he said, "What happened to this man, Sergeant? He is soaked to the bone. He looks like a wet walrus."

"Sir, he did not report until ten-twenty-one last night. The processing office closed at ten, so they marched him and the other late comers. It is standard procedure, Sir."

"Okay, okay, Sergeant," The colonel made a cathedral with his hands. "You may wait outside while I talk to Mr. Murfrey."

After the Sergeant left, Colonel Benson re-introduced himself, "Remember me back in Gulfport. You may sit down Mr. Murfrey or is it, recruit Murfrey? Sorry for the ordeal, but welcome to the U.S. Army. Not to sound trite, but the world awaits you son. We have a place for you, but first you will be taught soldiering, get some weight off with a trainer and learn how to shoot a rifle. It will be new to you, but when you finish your basic training, you will have a sense of satisfaction. I will be your commanding officer. If you have any difficulties, just come to me; we will work it out together. He looked at George's slovenly appearance and laughed. "George, may I call you George?"

George looked at the Colonel's name tag and laughing said, "Sure, and may I call you Alan, Alan."

The Colonel laughed. "Only in private George. You know we do have to maintain military decorum?"

"Sure thing Alan."

"Well," the Colonel looking out of the window, remarked, "Looks like it has stopped raining. How about a cup of hot coffee?"

"I would love one," quipped George who now felt he had found a home in the army.

The Colonel pressed a button and ordered two cups of coffee which were produced within seconds. They both sipped their coffee. George said, "Now this is more like it."

"George, once you have learned how to be a soldier, shoot a rifle and your trainer says you are fit, you will be assigned to Special Forces. Sergeant White has been assigned to see that you get your uniform and get settled in your barracks. He will see to your present needs. Any questions?"

"Alan, can I get some sleep. I am bushed. We drove straight here from Gulfport and then as you know I marched all night. I am about to fall out from exhaustion."

"I tell you what, George, the Sergeant will help you get your clothing, find your barracks and let you get some sleep. Then we will begin your orientation."

"Sounds good to me," said George. "I am already liking the army a whole bunch. What about my friends who came with me, Maybellene Modine and Mutt Hanson? I would like to stay in touch with them, Sir."

"No problem, George. Sergeant White will take care of all that. Get some sleep and I will see you back here at sixteen hundred hours."

Meanwhile at opposite ends of Fort Benning, May Modine had been assigned to a unit, was made a Private and was meeting her fellow female soldiers. Corporal Iverson Hanson, aka, "Mutt" had already been dubbed, the "old man" by his new comrades and was being processed into the army while giving helpful information and war stories to those who listened. Both May and Mutt would undergo aptitude testing letting known their desires as to what type of duty they preferred. Mutt, with past experience of such matters, slipped the Sergeant in charge a fifty dollar bill he had hidden in his wallet so that he could be assigned to heavy artillery or the armored division.

The sergeant did not see a problem in granting Mutt's request as he pocketed the fifty.

On the other side of the base, May's collegiate transcripts, which she had brought with her, were studied. "With exceptional grades like these, you should apply for Officer's training school," said the Officer in charge.

Meanwhile, George was given a cursory physical and assigned a bunk in Barracks 101. He flopped down on the bed and slept for four hours. He had noticed other men sleeping during the day. Since he was directly under Battalion Headquarters, any time he was not on duty, he could grab some sleep. Also, he was told, there would be no inspections of that Barracks, no KP. There was a catch: Each man had to contribute funds to the cleaning service bills.

When George was assigned to a cubicle and a bed, he met another soldier lolling around who had just gotten out of bed. This was around 9:30 A.M. His name was Skip Rogers from Trenton, New Jersey. He explained to George that no one would discuss what they did in Special Forces, so don't ask. He helped George stow his gear, showing him how to make his bed so that he could take his nap.

George was snoring peacefully in his newly made up bed when he was awakened by a hand grabbing him and shaking his shoulder. "Rise and shine," came a voice attached to the hand. "It's time to see the Colonel."

George shook his head that was full of cob wells and said gruffly, "Alright."

He dressed for the first time in his new soldier uniform and then was whisked backed to Colonel Benson's office, still in a foggy mind all he could remember about the Colonel was his name was Alan.

As he looked at the Colonel's name tag; it was Benson. He gave him a snappy salute and said, "Recruit Murfrey reporting for duty, sir."

The Colonel smiled, instead of laughing at the ridiculous salute, returning it in a less than snappy fashion. "Very good: Private Murfrey. Sit down. I have been studying your file. We have a lot to discuss."

George sat down and glanced at the thick file that was in front of the Colonel. Stamped on the front in bold letters was: "F.B.I." George shuddered. "Lets' get down to business, shall we? Before we do, I want you to promise me that you will be entirely blunt and truthful. Also,

243

from now on anything said in this room or coming from me will be treated as classified and Top Secret. If you slip up and pass information along you will be shot as a spy. Understand?" He paused and looked George straight into his eyes.

George nodded.

"You will have to do better than that," said Benson. His eyes were hard.

"Yes sir. I fully understand and I will not pass any information I get from this office--classified or unclassified." He added, "From all I have been through, the last thing I want is to get shot as a spy. As they say, Alan, if I didn't have bad luck, I would have no luck at all."

"Have you ever heard of Fannie Mae McBride?"

"Not that again," said George. "What is it with this McBride? I guess you have it all in that file on your desk. You see I got stabbed and shipped up to this loony doctor in Baltimore who asked me the same thing...at least I think he did. I was under heavy sedatives while in Baltimore. Alan, I swear I never heard of this McBride person until Dr. Aholie asked me about her."

"You don't have to swear to it George. We are friends here. Fannie Mae McBride was from Leslie, Arkansas. I knew her personally--she was my first one I trained." He went on to tell of "Big Fanny" as she was affectionally called. "She passed gas much like you, but hers were lethal. She wanted to join the army very badly. In short, I was put in charge of her; she became a hero and won the Medal of Honor. Her grave is next to the Unknown Soldier's in case you are ever at the Arlington Cemetery."

He went on into details of Big Fanny's training; how he accompanied her to Panmunjom to the truce talks; how she had gassed the North Korean generals, bringing the Korean Conflict to an end.

After going over the history of Big Fanny, Benson picked up George's file from the desk and held it up. "Looks like," he said, "that you have the same powers as Big Fanny. Maybe not as powerful, but your history indicates they seem to be increasing as you have gotten older,"

George started to tell him that he had not killed anyone and really did not intend to do so. Benson cut him off. He put his fingers to his lips.

"Don't try to deny it, George. I know you were responsible for gassing the Left wing of the Baltimore General Hospital when you were there as a patient. It had to be a quirk and good fortune that no one died because of it."

"Sir, I mean Alan, I can explain," said George.

"No need to George. It is all right here in these reports. It all adds up; no one killed, but the incident at Walmart was different." There went those hard hazel eyes of Benson into George's baby blues.

"Was this the first time you became lethal or did you know beforehand that you had the power?"

"Colonel, I mean Alan I did not know it then and I still don't know that to be true. That woman was already sick and ready for a heart attack or worse. I did not mean any harm. Many times I had gone into Walmart and even K-Mart, dropping my farts. No one ever got hurt. I bet I am not the only one who does that."

"I can vouch for that, George," said Benson who had experienced leaving aisles stunk up by some unknown before he arrived to purchase items. "Perhaps you have forgotten about those two employees who fell to the floor and could have died. I have seen the videos of it. You must have considered what I am suggesting. Remember, we are going to be truthful."

"I am doing the best I can. If you are right, then why aren't you scared that I will cut one loose right now and just walk out of here?" George's face was turning red blotting out his rosy cheeks.

"Now calm down George. Remember, I am your friend. We need to work together--for your benefit, our benefit, the army's benefit and for your country."

This talk of all the benefits seemed to calm Murfrey down.

"I am sorry, Alan, all this upsets me. So what am I going to do?'

"I am here to help you, son. Trust me. I will guide you just like I did Big Fanny McBride."

"What ever happened to Big Fanny? How did she die? Was she still in the army when she died?" asked Murfrey as he wiped a tear from his eyes.

"She was Honorably Discharged and went back to Arkansas where she died in an accident." The Colonel did not elaborate on how an angry pack of razorback hogs ganged up on her and pushed her off a cliff.

"George, let me ask you a question. How were you able to control your gas problem all that time you were locked up in jail and even right now?"

"Very simple, Alan, my friend Mutt Hanson was a trustee at the time I was incarcerated. He brought me matches."

"Matches?" the Colonel was incredulous.

"Yes, matches. Whenever I felt like it, I would go to the bathroom, strike a match and burn off the fumes as they came out. Would you like a demonstration?"

"You sure you won't injure me?" asked the Colonel cautiously, but curiously.

"Naw, I need to pull my pants down, though. I don't want to scorch my nice new uniform."

"Go ahead. I'll just watch from over here." Benson got up from his desk, closed the curtains and walked to the other side of the room. "Now don't set the place on fire. The army would not like that."

George dropped his trousers and his new khaki shorts exposing his big hairy ass. He took out a long wooden match striking it with his thumb nail like he had seen Mutt do. As he did this, he strained and out shot a bright blue flame that went "whisssh". It was three to four feet long and lasted fifteen seconds.

"Great balls of fire," exclaimed the Colonel. "I have never seen anything like that. Why you are a human blow torch! You are right. I don't smell a thing"

"I could have gone longer." said George. "I don't know if you noticed it, but I used those Big Star wooden matches. Those cardboard ones would singe the hairs off my hands."

"Okay, you can put your clothes back on and sit down. Quite a demonstration!"

246

George sat back down; quite pleased with himself.

"So that is how you kept your little secret since the Walmart episode?"

"Yes, like I said, as long as I have matches, I have got it under control from stinking up the place. I don't know about killing people. I am still not convinced that I am like Big Fanny."

"Not to worry, George. Just keep those matches handy. I will even get you some of those waterproof matches that the campers use. We don't need any accidents."

"I didn't know they made them, said George. "I keep my matches in a prescription bottle.

"George, I am impressed with you, your honesty and your willingness to work with me. I am going to show you something which is definitely classified." Benson reached into his back pocket and produced his wallet. He flipped it open showing a solid gold shield attached to it. "This is a gold shield that shows that I work directly under the Commander In Chief, the President of the United States. There are very few of these shields given out, believe me. As you can see I have incredible power to do my job. As a demonstration, and because I believe we will work well together, I am hereby promoting you to Sergeant First Class, which is an E-5 rating. Work with me and I promise you, that you will go right on up in rank."

"I know I am throwing a lot at you on our first briefing, but I want you to try these and let me know if they work. They worked for Fannie Mae McBride." He produced a prescription bottle much like the one George kept his matches in, but larger. He handed it to George.

George opened the bottle and poured out several large purple pills. "What is it?" he asked. Mutt had already discussed his future and how and why the army would use him. "You are going to be used as a spook," Mutt had told him. You know some kind of a spy or maybe an assassin. Why else would they want a man like you?"

"They are pills that control you gas problem," said Benson. "They do a better job than matches. Try them and let me know how they work."

"Whew!" said George. "I thought they might be cyanide pills I would have to take if the enemy captured me."

"I see it is half past five already. That will be all for today. Sergeant Ziegfield will be your new guide and a liaison for your duties. He will take good care of you. Tomorrow, you begin your training. You will get your physical trainer, learn to shoot a rifle and get the full basic military training. If anyone mistreats you in anyway, tell Sergeant Ziegfield or me. I will take care of it. Remember, how we use you is a military secret, so keep it that way. Again, can I have your promise on that?"

"Yes, sir!" said George with enthusiasm." Can I see my friend Mutt and girlfriend, May?"

I have already ordered Ziggy to take care of it. They will meet you at the PX at eighteen hundred hours." Benson stood up indicating the meeting was over. Out of the blue Sergeant Ziegfield came in and told George to follow him.

First, Ziggy took George to have his new sergeant stripes sewed on and then it was on to the Post Exchange. May and Mutt were already in the cafe, drinking cold drinks when George arrived. Everyone was excited as if Christmas had come. "I am going to try to get into OCS," said May.

"What is that?" asked George who had squeezed into the both next to her.

"Officer Training School silly."

"And what are you so happy about, Mutt?"

Mutt turned his arm and showed off his Corporal stripes. "I have it on good authority that I am going into the Armored Division for training. Whose ass did you kiss to get those Sergeant stripes?"

"It is classified, said George.

"Well, don't get too carried away." warned Mutt ominously. "It was just last night that we had that all night death march from Bataan."

CHAPTER TWENTY ONE

Training

The next few weeks went by quickly without incident; Ziggy saw to it that George was where he was supposed to be for his training. He even got marksman at the rifle range with the help of his pal, Mutt, who also just happened to be at the range firing his weapon that same day. Mutt would have qualified as "Expert" except he fired enough shots into George's target to pull him through. Instead, Mutt was listed as a "Sharpshooter".

May Modine took her tests to see if she could get into OCS, passing them at the top of her class. If George signed a waiver releasing her go to Virginia for her training, all she had to do was to wait for orders. The signing of the waiver meant that she could be sent over the sixty mile radius of where George was located, restricted in the buddy plan.

George could not believe it when the scales showed he had lost twenty pounds in two weeks through his training exercises and a special diet. Although he did not belong to any one unit, he was allowed to train with various ones that Sergeant Ziggy fit him into. Thus, he was able to get a taste of Army basic training. He even donned a gas mask and was put in a chamber where poison gas filled the air. This was ironic. He could have furnished the troops with his own brand.

One afternoon, George had been dropped off at the PX to meet Mutt. May had gotten her orders and was on her way to officer's school. He was entering the building and did not see the two officers approaching him since at the time he was searching for this friend, Mutt.

Ziggy had dropped him off and was pulling off in his jeep when he saw two officers standing George at attention. They seemed to be yelling at him. He hopped out of the jeep making his way to the altercation. One Major was threatening George with court martial while the other mentioned other punishments such as marching in a circle with his rifle slung over his shoulders for at least four hours.

249

Sergeant Ziegfield approached the two Majors, attempting to explain George's preferred status. This having not gone too well, Ziggy was told to get down on the floor of the Post Exchange and do one hundred push-ups.

While Ziggy was doing the push-ups, one Major asked, "How long have you been in the army, Sergeant Murfrey?"

"Two weeks and four days, Sir," said George in his high nervous voice. His belly had popped one of the buttons on his shirt. Upon observing the missing button hole, the Major called George a disgrace to the army while the other called him a fat pig. That officer pulled out a small pad and began to write George's name, rank and serial number. While the two were on George's case, Ziggy got up surreptitiously leaving the scene. George was told to report to Mess Hall number 18 the next morning for KP duty, until further notice. When George could not say what unit he belonged in, the decibels from the two Majors went up as they yelled loudly that they were just about to call the Military Police and Provost Marshall.

As George was sweating M-16 bullets in walked Colonel Alan Benson along with Sergeant Ziegfield.

The two Majors were so busy yelling threats at George that they failed to salute the Colonel who, if they had noticed, had a very hard look on his face.

"Attention!" said the Colonel in a loud authoritative voice. The two Majors looked to see where that voice came from. One spied Ziggy and said, "Sergeant, you disobeyed orders. Now you will be court-martialed along with this excuse of a soldier. The other Major started walking toward Colonel Benson when the Colonel focused hostile eyes on both the officers. "I said stand at attention!" said Benson.

The two Majors, out ranked and realizing, the command to come to attention did not come from Sergeant Ziegfield, came to attention.

"Let me explain," said one of the Majors.

"Did I say talk? You will address me as 'Sir'. See that wall? Both of you get in a brace against it, now!"

It had been long time since the two officers had been to officer training school as cadets, but they knew what a military brace was. Up against the wall they went.

"Give me a pencil, Sergeant Ziegfield." He was handed a pencil which was placed behind the back bone of one of the officer's neck. "You better not let that pencil fall, Major." He turned to the other Major and said, "Just, who do you think you are making my Orderly do push-ups in this public place?'

"Sir...."

"Shut your mouth, Major. I will tell you when to speak. Get into the green chair."

George did not know what the green chair was, but soon saw it in action. There was no chair, but the Major had gotten into an imaginary sitting position. He began to tremble as his muscles vibrated from the strain. While that officer swayed and trembled, Colonel turned to the officer in the brace. "Next time you start yelling at any of my men, you had better find out whose men they are. See those insignias? They are Special Forces under my command. You had better learn them before you go throwing your weight around. At ease!"

Gladly the two rebuked Majors stood at ease.

"Sergeant Ziegfield, give each Major my name, office address and have them appear before me at 0800 hours tomorrow morning." After this was done, Benson commanded, "Eyes right! Take a good look at both of my sergeants. You are not to bother either one again. Do you understand?" When they both nodded in the affirmative, Colonel Benson said, "Okay then. See you two in my office tomorrow while I decide whether or not to write you up and put it in your record. You are dismissed."

Later, within the confines of the booth at the Post Exchange, George was telling Mutt of the event. "I didn't know officers ate out anyone but enlisted men. Colonel Benson really unloaded on those two Majors. I almost felt sorry for them."

"I bet you did. They got what was coming to them. I will say one thing; did you ever notice that everywhere you go you create a disturbance of some kind? I have never seen anything like it. I will say this: I have seen Generals chew out other officers," Mutt added. "I have never seen a Lt. Colonel jump on another officer. Your boss must carry a lot of weight. Look, we don't have to be exposed to all this. We are both non-coms. In the future we will meet at the NCO club."

"Just look in the mirror, Mutt," said George. I have noticed that everywhere you go, you have to punch somebody out."

"Point well taken," said Mutt.

Although Ft. Benning is a large army base, nevertheless like in New York City, the word got around about the chew-out of the two Majors spreading quickly. Their names, Major Bland and Major Andrews were mentioned in the chit-chat that followed. George, who now met Mutt at the NCO club, never saw them again. It was rumored that the two Majors had been shipped to another base.

As the weeks flew by, George stayed on his diet and lost inches around his girth. He had to have his shirt and pants taken in at the cleaners. He underwent hand to hand combat and was taught to fire his M-16 rifle under every kind of adverse condition his trainers could think up. He fired in the heat of the day with sweat dripping down his nose. He fired the rifle in the rain and mud. He fired from an enlarged foxhole and from a kneeling position as well as prone. He learned to care for his rifle and could field strip it as good as anyone. He was dutiful in sleeping with his rifle. In short, Sergeant First Class George C. Murfrey took every bit of his training to heart. He even liked it.

But as with George's history of creating disasters, his par excellence was like a truck merrily rolling down-hill when the wheels rolled off.

Part of the training was going on bivouac. This meant pitching their tents, sleeping in the Georgia woods. During this time, the men were required to put to use what they had learned about navigating with a compass. They were required to be left by themselves among the Georgia pines and using a compass find their way back to camp.

George was struggling with his back pack and rifle when he remembered he had not taken his purple pills for three days; he had left them back at his barracks. Looking through his back pack he could not find his matches, either. While wandering through the woods, he was all alone. The forest was quiet. He spied two curious raccoons, with their dark circles around their eyes looking at him with curiosity, then ducking behind some brush.

It had been a long time, since he had cut lose with his foul smelling gas with abandon. He had kept it under control. Never had he wanted to take a life again if he could help it.

Frankly, George wasn't really sure he had caused that lady's death back at Walmart. That was eons away in time.

He had sat down to take a break, watching the antics of the raccoons. As soon as he would turn his head away from them, they would emerge to get a better look at him, but when he snapped his head back, they quickly disappeared; but not before George got a glimpse of them. Since he was all alone out in the wilderness; no one would be the wiser if he checked to see the effect of his gas on the raccoons.

Farts rose slowly and with his back turned to the two animals he mustered up a machine gun staccato as the gas spread from his rear end. Curiosity got the best of the raccoons; they advanced and sniffed. Then the two backed up, but the sniff got them. Both leaped high into the air, and fell on their backs as if shot. With paws twitching and jerking for about two minutes, they became still. White foam erupted from their mouths as they lay motionless.

George stood there looking down at two of God's little creatures who had never harmed anyone other than maybe turning over garbage cans and stealing food from humans.

Colonel Benson had been right. He was lethal. He had this awesome power!

George cried out in agony, "I am sorry! I am sorry God." He thought a minute and added, "But God, it is not entirely my fault. You had a hand in it. I am not going to take all the blame."

The stench was overpowering, even for George. He moved away. An owl that had begun hooting his head off for a mate fell from a tall pine tree hitting the ground with a thud. He recognized the awful smell as that of chum that had gone bad and had rotted. Anyone who used ground up fish and other trash from the sea to lure bigger fish and had ever let it rot would surely have recognized the smell.

253

George began to move out hurriedly following his compass.

He did what had been drilled into him; he let the compass guide him.

After detouring around pine trees, brush and other obstacles, an hour later, he stumbled onto the bivouac camp, hot tired and drenched with sweat. The master sergeant in charge was blowing his whistle and giving orders for everyone to pack up and get on the army trucks that had come to take the soldiers back to Ft. Benning.

The bivouac was over. Terminated!

Tents were torn down and removed. Like Indians moving to another location after creating unsanitary conditions, the troops did not take the time to police the area.

Trash was left scattered in their haste to leave.

The powerful smell that had struck down two nosey raccoons and one hooting owl had diminished by the time it had invaded the valley where the troops were trying to learn some new skills, but still the smell became unbearable. Further in the hot hills of Georgia, no orders were issued for the soldiers to bring gas masks. There was no way the troops could stay in the area. The Sergeant would send a clean-up detail to the area later after it was inspected.

"Come on Murfrey! Get a move on it," shouted the Sergeant. "We are moving out. While you were gone, this area has become contaminated."

George noticed that most of the soldiers had make-shift gas masks around their noses consisting of rags tied and a few drops of gasoline or kerosene placed on the nose area. This seemed to work well enough. Then he noticed a Red Cross field ambulance moving slowly off. "Well, maybe not that effective," he reflected

The next morning after breakfast, Sergeant Ziegfield escorted George to the office of Colonel Benson. It had been over a week since he had seen the Colonel. He was ushered into the Colonel's office and upon facing Colonel Benson George showed the results of his military training by rendering a very snappy salute. He stood at attention in his newly tailored uniform that did nothing to hide his protruding belly. Mutt had talked him into getting the uniform tailored. "As you slim down," reasoned Mutt, "you can get it cut away some more. Save you money in the long run."

Still snappy in military decorum, George said, "First Sergeant Murfrey reporting, sir!"

"Sit down George," commanded Colonel Benson. "We need to talk."

The Colonel smiled. George noticed that even though Benson was old, he was still a handsome man. He still had a full head of white hair which gave him character.

"Was that sudden exodus from the bivouac yesterday some of your doing?"

"I am sorry Colonel," said George in his high pitched guilty voice. "I was alone many miles from camp and just cut one loose. I hope no one was injured. I did not mean for anyone to get hurt."

"No, George, you did not cause any injuries. As a matter of fact, it was a good exercise. The men had to improvise gas masks and survived sickness. Only eleven went to sick bay with severe vomiting. That was minor."

"The Captain, in charge of the bivouac, laughed about it and said he would like to simulate attacks of that kind on a regular basis. He does not know it was you who did the dirty deed."

"George you know your abilities are top secret. You cannot let your guard down." Benson laughed. "You cannot let your pants down either, unless you strike a match. I want you to promise me not to let lose any more farts without first striking a match. Take those damn pills I gave you. They worked on Big Fanny; they will work on you. That is an order George. Verstehen sie?"

George did not know German, but he verstehen-sied.

"I sent a team out to investigate the damage done early this morning. Wearing special gas masks, they were able to find two dead raccoons and a dead owl plus numerous piles of dead insects at ground zero where you obviously leaked your gas. I would be right about the location, wouldn't I?"

"Yes, sir," George agreed. He was still not sure he was being praised or to be punished.

"Good, good," praised Colonel Benson. He picked up several sheets of printed material and handed them to George. "George, here are your new orders. For obvious reasons, I am cutting short your training here. You are going to Camp McClain, Mississippi. You will still be attached to Special Forces, where you will be specifically trained. Your buddy, Iverson Hanson, will, of course, be sent to Mississippi to Camp Shelby. Both of you will be under the 155th Brigade of the Mississippi National Guard. Hanson was been assigned to the 155th Heavy Brigade Combat Team, which he requested. He will be trained to operate a MIAI Abrams Main Battle Tank or a Bradley high speed fighting vehicle. As your orders show, you will both be transported to Keesler AFB after flying into Gulfport Airport and then a Jeep will take you to Camp Shelby in Hattiesburg, Mississippi. You are familiar with that area, right?"

"Yes sir. I know where that is. I grew up near Biloxi and am very familiar with Hattiesburg," said George. "Will Sergeant Ziegfield accompany us?"

"Yes, Sergeant Ziggy, as we nicknamed him, will still be your baby sitter. You will spend a few days at Camp Shelby and then on to Camp McClain for your special training. The 155th Brigade is now training at Camp Shelby, readying to be deployed overseas. Have you ever been overseas, George?"

"No sir, but I like the music in Spain and would kinda like to go there."

"I can't promise you Spain, but there is always the mid-east. I will see if you can spend a little time in Germany after you complete your training and have gone overseas. I want you to know that being in Special Forces means you are special, not only to me, but the army and your country. We will use your specialty in a way that will serve us best. I want to say I am proud of the way you have handled yourself while at Ft. Benning."

"Thank you, sir."

Benson handed George his orders. "That will be all, Sergeant Murfrey. Remember, you are top secret. If you spill the beans, I will have to kill you myself."

George wondered, "Was he kidding?"

When George exited Benson's office, Ziggy who had waited outside, held up three airline tickets and said, "I have got you, me and Mutt booked on a flight aboard Delta Airlines to Gulfport-Biloxi Airport for 2:00 p.m. So let's get a move on. Then we will arrive at Keesler Air Force Base, where a vehicle will be standing by to take us to Camp Shelby, where you and I will spend several days. Hanson will remain there for further training and we will move on to Camp McClain."

"What's the big hurry? I was beginning to enjoy it here?" asked George.

"We will be joining the 155th Brigade, which is in advanced training for overseas deployment. When they go, we go."

"So you are leaving these beautiful clay hills to go to God's country," joked George.

"You might as well get used to me. I will run interference for you in case of any problems. As the Colonel may have told you Special Forces is for special people --and you are one. You are one of Benson's boys and if you didn't notice it, an untouchable. It is my job to keep it that way."

"Will the Colonel come to Mississippi?'

"I doubt it," said Ziggy, who pulled the jeep in front of Barracks 101. "But I wouldn't be surprised if he showed up at your next army base. Benson was the one who accompanied Fanny Mae McBride to Korea."

"Alan, I mean Colonel Benson told me about her; said she received the Medal of Honor. He never told me the complete details as to how she did it. What exactly did she do?"

"It's classified. You will get a higher security clearance after you complete your training at Camp McClain. Then you may get the details," said Ziggy. "I have been given privy to all that happened with Big Fanny in Korea,"."

"No. No one told me." George looked at Ziggy in a new light.

"What will I do with my M-16?"

"We will turn it in. They will issue a nice new weapon at Camp Shelby."

Off they went. When they arrived at Mutt's barracks, he was outside waiting with his duffle bag.

"What took you so long?" grumbled Mutt. "I have been standing out here in the hot sun for fifteen minutes."

"You know: army red tape," said George.

"Oh," said Mutt, who knew about army red tape. It was always, "hurry up and wait."

The flight to Gulfport-Biloxi Regional airport and the trip to Keesler AFB was uneventful. On the way, George told about his last visit to the air base as best he could recall.

"I flew out of here to Baltimore, Maryland on a helicopter. Why are we going by jeep to Camp Shelby?"

"I guess someone did not think about it. Give me a minute." Ziggy dialed a number on his cell phone. "Colonel, we are supposed to go by car to Camp Shelby. "Why not make one of those helicopters here on base available?"

"Yeah," added George in the background, "Since they want us there so fast."

After Sergeant Ziegfield hung up, he said, "The Colonel said he would see what he could do."

When they reported into headquarters at Keesler, new orders had been cut to transport the trio to Camp Shelby by helicopter.

"I never cease to be impressed with Colonel Benson's pull he must have," said Mutt to Ziggy. "I heard about him chewing out those two Majors and how they took it like two recruits."

"You will probably never know the pull he has," said Ziggy.

"And I am not going to tell you even if I knew," said George laughing.

When they arrived at Camp Shelby the Master Sergeant who looked at the orders, said, "My, my, you guys must be something special."

"That is why we are in Special Forces," quipped George.

"What about the Corporal?" The Sergeant pointed to Hanson.

"He is all yours, Sergeant," said Ziggy.

"I see you requested armored division. What is your pleasure, Corporal?"

"I think I know where we will be going. It is really quite obvious. Heavy tanks won't be any good there, so put me down for those fast speeding Bradleys'." replied Mutt.

After Mutt left to join his assigned unit, Sergeant Ziggy and George found their new barracks which was much like the one in Ft. Benning except worse. There were cracks in the floor where the light shone through. The doors were beaten up and were hard to close.

"This barracks has suffered abuse!" exclaimed George.

"It is only for three days," said Sergeant Ziggy. We will not be in barracks with the regular troops because it is not good for their morale to have us hanging around getting special privileges while the rest are constantly inspected and punished for various infractions. By the way," said Ziggy trying to change the subject. "I heard that you caused the Second Platoon to evacuate their bivouac area last week and that you were responsible for the death of two raccoons and one skunk. Sounds like you really are lethal."

"It was two raccoons and one owl, not a skunk. I thought I was classified as top secret. I really don't want any of this to leak out."

"You forget I am cleared for top secret. You don't have to worry about me putting your secret on the street. Are you as lethal as they say?"

"I don't know who 'they' are, but to answer your question; apparently I am. I am not proud of it," said George defensively.

When George and Ziggy arrived at Camp McClain, George was given a dual assignment. He was to learn all he could about his role in secret missions that would come later. His cover so that he could blend in with other troops was to train as a "Watcher" for explosive devices such as roadside bombs while riding in the converted Hummer vehicles. Besides sitting in class with an actual instructor, he was shown video after video of actual I.E.D.'s as they were called. He watched actual piles of seemingly trash containing explosives and how to spot the telltale signs that were present. He learned to spot the wires that went to the detonators used to explode those bombs. Innocent looking structures or parked vehicles were ideal places to hide explosive devices. They learned to recognize rifle propelled rockets. Failure to recognize such dangers usually brought about the death of his fellow soldiers. "On the other hand," his Instructor said, "nature is unkind to the insurgents who plant those bombs. They have to wait for their prey after the explosives are hidden. It is very sandy along those highways and streets. After taking great pains to hide the deadly explosives and wires leading to them, the wind comes up, blowing the fine sand, exposing the wires or sometimes the explosive itself. These signs are there if you really look closely for them."

"How about the suicide bomber? I wish," said the Instructor, "that we had some former Custom agents working for us. These agents look for clues to catch smugglers and are quite good at it. They look for bulky clothing, walking funny, shifty eyes. It's body language that gives them away."

The class of about forty men watched actual films of suicide bombers approaching who detonated themselves first in normal speed and then in slow motion. There was that facial expression; that twitch of the eye, the suspicious walking and gestures which gave them away. It was easy to spot them in slow motion. The class was given a series of men on film approaching other soldiers. As a test, the "Watchers" were to recognize the bombers and give their reasons for the observation. Those not bombers were to be excluded. George only missed one on the first test. After that, George led the class in recognition of suicide bombers as well as spotting I.E.D.'s.

Recognition of these deadly men and women and sometimes children was not easy. They all seemed to have furtive eyes that darted suspiciously back and forth; all were foreigners dressed as Arabs. A decision had to be made in a split second when that "Arab" suddenly tried to reach for something under his clothing.

George's other classes consisted of learning to recognize the leader of a group of insurgents and how to deal with them. He was taught how to keep from being killed immediately after capture; how not to provoke them, but to make them think he was harmless. As a fat boy growing up with bullies in school, George had had a lot of practice in this situation.

He always looked harmless; his rosy cheeks, his blue eyes and sprinkling of freckles around his nose. His girth seemed to inspire a non-combative feeling. His only aggressive manner was the sarcasm that often came out when he felt defensive. Through psychological testing and confrontation, George was taught how to speak to his captors without creating animosity.

It was obvious to George, with all this emphasis on being captured, that somewhere down the line his superiors expected him to be captured on a mission. On the brighter side, George learned in his other classes that the older death trap Humvees were being phased out and when he reached Iraq, he would be a watcher on one of the newer and safer M.R.A.P.'s. Those initials meant Mine Resistant Ambush Protected vehicles. His chances for survival were greater than those who went before him. That was comforting.

Also, comforting was his issue of protective clothing which consisted of a outer vest weighing sixty pounds, a Kevlar helmet, fire retardant gloves and retardant uniforms he would wear out on patrol or in a convoy. George now had two duffle bags as well as a rifle to contend with.

Ziggy told him, "George, don't worry. I will help you with one of those bags. I did not know that they would train you as a watcher in addition to your other specialty."

"So what's next?"

"We are going to get our overseas shots."

"Sorry I asked. Well, lets' get it over with."

While getting numerous shots, the examining doctor took a look at George's obesity and said, "My God, man, some of you sergeants just let your weight go. You need to get on a diet. Did you know that you weigh three hundred three pounds?"

"I did not take the lint out of my naval this morning," said George who had an aversion to doctors after his treatment at Memorial Hospital at Gulfport; then at Baltimore General Hospital at the hands of Doctor Alphonse Aholie. He realized he viewed doctors as the enemy, resorting to his old sarcastic ways. "I am sorry, doc," he said. "I tend to get defensive and did not mean that. I am actually on a diet at the present.

When I joined the army I weighed around three hundred sixty pounds. At present I am the incredible shrinking man."

"How in the world did they let you into the army?"

My good looks, I guess." George grinned.

"Very good Sergeant Murfrey. When did you join?"

"Let's see. It has been about five or six weeks. Something like that. Time flies when you are having fun."

"What is this world coming to? How did you make Sergeant so fast?"

"Again it must have been my good looks. What can I say? Look doc, is this going to take much longer?"

"Actually, I am through. You passed all your tests except for your obesity. I would be glad to put you on a different diet, if you would like."

"No thanks, my job in the army requires a fat boy."

The doctor looked up from the file he had just scribbled something in. "I am glad you told me that. I won't ask how they are going to use you in Special Forces. Well good luck to you soldier. It's been nice talking to you." The doctor shook his head in dismay.

"Wouldn't do you any good, doc. It is classified," said George laughing loudly as he left.

The next day, George received more rifle training. This time, he did not shoot immobile targets. Instead, he attempted to hit pop-up targets. On his first try, he missed every one of them. So he started anticipating the pop-ups, hitting a few, including a family of four. On his final round, he did better--no innocents hit, only several fierce looking Arabs.

Ziggy came to pick him up, but first had an animated discussion with the sergeant in charge of the rifle range. After the chat, the sergeant reluctantly approached George and said, "Sergeant Murfrey, it was close, but you passed. I am going to recommend that you get more practice on the rifle range. Good luck shooting terrorists and try and miss the children." He chuckled at his joke.

"Very funny," replied George.

Even though, George, Mutt and May all had cell phones which they used each night to stay in touch with each other, while at camp McClain, The only call George could get through, was to Mutt.

"I will be through here by the end of the week," said George. "I expect they will turn me loose then."

"Better hurry. You don't want to miss the plane. On Saturday, we are having our farewell ceremony and then it is off to--you know where."

On Friday, Murfrey was brought before an officer in charge with the rank of full bird Colonel.

Colonel Franks congratulated him on his completion of training at McClain. He was told just how the army planned to use him in the future prior to his first mission. They had decided that Sergeant Murfrey would get a taste of combat before being sent on solo missions to let loose his lethal gas. He would put his training as a "Watcher" to use by riding in convoys in Iraq.

"We want you to learn the lay of the land in Iraq and what you are up against. There will be more training along the way. Rest assured, when the time comes, you will be fully prepared," said the Colonel who handed George a sheaf of papers along with new Sergeant stripes. "You are hereby promoted to the grade of E-7. Congratulations and good luck. We need one last thing from you to complete this assignment."

"What is that, sir?"

"As we told you when you started training here, you were not to take those purple pills furnished. That is right isn't it?"

"Yes, sir," admitted George.

"Then before you leave, we have a test set up for you."

George was led by the Colonel, himself, who wanted to witness this phenomena, to a well-lighted room, where there were ten cages containing squirrels, a tree monkey, skunks, rabbits, more raccoons, snakes, two coyotes, numerous mice rats and spiders.

"I will leave you to do your business," said the officer.

"Do you want me to cut lose or just a squeaker?" said George making conversation.

"Have at it."

"You had better have good ventilation. They had to shut down a whole wing of a hospital in Baltimore. Keep your gas masks handy. I don't want to cause any injuries to your personnel."

The officer, in unbelief, was getting impatient. "Go ahead. After you finish, we will seal off the room if it is as bad as you say."

Farts went into the room and without hesitation summoned up all he could muster. Just for fun, he played Dixie and ended with a machine gun staccato. He could see the staff peering through the glass panel in the door. When he finished, he opened the door quickly and stepped out. He continued to walk out of the building.

"Wait! Don't you want to know the results?"

"I already know the results. No need to tarry. Ta ta, so long it has been good to know you." With that quick goodbye, George hurried out and climbed into the jeep with Sergeant Ziegfield, who was waiting for him with the engine running.

Inside the building all eyes were focused on the surveillance camera which swung back and forth slowly scrutinizing each individual cage.

"One hundred per cent kill. That's our man." One of the technicians shouted in awe.

"God help the terrorists," stated another seriously. "I have never seen anything like it."

"Astounding!" remarked the Officer in charge. "Even the snake is dead!"

The next day Ziggy requisitioned a jeep from the motor pool and the two rode down to Hattiesburg and on to Camp Shelby. They arrived in time to view the Farewell Ceremonies for the entire combat team of the 155th Brigade which was arrayed in Battalion formations. Below where they sat, in the grand stands, were the dignitaries: the Governor of Mississippi, General McKeenon, and Brigade Commander Glasscock among others. There were about ten thousand spectators accompanying them. It was strictly pomp and circumstance; troops marching; the band playing vivid marching songs. This part of leaving the homeland, going off to war, seemed joyous. George wished he could have been down there marching with the rest of Mississippi's finest.

He looked for Mutt, but did not see him; they all looked alike. He remembered what one of his instructors had said in one of his classes: "We are the most lethal nation in the world. There has been no equal to us in the history of the human race.

"Now, they have another lethal weapon in their arsenal," thought George. "Me!"

After the long grueling training program in which the soldiers of the 155th suffered through, they were rewarded with a four day leave. They were due back at Camp Shelby by sixteen hundred hours on Wednesday.

Among those who came from all areas across the State of Mississippi, were Sergeant George C. Murfrey the Third aka "Farts" Murfrey and Corporal Iverson Hanson aka "Mutt" Hanson. Sergeant Ziegfield elected to stay on base at Camp Shelby and was made custodian of the duffle bags, property of the two Gulfportians, along with their rifles.

Mrs. Agnes Murfrey, who did not attend the ceremony, drove up to in her new used Buick LeSabre much like the Le Sabre May Modine owned except hers was brown, to pick up the boys. While George was away, she had decided to get rid of the notorious gangster-mobile, the 1939 LaSalle that made the locals stop and stare. She had good news to tell her son; she, and Betsy Brumfield, had come in first place in a duplicate bridge tournament.

Sergeant Ziggy issued his admonition in front of Mrs. Murfrey, "Don't you boys get into trouble down there."

"They won't," said Mrs. Murfrey. "I am gonna keep a watchful eye on Georgie. If Georgie is good, then Mutt will behave himself. You'll see." She turned to her son. "Where is your girlfriend May?"

"I forgot to tell you," said George. "She is in Virginia going to Officers Training School. Looks like Mutt and I will be out ranked. I can't wait to get out of this uniform. Did you make some of your delicious Shrimp and Crabmeat gumbo?"

"Not only do I have a large pot of Creole Gumbo in the refrigerator, I, also made you a pot of red beans and rice with Andouille smoked sausage."

265

"Maybe you had better lay off the beans," warned Mutt. "They give you gas and you know the result."

"Yeah, in my zeal for a good meal, I forgot about the red beans. Those beans may be why I am in this man's army. So bring on the Gumbo."

As they made their way to the Gulf Coast, George asked Mutt, "What are you going to do these next four days?"

"I have got a reservation at the Grand Casino and I am going to lie around and gamble a little until I run out of money. No more Wills Hotel for me. How about you? What are you going to do?"

"I dunno. Maybe, I will join you. We could see a floor show. I am not much on playing cards or rolling dice," said George who turned around in the front seat while his mother drove. "Say, I hear the Palace Pool Hall is back open. We could shoot a game of pool."

"I doubt if they will let us in, but we could try."

"Since the 155th is flying out of Keesler Air Force Base, Ziggy is going to meet me there. Why don't you meet him there also?"

"Not me George, I want to deploy with my platoon. By the way, I was just told that I will be assigned to a Bradley when we get to Iraq. I am to be a machine gunner. How about you? Do you know what you will be doing?"

"Vaguely; I have been trained as a "Watcher" in a M.R.A. P. I will do that until they come up with some other mission. So I will just be riding around in a convoy trying to spot bombs and terrorists," George said trying to act nonchalant about it.

Mutt laughed. "I would rather be in one of those Bradleys. They are too fast for the insurgents to hit. Maybe, I will come to your rescue if you get ambushed."

"Would you please?" said George. "I hear those M.R.A.P.'s are a lot safer than the older Humvees. That's what they told us at Camp McClain. So much for the buddy system we will be lucky if we see each other."

"We will see," said Mutt. "Keep your cell phone handy."

CHAPTER TWENTY TWO

Off to Iraq

Nothing much had changed on the coast. It seemed the same. The sailboat regattas with their bright sails still dotted the water out in front. Motorboats were being launched with fishermen cruising to the hot spots to catch the big ones. Always an abundant supply of tourists filled the casinos, playing the slots, rolling the dice or trying their luck on the roulette wheels.

It all looked good to George Murfrey, for it was home.

George finally got through to his girlfriend May.

"Guess where I am?" he asked.

"No telling."

"I am back in Gulfport--me and Mutt. We both got a four day leave from Camp Shelby before we are shipped overseas. Why don't you wrangle a three day pass and fly down. I really miss you. I have even lost over fifty-five pounds."

"I wish I could; I am in the middle of my exams. Besides," she joked, I will be a Lieutenant soon and we are not supposed to mingle with enlisted men. You are not the only one who has lost weight. I bet you won't recognize me when we see each other again. I miss you too."

"May, you know the problem I have and the trouble I was in at Walmart?"

"Yes, I know. What about it?"

"I have been tested and I, well I guess, I am lethal. That is all I can say."

"Oh? Just how lethal," she demanded.

"One whiff and pow! You are dead!"

There was a long pause. Then almost in a whisper: "George, how are you handling it?"

"That is classified. All I can tell you is that it is under control. I am certainly avoiding red beans and rice." He laughed.

She whispered again, "You poor boy. You really got a cross to bear; don't you?"

"Tell me about it," said George. "Anyway, I can't wait to see you when you get those bars on your shoulder. We never thought any of this would ever happen."

"I have been thinking, George. We really had some good times. You know--kept it light, but since we have been apart, I need to tell you something."

"Well, what is it?"

"I love you dearly," she blurted out.

"May, I love you too." He paused and after interminable silence said, "Well ain't that a pile of crap! I can't even kiss you or hold your hand. I would like to hop a jet and fly up there to see you; you know: tell you in person. I have plenty of money now. I have hardly spent a cent. I am at E-7 now in pay."

"I will be at E-11 when I graduate," said May softly with a giggle.

"I am going to see about that," said George. I have already had two promotions and am looking at upgrading to Master Sergeant. It is all because of the assignments I will get. Don't be surprised if I catch up to you. Uh, oh, my cell phone is beeping. I better hang up before the battery runs out and the phone shuts down. See you."

"See you," said May with a sob. "Love you, you big offal."

"Love you too." He closed the lid to the phone which hung it up.

It did not take Mutt long to go through his accumulated pay checks. Within hours after he hit the roulette table, Mutt had doubled, then tripled his money and at one point was ahead about twenty thousand dollars in chips. He was using a system one of his army friends has told him about.

"First, you stand and watch the roulette. If, for instance, you see red win five times in a row, bet on black. If red wins again, double your bet and bet on black. Keep doubling your bet until black wins."

"What if it keeps landing on red?" Mutt asked.

"The odds are it won't. Just keep doubling up until you win or are wiped out."

Unfortunately, using this system, it kept hitting red and soon the twenty thousand was gone plus most of Mutt's pay checks he had saved.

George came down and they left to go to the new Palace Pool Hall.

"You will have to pay for the games, George. That little white ball just kept dropping into that red slot. I am busted," explained Mutt. "...also the beer."

"That's alright. I have plenty. I even opened a checking account at the bank."

"Well bully for you. While I am losing my ass, you are salting yours away. Just remember all those times I used to pick up the tab when we went out."

"Mutt," said George. "Guess what. I spoke to my girl and she says she loves me. I am practically engaged. How about that?"

"You stupid ass! What is the matter with you? Doesn't she know what she is getting into? Look Murfrey, when we get to Iraq, we could both be dead in twenty-four hours. You don't have any business getting engaged. Hell, man that's one thing you don't need and that is getting serious with a woman. All they will do is spend your money and then dump you. I thought you had better sense."

"Don't get your bowels in an uproar."

"Ha! Now don't get yours in an uproar or you will wipe out half of Gulfport."

"Now Mutt," said George in a very low voice. "I told you before, all that was top secret. For all we know, I could be monitored by the F.B.I.. They did it before."

"Okay, okay, let's drop it. Let's go and shoot some pool like old times, for tomorrow we may die."

"Don't keep saying that!"

At the pool hall, Slim the bartender eyed, Farts Murfrey and Mutt Hanson as they entered. They were both in civvies, but looked different; they had that military look about them. Murfrey had lost weight; Mutt was sober.

"What are you two doing in here? You know you are barred," said Slim.

"Oh, come on Slim," said Mutt. "That was long ago. There have been a lot of changes since then. The statute of limitations has run out."

I don't know about no statute of limitations. All I know is that you are permanently barred. You can't come in here."

Mutt moved up to the new bar which lacked the scars and burn marks like the old one. He looked Slim in the eye and said, "Now look here, Slim. You can't bar us. We are both in the U.S. Army fighting for your scrawny ass to keep you free. Ain't that right, Farts?"

"That's right," said Farts who had reached into his wallet and pulled out his Army I.D. card. "And here is my military I.D. to prove it."

"Put it away, Farts. Slim knows we are Army." Mutt put both hands on the bar and sternly said in his deep voice, "If you put us out of the bar, you are putting Uncle Sam out. The Soldiers and Sailors Relief Act says you can't do it."

Slim whose life was spent tending bar for a vocation and reading girlie magazines for pleasure, had never heard of this Soldiers and Sailors Relief Act. His black whiskered face scrunched up in thought, while chewing on a toothpick, he looked at these two characters that once wrecked his livelihood. Trying to make up his mind he thought, "They certainly didn't look like those other two characters from the past."

Mutt broke the silence. "Besides, if we act up, all you have to do is to call the Military Police or the Shore Patrol."

"How long you boys gonna be in town?" Slim asked.

"Mutt leaves to go back to Shelby tomorrow; I leave to go to Iraq on Thursday."

Slim thought that over. The pool hall was empty except for two all day drunks in a stupor at the end of the bar and two teenagers banging balls on newly covered table three. He could use the business.

"Alright, I'll let you two in, but no funny business. Don't start nothing, you hear? Just walk away if there is trouble. I will be watching you--and Farts, no farts, you hear?"

"By the way boys, Fart's buddy was in here yesterday wearing an Army uniform. I kicked his butt out, so consider yoreselves lucky."

270

"What buddy?" squealed Murfrey. Mutt was his only buddy.

"You know, Big Jake. The one what stabbed you with his big knife. They were gonna send him to prison, but someone said he got the same deal you got, Farts, and he enlisted into the Army. He said he was on leave and going to Iraq in a few days with the Mississippi National Guard. He did not know about that Sailors Relief Act, so I threw him out.

Slim looked at the consternation on the face of Farts and the dropped mouth of Mutt and commented, "You guys didn't know that?"

"Naw, we didn't know that," said Mutt acting like it was nothing. "Rack 'em up. Let's shoot some pool and Slim give George a Heinekens and me a Bud Lite."

Murfrey stood there in a trance--not moving.

Mutt removed a pool stick from the wall and jabbed him in the ass. He added, "I'll break. The last time you broke, you bounced the cue ball off Big Jake's back."

George nodded automatically; in spite of the jab, he still was in deep thought. Just when lady luck had smiled on him again, he gets this news that not only had Big Jake joined the Army, but his nemesis was going overseas in the same Brigade. He had made it through rigorous training, lost weight, been promoted twice and his girlfriend loved him. His exhilaration was short lived; now this.

Big Jake, the meanest man on the Gulf Coast, was going to Iraq. Could he ever escape his past that followed him like a trail of bad gas?

George saw Mutt studying him. He said bravely, "I bet Big Jake will be shocked when he sees that I am a Sergeant." George took the blue chalking cube in his hand and began to chalk the tip of his pool stick vigorously, making it squeak loudly, blue dust falling onto the sticky floor just mopped by Slim.

"He will probably shoot you first," joked Mutt.

"We will see about that. I ain't scared of him anymore. I have had hand to hand combat training and I learned how to shoot terrorists. I can handle him. He even looks like a terrorist; don't you think, Mutt?"

"Yeah, sure," said Mutt. "Just leave him to me; he won't harm one kinky hair on your big fat ass."

"We will see about that too," grumbled George.

George became quiet and concentrated on his pool game. No more wild flying balls, no hitting the balls with great force, instead he settled down playing each ball with all the skill he possessed. He won every game.

The next day, Mutt left the coast traveling on a Greyhound bus for Camp Shelby. It stopped and let him off on Highway 49, several miles from the base. Just as he figured, with his wearing his army uniform, along came a bunch of G.I.s' in a yellow Mustang convertible, giving him a lift. He had not called his father while on the coast, otherwise he might have been driving his taken away, red Chevrolet Camaro sports car. He was too full of pride to do that.

George, on the other hand, was taking his mother out to eat at McIwanes' Seafood in Biloxi that evening. But first, he would look up his friend, Detective Ed Smallwood so he called at the police station and found him on duty.

"I don't think it would be wise to come out here to the station. Why don't I drive out to your house and pick you up? We can go have coffee at T.D. Drugstore."

T.D. Drugstore was on the corner in the heart of Gulfport. It faced the old Johnny's Bar, now closed again, across the street. In the back of the drugstore was a dining area that served breakfasts and hot lunches and outstanding coffee.

At ten hundred hours, Ed picked George up in his black Ford Victoria police car. At the drug store, each ordered coffee.

"Man, you sure look healthy, Farts. It looks, like the Army was a blessing." He looked at George with inquisitive eye and said, "How are they treating you?"

"Great. I have gotten two promotions since I enlisted. I guess you would say it was a blessing in disguise. I had not thought of it that way. I just finished my training and tomorrow, I fly out from Keesler to Iraq. Thought I would give you a shout; thank you for taking up for me in the Walmart deal."

"You don't need to thank me. I never believed for a minute that you were some terrorist. Isn't it ironic; now you are going over there to fight terrorists. They still talk about you and the trial. Carvin and Waddell never got over the fact that you beat them in court The D.A. fired Bum Ketch for messing up his case. I guess you heard about Jake Bannister getting off the hook."

The waitress refilled their cups. They sipped their coffee.

"I heard, but I don't know the details," said George.

"Bannister had been granted immunity for stabbing you, but as you know Big Jake did not come through with his testimony. Your lawyer made a fool out of him. D.A. Beekman was mad as all hell. He was going to try Jake for Aggravated Assault and Perjury. Even though you had left to go into the army, there were enough witnesses to convict Bannister. So what did he do? He hired your lawyer, Nancy Grace Best and she got him the same sweet deal you had gotten. She got all his three pages of misdemeanors purged and made the deal. Now she is the new City Judge in Gulfport and the army has another problem. Present company accepted." The detective leaned back and laughed. "He's in the army now," he sang. "I am surprised you did not run across him."

"We are in different units. You don't know what branch he is in, do you?"

"I heard he was in light infantry."

"Light infantry!" George cackled so loudly the other patrons turned their heads in his direction. "Serves him right. He will get his due. Those guys in light infantry run or march everywhere they go and believe me, they don't go light. When they run, or march they are fully dressed; pack on their backs and rifle in hand. What a laugh. If he thought he was getting off easy, he has jumped out of the frying pan into the fire."

"I take it you have it soft; what will you be doing?"

"I am what they call a "Watcher" or a spotter in an M.R.A.P. which is a newly developed heavily armored vehicle that took the place of the dangerous Humvees. My job is to ride in the convoys, looking for anything suspicious along the highways. If I spot anything suspicious, I point it out to our machine gunner who takes action. As long as we don't get blasted by roadside explosive devices or hit by a rifle grenade, there will be no problem. In that respect it is a soft job."

273

George did not mention that he was in Special Forces; that was classified.

"I guess the Boy Scouts helped prepare me for all that military stuff. I have even lost over fifty pounds to date."

"I can see that you still have that belly. No offense," said Smallwood. "How is Mutt Hanson doing? I heard he joined up with you when you went in. I bet Judge Best, is glad not to have him in her court. Every time I used to see him, he was drunk; except, of course, when he was painting curbs. By the way, the city doesn't hand paint them any -more. One of the winos was given that job and he wandered out and was smashed flat by a Mack truck. He sued the city for a lot of money; got a nice settlement; threw a grand party. They found him in his one room travel trailer dead and dead broke. All those thousands of dollars settlement money gone. So they cut that educational program out. No one knows where all that money he received from the settlement went."

"In answer to your inquiry about Mutt Hanson," said George. "He is doing okay. He is in the Heavy Combat Team Brigade assigned to one of those fast moving Bradley tanks, as he puts it. He loves it. I haven't seen him drunk since we entered training.

"That's great. How about that gal you went with. Maybelline Modine was her name. What became of her?"

"She joined up with Mutt and me and now she is in Officer training. That girl is a whiz. Soon she will be a Lieutenant," George said proudly. He then said in a low voice, "She will be fraternizing with an enlisted man if I have my say-so."

"Wow," laughed Ed. "With you three and Jake Bannister over there, I know our homeland will be safe. For a while I was worried. Now, what can I say? Maybe you can gas them like in the Boy Scout days, huh, Farts? You know of course, that we the citizens of Gulfport owe you a debt of gratitude. If you had not gassed the East Ward School when we were in the second grade, it might have taken years to get our sewerage system. And let's not forget Walmart. As a result of Mrs. Matthews dying and from your dropping farts in the aisles, they have widened the aisles so that when their customers pass bad gas, it doesn't accumulate, but is sucked off quickly." Ed laughed again.

"Lets' not go there. The army has solved that problem. Say whatever happened to Zach, Tom Bradley and Joe Wilson?" said George trying to change the subject..

"Zach joined the navy and is now a Petty Officer. Tom Bradley went into divinity school and became a preacher and Joe Edwards is still in college getting his doctors degree in Physics. Go figure."

"Looks like we all did well. You know, when I look back, even the bad times were good." George was silent a minute. He sipped his coffee and then said, "I am actually looking forward to going overseas. I feel I have been well trained. Uncle has been good to me. I may make the army a career."

Ed looked at George curiously. He said, "Is this the Farts Murfrey, I used to know? I can't believe it. For a while all you used to do was to hang out with Mutt Hanson, sip on Barq's root beer or something stronger and wander around Gulfport. Almost makes me want to join up, but I think I will stay here and fight crime."

"Every man to himself," said George. "I will be fighting not only for my country, but being attached to the Mississippi National Guard, I will be representing the Magnolia State." He made a fist and said, "Who-rah." In as deep a voice as he could muster startling the coffee drinking customers again.

About that time, the detective's pager went off. He called the dispatcher and then turned to George. "Look, Farts, it has been good to see you, but I have to earn my pay. Some man who lives on Second Street has been found with his throat cut. His car is missing. I will drop you off on the way."

*   *   *

Agnes Murfrey was thrilled that her son was taking her out to eat on his last night in town, having booked his reservation at McIlwanes Seafood House at the small craft harbor in Biloxi, she donned her church going clothes, a flowery dress with greens yellows and orange with a hat and purse to match. George wore his uniform with the new sergeant's

275

stripes sewed on the sleeves, belly sucked in and rigid like a true soldier; he and his mom marched into the crowded restaurant.

Feeling patriotic about the war in Iraq, their waiter took them to a special table overlooking the scenic Biloxi Yacht Harbor, where yachts, cabin cruisers and sailboats rested peacefully in the calm protected waters.

They sat down at the green cloth covered table with silverware rolled up in a cloth napkin to match, his large rear end plopping into the wooden chair with a scraping bump, his large pudgy hands grabbing up the glass of ice water recently poured by the obsequious waiter, his mother softly filling her chair that had been pulled out by the gracious waiter, her adoring face smiling at her son and the attention given them.

After studying carefully the plastic covered menu, George ordered the popcorn shrimp, a salad with blue cheese dressing and a baked potato with all the trimmings, his mom getting the broiled Flounder stuffed with crabmeat dressing along with peas and rice plus a salad topped with Ranch dressing.

"Are they sending you to Iraq?" asked the tall dapper waiter.

"Yeah," said George. "This is my last day in the U.S. of A."

"Hope you take good care of your troops, Sergeant."

"Actually," said George. "I am an Army of one."

"Oh, I understand. Good luck then. Just remember; we appreciate the sacrifice you are making for your country."

After the waiter left with their order, Agnes said, "Wasn't that nice? I am very proud of you son. You really recovered from your problems. I want you to know that I never stopped praying for you to be lifted out of that mess and here we are."

"Mom, I just did what you taught me," said George with a wry smile.

"What was that son?"

"I took my lemons and made lemonade out of them."

While waiting for the meal to come, George gazed out over the many kinds of play toys and vessels berthed in the harbor. Through the picture window he spied a young boy, maybe ten years of age, throwing pieces, torn from a roll, he had saved, into the air, tiny pieces he pinched

276

from the bread as George had once done, only smaller amounts. As in George's case, sea gulls with their sharp eye for food, swooped down to catch the morsels in mid-air, while other gulls cackling and screeching loudly entering the contest to snatch the prize away from the lead sea gull, who veered off to the left suddenly, while the others went to the right.

It was like yesterday; the loud deafening boom of the forty-five which instantaneously sent its' destruction to a sea gull he once knew by name, but now could not recall.

All he could think of was the question he asked himself: Would he receive the same fate in Iraq?

Would he be blown to bits by some Improvised Explosive Device in a strange country with its strange gibberish tongues and mysterious music?

His dreamlike revelry was shattered by the clanking of his dish against his water glass as the elegant waiter placed the sumptuous plate of popcorn shrimp before him, his mother admiring her stuffed Flounder with the relish of the hound dog.

"Will there be anything else that I can get you, Sergeant?" he asked.

"No. I mean no thanks," answered George who immediately speared a shrimp the size of popcorn, popping it into his mouth, a look of satisfaction spreading over his face; this delicacy not like those he had eaten in fast food restaurants that were all batter with only a tiny slender sliver of a shrimp inside; this one contained a tasty shrimp with only a modicum of coating of fish-fry batter, only serving to enhance the true delicious taste of freshly caught shrimp. He knew then that he would miss the Mississippi Gulf Coast where sea food enticed the taste buds.

He called back to the waiter, "I think I will also have a bowl of shrimp and crabmeat gumbo."

"Georgie," interrupted his mother. "Where are our manners? We forgot to say Grace."

George stopped chewing.

"Dear Lord, bless this food to our bodies and protect my son and his comrades from harm in Iraq and thank you for blessing us here today. Amen."

Georgie dove back in tossing the miniature shrimp into his eager mouth.

His mother continued. "Georgie, those sea gulls diving for food out here reminded me of seeing you on television on the beach the day that when you were arrested for murder when that awful deputy sheriff shot and killed that bird. For a moment it looked as if he was going to shoot you. Did you know he had his gun pointed at you when those sea gulls splattered him good?"

"Mom, I doubt that he would have shot me in front of all those people. Anyway, let's enjoy this fine meal; that was long ago--times have changed."

"Son," she said meekly. "Do you still have that--you know that problem with gas? I have not heard or smelled anything since you have been home."

George, nonplused, looked up. "That reminds me," he said. "It is time to take my pill."

He reached in his pocket and pulled out an amber pill bottle and from it produced a huge purple pill, large enough to choke a horse, showing it to his mother before tossing it down his gullet, washing it down with a swig of ice water, the pill joining the half plate of popcorn shrimp.

After polishing off a basket of fresh rolls and Gumbo, the meal ended with a slice of pecan pie on it a large scoop of vanilla ice cream.

"I am glad to hear that the army solved your problem and without hurting your appetite. That was the only thing holding you back. Now you can achieve success--with the Grace of God, of course."

"Of course," said George mockingly.

*   *   *

The next day, Sergeant Ziegfield was at Keesler Air Force Base waiting for him. After helping George with the two heavy duffle bags he had been struggling with, Ziggy pointed out the humongous aircraft that was to fly them to Kuwait, a Globemaster C-17, big enough to store three tanks, only this time it would be troops.

"That's our plane," said Ziggy. Let's get on board and get a good seat."

"I didn't know they had any good seats on that monstrosity," said George as he looked the airplane over.

"I saw you buddy, Mutt earlier with his platoon. They flew out of here about ten minutes ago. He didn't look all that excited either."

"You should have seen him," said George. "He really put on the dog, spending money like crazy, a girl on each side assisting him while he rolled the dice and played roulette. At one time, he was twenty thousand ahead, but those free cocktails got him. Soon he was down to nothing, the girls surrounding him, disappeared when his money gave out. He left the casino broke, even had to borrow fifty dollars from me."

"I spoke to Mutt," said Ziggy. "He said to tell you to kiss his ass and he would see you on sand dune number three.

After the C-17 with its' four propeller driven engines grabbing air, leaving the runway, the excited men, mostly youngsters, cheered as it circled over the Gulf of Mexico and headed northeast.

CHAPTER TWENTY THREE

Duty overseas

When the Globemaster C-17 took off from Keesler AFB, the temperature was in the nineties the humidity was in the eighties. This was cool compared with the oven the troops were greeted in Kuwait; the temperature being a torrid one hundred thirty.

"I didn't know humans could live with such heat. This should be against the law. I don't know if this fat boy can take it; maybe I will put in for a transfer for the mountains in Afghanistan. It has got to be nicer there," said George who was wringing wet moments after lugging his two heavy duffle bags tightly filled with its essentials for becoming one of America's warriors, supposed to save his country from unknown despots, angry fanatics, suicidal brainwashed nutcases and downright mean terrorists who would just as soon kill you as look at you.

"Here, take these," said Ziggy as he handed George a bottle of water and several salt tablets. "Cheer up. We are only supposed to be here for two weeks. I hear Iraq is much cooler."

"No wonder everyone is a religious fanatic in these countries. If hell is hotter than this, I am going to straighten up and go straight to heaven, if Saint Peter will take me," quipped George in his usual sarcastic way.

They threw their duffle bags into the army trucks waiting for them; the soldiers herded into a bus which took them to a tent city called Camp Buchring, after a long trip into the desert. George saw his first foreign soldier, a Kuwait soldier who took charge of the bus and told them in hard to understand English that they were going to be updated on their "instructions". George could not comprehend all that the soldier said, but did catch the word: "climatized".

Two hours later, the bus lumbered into the bleak desert land that stretched for miles without a sign of life or Bedouins or some kind of lizard one expects to find in such a desolated place; instead there was array of tents where the Mississippi National Guard would be acclimatized and prepared to do battle with up to date "instructions". Each tent held seventy soldiers, their temporary home for the next fourteen days bringing them closer to harm's way.

George found himself with a group of soldiers whose continued training was even more specialized, whose sole purpose was to relieve battle weary soldiers, counting the days and hours when they could return to their families, hopefully their jobs awaiting them after their tour of duty. He was rousted out of his exhausted slumber at some ungodly hour from his comfortable cot and instructed to put on sixty pounds of an armored vest designated as an Improvised Outer Tactical Vest or IOTV as the army liked to call them; his training taking place in an M.R.A.P., an armored vehicle, which protected the convoys, now being sharpened by his instructors, who had the battle skills from personal experiences, knowing what they were talking about.

To complete this dress rehearsal, George, with the rest of his group, put on Kevlar helmets and protective goggles; were given rides in M.R.A.P.'s, similar to the vehicles that awaited them in Iraq. George was designated a "watcher", riding each proceeding day into simulated conditions he might expect in the future his job spotting targets he would surely encounter. For the first time, George had second thoughts about joining this man's army; fun and games was over.

A team was formed. His driver was Eugene Gibbons, a lanky farm boy from Lucedale, Mississippi. The machine gunner was Rex Welby, a rugged welder who hailed from Pontotoc. Ed Stevens, from Meridian, was the radio operator and GPS man. He had worked in a dentist's office making false teeth, but his aptitude tests showed he had the skills not only operating the radio and GPS, but could take them apart and fix them if necessary. Finally, sharing the chore as a co-watcher, was Antoine Jones, a quiet black man from Vicksburg whose vocation had been a checker in a lumber yard which required a sharp eye to prevent unpaid lumber leaving the gate.

George had no vocational background, but with twenty-ten vision, he did have sharp exceptional vision. He was on loan from Special Forces filling in the time between assignments, hardening him physically as well as mentally for those dangerous assignments sure to come.

All were anxious to learn and work together; their lives depended upon it.

Sergeant Ziegfield did not participate in the training, but was there to assist George making sure he made it through his training as a watcher. As a watcher, George was expected to learn the territory in Iraq; to learn about the enemy; what he was up against. What better way to gain this knowledge than to ride in those armored M.R.A.P.'s with a convoy day in, day out, being part of the army as a regular combat soldier in contrast with his assignment in Special Forces.

Dressed in full battle gear, George was required to ride as a watcher while there were simulated targets which he must spot, before they blew him up along with the men in his vehicle. It was as real as actual combat to him. He would pin point the enemy in various situations, conveying the target to his machine gunner, riding on top of the vehicle partially exposed, firing the machine gun at targets before they could shoot him. There were simulations for the radio operator, who had the duty to call for help, when their position was being over whelmed or how to use the GPS when their location was in doubt before they got lost, suffering the fate of those who had made the wrong turn; were shot and killed by the ever present enemy; like young animals straying from the group only to be picked off by a pack of wolves.

It took several days of straining his eyes to locate those tiny wires that often led to a roadside I.E.D., but George began to catch on, becoming quite good at it; in fact, it became too easy and the instructors were hard pressed to disguise would-be bombs in sand dunes and trash piles which George couldn't spot.

He was rewarded with the "wand", a device that was being tested to explode the live secretly placed bombs. The device had the same capability the cell phones the terrorists used to send the message to their hidden bombs, exploding them at the right moment before the convoy was in critical danger. It, unlike the terrorist cell phone, dialed itself until it got the right number or signal. George enjoyed spotting, pointing and exploding the hidden bombs. There was a drawback: if a bomb was

282

missed and the instrument activated, the missed bomb might explode in another section of the convoy; also if there were several bombs with the same signal that could get tricky too. The fact that George was trusted with the device in simulation showed how accurate he had become in the spotting of the I.E.D.'s.

Spotting the enemy, whether a man with a turban or a woman wearing a berka was another matter. They could be seen walking down a street in their flowing full length garments and in a flash would be fingering a cell phone or some other gadget which triggered a bomb, but by the time the two week training was almost up, George had seen morning, afternoon or even night, the dangers of riding in a M.R.A.P and he had identified them all.

On the last day of his training, George experienced what a roadside bomb could do to a vehicle like the one he would be riding in. In a mock convoy, there was a radio controlled Humvee with dummy soldiers riding in it. George's vehicle was third in line. Before he could spot the I.E.D., the bomb was exploded stopping the convoy abruptly. Everyone was ordered out of their vehicle and with his ears still ringing, they saw the utter destruction of the forward Humvee, most of the vehicle blown to bits along with the mock-up dummies in it.

They all silently gasped. It hit home and that was when George asked himself, "What am I doing here?"

His specialty was doing what came naturally by letting out deadly flatulence which was supposed to kill the enemy. He was beginning to look forward to the special missions. So why was the army risking him as a watcher on a M.R.A.P. riding around in convoys drawing deadly fire, risking getting blown to hell and back? Go figure.

His biggest fear was the terrorist with a propelled grenade launcher. He had to spot the potential launcher, hoping his machine gunner was not firing at another target while the device or weapon came out from under a full length garment and then triggered to blast his vehicle. In such cases, since George carried his automatic rifle on each trip, he would have to tell the driver and radioman to stop the vehicle leaving him the responsibility of shooting and killing the man, woman or child with the grenade launcher. This was a responsibility he had not prepared himself for.

When he had the opportunity he vociferously expressed his concern to Ziggy. "What am I doing being trained to spot I.E.D.'s and perpetrators? Last week, I couldn't even spell perpetrator. Why I may get killed or injured and the army may never use me for my real reason of being here. This senseless riding around like Sally all day is for the birds. I would like to call Colonel Benson and tell him what is going on."

"He already knows. Yours is not to question why, yours is to ...just do it."

"You mean do or die, don't you. It's that last part, which I don't especially care for. I would still like to talk to the Colonel; can you make that happen?"

Sergeant Ziegfield laughed. "I am sorry George. You have a way with words, but don't quit your day job yet. The Colonel will be here in person when you least expect it. I am in contact with him almost daily. Have no fear. When we get to Iraq, your assigned vehicle will have two watchers and the other one will be me. My job is to assist you and be rest assured, I will do it. You see, I know the job. I was once a watcher when all we had were those Humvees with no armor requiring us to put make shift armor on them ourselves. I survived. Riding in the new M.R.A.P.'s with all that protective armor plus the newer helmets and vests; why your chances of being injured are miniscule."

"Sorry I brought it up," said George. "You sure know how to brighten things up for a fellow."

The day before leaving Kuwait, the mock convoy only went out on its training mission that morning. After returning, they were all called together and the chief instructor had his last word. "Men, I have done all I could to prepare you for what you can expect in Iraq. You have done well in what we call our Warrior Training Task Force and tomorrow you will put it to good uses. If you were alert and paid attention to your instructors, in all probability, each of you will return intact to your homes in Mississippi. I hope each of you has gotten to know the other personnel in your vehicle. From now on, you will eat with them, sleep in the same barracks with them and become brothers to each other. Your very life could depend on each of you working together."

"My self and the other instructors have done the best we could to prepare you. The rest is up to you. In the words of General Patton, that great warrior, 'I don't want you to die for your country. Make that other miserable bastard die for his' or in our case, let that miserable bastard die for his cause, whatever it is. Good luck and God Bless."

George realized that he did not really know much about the men he would be relying upon in case of life threatening danger since the training was so consuming, the weather so hot and the days so long that he and the others just bitched and griped a little before falling into the bed exhausted.

He had learned that their driver, Eugene Gibbons was only twenty-one, having been a truck driver, driving logging trucks around Lucedale; later having gone to truck driving school; then after graduation, hiring on with Rebel Yell Trucking where he drove eighteen wheelers from Mobile to Atlanta. Gibbons was single; all he ever talked about, was how he sexually pleased his women in every graphic way possible.

The machine gunner, Rex Welby spent his spare time hunting deer at his brother's deer camp. He was a gun fanatic with a collection of over one hundred guns, pistols, rifles and shotguns. Rex took care of his machine gun like it was a baby. He was a burly man with large hairy arms and legs. He could not wait until he bagged his first raghead. It was no problem knowing where he stood as he voiced his opinion on just about every subject; he let it be known that he scored expert on the rifle range at Camp Shelby as well as at Fort Benning, making him a reliable man to count on in battle.

Where Rex was a large hairy brute, Ed Stevens, the GPS and radio operator was only five foot tall and hardly weighed ninety-nine pounds soaking wet; he did not take up much room in the vehicle. He let everyone know that he had finished two years of Junior college and was going to finish college under the G.I. bill when he returned from duty in Iraq, having signed up for deductions from his pay to help foot his future college bills. While in Hinds Junior College, he had fixed, built and sold computers and other electronic gadgets to get the extra money needed.

285

When George showed him the "decimater" used to jam signals and explode bombs with a cell phone signal, Ed pulled the back cover off the instrument, studied it, explaining the printed circuit board and other components in a language George did not understand.

For the time being, Antoine Jones, his other watcher, was assigned to another M.R.A.P. which left Ziggy as his co-watcher looking out of the window to this left. He realized that he knew very little about Ziggy except that he was married, had two children, a boy and a little girl and was from New Jersey. Rex and Ed said they had been married, but had divorced; Rex was caught running around while Ed's wife got bored, leaving him for a successful dentist across town. Now Rex was married to his arsenal of weapons and Ed to his electronics. Ziggy was regular army with a chest full of medals and ribbons; outside of Mutt and Maybellene, he was now George's closest friend.

George kept his former life private. He did not want it known that he had been charged and tried for murder, much less for terroristic acts or that he would be on missions with Special Forces. The others knew that he was not a regular Guardsman but that was all.

Ziggy had told him, "It is a matter of time before your past leaks out. You need to be prepared for that occasion if it does. So start figuring out how you are going to handle it. If I were you, I would just laugh it off as if it was nothing; like nothing really serious happened."

"That's easy for you to say," said George. "I was tried for murder and act of terrorism and was never found innocent or guilty. The state's main witness who stabbed me and tried to get me convicted is now with the Mississippi National Guard and likely to run into me when we get to Iraq. I hear he is in Light infantry."

"A foot soldier," interrupted Ziggy.

"That is right. He knows I am with the 155th Brigade, but doesn't know what division. So what do I do about him?"

"Tell you what," said Ziggy scratching his head. "There are six camps in Iraq where the Brigade will be operating from. I will call the Colonel and let him make sure the two of you are not in the same camp. Chances are you two will never run into each other. As I said before, being a watcher on an M.R.A.P. is temporary mainly so that you can get the lay of the land and toughen you up a little. Then it is back to Special Forces and the soft life."

George locked his baby blue eyes on Ziggy's hard brown ones and said, "If facing Big Jake with a large jagged knife, being stabbed in the stomach, ending up in the hospital in Baltimore, Maryland where this mad doctor tried to cut my fat ass open to see if I had skunk glands then go through a trial for Capital Murder, while sitting in jail, with the death penalty on the table--if that didn't toughen me up, what would; I would like to know?"

"This is different," said Ziggy. "You will see. The fact that you did not break under those conditions is one of the reasons the army recruited you and put you in Special Forces. You will do alright."

"I hope so."

CHAPTER TWENTY FOUR

The Hero

After all those months of intensive training which included every conceivable situation the troops might encounter, the battalion was ready for duty, ready for combat, ready to fight, and ready to make that bunch of heartless fanatics called terrorists or by some, insurgents, die for their cause. Many of those so called insurgents were not local boys, but consisted of ready to die inhabitants from other countries in the area; some of those countries were considered friendly to the United States, but provided the funds secretly to those fighters who were slipping across the borders of Iraq in multiplying numbers. Like a giant magnet pulling in good and evil with both forces saying they were on the side of good and the other side dismissing that idea as pure foolishness, the Guardsmen from the State of Mississippi flew into Iraq landing at Baghdad International Airport or what was left of it, formerly the pride and joy of the Iraqis with once brightly colored commercial jets landing and taking off to all parts of the world, but now olive drab military aircraft met by heavily armed soldiers as the not so pretty dull khaki colored aircraft busily came and went to various parts of the earth.

George and the others on board his aircraft had gotten a brief view of the Euphrates River which ran through this great city when the pilot had graciously let them come into the cockpit one by one to catch a glimpse in violation of his rules governing the flight. They did not have time to check out the airport; dull tan army trucks were awaiting them as soon as the plane cut its engines whisking them away in the very convoys they had recently learned about. Instead of just sand and more sand, the city of Baghdad did sport vegetation and the air was not as hot; it was only 92 degrees Fahrenheit that day. George already having sweated off 25 pounds of water in Kuwait, could handle that, in spite of having to lug around two full duffle bags that were awaiting him plus the rifle he carried with him as part of his attire. Ziggy, of course, was there to give him a hand with the burden. Where was Ziggy's stuff?

288

On board the bus, everyone was upbeat, singing, joking, laughing seemingly without a care in the world.

George, who was seated on a bench, spent his time looking at the surrounding. A few street urchins stopped and stared; some waved, some throwing rocks at the passing trucks. The adults seemed to be busy with their lives only glancing occasionally as they passed through neighborhoods in the same type convoy that George would soon be a guardian of.

"You sure are quiet," said Ziggy who noticed George looking at the area as the convoy picked up speed. "Thinking about the job ahead?"

George turned his head to Ziggy and said, "That was earlier. No, I was thinking what are we doing here trying to change these people and give them democracy and Christianity. How would we react if an invader came to America and set up a dictatorship and told us we had to become Muslims?"

"If we don't watch out, it could happen. Islamic rule is spreading at a fast rate," commented Sergeant Ziegfield.

"These people have been under a dictator for thousands of years. They have no idea how to govern themselves. They have to be told. Saddam Huesein was a terrible and harsh dictator, but at least they had continuity and not chaos as they have now. That's what kind of government they were used to and you know what?"

"What?" said Ziggy.

"The Muslim religion goes hand in hand with their type of government. These people have no choice. It is either get on your knees and pray five times a day or else. And the women--they have no voice. They are not even to be seen-- all wrapped up in Berkas and gowns and such. If they get out of line they are beaten or have their nose or ears sliced off or maybe worse; they are taken out and stoned to death. And this has been going on forever from biblical times and as soon as we are gone, like weeds, the garden we created will disappear. And that is why I wonder--why are we here."

"I think we are fighting over here so that we won't have to fight them in our country. That is what our President tells us."

289

"Hogwash," said George. "Do you for a moment believe all that? If they could slip into our country, and take over, they would be there now. I was looking while we were riding, trying to spot the enemy that does not wear a uniform. They are a bunch of radical ragtag terrorists who prey mostly on innocent people. It is like the lottery from what I have surmised; each day someone's number is called and poof they are blown up along with the suicide bomber. If the population did not support them, they would not exist for long even with their intimidation they bring with them."

"Wow, George, you sure have thought that one out."

"Don't get me started," said George smiling. "I have a pretty good idea what we will be up against. All I said is between you and me. I wouldn't want to shatter the idealism and flag waving that goes on in most of these guy's heads. Don't get me wrong. I love my country and will fight for it, only this is a phony war and I know it." He leaned over and said in even a lower voice, "I know why I am here; it beats living in a small cell convicted of murder, facing execution by lethal injection."

The bus pulled into the large army base outside of Baghdad which was heavily guarded and surrounded by several sets of electronically wired fencing; much like those found in the penitentiary. The barracks, a large tent, had wooden floors, housing thirty cots. Was this to be George's home for the next twelve months?

That first night while everyone slept as if drugged, having tired out from the trip while getting settled in their new home, someone cried out, "Incoming! Incoming! Everyone get down." George was a wakened when a large hand gripped his shoulder, the hand being attached to a man in an olive drab T-shirt and olive drab boxer shorts, rudely saying, "Wake up! Wake up, man. You were having a nightmare."

The lights came on as George shook the sleep from his exhausted body to try and make some sense from the realistic nightmare he had just experienced. The veterans, survivors of the Vietnam War, had dived under their beds.

Someone yelled, "It's just a nightmare." Pointing at George he said, "That goon had a nightmare!"

This set off grumbling from those fully awake.

"What's the matter with that fat prick?"

"Somebody ought to tape his mouth up."

"I was sleeping so good. I am putting that fat bastard on my shit list."

While this grumbling and assorted complaints and derogatory remarks were being expressed, the night duty officer came into the tent to see why this particular tent was lit up like a Christmas tree. He loudly said, "Settle down everyone. It is 3:15 in the morning. I am going to turn out the lights so get back in your beds and try to get some sleep."

Just as the duty officer flipped the switch to turn off the main lights, the already awake occupants were startled by mortar fire as well as rockets being propelled into the camp.

Quickly the duty officer flipped a night light switch and called out, "Everybody fall out and proceed to the bunkers. Don't know where the bunkers are? Just follow me."

The men in the barracks quickly forgot their beef against Murfrey joining him as well as Sergeant Ziegfield, who had quietly appeared, quickly following the officer in charge, some still trying to step into their fatigues while stumbling and marching, others just going along in their skivvies.

The bunker was a 24 foot long by 12 foot hole in the ground with a tin roof covering it. It was in this flimsy structure that the men sat on long benches for an hour while rockets and mortars fell; the light infantry and marines, who had been called out, met the enemy returning fire against them, until the intruders stealthily faded from the area.

The all clear sounding, the men in the bunker stood up to file back to their barracks in preparation for breakfast and the new day, but when they attempted to open the door, it would not budge. Several of the men got behind the duty officer and gave it a push. This time it opened several inches and to their surprise fine tan sand trickled in like sand running through an hour glass. Another push and the door opened wider. One soldier got on his hands and knees and began digging out the sand letting it land on the floor behind him. The door opened wider and one of the skinny soldiers was able to slip through.

291

"You are not going to believe this," reported the skinny soldier on the other side of the door. "We have a full blown sand storm out here. I can barely see my outstretched hands!"

Soon the sand was dug out to allow the opening of the door. They were greeted by a whistling hissing sound as the storm blew the sand into their faces. It was a fine brownish sand that saturated the air. Murfrey and Ziegfield, who had managed to pull on their trousers, were able to produce handkerchiefs covering their faces enough to keep the sand out of their noses when they breathed.

The duty officer called out, "I know the way back to the barracks. Form a human chain. Each one of you, grab the hand of the man in front and I will lead you back. Try and cover your mouths and noses."

As they were led back, they noticed an eerie orange glow that lighted up the sand filled air where one of the incoming rockets had set afire one of the large tents. The wail of a fire truck, slowly moving to the fire, could be heard. Everyone was trying to see what was on fire, but visibility was so bad, no one could really tell.

"I hope it ain't the PX," shouted one of the men"

"Or the mess hall!" another exclaimed.

Forgetting that it was he who had awakened the troops, George said loudly, "How dare those insurgents disturb my sleep. Don't they know that we are the most lethal force on the face of this earth?"

This brought a loud chorus of laughter. Someone answered, "Maybe no one told them."

Another added, "They are kind of ignorant and backward."

Still another: "I am glad that fat bastard woke us up. He must be clairvoyant or something."

The duty officer called back in his heavy southern voice, "Boys, it looks like this dust storm will take a while to blow itself out. If you want, while I check out when the mess hall will open, those who want to can crawl back in your bunks. It could be around for several days."

To the man, the weary warriors climbed back into their bunks. Some soldier in a high pitched yelled, "Good night Mrs. Callabash where ever you are." Another answered, "Who the hell is Mrs Callabash? Your girlfriend?"

While the base was socked in with sand storms that came through the area, the buzz in George's barracks under discussion, was whether George was having a nightmare, or a premonition when he had hollered, "Incoming, Incoming," just moments before the incoming mortars, rockets and grenades actually hit the base where the majority of the 155th Brigade were sleeping. Was it some sixth sense he possessed or a coincidental nightmare for this was no ordinary soldier. The question was asked among the men: How did this overweight fat man get into the military, anyway? No self-respecting recruiter would sign him up with all that weight. Maybe he had psychic powers; at any rate, they quit calling him that fat bastard, smiling when he passed them by.

Although visibility was eleven feet, George and Ziggy were able to find the mess hall having no effect on George's appetite. He put away orange juice, coffee, pan cakes, scrambled powdered eggs, bacon, sausage and S.O.S. on biscuits. As the two were returning to their barracks, they ran into Mutt Hanson.

"I have been looking for you," said Mutt in his deep gruff voice. "Looks like we have a holiday; nothing much we can do this morning, so why don't we see if we can locate the PX?"

"Alright by me," said George.

"Tell you what," said Sergeant Ziegfield. "I have some phone calls to make. Catch you later."

"Do you think we can find it in this mess?" asked George.

"I found you, didn't I? Come on."

The tiny brown particles were suspended in the air giving the wooden buildings and tents ghostly forms while soldiers they met, appeared out of nowhere. When Mutt asked where the PX was located, some shrugged and others pointed in different directions.

"I hear there is no booze on the base. Because of the Muslims, it is forbidden," said George.

"Are you kidding me? After I got in early yesterday, I found this place that would put prohibition joints to shame. Don't believe that bull for a minute. I have already sampled some ice cold Heinekens and even drank some imported German beer. It tasted pretty good." Mutt looked over at George and laughed. "Look, I didn't get drunk or even high; those days are over."

"I will believe that when I see it," murmured George under his breath.

"I heard that! Guess you know, the tent that got hit, was occupied by Arkansas Guardsmen. Ten wounded and one dead. You never know when your number will come up."

Three days of wearing bandanas, make-shift masks and even rags ended when the sky cleared making it possible to clear the sand from the barracks, latrines and foot lockers as well as the piles of sand on the walkways. Later that day, after the clean-up detail, the men were drawn up in their formations to witness the memorial for Private Johm F. Caballo of Fort Smith, Arkansas, the one casualty from the other night. The men faced a rifle with its barrel driven into the ground with the deceased's helmet placed over the stock. After the eulogy the men were dismissed walking quietly back to their barracks.

Instead of the platoons being designated by numbers, they were given descriptive and exciting names. George's platoon was called Task Force Swashbucklers. Their job was to ride in their Armored Mine Resistant Personnel carrier.

Task Force Swashbucklers were notified to meet for duty at fourteen hundred hours where they were told they would accompany a convoy on a thirty mile run.

"This is it, said Sergeant Ziegfield.

"So soon, said George. I don't know if I am ready to meet our neighbors."

"The training is over; now we will see if you learned anything."

The two watchers, George and Ziggy met their driver, Eugene Gibbons, Rex Welby, their machine gunner and Ed Steven, the GPS and radio operator.

They were told their mission was to escort a platoon of foot soldiers to an outpost thirty miles away, their vehicle being third in line of a small convoy of six. Then they were brought over to see their vehicle a brand spanking new CAIMAN M.R.A.P. vehicle. In a staccato voice the motor pool sergeant informed them that this was the newest

M.R.A.P. which had the capacity to carry a ten man crew, having a full time all-wheel drive with fully automatic transmission, an electronic tire inflating system, auto-locking brake system, a highly survivable and sustainable M.R.A.P. vehicle designed to defeat current and future improvised road bombs.

"You men are lucky to get this vehicle since it was originally assigned to the marines, but our procurement officer talked them out of it. So don't let the enemy, harm this beauty."

George looked at that "beauty" which was painted the typical dull tan with six humongous truck tires, a metal box mounted on top with a machinegun barrel sticking out from it. He noticed that it had three small windows in the area he would sit as a watcher. A larger and more fortified vehicle, it actually bore no resemblance to its predecessor, the inimitable Humvee that had cost so many lives due to its flimsy body structure.

Ed Stevens spoke out, "How come we could not get one of those M.R.A.P.'S with a ceramic V-shape bottom that is said to cause roadside bombs to glance off when exploded?"

The sergeant responded, "Believe me, you are getting one of the best made. Those ones with the ceramic bottoms are not what they are cracked up to be. You will see. Now, if there are no more silly questions, how about you men manning the vehicle and joining the convoy."

The convoy moved out traveling at a moderate speed over a paved road, but after three miles it became a gravel path covered with sand which remained from the recent sand storm. They were soon eating dust with almost zero visibility from the dust kicked up from the forward vehicle. On top of that the wind had kicked up and was blowing the tops off the sand dunes present on each side of the road making traveling hazardous since these vehicle were made to travel roads, not sinking sand. Ed Stevens was earning his pay keeping the vehicle on the road through GPS readings, staying in radio contact with the other vehicles in the convoy, twisting knobs and hitting levers on his electronic equipment, busy as the proverbial one-arm paper hanger.

295

The convoy was about ten miles from the forwarding base when George spotted wires exposed in a sand dune,

He quickly hollered, "Halt! Stop the vehicle!"

About one hundred feet behind the vehicle in front of them, they halted. Rex the machine gunner had not seen the wires. He said, "What is it Sergeant Murfrey?"

"I see wires going from that dune about one hundred yards at three o'clock. We should check them out."

"I don't see anything," said Rex. "Look, Sergeant Murfrey, this road has already been closely covered by the Route Clearance Platoon. If those wires were there, they would have found them. We are holding up the convoy. Don't make us the laughing stock of the base on our first time out."

By the time Rex had delivered his short speech, George had opened the door to the rear of the M.R.A.P. and was running toward the wires with his rifle slung over his shoulder and wire-cutters in his left hand. He quickly tugged on the wires which exposed five crude pipe bombs, cutting the wires while lifting the trophy for all to see. It was then that he noticed a crude stone wall partially covered by sand that had blown up against it when suddenly an Arab rose up with a rifle that had a grenade attached to it. Before Rex could fire his machine gun, George had un-slung his rifle, pointed it at the man who was in the process of pulling the trigger, George's rifle barking just like in training at Kuwait; only George did not miss this target; the Arab toppling forward with the grenade rifle falling into the sand.

Finally, the machinegun rattled its deadly fire kicking up sand all around the fallen man some finding the prone body lifting it up as it was riddled. Rex next, trained his powerful gun on the stone wall, reducing it to gravel as chunks of stone flew into the air until he ran out of bullets revealing that there were no more insurgents hiding behind the wall.

"That was some fine shooting, George," said Ziggy.

"Yeah," broke in Ed Stevens. "I have never seen such sharp shooting. I called in the coordinates and the bomb squad is on their way. You are lucky Ole Rex here did not shoot at the grenade or you might be picking shrapnel out of your teeth."

"My ears are ringing," said George. "I guess I was just lucky."

Rex, who had come down from his turret said, "Next time, Sergeant Murfrey, let me do the shooting."

"I am sorry," said George. "I just reacted. Next one is yours."

"Damn right," said Rex indignantly. "That's my job. You spot 'em; I shoot 'em. Okay?"

"Sorry again," said George who was getting tired of Rex's ego when he had warned him of the wires beforehand. "Just trying to do my job the way I was taught. But like I said, the next one is yours."

"Hummp!" was all Rex said to this fat bastard who had stolen his thunder. He would wait to see if the next one would really be his.

The machine gunner's wait did not take long. The convoy continued toward its destination over the gravel goat path entering a small village where children were playing soccer, kicking the ball. The kids stopped playing to watch the huge vehicles belching diesel fumes as the first one, an M.R.A.P., lumbered through kicking up sand and dust. Women with their faces covered except for a slit showing their flashing eyes looked on warily. There were men in their dirty pantaloons type trousers and some with flowing robes and dirty turbans standing around trying to look nonchalant never taking their eyes off the convoy invading the perimeters of their town.

Watching back intently was Sergeant George Murfrey who studied their body language. Not liking what he saw, looking into their hard eyes, glaring at the soldiers with open hatred, the convoy passing before would be insurgents. Without thinking, George nervously reaching, for his M-16 rifle his hand finding the trigger mechanism sensing danger knowing that any second a violent attack could come, he called up to the machine gunner, "Get ready." But Rex either did not hear him or simply chose to ignore his warning, looking straight ahead like some majestic statute, the conquering hero.

The convoy was brought to a sudden halt when one of the rag-a-muffins kicked his beat-up soccer ball in front of the lead vehicle and ran in front of it to retrieve the loose ball.

While all eyes of the soldiers were on the young kid grabbing the dirty well used ball, George stayed focused on one of the bearded men

297

noticing that he too was not watching the child run in front of the mine resistant carrier but was walking slowly toward the convoy that had stopped; "Blackbeard" separating himself from the group of men he had been standing with. George noticed Blackbeard's comrades had now turned, walking away toward the shabby sand stone structures that resembled buildings, wind- blown and pocked.

As the man strode silently toward his vehicle fifty yards away, George reached over and hit the button that opened the back door of the carrier and as he had done before, letting himself out. By the time he had leaped out with rifle in hand the man was now running straight toward George shouting, "Death to America!" over and over in a highly distorted voice."

George quickly raised his rifle, easing his finger on the trigger, hearing, the rifle boom, feeling the shock of the rifle stock as it recoiled against his shoulder,

The man crumpling slowly, half his head blown off as George spit the words out, "Halt! Halt!"

Rex hearing the explosion swung his machine gun around toward the area the villager had once occupied in seemingly normal fashion; they had vanished. Even the children had scooted behind the structures leaving only George standing with rifle pointing at the form that had been a live human seconds before.

Rex muttered under his breath, "That fat jerk has really done it now. He is going to get it. That trigger happy bastard is gonna get it."

Still stationary, all guns in the convoy were trained on every conceivable target. Sergeant Ziegfield quickly hopped out of the open door pushing the M-16, George held, aside. Ignoring danger he next ran to the body of the fallen Arab and finding the Arab's right hand clenching a cord, unclenched the fingers from the dead man, releasing the cord. He then cautiously flipped open the robe covering the man's body, revealing a vest made of explosive sticks. Carefully, he began to remove the vest that was tied crudely around the dead man's body with a rope.

Breaking the silence, Ziggy said, "George, bring me those wire cutters if you please."

298

George brought the wire cutters on the double, his fat belly bouncing up and down, pig tail navel poking through, thinking he needed to get back on his diet abandoned since he had left the states,

Ziggy snatched the cutters and adeptly cut the wires that were attached to the firing mechanism only then after a few snips did he pull away the improvised explosive device and hold it up like a trophy for all to see.

"Give me a hand with this." George helped lift the body as Ziegfield searched for other weapons. "Been awhile since I have seen one of these devices   It is one of the older ones; most men never live to see one." Looking at George's shocked expression, he said, "George, how did you know?"

"I just knew. It was the way his eyes moved back and forth fluttering. His body's movements were unnatural. I just knew. That's all."

The other soldiers had come out of the back of their trucks, guns drawn. As before, someone brought a body bag and they scooped up the corpse now gathering flies in the hot sun taking him unceremoniously away. Sergeant Ziegfield carefully laid the unarmed explosive device in the back of the carrier.

"It's okay," Ziggy told the alarmed men. "I have deactivated it. I am taking it back for the experts to examine. It is a very old device. I bet they haven't seen one of these in a long time either. Stevens, give the okay for the convoy to move on."

As the convoy revved up the powerful diesel engines belching black smoke, the convoy moved slowly out of the tiny hamlet. None of the residents had ventured out as the convoy pulling out, was soon out of sight, kicking up dust and sand behind it.

As George sat there contemplating, no one said a thing, not even Rex, the machine gunner. "My first day out and I have just killed two men now totaling three lives I have taken, one by mistake and two on purpose", thought George.

Turning to Ziggy, he said, "I hope it won't be like this every day!"

"Outstanding and astounding!" shouted Ziggy over the roar of the engine. "On my last tour of duty here in Iraq, I witnessed only one insurgent killed. I saw a lot of our boys shot up, killed while others lost their legs and arms. You did good my friend. It could have been us instead of that suicide bomber. "

When the convoy pulled into operating base compound, the men in his Caimen vehicle crowded around George; after inspecting the disabled bomb more closely. Rex, who was shaken by the size of the device and the dead man's blood and parts of his brain now drying on the bomb, said, "It is alright by me how many people you shoot. Don't let me stop you. If that man had pulled that cord, we would have all been blown to bits. Sorry I ever yelled at you Murfrey."

"Yeah," chimed in Stevens. "You can be my watcher from now on. Thanks!"

"Same for me," said Eugene Gibbons in his soft country voice. "I never expected anything like this. You see all those training films and hear all that gobble-de-gook about the dangers, but it happens so fast!" He stuck out his hand to shake George's. "Thanks Murfrey."

By that time the rest of the convoy were crowding around George shaking his hand and patting him on the back until they were ordered to "Fall in!" and marched to their new quarters. Twenty soldiers had arrived to take the place of twenty anxious men waiting to be relieved from their duties at the compound which consisted of an area about one acre fenced in with razor sharp barbed wire on the bottom and the top. There was a tower thirty feet high, several plywood buildings that housed the men, and a small mess hall/recreation facility. The other shacks, as George called them, contained spare weapons and ordinance for weapons, and supplies. Other buildings contained the radio and radar scanners; another contained the diesel generators.

It was a cozy little place in the middle of nowhere, irresistible to the insurgents for attack.

"They always come at night," explained Ziggy. "In the day time they can be seen for miles before they could get close enough to attack. What they don't realize is that we can see them at night with night vision glasses, radar detectors and infrared devices. Depending on the size of the attack, a large force would be bombed by our air force and then helicopters would land additional light infantry to help out the soldiers here. So far every attack has been wiped out before they could do any real damage. I was surprised that we met the resistance on the way here. Maybe they are stepping up their attacks out here in the desert. They definitely did not want the convoy to reach this base."

"How long will these new troops have to stay here before they get replacements?" asked George.

"Generally, one or two months."

"Sounds like great fun."

The next morning the convoy headed back with twenty battle hardened men glad to leave the compound. They had been lucky; no casualties, no insurgents had made it within a mile of the perimeter of the compound.

On the way back, they passed through the same village where George had shot the suicide bomber the day before. There were no spectators or children playing this time, the convoy passing through it without incident. Back on duty George scanned the various dunes off the road. He spotted a suspicious one, reporting it to Sergeant Ziegfield who radioed the convoy to speed up since there seemed to be no visible wires, or visible personnel lurking in the area. Even then all guns were trained on the area in case anyone moved.

After the convoy passed, Ziggy said, "I guess you misjudged that dune."

George pulled out the wand, the decimator, and began pressing buttons to activate phone codes. Suddenly there was a loud "whump" behind them and a ball of flame shot up into the air one hundred feet showering the desert with shrapnel like hail. None reached the speeding convoy.

Rex, the machine gunner climbed down from his turret and said, "Damn, Murfrey. You did it again. You must have a sixth sense. I looked at that pile of sand and it looked alright to me. What tipped you off?"

"See those ripples in the sand made by the wind? There were no ripples around that dune. The sand had been brushed clean; that is what made me suspicious."

Rex turned to Sergeant Ziegfield and asked, "How come you didn't see it too? You are supposed to be a watcher."

"Oh, I saw it alright; I just thought I would let Sergeant Murfrey get the credit."

"Yeah! Sure. What kind of a watcher are you?"

"Why I watch Sergeant Murfrey," said Ziggy which was actually the truth.

CHAPTER TWENTY FIVE

The warrior

The dusty convoy pulled into the main base outside of Baghdad around mid-morning. While George was stowing his heavy duty armor, he was told to report to building MM immediately; a jeep was waiting to take him there. "What's this all about?" asked George suspiciously.

"You will see," said Ziggy, obviously in the know. "Go ahead. You don't need me. I have got to make my report and turn it in."

The sky was clear blue and the temperature was into the nineties when George, all dusty and sweaty walked into building MM, a small plywood shack much like those he had left that morning thirty miles away at the compound, a sign that the Americans did not plan to stay permanently which was a joke since it was a habit of the U.S. occupying forces to never leave completely except when forced out as in Viet Nam. A window air conditioner was chugging away keeping the one room noticeably cool.

He saluted the officer seated across an unpainted plywood table and was motioned to sit in one of the wooden chairs facing the small bald headed man with curly red hair surrounding his shiny dome and a short red beard at the bottom of his chin. After sitting down, he briefly took in his surroundings, a décor of unpainted plywood which surrounded him from the floor to the ceiling, wall to wall. Only two bookcases were stained light brown, emphasizing the wooden knotholes imbedded therein. On the desk were two LCD computer monitors facing the officer; one attached to a HP notebook and the other to a PC under the table. Several books on psychology leaned against each other in the bookcases props no doubt as they appeared new and unused while on the wall were framed degrees issued to Alfred Gustov Herringbone from several universities in the field of Psychology. The small man dressed in army fatigues, picked up his wire glasses and placed them on his face in order to examine this specimen more carefully. Instantly George knew he was in the office of a shrink; the plywood shack and the fatigues did not fool him a bit. The set of gold bars told him the officer was a captain, confirmed by a brass metal name plate on the desk stating that he was Captain Alfred G. Herringbone. The only luxurious item in the room was not the metal filing cabinet next to the shrink, but a high back leather swivel chair much like the one used in the Harrison County Circuit Court room by the presiding Judge at his trial so long ago.

George had a puzzled look on his face. Was this the same shrink he had encountered at Baltimore General Hospital? To George they all looked alike, except this one had red hair.

After the Captain identified himself, George asked in a quivering voice, "Do I know you? I mean, have we met before?"

"Why do you ask?"

"You look like a shrink I met once before in Baltimore."

"You mean Dr. Iskara Meanie at the Baltimore General Hospital? No I am not him, but I know of him."

"How did you know?"

"I have your complete psychological and medical file before me. Ours is a small world both for us "shrinks" and our patients. Do you know why you are here, George? You don't mind if I call you George?"

"Of course not; call me anything but call me for dinner." He laughed nervously at his own over used joke. "As you can see doc, I tend to laugh and joke when I get stressed out."

"No reason to worry, Sergeant," said the psychologist. He rose out of his chair and extended his hand across the plywood table in a gesture to shake his hand.

"It is my pleasure to shake the hand of a real hero--before we get down to business. Just relax, George. The Army is proud of you. I am proud of you, but you see; now when a soldier takes the life of the enemy, the army wants to know how it affected that soldier. Was this your first mission?"

"Yes Sir."

"How did it feel to have killed two insurgents?"

"It happened so fast-it was just a reflex–I really haven't had time to think about it. When I have a lot of time to worry about something, that's when I get really stressed out. So far I don't have a problem."

"Your file shows that you were charged with the death of a woman back in Gulfport. How did you handle that?"

"Being charged with it when I did not think I was responsible, did cause me a lot of stress, but as you know the Army took me in; now I have another life; Now I get praised for killing someone. Go figure."

"I have a note in the file that upon arriving here in Iraq, you had a nightmare that night. 'In coming!' What happened there?"

"Just a dream, Sir. We have had such intense instructions, movies, pictures and simulated combat in Kuwait, that I dreamed it was really happening; so real I thought we were actually under attack when I woke up. You want to know what is so strange? Within a minute later we were under attack. At first after I woke up the whole barracks with my yelling, the men began to curse me and call me names, but after the barrage began within seconds, they gave me credit of being clairvoyant of something. Now I am greeted with respect and awe; now isn't that funny."

"Do you think maybe you do have certain precognitive powers?"

"Not no but hell no! It was just a bad dream, but don't tell those believers that; I kinda like the respect; which in truth I never ever had in my whole life time."

"Well George, it is my opinion that you are indeed very special. It looks like you have found your niche in life so go do your duty and defend your country. But should you have any stressful problems don't hesitate to come in and see me. Meanwhile go back to your battalion with my blessing and follow your gut instincts; they seem to be on the money."

"Thank you Sir, but I am really only a product of excellent training. I reacted without giving it much thought. It was kill or be blown to bits; I had no choice."

After the interview, George was given psychological profile tests which a third grade student could figure out. He could see that if he marked the box at the end of the question one way, he was a well-rounded happy person; if he marked it the other way, he would be judged a depressed psycho ready for the nut house. He chose to be a happy person which pleased Herringbone considerably.

Next Herringbone handed him a series of pictures, more the same as the profile test. In one picture a man was leaning over a bridge peering down into dark gloomy waters, a barely visible moon up above obscured by grey clouds. It was obvious that the scene depicted a man contemplating suicide getting ready to jump into the dark pool below. He said, "It looks like a man looking into the water thinking about his girlfriend and the happy life ahead for him and her."

The rest of the pictures were more of the same and the answers given were all optimistic. Captain Herringbone congratulated him and told him he was recommending that he go back, resuming his duties as a watcher. He added, "By the way, George, did you know that you will probably be up for a medal?"

"A medal sir?"

"Yes, probably the Bronze Star from what I briefly heard."

When George ambled out of the Psychologist's office into the dazzling sunlight sending the temperature soaring into the high nineties, he noticed that his driver and jeep had disappeared causing him to have to walk back to his barracks. He found sergeant Ziggy sitting on his bunk reading a packet of what appeared to be orders.

Ziggy looked up. "How did it go?"

"Alright, I guess. I saw a shrink who said I was nutty as a pecan tree, but that was okay since while it is not a requirement to be here, it sure is an asset. I told him if he thinks I am bonkers, he should meet the fellows I hang around with. He wrote something down in his note pad and said he would try to get to you and Mutt later when he has time. So what are you up to; that looks like orders."

"They are. While you were off proving what everyone already knew, I was in contact with the colonel. You remember him? He wants me back, says I have done all I can do for you for the moment. He is quite proud of you and your progress. Looks like you did too good; now he is sending me back to the states, so you are on your own-at least for the next three months."

"Ziggy, I kinda got used to having you around. We made a good team."

"I know," said Ziggy. "I'll be back; you can count on it. By the way, you are the talk of the base getting two kills. It seems even good news travels fast, at least over here, but don't get too used to it. You are still with Special Forces. After the three months of riding around with convoys, you will be used for what you were really sent here for; so don't forget it. Being a watcher will prepare you for the mission that is sure to come. Memorize the lay of the land including each street you travel through. Being familiar with the territory may someday save your life. Hey, on the light side, I am not leaving on the convoy until fourteen hundred hours so why don't you come with me. I want to show you something."

George followed him walking through the dusty sand for about a half mile through rows of tents until they came upon a block filled with plywood shacks much like the one that was the psychologist's office. Inside was entirely different. All around the walls plywood shelf tables were fastened; on them were computers with web cams attached to the computers. Mostly officers were talking into the web cams as they sat in wooden chairs. There were about twenty soldiers using the computers as if it was a command center.

"Welcome to Skype," said Ziggy.

"What is that?"

"It is a free phone system where you can call long distance just about anywhere in the civilized world; that is provided the person you call also has a computer, web cam and the program Skype installed on their computer. I'll show you how it works."

Ziggy sat down at an unused computer, turned it on and with the mouse double clicked on the desktop icon on the computer monitor. When the program came up Ziggy, identified himself and then clicked on the name, Sarah Ziegfield.

He turned to George who was watching intently and said, "I am calling my wife. It is about two in the morning in New Jersey, but I have told her not to turn her computer off; which is next to her bed. This computer does not have a web cam, but you can get one at the PX and then you can see the other person.

"Hello," came a sleepy voice. "Is that you Ziggy? Do you know what time it is here? You woke me up."

"Hi, sweetheart. I've got George Murfrey with me and I am showing him how Skype works. Also, I am leaving Iraq today and should see you in about two days. Okay, I am hanging up; go back to sleep. Love you."

"Love you too." Click

"Man that is cool," exclaimed an excited Murfrey. "I am going to make sure that my mother and my girlfriend both get a computer and put Skype on it."

"As you can see these computers are used mostly by officers. If anyone questions your right to use them, just show them you ID card which lets them know you are in Special Forces and not to be trifled with. Be sure to buy a web cam at the Post Exchange; as you saw, not all of the computers are equipped with one."

Being in Special Forces had its perks. Actually George was a hybrid soldier, a watcher with the National Guard perhaps soon to be an assassin with the Special Forces. Unlike the other soldiers in his tent, he did no KP, no menial cleaning duties, no drills, and no parades, sleeping in the daytime when he felt like it; all of which was not questioned by the other soldiers, who now treated him with reverence.

After Ziggy departed, he found himself with time on his hands with nothing to do; maybe he would take a nap or go to the gym and work out. He had no idea where Mutt was located; maybe he would go and find him. Just as he was considering where he might find Mutt Hanson, in walked Mutt.

"Speak of the devil," said George. "I was just thinking about you."

Ignoring the remark, Mutt said, "Come on lets' go to the NCO Club and get a beer."

"Not me, I am not drinking beer at this time of day; besides it is illegal."

"Illegal! Meelegal. Come on; you can get a cup of coffee, wimp."

As the two walked to the NCO Club, George asked, "How come you aren't on duty today?"

"I thought I was smart and would see some action choosing the tank corps, but we don't use them unless it is in one of the big cities with paved streets. They bog down in the sand and the sand is always clogging up the mechanism. Grease and sand don't mix so they have us doing a lot of other things that don't make sense just to keep us busy. To answer your question, I paid a private to take my place and that is why I am here. Anymore questions?"

"Nein, Herr Kapitan."

They entered the club which was dark as a movie theater after coming in out of the sunlight. A few minutes later, it appeared that the club was empty except for a bartender in uniform polishing glasses with a dirty rag. Mutt went to the bar and returned with a beer and a cup of coffee.

"Guess who I ran into yesterday."

"No telling, but I am sure you are going to tell me."

"Your old pal, Big Jake Bannister and he is just as ugly looking as ever except he has a nice tan and is pissed off having to run everywhere like a goose with those other light infantry morons. He still blames you for all the trouble he got into, vowing to seek you out and beat your brains in. I told him if he messes with you, he will have to deal with me later."

"I am sure that put the fear of God in him," commented George dryly.

"Maybe it did and maybe it didn't, but it gave him food for thought. I wasn't kidding."

"Maybe he doesn't know that I am a member of the Swashbuckler Task Force and have already shot and killed two insurgents and you know what? I think of Big Jake as a terrorist. Maybe I will shoot him too. Just tell him that if you happen to 'Run' into him again."

"Is this my old friend George "Farts" Murfrey talking? You must have been hanging around me too long; how you have changed. I heard about your encounters, but I said to myself, "Was that some fluke?" I could not believe my ears. Maybe you don't need me to protect you anymore."

"I am in line to get the Bronze Star," said George changing the subject.

"That and a dollar will get you a cup of coffee here at the club. What pisses me off is that I haven't seen any action since I got here. There is not too much call for tanks out here-another government goof-up."

"I am sure your day will come," said George. "What about your action when you got shot by a Punjab? I am not sure such a place even exists. Did you make that up from reading Rudyard Kipling?"

"And I tagged you for being smart; you must not have taken world geography. When I refer to Punjab, I am talking about one of the richest and largest territories between Pakistan and India. Let me educate you a little. As you may know Pakistan and India don't like each other. They quarreled over Punjab so the British stuck their noses in the dispute and divided up the land giving the bulk of it to Pakistan. Sixty per cent of Pakistan's wealth lies in Pakistan-Punjab. I know you have heard of Islamabad; well that city is in Punjab."

"Is that where you were shot?"

"No, it was in the city of Lahore which is in Pakistan just across the River Ravi which divides India and Pakistan. You see, I was serving as a peace keeper."

"Hah!"

"Don't laugh. Maybe I wasn't trying to keep the peace, but anyway, I was curious since I heard that the people in Lahore spoke English so I stashed my rifle and crossed the river, entering the city. It is a large city with around eight million inhabitants. I had heard they had excellent restaurants and bars plus lots of good looking women."

"I know George, I should not have left my post, which was literally out in the middle of nowhere, but I was alone and bored and thought no one really cared; besides I wanted a T-bone steak. To make the story short, I found this great restaurant-bar which had a western décor. The waiters wore cowboy hats and they even had the skull of a dead cow nailed to the wall, which of course flies in the face of India with its sacred cows. Anyway I had the T-bone steak, something you can't get in India, and a lot of drinks. I even latched onto a brown skinned beauty with flashing brown eyes and a fine body; all was well except her boyfriend came in demanding she leave. They threw him out, but she slipped out the back door and when I left…bang! I got shot in the right buttocks. It just grazed me, but it bled a lot. I stuffed my handkerchief in the bullet hole, called a cab and made it back across the river in time for my relief to come on duty. They assumed I had been shot by a Pakistani from across the river breaking the cease fire agreement and when they asked if someone from Pakistan shot me, I told the truth: That was where the bullet came from. I did not tell them I was actually in Punjab, Pakistan at the time I was shot. I was taken to the hospital and spent a night there. It almost caused an international incident. I was sent back to Scotland for further healing and inquiries when somehow it leaked out that I had been over in Lahore. It had caused so much stink already that the Brits and the Scots were glad to be rid of me, so they gave me a medical discharge telling me not to ever say a word to anyone about what really happened.. I was given the small pension with that understanding; to keep my mouth shut or lose the pension—hush money so to speak. So now you know the truth so you have to keep your big trap shut if you want to get along with me."

"Not to worry. You haven't squealed on me being charged with murder in the states, so I owe you one."

"More than one George more than one."

When George returned to his barracks, a shave tail, Lieutenant Adkins, in charge of his platoon, sat on the side of his cot waiting for him.

"Where have you been?" he demanded. Before George could answer, he continued. "I don't know what kind of pull you have around here, but this has got to stop and I intend to put a stop to it."

"Better men with more rank than you have tried Lieutenant," said George smiling.

"What did you say? We will see about that!"

George remembering what Ziggy had told him what to do when an officer got on his case, seeing that this would be a good time to test it, he pulled out his I.D. that designated he was of Special Forces, handing it to the Lieutenant who rudely snatched it.

"What is this?" said the Lieutenant reading it over and over and mistaking him to be in another branch. "Uh, oh," said the Lieutenant. "You are not here investigating anyone are you Sergeant Murfrey?"

Enjoying the sudden change in the atmosphere, George said, "Now Lieutenant Adkins, you know I can't tell you that. I am sure we can work this out without me calling the Pentagon." It was all George could do not to laugh out aloud. "Now what was it you wanted?"

"There is a convoy forming up, leaving in forty minutes; your M.R.A.P. has been designated to be the lead vehicle. I am sorry, but when I could not find you, I panicked since you seem to be an integral part of the Swashbuckler Task force. My jeep is right outside, so I would appreciate it if you grabbed your gear and rode with me to the area where your comrades are waiting. This is an important mission. I have been informed that a battalion of marines are being flown in to try to deal with the stepped up effort by the insurgents; with them there are Senators and Congressmen plus other dignitaries who are on a fact finding mission. So you see how important it is that everything goes right."

"Thank you for sharing that with me Lieutenant; I am ready to go."

When George Murfrey was assigned to the position of a watcher in the M.R.A.P. that protected the convoy, he was of the misguided opinion, that the purpose of the convoy was to act as a decoy to draw the enemy out so the army and marines could fight back. The earlier convoys consisted of trucks and Humvees trying to fight back when all it took was one man pushing a button or pulling a trigger to blow the Humvees to kingdom come. When the insurgents became really serious, they used rockets, rifle grenades trucks and cars packed with explosives to knock out the convoys obliterating the troops, except for the maimed solders that survived. It was like living in the jungle, riding in the convoys, where no one knew from day to day if he or she would be around the next day either, being placed in a body bag or flying to Germany for immediate treatment and then home without vital body parts. The insurgents posed all kinds of dangers sending women and children out to blow themselves up killing everyone in close proximity. Their trucks failing to stop at check points were filled with explosives that leveled whole blocks. Mortar shells fell and were still falling at night on the various camps. Instant destruction that brought about shock and chaos was the result. The lucky soldiers just suffered traumatic stress syndrome disorders.

With all that destruction going on, the only way the coalition troops could be sustained was through convoys—the life blood of the occupying army in Iraq. This notion that the main purpose of the convoy was to act as a decoy, as George found out first hand, was pure bull. In order to bring in soldiers marines and civilians and take them to various designated areas, the responsibility rested with the convoy. If the convoys were blown up and destroyed, the supplies they protected, did not reach the troops. That the convoy was the life blood of the army was an understatement!

After becoming part of the convoys, George came to realize that to kill the convoy was to stop the army in its tracks. Without the convoy this torn country could not be rebuilt.

Being chosen to be the lead vehicle in a convoy traveling to Baghdad round trip was an honor that went along with the great responsibility. The Swashbuckler Task Force had acquitted themselves well in the countryside; now was the time to be tested on the city run.

George tapped Rex on the back seeing that Rex was half in and half out of this turret crouched down. "See that ledge over there at 2:15," he shouted. Train your machinegun on that ledge."

Rex shouted back, "I don't see nothing, but I'll play your silly game." He swung the turret around facing the ledge, his fingers on the trigger ready to fire. "How do you know, Murfrey?"

"Just a hunch; it is a good place for an ambush. Watch out!"

Like in the drills the machine gunners had gone through, up popped the target, except this time the target was a real man wearing a turban, a stripped gown along with a rifle sporting a deadly grenade at the end of the barrel.

Rex was ready. Before the insurgent could lock in his target, Rex squeezed off three hundred rounds in a second and watched as the man and the wall in front of him being torn to pieces.

"Any more?" asked Rex who had come down from the turret and was blowing imaginary smoke away from his index finger.

"Could be, but after that blast I don't think anyone will stick his head out for a repeat performance," said George.

"You are a damn good watcher," said Stevens.

The convoy continued down the highway crossing the Euphrates River and into the airport where the incoming troops had already arrived along with supplies The guardsmen, that were leaving Iraq, made their way to the large C-17 airplanes waiting to fly them back to their loved ones while the fresh incoming soldiers and marines looked on in amazement as they heard words spoken of gratitude directed to the Swashbucklers and the other M.R.A.P.'S that had been a part of the convoy. What they did not know was that the greatest danger was usually on the return trip. Nothing would demoralize the fresh troops more than being shot up, killed and arriving at their new base without the necessary supplies-very disheartening indeed, to see your best buddy taken away by the medics with his legs or arms blown off and not even seeing the enemy who always seemed to slip away unscathed.

George was the only watcher in his Caiman vehicle; Sergeant Ziegfield had not been replaced. Thus, he was given the duty of having to watch both sides of the road and beyond. On the outskirts of Baghdad the returning convoy traveled down the bleak highway which was level except for a few sand dunes on each side where I.E.D's could be hidden-not to mention the debris and trash scattered everywhere seemingly never cleaned up.

This scenario reminded George of the wild west movies he had seen as a child where the Indians, who knew the troops were coming, covered themselves up in the sand, springing up to ambush the "blue coats" when they passed.

"Put a few shells into that pile of trash about one hundred yards ahead for good measure and then train on that sand dune almost across from it."

Rex, who enjoyed firing the machine gun, quickly fired on both targets and instantly there were two explosions, the one on the right producing a huge ear shattering ball of orange and black flame and the dune on the left throwing out shrapnel that could be seen as it cascaded across the highway in front of the convoy with only a few steel balls and pieces of metal, having their force dissipated, bounding off the protected Caiman Medium Tactical Vehicle.

One of the metal balls put a star type crack into the windshield; Eugene Gibbons swore with a country twang, "Damn it all to hell! They done cracked my windshield."

Rex, dropping down from his turret, said, "One of those ball bearings bounced off my helmet; I am lucky one didn't hit me in the face."

"You better get back up there Rex," said George. "I don't think they are through. Ed I think it would be a good idea for you to call for air support to stand by in case we need them."

As the convoy ambled on down the dusty road, out of nowhere, came a beat-up tiny old worn out Toyota pick-up truck heading from the opposite direction.

"Fire a burst of rounds in front of that truck and warn them off, Rex."

"I see it, Murfrey." The fifty caliber machine gun sounded off as the two vehicles closed on each other. The Toyota slowed down, but did not stop. The Toyota continued to creep slowly forward.

Rex hollered, "What do we do now, Sergeant Murfrey?"

"When he gets within a quarter mile, let him have it; he knows better and he got the message."

As the Toyota crept closer, the drivers' door swung open and the driver jumped out in a roll and got up running across the sand.

Gibbons, the driver brought the M.R.A.P. to a screeching halt while Rex pulverized the vehicle with a swarm of flying bullets and suddenly the unmanned truck blew up sending shock waves and ear shattering sound over the area with another large orange ball of fire followed by thick black smoke, rising into the air several hundred feet. Then out from behind a large sand dune on the left about twelve men rose up, their bearded faces covered with sand; they we shooting something in Arabic and charging with AK-47's and rifles with grenades. George looked to the right, seeing the same scene repeating

315

itself. Bullets were bouncing off the armor plate of the Caiman; Rex was firing furiously enjoying himself while Ed Stevens excitedly called for air support.

It was a full scale battle.

As the smoke cleared in front where the banged-up Toyota had detonated, George could see a large crater where the road had once been; it had to measure fifty feet across. There was nothing left to do but fight; they were caught in a cross fire. All the other M.R.A.P.s' were firing at the insurgents who were dropping like fly spray hitting a swarm of flies from the deadly machine gunnery. It sounded like bees zinging and pinging as the AK-47's bullets hit the vehicles. All of a sudden one tore into Rex's helmet dropping his lifeless body down into the Caiman interior. Blood was pouring out of the left side of his head. Gently Eugene and Ed grabbed Rex and eased him into the seat next to George.

"Take care of him and stop the bleeding. I am taking his place." George then climbed up into the turret and began to train the powerful weapon on the closest insurgents, cutting them down like wheat. He swung the gun to the other side and began to fire on men who had grenade propelled rifles. One got his grenade off, but luck was with the convoy: his aim was bad and the grenade exploded twenty yards away without wounding any one.

George could hear the put-put of the helicopter that suddenly appeared, firing on the insurgents from up above. As one insurgent tried to train, his rocket launcher, on the copter, George blasted the man fire the device. He could see the open space in the Blackhawk and saw the machine gunner giving him a "thumbs up".

Just as quickly as the battle began, men's bodies having been cut into, turbaned heads destroyed, bloody splotches being absorbed into the thirsty sand, no more fanatic shouts, guns silent, the flying gunship turning back to its base; it was all over.

"What happened?" mumbled Rex who was conscious now wore a bloody makeshift bandage around his head resembling a turban. "It's hot in here!" Then as George slipped down from the machine gun turret, Rex said, "Why were you up there with my machine gun?"

"Just checking it out Rex; you can have it back. Good to see you made it. Looks like you earned a Purple Heart. Congratulations."

The marines in to convoy helped build a temporary road around the crater while the soldiers took care of the dead and wounded. Within twenty minutes the task was complete; the convoy rolled on intact, a few wounded, but no causalities, the seriousness of the war learned quickly by the new green troops being brought in to take over where those who flew out that morning yo go home.

Rex was gathered up with the other wounded including five insurgents captured and in bad shape. The convoy had greater success than the insurgents, whose count was nineteen dead. Sergeant Murfrey as the new machine gunner fired his weapon five times during the trip to the main base; two of his short bursts exploding two suspicious trash piles in the distance. Other than those two explosions, there were no more significant incidents to report.

Lieutenant Adkins, who had been displeased with Sergeant Murfrey, now congratulated him, telling him he was now the machine gunner and Antoine Jones, the black man from Vicksburg, Mississippi returning to fill the vacant position left by Murfrey, was now the watcher. Rex Welby was out with a severe concussion, sixteen stitches in his head and complaining of diminished vision; whether he would make it back was anyone's guess including the doctors who treated him. He was given light duty.

Every other day the Swashbucklers lead the convoy to Baghdad International Airport to pick up incoming troops and needed supplies. The insurgents had no success in stopping the trips, now using snipers who focused on the fat machine gunner who fired back with such accuracy that they pulled back from shooting at one hundred yards to two hundred yards. Even then George pinpointed the snipers and injured or killed some daily. He had an uncanny ability to anticipate their exact presence and was ready when they exposed themselves to try a shot: it was them against George Murfrey, whom they concentrated on, trying to remove him from his protected turret being only able to inaccurately hit the armor plate with their bullets zinging like buzzing bees. One bullet did strike George's kevlar helmet and another struck his bullet proof vest which merely left a bruise about the size of soft ball, but George's bullets put that shooter out of commission permanently as the force of the fifty caliber bullets threw the insurgent backward, brutally tearing his body apart.

Soon, the insurgents just left the convoy alone; they had gone back to the drawing board, cooking up some new idea of how to solve the problem of the fat accurate machine gunner who was losing his girth through diet and exercise at the gym, now being able to squeeze into the turret without any trouble since he was down to two hundred ninety pounds having lost sixty pounds since joining the army and gaining some back; it was a see-saw battle of the girth.

Sergeant George Murfrey, 155th Brigade, Mississippi National Guard with the U.S. Army in Iraq had found he was good at what he did: shooting and killing insurgents. He did it on reflex without thinking of the consequences having all the necessary attributes and qualifications that it took: twenty-ten eyesight, a steady hand, and the ability to spot road side bombs and highly suspicious suicide bombers plus he did not flinch under fire mainly because he had a don't give a damn attitude. He had learned his instructions well; plus using his past knowledge of spotting various fish while fishing in the Gulf of Mexico, he utilized his knowledge and experiences without realizing it. Now he was combat hardened; educated further in battle.

The Swashbuckler Task Force was the number one M.R.A.P., leading the convoys. The high command took notice along with the insurgents, who, when they saw Sergeant Murfrey manning his machine gun, after losing valuable sharp shooting snipers, decided to prey on the easier convoys leaving the Swashbucklers alone. Thus, the insurgents refused to make Sergeant Murfrey more famous; they left his convoys alone, letting them pass through without incident for the time being.

Colonel Benson received daily reports about his man in the field who like a duck taking to water, was getting his feet wet. Soon the three months "feel of combat" would be over and George would be pulled out to rejoin Special Forces where his other skills could be utilized on secret missions.

The order came through for Sergeant George Murfrey to be given the Bronze Star for his meritorious service and bravery, but George was not allowed to receive it publically on the parade ground; Colonel Benson, for security reasons vetoed that. He did not want Sergeant Murfrey to have any more publicity than he already had. Murfrey did not exactly blend in with the other soldiers being that he was overweight, a poor example for the other men. And there was the enemy who had their eyes and ears all over the base in spite of efforts to the contrary. George would get his medal in a very private ceremony, being told not to wear it in Iraq.

"Not in my wildest dreams," said Colonel Alan Benson. "Next thing I know Murfrey will be up for the Medal of Honor."

"I tried to tell you when I came back to the States," said Sergeant Ziegfield. "I have never seen anyone so cool under fire. It was just like he was going about his business. He hit the button, popped open the rear door of our M.R.A.P., got out without a howdy do, after clipping wires to an I.E.D. taking aim at the rag head who was trying to shoot a propelled rifle grenade into our convoy, shooting him right through his forward, a clean shot that removed the man's head. You should have seen it Alan. Then later he sees this insurgent all trussed up with turban and billowing robe coming at us like he was some greeter. So what does our George do? He shatters his head or part of it with another clean shot. I got out and was going to remove the explosives under the robe, but I needed the wire snips so I holler to George, 'George, bring me the wire cutters' and with every one looking on but not about to get out of their vehicles, George is back with the wire cutters. He is a cool one, our George."

"Are you going to pull him out of the field before his time is up; he is ready now."

"No. Ziggy. He has three more weeks before he goes back to Special Forces. I think I will leave him there," said the Colonel, thoughtfully as he stroked his chin. "My latest report shows that the insurgents don't fire on those convoys when they see George manning the machine gun. Their conclusion: There are too many others for easy picking, but when they pick on George, they lose their sharpshooters.

Several weeks ago there was a real battle where Rex Welby his machine gunner got hit and George took over as machine gunner mowing down-- we don't know how many of the charging insurgents he nailed, but the insurgents came off quite badly that day. I am telling you that boy is a one man wrecking crew. At least it will be peaceful and safe for those traveling in George's convoy. Those three weeks will go by quickly. I don't think there will be much more action for our boy Sergeant George Murfrey until we use him."

"Don't count on it." was Sergeant Ziegfield's prophetic utterance. "That man has a history of being in the midst of stuff happening and when it is quiet, he starts something on his own. Maybe, I ought to go back to Iraq to oversee the next event."

"That won't be necessary, Ziggy. We need you here. Just three more weeks and you can be back in action."

While the Colonel and his trusted right hand man were having their discussion, the intercom blared, "Colonel there is a Captain Shirtain calling from Iraq."

"Colonel Benson, here," said Benson while putting the phone on speaker. "How may I help you, Captain?" He continued to sip his coffee placed before him.

"Colonel, I note in Sergeant George Murfrey's file that any changes in his duties, you are to be notified."

"That's right Captain. You are a little late; I already found out that he was made a machine gunner. No problem. Do I detect a Mississippi Delta drawl?"

"Sir, that is not why I am calling; we are cutting orders to send Sergeant Murfrey to Kirab, Northern Iraq."

"What! On whose orders!" roared Colonel Benson spilling his coffee, while rising up from his brown leather swivel chair. Ziggy was openly laughing with an "I told you so" look.

"From Headquarters, 155th Brigade, Major General Emanuel McDougal. Don't shoot me, sir; I am just the messenger."

Benson sat down composing himself and with a quiet voice said, "And do you happen to have General McDougal's phone number? I would like to talk to him."

"Yes sir," said Captain Shirtain snappily. "He is right here at this very moment in the Headquarters' building. Would you like me to connect you to him?"

"Yes, but make sure we are connected on a protected phone. The special code is SPL0z55."

"Just a minute, Colonel Benson," said Captain Shirtain from Indianolia, Mississippi smiling to himself.

After about a three minute wait while Shirtain walked down to the General's office, relating what had transpired so far, coding the phone for protection from enemy ears, putting the instrument on speaker phone so that he would not miss any of the conversation, the General came on the phone. He drawled, "Colonel Benson, you got a problem with our assignment of Sergeant Murfrey to naughthen Iraq?"

"Yes, I have, but first let me ask you why he is being transferred. Did he do anything wrong?"

Major General Emanuel Horatio McDougal was one of the good 'Ole boys found in Mississippi having been appointed to his position of Supreme Commander of the 155th Brigade, National Guard by his drinking buddy, the Governor. When he saw Sergeant Murfrey, he was delighted with his look-a-like; both having almost identical pot bellies; only the General's girth was earned through hard drinking of beer and whiskey at social events, deep sea fishing expeditions and poker games plus a little "high on the hog" eating.

"Why Cournal Banson, Sergeant Murphy has been wourking havoc…" He paused to take a puff on his big fat stogie, a product of Cuba, and continued, "on the enemee that is. When it comes to leading a con-voy, he has utterly demoralized the Al Kite-ter. He is head and shoulders above any one we have. Why I am proud to call him a Mississippian; wish we had more like him saving lives of those Yankee boys you all send over hear to fight. If it wasn't for him, I might not be smoking this here seegar. Since he has been in the lead M.R.A.P, we have had no loss of life on his con-voys in over a month."

The General laughed.

"Say Colonel, where did you find that fat fucker, anyway? I believe he has me beat. You know he was awarded the Bronze Star.

Was that on your orders that I could not give him the metal on the parade grounds, having to give it to him in my office with instructions not to wear it? You spooks in Special Forces sure try to be klan-dest-tine. When I saw that porker squeeze through the door, I thought to myself, that boy's belly is bigger than mine and I got mine honestly. What have you all been feeding that boy?"

"With due respect, General, I know all that. He is a member of Special Forces, recruited and trained by me. We have great plans for Sergeant Murfrey and it doesn't include losing him in northern Iraq. By the way General, our plans for Sergeant Murfrey out-weigh yours. You can check with the Pentagon on that if you wish."

"No need for that. Look Colonel Bensong," the General drawled. "We are literally getting killed with our convoys in Naurthern Iraq. It is disgraceful. Our boys do everything they can to get out of being on the con-voys; you know: sick calls, vehicles that won't start and any other ingenious excuses they can think of. We are getting blasted and it breaks my heart to award the Purple Heart to those brave men who lost their arms, legs and other body parts. We are running out of medals."

"Now Colonel if you will release 'Ole Murphy, maybe we can have some success in stopping this carnage as we have in South Iraq. I am rounding up look-a-like fat boys to take his place in the South so we won't lose the momentum. So how about it?"

Colonel Benson was silent while he studied the request. Finally he said, "Can you do it in three weeks? In three weeks we start operation flatter blaster. I have to have your guarantee we can have him back in three weeks."

"Wal Colonale, I guess three weeks is better than none. Are you sure you can't give us more time; three weeks is not much time."

"Not on your life. The operation I mentioned, which by the way is highly classified, is being drawn up as we speak. Everything has to fit into place precisely in order to go off without a hitch. Another thing, when Sergeant Murfrey joined the Army; he went in on the buddy system bringing his buddy with him. The Army is committed to having his pal, Corporal Iverson Hanson no further away than sixty miles at all times."

"No problem; I will see that Orders are cut that include Corporal Hanson going to Naurthern Erak too-day."

"What about the other members of the Swashbuckler Task Force, will they be traveling with Murfrey?"

"Wal, the way I see it," drawled the General as he blew a satisfied smoke ring from his cigar. "It would be better to let those boys learn to get along without Sergeant Murphy since you say they will lose him in three weeks. Between you and me, Colonale, we got us a look-a-like fat boy from the mess hall to sit up there in the Sergeant's place. That oughta fool them for a while until they find out he can't shoot too good."

Colonel Benson smiled; the Mississippi General may talk southern, but was no dummy. He liked the General's thinking.

"I like your sneaky way of thinking, General McDougal; ever thought of joining Special Forces? I would like to look you up when I arrive in Iraq in three weeks."

"You are cordially welcome, son. You just come on by and I will have a glass of Southern Comfort waiting for you."

"Throw in a Mint Julip and I will surely drop by."

CHAPTER TWENTY SIX

Battlefield conversion and commission

The Swashbucklers had just pulled into camp, depositing their M.R.A.P. to be checked, repaired, gassed up and made ready for the next convoy. It was three in the afternoon and everyone was tired as they shed their heavy protective gear wet with body sweat, crashing to the wooden floor.

"Another quiet day; thank the good Lord," exclaimed Eugene Gibbons.

"I just hope we don't get complacent," said Ed Stevens. "I think I will go down to the firing range and get in a few targets. Anyone want to join me?" He looked at George.

"Don't look at me," said George. "I am meeting my buddy Mutt at the NCO Club. Don't worry about me getting stale. I am so keyed up, I am about to jump out of my skin."

"All you will leave is a tub of lard," said Ed Stevens, dryly. "I will say this: no one calls you fat bastard anymore."

Everyone laughed.

About that time a jeep pulled up in a screeching halt, throwing a cloud of tan dust over the area; those who had already pulled off the heavy protective gear, were out of uniform. Out stepped Captain Shirtain from Headquarters and in his hand was a fist full of papers.

"Attention!" shouted Sergeant Murfrey in his best military manner causing each man to drop his heavy gear and snap to attention.

"At ease men! Go about your business; except for Sergeant Murfrey."

"Oh my," said George in his inimitable way when stressed. "What did I do now? Forget to shoot some Arab?"

Ignoring the attempt at humor from this man who did not even flinch when addressing a superior officer, remembering who he was; an exceptional soldier tied in with Special Forces with a lot of pull, the Captain said, "Get your gear together, Sergeant; you are being transferred to Kirab, Northern Iraq. I will drive you over to your barracks to get the rest of you stuff. We have a helicopter standing by to transport you and Sergeant Hanson up there."

"Did you say Sergeant Hanson, sir? There must be some mistake."

"No mistake. I saw the paperwork," said the Captain smiling. "You are not the only one with pull. What do they put in the water down there in Gulfport? Don't answer that, we are in a bit of a hurry."

"Captain, in all due respect," said Ed Stevens who had been listening in. "Just what are we to do without our machine gunner? Are we confined to the base?"

"No such luck, soldier," said Captain Shirtain. "Tomorrow you will have a new gunner. You all will be alright."

"That's easy for you to say," said Stevens under his breath kicking the floor with his left foot in disgust, raising a small cloud of tan dust The Swashbucklers had been given a new watcher who did almost nothing in spotting roadside bombs and insurgents, letting Murfrey do all the work; now Murfrey was being transferred. When the insurgents find out the fat man was gone, they would be the target in the convoy shooting gallery once more.

Three hours later, Murfrey and Hanson were on the ground at Camp Taji, Iraq; another dusty lifeless hot hell hole but at least with some sparse greenery. They were separated upon landing; Sergeant Murfrey hustled to meet his new crew and recently promoted Sergeant Hanson went to his new unit where he inspected the Bradley tank he would be driving, a machine that looked as if it had not been properly maintained for quite a while. Because he had taken charge, seeing that the Bradley's at his former base, were properly serviced and maintained he had been promoted to Sergeant and given that responsibility. Now he could put his skills to use at the new base and the equipment ostensibly showed the need of it.

He had told George, "I took over inspecting the Bradleys out of self-preservation and they promoted me and made me in charge. How do you like those apples?"

At another large tent called a barracks, George let his gear and duffle bags crash to the floor in front of the bunk assigned to him.

325

"Are you the new machine gunner? Let me be the first to greet you. My name is Jolly Carter from Anguilla. I will be your driver."

George looked at this lanky country boy; must have been six foot four.

He shook his extended hand. "I am you man. Where is Anguilla?"

"It is a small town out from Rolling Fork."

"And where is Rolling Fork?"

"You don't know much about your state. You are bound to have heard of Yazoo City where our Governor is from. No? How about Jerry Clower?"

"Oh, yes. I have heard of Jerry Clower, the comedian—loved that joke about the wild cat and the man in the tree. Guess I don't know much about Mississippi. I did not travel much before joining the army except to Baltimore, Maryland, a town I want to forget."

"Era, era, Youse sposed to be our new machine gunner; the last one got his head blowed off. I am your watcher, I am Samuel Skinner from Arcola, probably never hear-tell of that town neither, but neither has no one else—it's out from Greenville."

"You got me there. I am from Gulfport." George was looking at the blackest man he had ever laid eyes on and shook his hand.

"My friends call me 'Sambo' but not little black Sambo."

Before George could say, "Glad to meet you," a stumpy heavy set soldier stuck out his hand and said, "I am Jason Williamson from Tupelo. They call me Stumpy."

"I know about Tupelo, the birthplace of Elvis Presley, but never been there. Glad to meet you Stumpy. I bet you are our radioman."

"How did you know?"

"A wild guess," said George laughing along with his new crew. "What happened to the last machine gunner?"

"We wuz in our Humvee and Eggerton Phillips, he was firing at some terrorists and they were throwing everything at us they could dream up. We had welded these here steel plates on the side of our Humvee or we would not be here shaking hands with you today," said Stumpy. "Anyway, we don't know if it was a roadside I.E.D. or one of those rifle grenades, but an explosion rocked the Humvee and when we all came to, the top was blown off along with Eggerton's machine gun and head. Only good that came out of that battle was we got us a new M.R.A.P. which our Lieutenant says can't be exploded, but we know he is lying. We ain't ever used it yet; been waiting for our replacement gunner to arrive."

"You wanna go over and do a look see?" said Sambo, their watcher.

"Naw" said George. "Seen one-seen them all. Sorry about your machine gunner. Ours got hit also; that is how I got my job. I have been hit twice by bullets, but no flesh wounds. I took one in the helmet and my vest stopped another bullet."

"How many missions you been on?" asked Jason Williams, the radioman in a quiet voice.

"Thirty-six so far."

"Never got blowed up?" asked Samuel Skinner aka Sambo.

"A few close calls, but I am still here aren't I? Like I said, I have been pretty lucky," said George.

"Better to be lucky than good," commented another.

"I am both lucky and good," said George.

They all laughed.

"Glad to hear that; hope your luck holds out. Most of us are scared to go out on those shooting galleries they call convoys. Glad to have a machine gunner who is both lucky and good even if you don't know where Anguilla or Arcola are located," said Stumpy.

The next day, Sergeant Murfrey met Lieutenant Leonard Cubbertson fresh out of Officer Training School. From Magee, Mississippi, Culbertson was revered by his men for his reputation as a football player who had led Magee to a State championship, had gone on to play for Ole Miss getting Honorable mention, All SEC as a quarterback. His wide receiver, Marlon Jefferson, also from Magee High School followed him to Ole Miss and was both all SEC and All American. Both had joined the National Guard and instead of pursuing a career in pro-football, were called up and found themselves sweating it out with a one year tour of duty in Iraq.

In twenty-two days, their tour would be up.

327

Culbertson had met Sergeant Murfrey later on the day of his arrival. George was told that he was welcome, but that although he came on good recommendations, his M.R.A.P. would not be the lead vehicle the next day, because he wanted George to become more familiar with the territory. That made sense to George who was used to decisions by officers, even if they weren't always right. The saying among the enlisted men was: "I will play your silly game."

"I have got something for you, Sergeant Murfrey. Let me have your rifle."

George handed over his M-16 rifle. In turn the Lieutenant handed over a brand new M-16 A-1 with a 4X scope.

"Do you know a Colonel Benson?" asked Culbertson. "He sent you this rifle with the message to use it when necessary. I guess you know what it is, Sergeant."

"Yes sir; it is a sniper's rifle that will shoot eight hundred rounds a minute and has a range up to one thousand yards," said George.

"Well, good; I hope you don't have to use it. Stick to your machine gun for now; that is your job." Culbertson shook his head when he looked at this cocky, roly-poly fat man who was now given a sniper rifle; maybe he was what he was cracked up to be, as he was highly touted for his skills at spotting and dispatching I.E.D.'S, suicide bombers, grenade launching insurgents and snipers. According to his records, Sergeant Murfrey had even received the Bronze Star, a medal not given out lightly. "You never know", he thought.

The next day the convoy was formed, bringing wounded, who could be returned to duty after treatment, at Najaf, where they had hospital facilities. The sun was already making it hot and the men were sweating and drinking from water bottles. Lieutenant Culbertson was tempted to put Murfrey's M.R.A.P. as the lead vehicle, but decided to use the one where his high school and college buddy, Marlon Jefferson, also a machine gunner whom he knew well, respected highly and could be counted on when the going got tough. Meanwhile, he would keep an eye on this newest machine gunner to see how well he handled himself.

Both machine gunners, Jefferson and Murfrey would man the newly provided M.R.A.P.'s. The men, who were to use them, believed them to be almost indestructible; that day there were less sick calls and absentee's.

Besides the M.R.A.P.'s protecting the convoy, there was supposed to be a Bradley light tank, a high speed fighting vehicle, but it was delayed as it did not pass inspection by newly promoted Sergeant Mutt Hanson because of numerous mechanical problems such as clogged carburetors, brakes that were very soft, water in the fuel tank and the gun turret would not turn.

If they could get the Bradley started, they would ignore the brake problems and the stuck gun turret, joining the convoy later.

Lieutenant Culbertson would be riding in the medical supply vehicle; several vehicles behind the one Sergeant Murfrey occupied. Culbertson was hoping that today they would be lucky and not be hit by the insurgents. As they were climbing into the respective vehicles, George told Stumpy, "I don't know why I was sent up here if they are not going to use me."

Overhearing the remark, Lieutenant Culbertson retorted, "You will get your chance, Sergeant; don't you worry."

The insurgents did not even wait until the convoy was returning with medical supplies; hitting the convoy when it was about fifteen miles out. They were coming into one of those small villages George had learned to distrust with its debris, garbage and burned out automobiles strewn along the road. This day there seemed to be more trash than usual, but George did not know what was usual on this particular road. Behind the piles of trash and debris were rather large sand dunes; the perfect place for an ambush.

Suddenly the M.R.A.P., where Marlon Jefferson was the machine gunner seemed to explode and rise up into the air about fifteen feet. The sound was deafening. The men in the convoy stunned into silence; could not hear the guns firing on them.

The convoy stopped dead in its tracks.

Men in Arabic clothing suddenly arose from behind the sand dunes where they had been hiding. There seemed to be about fifteen to twenty of them on each side of the convoy. George had not time to count them as they rushed toward the convoy, some with automatic rifles and others with rifles that propelled grenades. Immediately George opened up on the charging insurgents with his machine gun going clack-clack- clack as it struck home on men on each side, swinging his gun from side to side. This sent the attackers back behind the protection of the sand dunes while their snipers began to fire on exposed soldiers in the convoy including, Sergeant Murfrey who fired back. Bullets were zinging and pinging around George's turret; so far he had been lucky catching the insurgents off guard who expected this to be an easy attack.

They had been shouting "Death to America" in English before being driven back. Soon they would set up a mortar attack and the convoy would be doomed. Like a busy cat covering up the results of its bowel movement, George turned his gun on three men to his left; two had AK-47's and one with a propelled grenade rifle. They went down like weeds being cut with a scythe. On his right side in a window of one of the villages' two story houses made of concrete, a sniper stuck his rifle out to fire on George. George ducked down and came up with his new M-16 A-1 sniper rifle, training his rifle through the cross hairs of his telescope, firing a burst at the sniper, seeing him flung back inside the house. Next, a suicide bomber came out from behind the same house; George shot him also, creating a loud explosion. George could hear his radio operator calling in for help. "Where was that Bradley? We are taking heavy fire!"

George could hear the machine gun's clack-clack-clack from the M.R.A.P. several vehicles in the rear. He stuck his head down into his vehicle and shouted to his watcher whose name he could not recall, "Get up here and take over this machine gun. I am going up front to see if we can get this convoy moving."

Taking his sniper rifle with him, George hopped out of the left side firing short bursts into the dunes on that side while sticking close to the vehicles on his right. It seemed the sniper fire had come from the houses in the village which were situated on his right. He had heard someone yell, "Help is on the way. He fired on suspicious debris up ahead and out of the two, one exploded. This ambush area had been mined with explosives. Shrapnel scudded across the area in front peppering the stalled vehicles where the personnel chose to remain inside for protection.

When George reached the lead vehicle, what was left of the invulnerable M.R.A.P., shocked him at what he saw. It looked like a tragic car wreck tangled and mashed and torn with pieces of it laying on the ground as far away as fifty feet. Behind him, bumping into him knocking him forward as he halted was Lieutenant Culbertson who had come running.

He turned to Culbertson and said, "We have got to get this convoy moving out of here."

The Lieutenant seemed not to hear what he had said. Bullets were firing around them. George saw the lieutenant find what was left of his friend Marlon Jefferson, pulling the torso from the wreckage, cradling it in his arms while crying and weeping loudly; almost like a wail of agony.

George tapped the Lieutenant on the shoulder. He said, "Lieutenant Culbertson, we have got to get this convoy out of here."

This fell on deaf ears. He looked inside the remnants of the M.R.A.P. and saw the others-all were dead.

Turning to the Lieutenant he said, "Here let me help you get him back to your medical vehicle."

The Lieutenant looked up crying. He said, "I can't leave him here to be drug through the streets of Baghdad."

The watcher, Sambo, turned machine gunner in George's vehicle, had taken his new position to heart; he was firing the machine gun indiscriminately at sand dunes, but it seemed to work as the insurgents were now pinned down behind their dunes for protection. With the weeping officer back in the medical vehicle with what was left of his dead friend, George got back through the back door into his M.R.A.P., tapping the driver on the shoulder telling him to pull around to the front and then ordering his radio operator to notify the rest of the convoy to get in behind his vehicle and follow.

"That is the best news I have heard all day." Said Stumpy the radioman as they began to pull out and head to the front of the now burning destroyed M.R.A.P.

331

About that time the Bradley, that had been repaired, speeding up to the scene, firing its 25 millimeterM242 Chain gun at the structures of the village where suspected insurgents had been firing, reducing that area to ruble. Next, it trained its 7.62 millimeter M240C machine gun on insurgents who were firing on the fleeing convoy. What was left of the insurgents, as they fled for cover, were met with deadly fire from a gun ship helicopter that had also arrived, picking off the remnants of the fleeing insurgents.

Just a quickly the battle had begun; it stopped. The convoy minus four soldiers, one of which was the All American wide receiver from the University of Mississippi, the insurgents minus twenty-one young men some of which had traveled from Saudi Arabia, Syria, Yemen and Iran, all dying in this hot lonely desecration in the desert of which none of the fighters knew its name. The fire power of the American Army and the air support group had been too much for the insurgents who had hoped to catch the convoy unprepared, destroying it before help arrived. It almost worked, except for the quick witted efforts of George Cedric Murfrey who was given a battlefield commission for his heroism that day. Like most heroes, he had acted instinctively doing what had to be done for the moment.

Lieutenant Murfrey accepted the promotion without argument; it did not dawn on him that he was not like the others he slept with, ate with and traveled with in this unfriendly land; he simply did what he had been taught. He could not figure out why the others who sat next to him in class after class did not respond in the same manner.

The rest of the trip to Najaf and back had gone smoothly over the rocky gravel road that had once been used by caravans of camels in former days. At Camp Taji, George was summoned to the base shrink for a session like the one he had received at his former base. This time he was startled by two other men who would take part in the psychological testing and counseling. There sat Samuel Skinner, a.k.a. Sambo, the watcher George had turned his machine gun over to, spraying bullets at anything that moved, and also sitting there with his arrogant smile was newly promoted, Sergeant Mutt Hanson who must have fired the M240 machine gun in the Bradley. Before George could ask why those two were there, it was explained that it would be a group session since all three had a background of having a history of dispatching his fellow man. Sambo had killed a man several years back in self-defense from a home invasion by another of his race who had broken in his house, proceeding to rape his sister; the rapist was so put out with Sambo interrupting his dirty deed that he attempted to knife Sambo, but came off the loser. Mutt Hanson had seen action while in India with the Scottish Brigade having eliminated several "Punjabs" while in a real battle in which he had never talked about; nor the shooting incident in Lahore, Pakistan. All three knew the right things to say to the Psychologist and were dismissed within twenty minutes with the admonition to come back should they experience any problems.

As they were leaving the shrinks' office there sat Lieutenant Culbertson ashen faced and shaking; it did not look like one session with the shrink was going to do the Lieutenant any good. George wondered how he would feel if he witnessed Mutt's death in a similar situation. The death of his other best friend, Woody had altered his life so he had some inkling what the Lieutenant was going through. It made a difference when someone dear was killed, than someone who was trying to kill you or your comrades. Still just thinking about it, made him shudder as if a rat had just run over his grave. It was then that George turned to Mutt on the way to the small NCO club and suggested, "You know Mutt, I think we should go to church this coming Sunday."

"Alright by me," said Mutt shrugging his shoulders and that was that.

The next day, George was formally informed that he had received the battlefield commission, but he would continue to act as a machine gunner until it was confirmed through orders from headquarters. He was now Lieutenant Murfrey in name only, having no idea of how to be an officer or a gentleman, but that did not stop him from determining to lose more weight and square his shoulders like a man. It was as if being among men, who respected him and being in another land far from his past, that all the derision and humiliation he had endured was now gone, vanished; out of it came a new person being called a war hero.

He was assigned the living quarters of Lieutenant Culbertson who was cleaning out his belongings. A helicopter was standing by to take the Lieutenant to Baghdad International Airport and on to Germany where he could get better therapy treatment. George had heard from the scuttlebutt, that the Lieutenant was shell shocked.

"Sorry for your loss," said George to Culbertson as he entered the small wooden building reserved for officers.

"He was the reason we won the state championship. Marlon could snag a pass with one hand. He was my best friend," said Culbertson. "The pro scouts approached him wanting to draft him, but he elected to follow me to this God forsaken desert. We only had twenty-one more days here. I should have let you have the lead vehicle. You have the skills and experience to find those roadside bombs, but I ignored it."

"Sir," said George. "It could just as well been my vehicle if you had let us go first."

"No, I don't buy that. I have looked your orders over and over with your history right before me. You were qualified; you had the skills and you proved it. I made the wrong decision and Marlon paid for it."

"I hope you will be alright, sir. Good luck," said George as he clasped the broken man's hand with both of his.

"Thanks. Congratulations on your promotion. You saved the convoy and I wasn't any use at all," said the Lieutenant in a monotone voice who now had tears streaming down his face as he quietly closed the door behind him, shoulders slumped.

At the NCO Club, Mutt asked George, "What is going on about your suddenly wanting to attend church? This is not the George Murphy I know. Did you have a battlefield conversion?"

"When you see how fragile life is over here, especially when riding in these shooting galleries, we call convoys, it makes you think; it makes you think a lot. Besides, with being able to talk almost daily with my mother and Maybellene through Skype, with them urging me to start going to church and how they are praying for me, it has finally sunk in. Since we are sidekicks, you might as well go with me," said George.

"Boy! No telling what you will come up with next. It is like some kind of metamorphosis with you. I can't keep up with you and the changes. First you start losing weight and every time I see you, I see less of you." He laughed and continued. "You are becoming lean and mean, shooting all those rag heads and spotting roadside bombs. It is uncanny. How do you do it, and don't give me all that crap about paying attention in those classes at Camp Shelby, at Camp McClain and Camp Buchering in Kuwait."

"Sometimes I am just as confused as you are Mutt," said George smiling in a condescending way. "I know how I spot those I.E.D.'s. You are partly right; it was not just the army's intensive training which sunk in; it was more. When I was a boy, I used to wade down along the beach at night and pick up soft shelled crabs, bringing them home for my mother to cook and let me tell you, she knew how to cook them. Her good cooking may have been why I got so fat. Anyway, you learn to train your eye for the crab shell that has recently been shed. You only have a short time period before the new shell gets hard again: That is when they are vulnerable for fish who like to eat this delicacy. I learned to follow the trail to the spot where the soft shell crab tried to hide and just reached down, picking them up. Later, I got a special light and a gig and went after Flounders. Before I got the light, I relied on the moon light to show me where soft shells were hiding and that includes Flounders. Now, Flounders, they also bury in the sand, waiting for a meal to come by. They move to another location when business is bad. I learned to follow their special trail they left and there would be those two beady eyes sticking out of the sand where they burrowed. Later, when Woody and I went fishing off shore, I could tell you what species of fish there was in the water just by looking at the water's ripples they stirred up. I could tell if it was Speckled Trout, Spanish Mackerel, Lady Fish, Red Fish and even Flounder by the way the water looked. This was transferred to looking for hidden bombs along the wayside; same thing. Now shooting suicide bombers was different: I watched their eyes, facial expression, nervous tics and their body language. Most of them give themselves away by picking up speed as they walk toward their target. Believe me they are not hard to spot. I do have exceptional vision-twenty ten in both eyes. So does that help answer your question?"

"Whew! I need another beer after that. How do you explain your calm nerves when you are in battle?" Mutt held up his hand and pointed to another beer. The bartender nodded.

"Mutt, I concentrate on what I am doing. You could be stabbing you mother, or at least somebody's mother and I would not even look your way. I don't care what commotion that is going on, I stay focused on what I am doing; it is that easy. Now let's get back to God; I feel the need to learn the power of prayer and draw from that power, like my mother says. You know she prays for me every day. I am serious Mutt."

"Alright! Alright! I didn't know we were going to get so serious, but I guess seeing that other M.R.A.P. blown up had an effect on you. Sunday, if we are not in combat, I will go with you to the Chapel services."

"You don't know the half of it," said George grimly. "Seeing good men die, changes a person. I have found out that I was damn good at something when I thought I was no good at anything excepting farting to the tune of Dixie."

The next two and a half weeks went by without any more ambushes and without any more loss of life and M.R.A.P.'s. George's Marauders, as they called themselves with pride, led each convoy with George doing his best to train Samuel Skinner to take over as the machine gunner, since that was what Sambo wanted to become. He rode inside with their new watcher, Ben Blankneship from Natchez teaching him how to spot I.E.D.s'. He demonstrated the "decimator" showing Ben how to work that electronic marvel. All in all, they blew up eleven roadside bombs.

What had been hellacious treacherous trips, settled down to peaceful rides through the desert. When the time came for George to return to his base in South Iraq, he gave Ben the decimator as a going away present.

CHAPTER TWENTY SEVEN

Reporting to Special Forces for Duty

The days, of being a watcher/machine gunner in an M.R.A.P., riding in a convoy in Iraq, were over. George had come out of it with no injuries, a battlefield commission and a maturity that surpassed all past experiences. He was battle hardened, able to make quick decisions, and self confident. For the most part he had done it on his own; he had found himself; he had self respect.

Actually he would have preferred to stay with the Mississippi National Guardsmen protecting convoys in Iraq, but he knew that was not possible; he had an obligation to fulfill, secret missions to accomplish, for which he only could do. There was no way out of it. Nature had dealt him an unusual deck of cards and he must play them and most probably no one but a few would ever know about it. Until then, he would bask in his successes and the accolades that went with them; right now he was a hero and had the medal tucked away in his duffle bag to prove it.

George learned from his orders that he was being sent to Forward operating Base Kalsu where the 155th Mississippi National Guard combat team Headquarters was located. He and his faithful friend, Mutt Hanson flew in a noisy Chinook helicopter which whisked them quickly to Kalsu. At least that is what George thought, until he saw a jeep awaiting him and standing by it was Sergeant Ziegfield with a disgusted look on his face.

"You are late," said Ziggy. "You were supposed to be here ten minutes ago. What happened?"

"We had to fly around some dust swirls," said George. "What's up?"

"The Colonel wants to see you right away."

"Man, can't the Army let me catch my breath; I am grimy and tired. No rest for the weary, I guess."

"I think the saying is 'No rest for the wicked'", said Ziggy laughing. "Anyway, you have had it soft far too long; now the Army wants you to start earning your pay especially since you are now a Lieutenant."

"You heard. If that was soft, then I would hate to see what is hard."

They arrived at the Headquarters Special Forces building where Colonel Alan Benson was waiting in his office.

George entered giving the Colonel a snappy salute. He stood at attention and said, "Sergeant George C. Murfrey reporting for duty, Sir."

The Colonel returned the salute halfheartedly, smiling. "That is enough of that George. I am glad to see you perfected your military bearing these past three months, but save it for the outside. Here you are George and I am Alan, or did you forget?"

Alan rose and went around his desk to give George a solid handshake. He stood there looking George over before retreating to his desk. They both sat down.

"George, I can see you have done quite well these past months and from what I have heard of how you handled your duties, I made the right decision. What I see standing before me is a Soldier. I see you have lost weight and that's a nice sun tan you have now."

He tossed a couple of gold bars across the desk. "Here Lieutenant Murfrey are your bars; you earned them." He picked up a sheet of paper and read: "Sergeant George Cedric Murfrey is hereby awarded a battlefield commission of the rank of Second Lieutenant for taking charge of his convoy when attacked by overwhelming forces in which the lead M.R.A.P. was destroyed and the officer in charge was unable to perform his duties while the convoy was under heavy fire by the enemy being in danger of being destroyed. Through the efforts of Sergeant Murfrey, the battle was won and the convoy saved."

"Welcome back to Special Forces, Lieutenant. Don't get too used to those gold bars, George. If I know you, it won't be long before I will be handing you silver bars and promoting you to First Lieutenant."

George smiled and said, "Thank you, sir. I hate to be trite and say I didn't do that all by myself. A lot of good men joined me in that moment. What I did, I did, without even thinking of the consequences; it was purely a reflex action." With at twinkle in his eye, George added, "Someone had to do it. I must say, however, I really needed those gold bars."

"How is that, George?"

"You see, sir. I mean Alan. My girlfriend Maybellene has made it through OCS and is now a First Lieutenant. She informed me the other day that since I was a non-com, she could no longer consort with me."

"Not to change the subject, George, tell me how through all that, you managed to take your purple pill. I guess you were taking it, since I did not hear of any occurrences like back in Georgia when you polluted the area."

George pulled out of his pocket, a long blue plastic box and showed it to the Colonel. "I carry my pills in this pill box with the days of the week stamped on it. Each morning I religiously take one so there are no slip-ups. Those pills really work. It has been nice being normal."

"George, you are far from normal, but that is beside the point. I want you to hand over that pill box. I am taking you off those pills. In five days you will have a mission and we need your other skills. You will be billeted in quarters at the edge of the base and when your gaseous prowess returns, just use the wooden match method and burn of the fumes until you go on the mission.

Tomorrow you will start your training for the mission and will be briefed accordingly. Don't worry; it will just be a small mission to see how well you will do. You have to start somewhere; now is the time."

"I know," interrupted George. "You want to see how I do under dangerous conditions "

The Colonel stood up grinning indicating the meeting was over. "Exactly! You got it, George. I have great faith in you. It will be a sleigh ride."

"Alan, do you know why it will be a rough sleigh ride?"

"No. Why?"

"No snow."

339

"Ha! A little humor doesn't hurt."

George remained seated in spite of the clue to get up and leave. "One other thing, Alan: I am kind of tired of killing people. No let me correct that; I am sick of it. Wanta know how many I have killed? Lets' see: Counting the one at Walmart and those in Iraq: ten. I know they were trying to kill me along with the troops, and that makes it alright, but still I do not like it. Just thought I would let you know. Mano to mano."

The Colonel walked to the door and opened it. He turned and said, "Look George. Lets table this discussion for now. Get your briefing and extra training and we will have this discussion before your mission."

George got up and as he passed the Colonel, he said, "You are the boss. See you later."

Back at his new one room barracks in exile, he mulled over the circumstances deciding to play their silly game; after all it beat the alternative; so far the Army had been good to him.

The next five days put George back in the class room except he was the only student; it was one on one and it was boring.

Was the thrill of battle getting to be a habit or an addiction?

Over and over he was shown still pictures, videos and maps that depicted known terrorists, and streets in the area of Baghdad. The area covered was outside the green zone where civilians, employees, contractors, security guards and visiting dignitaries resided in exclusion from the general population. The videos showed various bomb making facilities as well as the bombs themselves being manufactured.

George viewed the streets, stores and residential buildings so much, he felt as if he had lived there. Over and over he was shown pictures of known terrorists for al Qaida and then shown their handiwork as they tortured prisoners, beheading them at the end. It was not a pleasant or pretty scene leaving George grim faced after those sessions, thinking maybe he had been a bit premature in telling the Colonel he was sick of killing. Those evil bastards needed killing!

After viewing the bomb making videos, George felt he could not only make one of those bombs, but could dismantle them if required. The stockpiles of weapons and bombs, that had been found by the marines and soldiers was in such quantity that it shocked him. It was almost unbelievable.

Even the pick-up trucks and vans used by the terrorists were shown him, over and over, until he was sure he could recognize one by the dents, scratches and battered paint jobs.

George wondered how they ever got those graphic pictures and videos. He knew he would not be taking any pictures on this mission. With the discontinuance of the purple pill, the gaseous problems he had almost forgotten plaguing him all his life, were back in full force. The living nightmare had returned to haunt him. Each day the amount of gas increased, causing him to light a match to burn off the lethal vapors, rendering them harmless, throwing out a brief blue flame. He had no doubt of his potency; maybe he was the "skunk man" but with an ability to exterminate certain persons who needed extermination.

In his mind it was good versus evil, but it was hard for him to tell who they were. Some were Iranian backed Shiites; others were young boys, led by older men from other countries, almost all sporting black beards making them easy to spot except for the fact the local men also had black beards and they were not necessary the bad guys; it was all so confusing.

Since George only had one instructor, a Harley Moak, from San Francisco, he sweet talked him into an extra fifteen minutes during lunch, which was used to call Maybellene over Skype. There was an eight hour time difference which made it about eight p.m. in Virginia. Looking at each other on the computer monitors was revealing. May in spite of wearing no make up looked beautiful to George. George had brought his weight down to a trim two hundred seventy-five pounds.

"George, have you lost more weight? Your face shows it." The web cam showed just his face and upper body.

"I guess I have," sighed George. "You haven't said anything about what is on my collar. Notice those gold bars?'

"I noticed them, but I figured they were just part of your get up with Special Forces. They are not real are they?"

"They are real alright; earned fair and square on the battlefield. They came with a pay raise too, so what do you say about that?"

"Well!' she said in a huff. I went through tedious officer training to earn mine and you got yours through some little 'ole battle. Doesn't seem quite fair; you haven't said anything about how much I have slimmed down Can't you tell?"

"I can tell alright; you have changed. Why you are beautiful. You know in some ways the Army has been good for us. When you finish over there, tell the Army that you are invoking the buddy plan and want to come over here. I see Mutt almost every day. We are both going to church now; you and my mother have gotten your wish."

"I can't believe my ears. Hallelujah! They are talking about sending me to Afghanistan, but I will let you know."

"Can't be any worse than here. We are supposed to be pulling out of this forsaken country soon. Maybe, I will get them to send me and Mutt there."

"Ya'll come," said May and she clicked off.

When George reported to the Special Forces training building, the men he saw entering the building were serious looking with hard faces and cold animal eyes, much like those of the enemy, the kind of people he had learned never to mess with, much less stare at. That did not keep them from staring at him and smirking as if he did not belong there. Some carried sniper rifles which George recognized to be Winchester Model 70's 30.06. Others had sniper rifles like the one he had used on the way to Najaf; he still had his, but left it back at his isolated one room shanty, as he called it. Maybe he would carry his M16 A-1 with scope around slung over his shoulder and stop all that smirking. Others, he passed in the hallways paid no attention to him while conversing about explosives designating them by letters and numbers. Unlike those men, he was one of a kind and had absolutely nothing in common with them. He had heard that those Special Forces snipers actually killed more insurgents, that the infantry in Iraq. They would probably turn those rifles on him if they knew of his special talents in which he was certainly glad to keep quiet.

Years ago back during the Korean Conflict, Alan Benson had successfully guided his pet project, Fanny Mae McBride, using her special talents similar to those of George Murfrey, to a conclusion that resulted in cease fire armistice; now he had George Murfrey to use, but there were no peace negotiations taking place. He also had a problem: If anyone from the press, watch dogs from Congress, al Qaida, the Taliban or even our allies found out about the use of gas warfare, which was banned, then there would be repercussions that could end his brilliant military career. Times had changed; secrets were leaked. It was difficult to keep secret programs, secret. Big Fanny had been a one time mission. The case of George Murfrey was different; he had to be tested with small missions in order to send him on a big one and Alan Benson, who was up in age, could not be with George on those missions as he had with Miss. McBride. Already someone was snooping around asking why those purple pills were being used and who was using them. The Colonel worked directly under the President at the Pentagon, carrying a special gold shield which backed off the investigators, but still this did not stop those inquisitive snoopers. Those two Major back at Fort Benning which he had chewed out, had tried to find out what was so special about Murfrey to deserve their humiliation; they were unsuccessful. Then there was General McDougal, commander of the 155th Brigade of the Mississippi National Guard who had friends in Washington, and it came back to Benson, were asking questions. The General had a lot of cigar smoking friends who backed him completely. Finally, there were those lab technicians who carried out those awesome tests in which George let loose his lethal gas killing chickens, birds, insects, animals and other live creatures within seconds. If one of them blew the whistle-well, he did not want to think about that. And what about the dossier the FBI had on George? He had had it suppressed, but one could not be sure a copy had not been saved and was in the vaults of the FBI for someone to discover. Classified documents were being unclassified every day.

George himself attracted attention; his gross obesity out did those lazy mess sergeants with their fat guts hanging over their belts. George further attracted more attention winning the Bronze Star and then a battlefield commission for his heroics. Benson never counted on that. As a watcher/machine gunner/sniper, George was exceptional. Maybe he should let George serve out his enlistment protecting convoys while leading them in an M.R.A.P. That would be easy enough to issue the appropriate orders and stamp on his secret file: "File closed".

No George Cedric Murfrey was too valuable to waste protecting convoys; he would proceed to use him on secret missions until he was told to stop. Then there were those purple pills. George had been on them since he had enlisted. If Murfrey developed immunity to them and their effects wore off, our soldiers could be wiped out with one gaseous blast and there would be a terrible consequences..

Lieutenant George Murfrey was having his own set of reluctance and doubts; he was tired of the killing, now turning to religion for answers. As he entered the outer office, his friend, Sergeant Ziggy was leafing through a sheaf of papers. He glanced up and said, "You can go on in George. The Colonel is waiting."

George smiled and said, "Don't you salute a superior officer?"

Ziggy lifted his right arm saluting him half heartedly. "Only when I see one George; only when I see one. You know we don't stand on ceremony around here."

"I know Ziggy. I just wanted to try my new rank on someone."

"Don't forget where you came from, George. Now you must not keep the Colonel waiting or you won't have those gold bars very long; you saw what he did to those two majors that time."

George entered the office still laughing. The Colonel was dressed in civilian clothes wearing a double breasted grey suit, a white stripped tie and a light blue oxford dress shirt with a button down collar.

"Come in George; have a seat. Those gold bars look good on you. How does it feel to be an officer in this man's army?"

"No change--actually."

"George, I have been thinking. Do you feel that you need to be tested before you go on your mission?"

"Not really. I am sure I can still perform; besides I don't like to kill little animals. May I ask why you asked?"

"Sure. The more we run tests, the greater our secret may be found out. The smaller the circle of people, who know about our missions, less is the risk of that secret getting out."

"That makes sense."

"You said something about not wanting to have to kill anyone and I said we would talk about that later. Now is the time. Would you like to elaborate?"

"Alan, I had just come in from the battle field so to speak and had seen many die, some at my hand, but I am okay on that as long as it is the enemy. I saw those films on what they do to our boys when captured, also their killing of innocent people. I went to see Chaplin Timothy O'Malley before coming over here. He says God is love not hate. Those who hate in the name of God are impostors; God will not be mocked. He also pointed out all those weaklings whom He made strong such as Gideon and Moses, defeating the enemy. I no longer have a problem when it comes to defending our country; I guess I was a little battle fatigued."

"Good. This afternoon, I am sending you on your first mission. It will be more like a trial run to see how well you do.-no big wigs."

"Any danger in it?"

"I won't lie to you George; there is always some danger, but I can assure you, the danger will be less than going on a convoy. You will be fitted with a GPS honing device located in your belt—a tiny chip, monitoring where you are at all times so we can come and get you if things go wrong. It will be a simple operation that will not last more than a few hours."

"Here is the plan: Sergeant Ziegfield will drive you into Baghdad, drop you off about three or four blocks from the green zone. You will be in civilian clothes, looking for a woman and will let yourself be captured. You will gas your captors and then walk out to a designated area to be picked up by us."

"Sounds simple."

"It is. Go to the mess hall where they will have pinto beans and rice waiting for you; they did not have red beans and rice, but like they say: 'Beans is beans'. Change into the civilian clothes and be back here at seventeen hundred hours. I will see you tomorrow for debriefing." The Colonel then smiled in a fatherly way and said, "Good luck and God Speed."

CHAPTER TWENTY EIGHT

Special Forces secret mission

George had changed in to tan slacks, a loose fitting light green sports shirt and loafers with tassels. He nervously waited for Ziggy to arrive and take him into harm's way. This was different. Riding in a convoy in spite of the serious dangers he faced, there were others facing the same dangers with him. Now he would be alone. Could he react the same way as in the convoys? Then his reactions had been without thinking; he merely did what had been drilled into him to do, like in a dream he acted and thought about it later. Now the longer he waited, the more scared he became. Would he revert back to his old self where he had become so frightened, running and squealing as he tried to get away from Big Jake in that Quick Stop only to be caught and stabbed in the belly?"

He gave a sigh of relief when Sergeant Ziegfield pulled up in the most beat up, battered 1946 Ford sedan that had once been painted black, but now had grey undercoat covering dented fenders and knocked in doors. The front windshield had a shattered area the size of a baseball which looked as if someone had thrown a large rock at it and they probably had.

Ziggy read him right. "Having second thoughts, are we?" he said.

"I was until I saw that excuse for an automobile," joked George. "Where did you get that wreck? The demolition derby?"

"Didn't you know? It is standard Army issue for Special Forces; you know, just the sight of this car scares the enemy. It does not look good, but it runs like a top."

"I bet," said George as he climbed into the old relic and sat on the ripped up front seat.

346

To his surprise, the ancient Ford sedan had been modified where it counted; in the suspension and the engine. The old car rambled through the pot holes, cracked streets and the ubiquitous trash and debris that was part of Iraq's heritage from aerial bombings, shoot-outs, suicide explosions as well as a sign of a defeated country still in the throes of more conflict between the insurgents/terrorists/ religious fanatics/ war mongers/adventurers /profiteers and the occupying forces that had entered under the pretense that non-existent weapons of mass destruction were being hidden somewhere and would eventually be found. Meanwhile the Ford engine purred like a kitten as Ziggly expertly dodged through the obstacle course that passed for a road.

As the jalopy that passed for an automobile swerved right and left trying to go around small craters, a few were not missed jarring Murfrey back into reality. It had been over a year since the Walmart incident that altered his miserable existence when he, at one time, had taken every remedy to thwart his gaseous problem without success, amusing himself with dropping his little bombs which proved deadly to a woman who afterwards dropped to the floor-dead. At his trial for murder, before the jury could find him guilty, Colonel Benson had suddenly appeared, somehow convincing the District Attorney to let him join the Army, his surrogate father, Benson, giving him the Purple pill stopping his gas attacks better than any off the counter medicine, doctor's prescription, cork or cheese could do. Now he was off the pill and on the way to gas some unsuspecting human who supposedly needed killing. It was like a crusade.

It did not make any difference that he had already killed nine or ten of those need to be eliminated persons while he defended the convoys, nor did it matter that he had been awarded the Bronze Star, which was hidden away in his duffle bag, or his battlefield commission and subsequent jump from Sergeant to Second Lieutenant without any training in etiquette or manners, but yet he was expected to be suddenly transformed into an officer and a gentleman. He had heard that through his past heroics, he might even be awarded the Silver Star.

But all that meant nothing today. Today he was transformed into a chameleon in civilian clothing and was to draw out the bad guys like

offering candy to a baby or whiskey to an alcoholic. His lifetime curse
was now a weapon. What was that Chaplin O;Malley had told him in
his brief session earlier? "Through God, your weaknesses can become
your strengths".

Bam! The vehicle shuddered as it recovered from that last pot
hole, jarring Special Forces Murfrey back to the real world where he
could die at the hands of some bearded monster filled with so much
hatred that it would engulf George. And if that did not happen, there
was Big Jake Bannister now somewhere in Iraq who had once tried to
take his life and probably had no qualms of trying it again.

George realized that they were already traveling through the streets
of darkest Baghdad when Ziggy broke his revelry by saying, "You need
to pay attention to our whereabouts so you can find your way back to the
area where I am going to drop you off. Don't make me have to come
looking for you. I don't want to risk my life any more than I have to."

George thought, "Yeah, it is alright for me to risk mine", but kept
quiet.

Earlier they had crossed the Euphrates River continuing in the
direction past that part of the sprawling city designated the "Green area".
The sun was rapidly going down dragging darkness behind it. The few
street lights, that existed, began to flicker on. The green area; that was a
good one! Was it called that because in this arid country, there was not
much greenery or was it called that because the money being generated
through civilian contractors, construction engineers, security services,
business men and dignitaries were concentrated there?

George's mission was not assigned to the green area.

"We are almost there," commented Ziggy.

Four blocks later, Ziggy brought the car to a stop, brakes grinding
and tires dropping into small pits with a crash. George could see people
peering at them from behind walls and windows; others just turned
around and stared. George had read that in Sweden, it was considered
impolite to stare, but here it was a national pastime. With a creaking
from the un-oiled door, George pulled himself out of the car. He had
managed to locate a New Orleans Saints baseball cap and pulled it over
his head.

This was it!

He walked away as the battered old Ford whizzed past him, rear end bouncing as it smashed into pot holes. This amused George causing him to laugh out aloud when he remembered one year as a child, he had witnessed a series of pot holes in his home town, Gulfport, where someone planted small trees in the deeper holes and how they were all filled in and paved just about election time. While he was looking around for a taxi, he noticed a car cruising slowly behind him. As it approached, he recognized the car as a green French Citrogen, one of the ones he had viewed on slides in his preparation for this mission. When he saw the driver he recognized Ali-bey Kazani, who was a double agent for the Americans and al Qaida. On the door of the Citrogen painted in long hand were Arabic letters and in English: "Taxi".

The Taxi pulled up beside George and he got in. "Where to?" asked Kazani in excellent English as he turned around to greet his passenger. He wore a striped blue and tan turban peering at George with small black beady eyes that mocked his pocked face partly covered with a cold black beard flashing a fake smile to cover up his cruel face.

As rehearsed, George answered, "I am looking for a woman; you know, ladies of the night."

"I know just the place; all are beautiful women," said the small driver whose head of dark black hair was sticking out from under his turban, his ears filled with the same black hair that ran down the sides of his face into a mustache and chin beard; no doubt this was Kazani, whose picture on various slides had been drilled into George's memory. It was all he could do not to address him as Mr. Kazani.

The Citrogen smoothly entered traffic and after three blocks, made a left turn on a street revealing an even shabbier less populated area. "Where you from?" asked Kazani.

"I am from the State of Mississippi, a town called Gulfport."

"Now that is, how you say it, a coincidence. About three hours earlier, I picked up a large man who said he was from Mississippi; he, too, was wanting a woman. I take you to the same place; maybe you two meet up." The driver gave George a sly smile. "You like Iraq?"

"It's okay," said George.

"Say I think I know you," said Kazani. "You are with the Mississippi National Guard. You are that fat G.I. I see on television. You shoot many terrorists. What's your name?"

"Smith."

"No, no. I remember now. On television they say you are with the 155th Brigade and your name is Murphee. You're Murphee. You are that man nobody like. You the talk of Baghdad. I carry many passengers, but never forget a face."

George was shocked. How did he get on Iraqi television?

"How did you see someone who looked like me on television?"

"Iraqi television uses amateur movie cameras to show the news. Many people have movie cameras and take pictures; you famous like John Wayne."

The driver picked up his microphone and began to jabber in an incomprehensible language pausing and laughing except when he said: "Murphee".

George considered calling the mission off, but they had taken the bait and it was his first mission; he did not want to come up empty.

A few minutes later, the driver pulled to the curb. He said. "Here you are Murphee. Many pretty girls." He pointed to a run-down tan stucco building that had a dim light over an open door. "Tell them Rashad sent you. That will be twenty American dollars."

George reluctantly left the cab hesitating as he walked toward the door. He felt a rush of cool air hit him and again had second thoughts about the mission. The story about seeing him on TV was plausible since it seemed that all the gawkers wherever he went, had small video cameras and cell phones. Strange he had not been briefed to expect recognition.

He heard Kazani call out, "You want me to wait, Murphee? I wait for another twenty dollars."

"No. I don't know how long I will be."

Without another word, the driver calling himself Rashad sped off, vanishing in the darkness. Entering the building, he walked down a dimly lit hall, smelling as if deserted, no sign of life except for a small red light over a door to his right and faint sounds of belly dancing music.

George never got far enough into the room to find out; something crashed on his head and all went black.

When he came to, he was being dragged by two men, one on each side. His eyes were covered with a sweaty rag tied around his head, a make shift blindfold that only partially blocked his vision, much like when as a kid, he was blindfolded playing "pin-the-donkey", pretending he couldn't see, but catching glimpses now and then.

"Where are the girls," he mumbled.

The two men dragging him stopped. The one on his right understood and spoke English. He said, "There are no girls, Murphee." Then he translated what was said to the other man in Arabic. "You too heavy. Walk. I guide you." He gave George a hefty push that propelled him stumbling forward.

He had no idea where he was or how far he had been dragged by his captors, only getting a glimpse of the area when he bobbed his head. They were on a gravel path, going around large rocks and pieces of destroyed buildings. George could see a very large crater, the results of an I.E.D. or maybe a bomb dropped earlier in the war. He would remember this crater as a landmark. Now he heard the opening of an iron gate that squeaked loudly, in need of oiling and then all was quiet again except for the heavy breathing of the two men obviously not in good shape. He got glimpses of shrubs and bushes as they passed through a court yard, then stumbling, almost falling. George said, "If you would take off this blindfold, I could walk better."

"Shut up!" snapped the one on his right. George stumbled again; they were now going down a hill and as he stumbled, he saw an Arabian moon and the black sky lit by stars, no street lights in this desolate area to show the way.

Finally, they came to a three story building where George had to climb three steps go through a doorway, walk down a long hall and then up more steps.

George was now out of breath.

"Can't we stop for a second?" George protested. "I am winded."

The man on the left hit him on the side of his head with something hard like a pipe causing George to see a shower of stars that were not in the heavens.

They reached the third floor and stopped. One of the captors knocked three times, then two and then three again; a clever code. A light was streaming out from under the door.

When it opened, someone said, "Another one? This is a busy night."

The makeshift blindfold was removed from George revealing a tall grubby partially graying bearded man wearing a skull cap and a long dirty robe, glaring at him with two cruel eyes, causing George to shudder; eyes that said, "I hope I get to kill you soon." His two captors were excitedly talking in Arabic which he did not comprehend except when his mispronounced name, "Murphee" was used. When they finished, for no reason at all, the tall Arab hauled of and backhanded him.

"So you are that fat American pig who has everyone scared when you are with the convoys; you don't look so tough to me."

The room, he had been rudely pushed into, had a naked light bulb hanging from the ceiling; the bulb attached to a brown plastic socket with a bead chain hanging from it. There was a four by four wooden table covered with blood stains that had turned brown with two wooden chairs to accompany it. George looked around and saw blood splatter and streaks left by someone's hand on the wall and more signs of blood on the concrete floor no one had bothered to clean up. The room had a sickening coppery smell which no one seemed to notice but him. Was this a human slaughter house?

After George had studied the repulsive room, he heard someone say, "Have a seat, Mr. Murpee." He was thrust into one of the wooden chairs. He noticed one of the men putting on a black ski mask while the one who had greeted him at the door set up a tripod with a video camera attached to it.

He began his interrogation. "Tell us your name!" shouted the tall Arab.

"John Smith," said George.

"You lie!" shouted another one who also had donned a ski mask which showed only his mean eyes and harsh mouth. In front of the camera, the two masked men pointed their weapons at him; one with an automatic pistol and the other brandishing an AK-47.

"Tell us the truth or they will blow your fat ass to pieces," said the one operating the camera.

"Okay. Have it your way. You already know my name is George Murfrey. I am with the U.S. Army 155th Brigade."

That's better, George Murfrey. You interrupted my interrogation of one of your fellow soldiers. See what we took off him."

The interrogator brandished a large Bowie knife, which he, with great force stabbed the wooden table a foot in front of George, causing him to pull back quickly. George glanced at the large wicked knife which looked like the one he had been stabbed with eons ago. Only one man, he knew, carried a knife like that with a blue and tan stained bone handle.

"Now George Murfrey, you will see what we do to invaders of our homeland who refuse to tell us what we want to know." The tall Arab said something to the two masked men in Arabic who then opened a door to another room and went into it from which he could hear someone kicking a body which grunted after each kick. After a few minutes of kicking and grunting, the two men dragged in a large man covered with blood on his face, shoulders and parts of his torso.

George almost did not recognize the man who was dumped on the floor; now the object of the video camera.

On the floor just to the side of the table was to his surprise, what was left of Big Jake Bannister. One eye was swollen completely shut, his nose lain to one side having been broken, the lips were grossly enlarged, blood trickling out of his nose and mouth.

He looked up at George with his good eye and said feebly," Farts, how did you get here?"

"Shut up!" screamed the tall Arab. One of the masked captors gave Jake a swift kick to Jake's shoulder which brought forth another loud grunt.

"You see the shape your comrade is in. He won't last long; we are tired of trying to get him to tell us what we want to know. See that knife we took off him? I am going to use it to cut his head off. We don't need him anymore and now you will see what will happen to you if you refuse to talk."

He nodded to one of the masked men, who yanked the knife from the table and brought it in front of the camera slicing the air with it.

"Wait!" yelled George. "I know this soldier; he is one of my men. Let me talk to him. I will order him to tell you what you want to know."

"You better talk fast. We have been trying to persuade him to talk for three hours and we are tired. If he doesn't talk, I am personally going to take his head off in front of this camera." The one with the knife made a cutting motion for the camera.

"Set him up so he can see me talking to him. I have to see if he understands what I tell him."

They grabbed Jake and roughly dragged him to the blood streaked wall, propping him up.

"Talk American infidel or you die," shouted the English speaking Arab.

George was allowed to get up and walk over to Jake whose eyes were glassing over, his chin resting on his chest.

George knelt down and shook Jake by the shoulders. "Big Jake," he said. "Look at me."

Jake lifted his head slowly looking at George, recognition coming again. Through thick bloody lips, he mouthed, "Farts."

"Jake nod if you remember what I did at the Palace Pool Hall causing everyone to evacuate the place. Remember?"

"I—I remember," gasped Jake, nodding slowly.

"Well I am going to do the same thing again. Only this time you have to hold your breath for over thirty seconds."

The tall English speaking Arab said. "Get on with it. What's this holding your breath stuff?"

"You will see," said George. "I am testing his comprehension. If he can hold his breath that shows he understands and then can answer

354

your questions better. I heard that by holding your breath, it clears the head."

That seemed to satisfy the tall Arab who then explained to his co-harts in Arabic what George was doing. They nodded in agreement, saying something in the affirmative.

Crouching down closer, George said in a low voice, "Jake when I count to three, hold your breath for thirty seconds. Nod if you understand."

Big Jake nodded slowly.

"Okay. One-two-three."

George began pulling himself up and as he did he let out a loud flatter blaster, shattering the silence. Two laughed and the third started to say, "You fat bast—". A whiff later, each one silently collapsed, vomited and started jerking spasmodically.

George reached down and began to pull Jake up from the floor. Jake grabbed his arms in an effort to help him as he watched in awe as the three captors lost consciousness; they did not have much time to get out of that room or they would end up like the terrorists. True to his word, Jake held his breath as George helped him to the door and to fresh clean air. On the way, Jake reached over and grabbed his Bowie knife while George snatched the video camera with the tripod attached to it using it like a steadying cane.

Outside the two leaned up against the hall wall catching their breath and after a while hearing no sounds from inside, Jake spoke through two swollen lips, "Thanks, Farts. Now I need to go back in there and finish the job. Do you think the air has cleaned enough for me to go back inside without me getting sick?"

"Why in the world would you want to go back in there. They are all dead."

"No Farts, I have got to make sure. You don't know what those dirty bastards did to me. I thought I was a goner; they were going to cut my head off. Now I want to complete the job; I am going to cut their throats; those dogs will never hurt anyone again."

George grabbed Jake by the arm to hold him back. "No need to do that, Big Jake. I can assure you they are dead, you know, like that lady in Walmart."

"No, Farts. I have to make sure. I don't want them putting a price on my head when they revive—you know some kind of Jihad."

Jake who was getting his strength back, jerked his muscular arm away from George and started toward the door.

"Hold your breath; whatever you do, don't breathe," shouted George.

He could hear Big Jake whacking away, coming out of the room, slamming the wooden door, his Bowie knife dripping with fresh blood.

While Jake slide the large heavy knife into a scabbard located under his trousers in the small of his lower back, George unscrewed a small Sony mini DVD camera from the tripod sticking the camera into his pants pocket, discarding the tripod.

"Come on Big Jake. I think I know the way; at least a little of the way. If we don't get captured again, there will be a car to pick us up. Think you can make it?"

"My ribs are broken. If you help me a little, I can make it. If that car you have waiting is that skinny little Arab with the dirty turban, that rotten cab driver; I am going to slash his throat too. Did that sorry bastard take you to get a whore? Wait 'til I get my hands on that rotten dog," said Jake. "Farts, I am sorry I ever stabbed you. You can believe me; I will never stab you again. I owe you my life. I am glad they are dead. They will never cut anyone else's head off. You can count on that."

"You need to be quiet, Big Jake. Now is not the time to be talking in English. Stay in the dark shadows and try to walk normal."

The two stumbled in the dark as they backtracked through the courtyard and then up and down the hill through the squeaking gate that was now closed. When they reached the area where the huge crater was located, George knew he was going the right way; the same path his captors had brought him earlier. From then on while looking at the ground and occasionally upward, the two came down the street where George had been dropped off by the so called double agent calling himself, Rashad. "That is where that rotten cab driver dropped me off promising me a pretty woman," said Jake, pointing to the same building red light still burning weakly—the same belly dancing music emanating from the front door.

"Come on," urged George. "We are almost there."

As they walked side by side, the natives, who were on the same sidewalk took one look at Big Jake with his one closed eye, blooded face, nose over on one side and after getting a whiff of the smell that the two broadcast in advance, hurriedly crossed the street. All of a sudden the grayish black dusty sedan driven by Ziggy, pulled to the curb in a grinding halt.

He reached across the seat, yanking the creaking passenger door open with one hand and said, "Get in."

After the two miscreants were in, Jake in the back and George up front, and under way, Ziggy said, "George, where did you find that guy? He looks like he has been in a meat grinder. Boy you two smell like warmed over sewerage, but that is to be expected. Why do I always get the dirty jobs!"

"Just picked him up along the way," said George who always had an answer.

"Big Jake, we are going home."

Jake, who had closed his eyes mumbled, "To the Gulf Coast?"

"No, to the army base," said George as he leaned over the seat facing Jake. "You will have some explaining to do, but I will put a word in to my Colonel."

"I take it that you accomplished your mission. Everything go alright?"

"Mission accomplished; we left three dead Arabs back there. I would not want to go back there; the neighborhood is contaminated.

"I killed those bastards," said Jake. "They were going to cut my head off."

"Sure you did," said Ziggy.

"I did! Farts helped me a little. Tell him Farts."

"Yeah, Big Jake stabbed them or cut their throats. I will explain it all when the Colonel debriefs us." George pulled out the small video camera showing it to Ziggy. "Most of it is on the video."

"I have never been so scared in all my life. Those Arabs were going to cut off my head, but Farts saved my life." Jake closed his eyes and was soon heard snoring loudly through his broken nose.

Ziggy asked, "You know this guy?"

"Yes. I will tell you all about it when we get debriefed. That is Big Jake Bannister from Lizana, Mississippi. He is the one who stabbed me at a Quick Stop."

"I think I read about that in your file."

"He is the one," sighed George.

CHAPTER TWENTY NINE

The Headhunter

The debriefing was thorough with the exception that Jake Bannister was not present; he had been sent to the hospital for his injuries which included a concussion, three broken ribs, a broken nose and various abrasions and contusions, leaving him for later debriefing after he had been patched up. All the while at the hospital Big Jake was vociferously telling anyone who would listen; that he had dispatched three terrorists with his Bowie knife, the story getting bigger and bigger. The Colonel did not try to stop Jake's braggadocio, as it served his interests to let the public believe it was he who caused the deaths of three recognized al-Qaida terrorists, discovered from the unedited video brought back by George Murfrey. George, although sore, had suffered only bruises a few cuts to his head and face and abrasions from the ordeal which pleased the Colonel immensely.

They were not pleased to learn that their agent, who now called himself Rashad, was really working for al-Qaida, almost could have been responsible for the lives of two American soldiers, almost getting away with it, and suddenly dropping out of sight. Unfortunately George spilling the beans about Rashad, no longer a double agent, was now rendered ineffective and had a price on his bushy black head.

The tall English speaking Arab, the leader of the trio, known in the Interpol as the "Headhunter" with a price on his own head, had now been sent to his heaven where he would be rewarded with seventy virgins. There was a lengthy list of the Headhunter's activities whose real name was Ali Zadak, a Saudi citizen, but with alias Passports under other names traveling all over the world. Internationally known, the son of a French arms dealer and a Saudi mother, educated at Catholic University in Washington, D.C., was responsible for assassinations in at least five countries. He was formerly an expert at constructing bombs out of available materials; he also taught others how to build the I.E.D.'s not to speak of his enjoyment in beheading captured soldiers, members

359

of the press and any other American, British, French, German, Spanish and even Iraqi citizens who in his determination needed to be displayed on the Arab television without their heads attached to their bodies.

The Colonel was delighted with the news that one of the most wanted terrorists in the world would not give them any more trouble.

"Talk about luck," said Colonel Benson. "Your very first mission, you brought down the Headhunter. I cannot understand how a man of his education could become what his nickname suggests. The DVD you brought us was invaluable; not only did it record most of your incident, George, but it had on it videos of several other beheadings of persons recently missing. One was Geoff Armistead, a news reporter for Reuters News Agency and the other an important Sunni from Iraq. And, of course, pictured on it was your buddy, Jacob Bannister. Amazing; I don't know how he took all that physical abuse without cracking."

"What is going to happen to him?" asked George.

"At first we were going to suggest court martial; we don't need our G.I.'s chasing around for prostitutes—at least not without our permission, as was your case, I might add. We even considered taking that big knife of his away, but he would probably just get another one. So after much deliberation, we decided to promote him from Private to Corporal and let him go on thinking he killed three insurgents which takes the heat off of you for the present time: Out of the limelight so to speak. You have had enough of that; we can't use you in Iraq any more since your convoy heroics have been broadcast over Arab television making you a well-known target by the enemy. Yes, Big Jake, as you call him may even get a medal."

The Colonel, now in military fatigues leaned back in his swivel chair and twiddled a sharp pencil. He scrutinized George whose facial bruises were beginning to turn greenish from dark purplish blue in places, facial cuts scabbing over. "How did the bruises and lumps you took affect you?" He offered a bottle of water to George.

"Thanks," said George as he unscrewed the cap and took a swig. "I had a headache, but took some pills for that. My main concern is the lightheadedness I got when I breathed in some of my polluted air. That was the first time it affected me; I always thought I was immune from my own gas maybe getting whopped on the head was a part of it. I just don't know."

Sergeant Ziegfield said, "Maybe you are like a scorpion, stinging his self to death. I am going to make a note in your file that your code name be changed to Scorpion."

"What was it before?" asked George.

"Fat Boy."

"Scorpion is alright by me," said George with a smile. "So what happens to me now; do I go back to riding in convoys?"

"No, George, we have found out from reliable sources, that there is a death threat out on you to kill you on sight no matter where you are seen—even on the base. As you know we employ lots of Iraqi's on the base and one of them could possibly see you and slip a knife in your back."

"So what do I do; start wearing a disguise?" George's voice was getting higher as that old feeling called fear came creeping back.

"That won't be necessary. We have already taken care of the problem. As we sit, your Orders are being cut for a thirty day furlough to be spent in Europe. Of course, your Siamese twin, Sergeant Hanson, will accompany you. After you get some R and R in Germany, which is well deserved, I might add, both of you will be transferred to Afghanistan for duty. Details will follow. Sergeant Ziegfield will accompany you to your barracks so you can grab your duffle bag, meet up with Sergeant Hanson and on to Baghdad International Airport, from which you two will be flown to Templehof, Germany. I will see you in Afghanistan after you get settled there. Have a nice trip and enjoy Germany."

When George returned to his isolated barracks, he found a Sergeant Whittman waiting for him. Dressed in fatigues, the Sergeant got out of his Jeep walking over to George. After saluting Lieutenant Murfrey, he identified himself. "I am Samuel Whittman, sent to you by Chaplin O'Malley to be your mentor."

They shook hands and George told Ziggy to go ahead and pick up Mutt and then come back and pick him up.

"We haven't much time, Lieutenant Murfrey; your flight to Germany will not wait."

"That is alright," said George. "I will be ready when you return. I need to talk to Sergeant Whittman for a moment."

Ziggy threw up his hands and drove away.

"Come on in, Sergeant. We can talk while I pack my bags. As you can see I am flying out of Iraq within the next two hours, so this will have to be brief."

"First, let me congratulate you for your decision to become a Christian. I know it was what they call a battlefield conversion and that is why I am here. Let me present you with this English Speaking Bible. Feel free to pack it and bring it along with you. If you have any questions, I will be glad to answer them. Let me say this to you: Don't think that just by converting or joining a church that life will be a bed of roses from now on. It could get worse. In the New Testament you will meet Paul, once called Saul before his conversion and after he became a Christian, he was arrested, thrown into jail, beaten, and shipwrecked, plus spending a great part of his life in prison. You might think that he was being punished by God, but the contrary was the truth. In all probability, if he had not been imprisoned, Paul would not have written two-thirds of the New Testament. When you have time to read the 'Good Book' I will be glad to talk to you further and answer any questions you might have."

"I have one now," said George. "Is O'Malley a real preacher?"

"Captain O'Malley is definitely an ordained Preacher having gone through Divinity College gaining a Master's Degree. After that he was a Pastor at Antioch Baptist Church in New Albany, Mississippi, my home town, and preached there for four years before joining the Army. He had to go to the Army's school for Chaplains', so come to Sunday services; we also have mid-week Bible study."

"I am with Special Forces," said George. "And I have to go where they send me, so I can't promise that I can attend regularly. Thank you for the Bible; I promise that I will read it."

About that time Sergeant Ziegfield and Sergeant Hanson walked into the room. Sergeant Ziegfield said, "Lieutenant, we have got to go or you will miss your plane."

Sergeant Mutt Hanson said laughing, "I see you found that lost sheep, Sergeant Whittman. Good luck with him. I have tried to get him to mend his ways, but to no avail."

"You two have met?" asked George.

"Oh yes," replied Mutt with a sheepish grin. "You don't think that you are the only one who needs some supernatural help?"

George shook his head. "No, I guess not."

On the military transport plane after the two had stowed their baggage and had stretched out, Mutt turned to George and said, "Just when I was getting those slackers down at the motor pool straightened out, getting all our Bradleys running like tops, so we could come to your rescue if needed, I get orders to join you in Germany on a thirty day leave. How did you swing that?"

"You don't want to know, believe me," replied George. "Besides it is classified. Lets' just say I have become persona non gratis in Iraq."

"Classified my ass! I know more than they think I know. For instance, I hear your old enemy by the name of Jake Bannister has been telling everyone how he rescued you singlehandedly killing three terrorists at a whore house that had no women. I won't ask what you were doing there; I have seen you in action when it comes to loose women and –well I can fill in the rest: he did identify you as Farts Murfrey. I bet he doesn't know how lucky he was to survive if you reenacted what happened in Baltimore. As Pee Wee Herman said, 'It's déjà vu all over again'."

"It wasn't Pee Wee Herman, it was Pee Wee Reese or was it Yogi Berra," said George. "More like the Palace Pool Hall and Walmart combined."

From Templehoff, they went to Hahn, Germany and were assigned a room in a barracks formerly occupied by the German Gestapo, another time, another war; the accommodations nicer than anything they had seen in Iraq or Kuwait or at any in the states. The next day they rented a sawed off Mercedes; it looked like a half car, but it drove good and was comfortable besides getting good gas mileage.

Mutt became the designated driver since he had had experience driving in Scotland and India plus driving Bradley tanks adding the autobahn to his repertoire as he called it. They visited Wiesbaden, took pictures, ate Vienna Schnitzel and then on to Rotenberg, a medieval walled in city with its tiny cobbled streets, impassable to automobiles, but walked by numerous tourists who came to get a good deal in buying cuckoo clocks and other authentic relics that would be shipped home. George shipped a cuckoo clock to his mother and another clock that had precision gears turning golden weighted balanced balls inside a glass dome to his girlfriend, Maybelline. Mutt bought a beer stein that was a miniature castle complete with handle and a hinged turret top. At Frankfurt-A-Main, after a meal consisting of German sausage and Sauerbraten, plus Apple Strudel, Mutt said that he had had enough of the tourist stuff; it was time to meet the locals.

Mutt, using his charm as a big spender, soon had two beauties, both blondes, who directed the group to a dance hall.

The establishment had a dance floor filled with couples dancing to Germany's version of rock and roll. Upstairs, couples sat at tables next to a wooden railing where they could drink their beer and watch the dancing below. The foursome found a vacant table upstairs and began drinking German beer from huge oversized glass beer steins. On each table there was a telephone.

"I wonder why there are telephones on each table," said George sipping his beer.

About that time the phone rang, Mutt picked it up and said, "Hello."

In broken English, one of the male locals demanded, "I want to speak to Blondie. Put Blondie on,"

Mutt said, "Go to hell; get your own girl!" He slammed down the phone.

The phone rang again. The same voice said drunkenly, "I said put Blondie on the phone or I will come over dere."

"Listen, you Kraut; go get your own girl. If you come over here, I will pop you up beside your head and ring your bell. Jackass!" Mutt slammed the phone down again.

"Who was that?" inquired George.

"Just someone who wants his ass whipped," said Mutt in a loud voice.

The girls picking up on Mutt's belligerent attitude got up without a word and took off. About that time the blonde headed Kraut staggered up, facing George whom he believed to be the voice over the phone and said, "Here am I American. You want to whip my ass?"

"Not me; him." said George pointing to Mutt who meanwhile had gotten up without a word threw a right uppercut Mike Tyson style, connecting with the German's chin. This blow sent the Kraut flying backwards until he hit the wall in back of him where he slid down completely dazed. All that was needed was a small yellow bird above his head making tweet-tweet sounds-"déjà vu all over again", George remembering the time Mutt had given two American airmen the same treatment outside Keesler AFB at a barroom in Biloxi..

Behind the first German came his buddy, who also, wanted him a blondie and was his "back up".

"You can't do that to my comrade," he said as he advanced on Mutt, fists balled up ready to strike. This one was several inches taller than his unconscious friend. Before he got the words out of his mouth good, Mutt connected with another uppercut and he went staggering back hitting the wall, sliding down beside his comrade with glazed eyes as history repeated itself all over again.

All eyes were on Mutt and George. The loud music had stopped for a moment of silence which was broken by someone heard stomping loudly on the wooden stairway on the way up to the second floor. Out stepped a large bruin Hilda barmaid with a stern look on her face. She looked at Mutt, then at George and finally at the two unconscious men sitting against the wall.

She never said a word, but raised a large fist, popping it into her other hand, then grimly pointing to the door. She repeatedly pointed at

Mutt and George, swinging her arm around pointing at the door several times.

"Alright, we get the message," said Mutt who had learned through the years that the victor in fights was hardly ever blamed, but why push it. "Come on George. I think as you say, 'we have worn out our welcome.' Lets' go!"

No one followed as they left and as they got into the Mercedes, the loud beat of a base fiddle could be heard pounding away.

The next day, they decided to go on a tour bus that included a ride on a large converted barge down the Rhine River viewing ancient castle after ancient castle. At the end of the tour of castles, the bus was there to pick them up along with other tourists; then it was on to Brussels Belgium.

In Brussels, the tour taking the group down a side street, where a brass band was playing to a large crowd of other tourists. The tour guide, Axelrod Hess, gathered the group in back of the crowd, already formed, snapping pictures explaining that this was the famous Mannekin Pis statute of which there were many legends. One legend he explained, was that in the year 1142 during a battle, a two year old boy was hauled up a tree in a basket where he urinated on the Berthouts, the opposing troops. Another legend he told them, was that in the 14th century a little kid named Julianske, went outside the wall at Brussels, found a lit fuse connected to explosives, pissing on that fuse putting it out. George liked that version.

Then there was the most popular version that a visiting wealthy merchant, was separated from his little boy, frantically searching the city for his lost son in vain, but finally finding him at the very street corner the group was on, taking a leak into the street, erected the pissing statute to commemorate the event. Mutt's loud comment was: "And they should have erected a statute of that drunk One-eyed Joe and me when we took a leak on Fourteenth Street in Gulfport; instead they locked us up."

Someone in the crowd said with an English accent, "They should have kept you 'ole boy." But Mutt did not hear the comment, for he had seen the statue, a small golden boy and had heard that the kid, today, was pissing from a keg of beer that had been hooked up to the boy instead of running a stream of water. Mutt pushing through the crowd, the brass band playing loudly, upon reaching the stature quickly climbing up to get a mouthful of the yellow beer dribbling out of the boys golden penis, doing quite well until he was yanked down by some indignant local. Everyone in the crowd took pictures, including George, recording the event which also appeared on the front page of Brussels newspapers as well as on television.

Several times a year the small bronze boy would be dressed in various clothes including karate suits, and uniforms of various military units around the world. It just so happened that on this day as Mutt Hanson got his share of tap beer, the youngster was dressed in a small uniform that imitated the battle fatigues of the U.S. Army.

The headline from one newspaper, L'Anglophone, read: "G.I. drinks Pis from Mannekin." Other newspapers, Euractive and Mondo Times , of which Mutt purchased copies, had similar stories with Mutt's face clearly shown.

"Now it's you, who had better stay out of Brussels as well as in Europe," commented George. But Mutt did not mind; for a brief moment he had gained fame, but when people began to glare at him in recognition, he was glad when they loaded the tour bus to travel to Bruges, Belgium one hundred forty-five kilometers down the road. Again they saw a city from tour boats filled with tourists who gasped in awe at the number of cathedrals and churches, with their high steeples, buildings that looked like castles plus statutes and monuments of great men too numerous to count.

"Maybe they will erect a monument of me," said Mutt.

"I don't think so, unless you are assassinated here; some of those people did not look too happy with you desecrating their beloved statute, especially when they found out you were some brash American soldier," said George.

"I bet that tour guide gave out my name; I wish he had not done that."

"Now you are infamous, Sergeant Mutt."

More pictures were taken with a Canon camera George had purchased. A set of blue china dishes, which one of the old ladies on the tour said were something special, were bought by George, shipping them to his mother. The tour took them to Amsterdam where they were put on another river barge passing various houseboats and significant sights too numerous to remember as now it was becoming a blur. They dined at an Indian restaurant, picked out by the guide, Axelrod, where they ate curried food so powerful that it over rode George's purple pill causing him to go into a stall in the men's room where he burned off the vapors with a cigarette lighter singeing the hairs on his rear end. Fortunately, for all, the lavatory was vacant at the time. A 'swoosh' was all that was left after the event and the chatter of the patrons at the crowded tables drowned that out.

In Paris, George purchased a large bottle of the latest, most popular and expensive French Perfume called Indecent, shipping it to Maybelline. They climbed the Eifel Tower, went to the Louvre Museum where they found the Mona Lisa and Venus with no arms along with so many other pieces of art, that it made them dizzy. A lot of those serious tourists from their bus as well as others within hearing distance did not particularly like the rendition of the song, Mona Lisa, as sung in deep baritone by that drinker of yellow piss back in Brussels, "Manequin Mutt" as he now called himself. At the Moulon Rouge, Manequin Mutt consumed a liter of the cheapest French champagne he could find on the menu and broke out with his own special loud deep voiced version of Malaguena and then onto the ditty, "What do you do with a Drunken Sailor 'Earli' in the Morning". No one knew what to do with that drunken soldier on onboard the bus as they headed back to Germany, fearfully letting him sing until he fell asleep.

Before they knew it, the tour was over and it was back to Hahn, Germany to await a flight that would eventually take them to Afghanistan.

CHAPTER THIRTY

Off to Afghanistan

When the C-17 landed at Bagram Air Field in central Afghanistan, Mutt Hanson was dead broke without a clue as to how all his accumulated money while in Iraq, had been spent during the last thirty days having in his possession only a beer stein that could pass for a miniature castle and a stack of Belgium newspapers which reported one of his many noteworthy misadventures. He was not one to account for each dollar spent, for money to him only had one purpose: To be spent. The trip had also made a huge dent in George's savings, but the items he bought were tangible; nothing came cheap in Europe. Both had memories that would last a lifetime; the pictures which George took, proved it. As they marched down the ramp that let down at the rear of the airplane, they marveled at the change of scenery from that of Iraq; greeted by serene majestic white capped mountains in the distance. The air was cool and although the landscape was filled with rocks and boulders, they saw significantly more trees and shrubs that had pushed through the rocky layer of ground. Miles away in those serene mountains were caves that housed irate members of the Taliban who went around repeating, "God is Great!" as they fired mortar rounds nightly on to the invaders of their homeland and in this case more particularly Bagram Air Field and the area that housed the infidels.

Aircraft were landing and taking off at the busy airfield, which they found out was the nerve center of the operations in Afghanistan. They would stay in Bagram each for several days having been given quarters together. Mutt quickly learned there was no beer or liquor, but at least there was a Pizza Hut and a Dairy Queen in the vicinity of their wooden barracks; quarters which even had a divider between their ten by ten rooms. Along with running hot water, the facilities were more comfortable than in Iraq, but they still had to walk a hundred yards to the latrine which included brisk walks in the frozen air if one had to pass urine during the night or shower in the mornings.

The Army was a little liberal in its interpretation of the sixty mile buddy rule; George was to be sent to Sharana, a small base thirty miles from the Pakistan border and Mutt was supposed to be sent to a secret a base outside of Kabul that was readying itself for spring clearance of the Taliban in southern Afghanistan, but George insisted that those orders were incorrect and somehow got them changed with Mutt being his temporary aide in Sharana

After settling in his new home, the first order of business for George was to locate the wooden building that had computers loaded with Skype with its free phone calls that included a web cam where both parties could converse miles away while seeing the face of each other.

The camera, focusing on George's face was obviously a good one: There were still faint signs of healed cuts to his battle hardened face in spite of the time that had passed from his mission in Baghdad. May said, "George, what happened to you. You have scars on your face that were not there when I saw you last. Were you in a fight?"

"You should have seen the other guy," said George. "I bet you can't guess where I am and to be correct, don't even try."

"If you are not in Iraq, I can pretty well guess. I got your post card you sent from Germany. How come you haven't called me?"

"I tried, but Mutt and I went on a tour through Germany, Belgium, Holland, Amsterdam, and France and I never got the chance due to our time schedule and the language barrier, but I sent more post cards and you should be getting some packages of stuff I bought for you."

"If they catch up with me," said May. I will be leaving for Hanau, Germany before the end of the week. Maybe I will be assigned to Afghanistan after I complete my training in Germany."

"Thanks to the Army's buddy system we signed, Mutt is here with me; he is my Siamese twin going where ever I go. Hey, I am no longer a machine gunner riding in M.R.A.P.'s; I have a new assignment."

"I see." May's facial expression became stern. "So that's it. I am sure the Army will get its money's worth."

"They already have. That is why I had to get out of Iraq, if you know what I mean."

"I miss you. Maybe we can take a leave together. Had I known you and Mutt were getting a leave, maybe I could have joined you."

"It was one of those R and R leaves. Like I said, I had to get out of Iraq in a hurry."

"Oh. George, take care of yourself. When you get settled, maybe I can get stationed there also, if I can find your location."

"We will see. I will write you. I have to get up early. We have a ten and a half hour time difference so I need to sign off." He added sweetly, "Love you--baby."

"Love you too—baby!"

"Sorry I can't tell you more, but everything I do is classified."

"You did alright," May said with a broad smile seen on the computer screen. Call me when you can."

George found Sharana Forward Operating Base to have similar facilities as Bagram except less of it. They had a Pizza Hut which was housed in a trailer and the gymnasium was smaller; the plywood building that had the Internet computers had only a few computers. That night he was awakened by a barrage of rockets that sent him into a crowded bunker with other men who gladly explained that this only happened once or twice a week.

It wasn't hard for Lieutenant Murfrey to find the building that housed the Special Forces headquarters as well as a grumpy full bird Colonel Sanders in charge who said, "Sit down Lieutenant and no I am not kin to Colonel Sanders of the Kentucky Fried Chicken family. I will tell you this: I don't know what you are doing here. You just show up without any notice and then I get this cock-a-manie Lieutenant Colonel Benson who calls himself Benson and acts like he out ranks me. This is a pile of Shit, if you excuse my French. He obviously is your handler, but won't tell me a thing. The only thing he has told me is that he is standing by and wants me to have you call him on this secure telephone." Colonel Sanders pointed to a grey telephone on his desk.

He was dressed in camouflage battle fatigues; a large black 45 caliber automatic pistol hung across his chest. The large gun had a chain attached to what looked like a curled up telephone cord. Under the holstered gun was a large web belt with three also camouflaged canvas packets that must have held shells for the forty-five. There were several other packets attached to his gear as well as a black decimeter which George immediately recognized. The outfit was much like the fishing vest George wore when wade fishing for Speckled Trout out on the islands in the Gulf of Mexico; only his fishing vest carried hooks, lures, scissors and pliers, doubling as a life preserver. The Colonel did not mind identifying himself as "Sanders" in large letters sewn on his fatigues or above that was sewn a large Silver Eagle indicating his rank. His head was neatly shaved Yul Brenner style, but his fifty year old face had a three day old shadow.

George reached over and picked up the receiver which automatically set off a buzzing sound. He said guardedly, "Hello." Surely Colonel Benson would not answer on the first buzz; but he did.

"Lieutenant Murfrey, Benson here. Did you have a good leave?"

"Yes. Yes Sir. It was quite …." Benson cut him short.

"George, I see you brought Sergeant Hanson along with you. You know he was supposed to report down south Afghanistan. How did you manage that?'

"Sir, let me explain," said George nervously.

"That's' alright, George. You learn fast. You just tell your buddy, "Manequin Mutt" that he is now a member of the Spook Club and that I am cutting orders to make it legal. He can be your aide and Sergeant Ziegfield will be freed up to help where he is needed somewhere else; so you see this has worked out fine and he won't have to baby sit you this time. Besides, from what I understand, Mutt knows all about your duties in Special Forces."

"Thank you sir. He is my best friend even before I joined the Army."

"Look, George, it will be several days before I fly into Bagram to go over you next mission which was being worked up while you and your friend were on leave tearing up Europe; I got a full report on your nefarious activities—always making a splash. Now we will get down to business. I will give you a new secure phone number. If you or your "aide" have any questions call me. Now let me talk to that pompous buffoon in front of you. Is he armed to the teeth?"

"Yes sir. How did you know?"

"Tell you later."

George handed the phone to Colonel Sanders. After George left the building, Sanders called his Orderly into his office. He said, "Get Congressman Locker on the phone; he will probably be at home. I want to know everything there is about this Lieutenant Colonel Alan Benson and this so called Special Forces soldier, Lieutenant George Murfrey. I am in command of the Special Forces here which is a sniper unit and this Murfrey or whatever his name is, doesn't look like any sniper I have ever seen or an army man either. Something peculiar is going on here and I want to know what it is."

Three weeks passed and no word from Colonel Benson with details of the mission.

George was kept busy back in school with an Afghan tutor who taught George Afghan words and sentences as well as the Afghan customs, codes of conduct. Again he was treated to a photo gallery of the area which included the mountainous paths, various caves in which the militants, as they were called hid. Map after map were shown him until the tests identifying the area which also included Western Pakistan; his quizzes were passed with flying colors. George knew how important it was to pay close attention as in Iraq where his very life depended on his knowledge of the area and his ability to understand the language spoken.

With his battle field conversion, George started reading the Bible, given him, and when he did not understand certain passages, he called on the local Chaplin who was more than glad to explain them to him. He did comprehend the passage: "My people perish from lack of knowledge." He did not intend to perish.

The second week of his intensified training concentrated on Pakistan whose border was only thirty miles away. When that week ended, he found that he could speak a few words with the instructor both in Afghan and Pakistani; he was able to identify the roads, paths and areas of Afghanistan and Western Pakistan and even certain Taliban leaders believed to be in the area. It became obvious where his next assignment would take place.

During this intensive learning period, George did not see much of his aide, Sergeant Hanson, who was not idle either, having been placed temporarily with a unit that went out on patrol daily into the mountains to ferret out pockets of Taliban fighters. These excursions came later each morning after the air force, out of Bagram, sent out airplanes and helicopters that bombed, shot rockets and strafed suspected Taliban strongholds and camps. Then the troops, including, Mutt moved in to finish the job.

When each incursion ended, Mutt would come dragging in greatly fatigued, complaining vigorously.

"I wish I was back in Iraq where it was safe," said Mutt in a tired voice throwing his helmet across the room, hitting the wall with a loud thud, while standing his rifle next to the door. "The Afghan fighters are nothing like the insurgents in Iraq; they don't come at you head on, but from each side trying to out flank us. They are tougher and smarter than those wimps we faced in Iraq."

"They have been fighting somebody for hundreds of years; they ought to be experienced by now," commented George who would soon have troubles of his own and really did not want to hear the scary stories related by Mutt.

"The other day, you know the time I was gone three days, the militants as they call them here, out flanked us completely in an ambush killing four of our men. I thought I was a goner when they tried to over run our position, but fortunately the Calvary showed up in the form of Blackhawk helicopters who blasted those bastards to smithereens and got us out of there with the wounded and the dead. I was lucky that time." Said Mutt normally reticent, but now really running off at the mouth. "And they are accurate when they shoot—you know like sharp shooters with scopes and long range rifles—and those nightly mortar and rocket attacks keep me awake. How do you sleep through all that racket? This place is a hell hole. Damn if I like being your Aide; I should have turned down that privilege and gone down to the troops in the south where I would be driving my Bradley tank."

George who did not have an answer to Mutt's plight simply said, "It is classified; no comment."

"I bet! At least I got promoted to Sergeant. Now I get Sergeant's pay, overseas pay, combat pay and TDY pay. I sure need it; I am so broke I can't pay attention, not that it would do me any good. There is really nothing to spend it on even if I had time. I hope I am still around when they rotate us." Mutt threw up his hands and slapped his knees. "Well, I have got a foray in the morning. Hooray for the foray! I wish I could find a bar around here. No wonder these people are so mean; no beer and I am starting to get just like them." With that speech, he left George's quarters. After boots and clothes hit the floor in the next room, George could hear Mutt snoring away.

The next morning George stepped out into a breath taking chill that reached right into his bones as his slippers crunched on the snow coated ground on his way to the latrine a football field away. The tall mountains that surrounded the valley were completely covered white with snow, overhead the sky was turning blue as twinkling stars began to fade away, darkness being pushed away by the sun peeking out through the very mountains Mutt would be patrolling in an effort to dislodge the elusive Taliban fighters who shouted "God is Good!" every time one of Mutt's fellow soldiers was struck down by shots fired from the unseen enemy. Already American airplanes were flying in the vicinity dropping their bombs in areas suspected of hiding Taliban militants who would come out of nowhere to ambush the troops the moment the airplanes left, a new sounding boom echoing through the valley announcing that now was the militant's turn as Mutt and his comrades at arms passed through a gap in the mountains on their way to meet the enemy.

"This is the day that the Lord has made; I will rejoice and be glad in it." Said George back from the latrine, while he read aloud from Psalms eighteen and then from Proverbs eighteen, mainly because today was the eighteenth of November and his Chaplin had suggested the reading of passages from both books of the Bible that corresponded with the days of the week. He pondered about the difference between the two religions; one based on God's love and freedom to embrace it while the other ordered the killing of all infidels, Jews and Christians who refused to renounce their religion and convert to Islam; a religion where extremists such as the Taliban grew beards, beat their women, failing to correctly follow their edicts or were stoned to death if they were adulterers, while the man went free unharmed even when he raped and ravished them. He could not understand how one religion preached forgiveness and Grace while the other encouraged blowing oneself up as a suicide bomber. While he was considering ordering a copy of the Koran over the Internet to check this out for himself, he was notified that Colonel Benson had arrived from Bagram; that George was to proceed to building 1009-B, a newly built addition to 1009-A.

As he entered the wooden building and clopped across the wooden floor, he noticed the Sergeant seated at the wooden desk that was facing him was a cute brunette around twenty years of age.

"Lieutenant Murfrey to see Colonel Benson," snapped George. "Where is Sergeant Ziegfield?"

The pretty Sergeant whose name tag read 'Branson' said, "Sergeant Ziegfield's wife was due to have her baby so he went on leave. He will be back as soon as the baby is delivered. You may go on in; the Colonel is waiting for you."

When George entered, he was greeted with "How is it going George? Have a seat."

As he sat down, he noticed that Benson was dressed in civvies the same as the last time before he went on his mission in Iraq. Did this have some superstitious meaning?

By-passing that question, George asked, "What happened to Colonel Sander's office? Did he move you out?"

"I thought it best that we conduct our business here. That arrogant bastard resented me using his office and wanted to know too much about our mission. He even contacted a Congressman wanting details about what we were doing in Afghanistan. I had to show the Congressman my gold shield given to me by the President and directed him to the Oval Office. That Congressman did not like that and left mumbling: "We will see about that.""

"Enough of that, George, at 0900 hours I have a briefing team coming who will go over your next assignment I thought we might chat before they arrived." He shuffled through a file and said, "I see you have had further training and according to your instructors, you did quite

376

well and are good to go. I have good news and bad news; the good news is that you get to go on another mission of great importance which could affect the war."

"Where have I heard that before?" muttered George. "And what pray tell is the bad news, Alan?"

"Don't get too smart, George; I am still your commanding officer and as you know you were welcomed into the Army because of your unique abilities when in fact, you were unfit to serve as a soldier. Being an obese pot-bellied soldier walking around each base you were assigned, raised many eyebrows and many questions from which I caught a lot of flak to say the least."

George shifted nervously in his chair; he did not like where this was going. He said, "I have lost over seventy pounds."

"I know you have, George and I am proud of you. You have taken to the Army like a duck to water. Well here is the bad news: Gas warfare is illegal under the Geneva Convention." Benson shook his head. "I know what you are thinking: They meant the manufacture and use of poisonous gas such as mustard gas. Somehow it has gotten out that your flatulence may be deadly to humans or at the least harmful. There are records that can be obtained about your ability even before you joined the army. There are pros and cons about all this. We have that wacky doctor Aholie still maintaining that you are the 'Skunk man', a freak of nature and there is plenty of proof to back that up. On the other hand your record as a watcher and then a machine gunner on an M.R.A.P. in Iraq without any gaseous occurrences, thanks to that pill I gave you, has them baffled. The probe goes on, but as of yet, they have not learned about the pill. I tell you this to prepare you in case they get wind of the pill and put two and two together." Alan smiled.

"The bad news is this: I am afraid this may be your last mission under Special Forces. We were lucky that that stupid Jacob Bannister got himself caught, was tortured, then stabbed those three terrorists with that Bowie knife of his, insisting that he killed them and that you had nothing to do with it. What you and he don't know was that when we sent our men to clean up the mess, there were two other dead terrorists, who had arrived before our men, entering the room without gas masks, dying also. I had them stabbed with the same Bowie knife taken from Bannister; which ought to confuse them for a while, but keeping a secret like that is as difficult to do now-a-days as keeping sex between a man and a woman secret. Someone always wants to blab and it is usually to the wrong person. When our boys entered with gas masks intact, they had to clean up the vomit and blood on the floor, but when they got outside they noticed the smell had followed them outside, like a skunk's scent-mind you- so I ordered the building burned to the ground, but that section of town stunk for several weeks in spite of the smoke."

There was a tap on the door and Sergeant Brunson entered. "Colonel, the men you were expecting have arrived," she said.

"Have them take a seat, Mary. I will see them in a minute." He arose from his desk and continued. "So you see we have a dilemma; If this mission was to get out, there would be a greater stink around the world than any you are capable of expelling. In short this has to be your last mission. Again you will be furnished with an implanted GPS instead of putting it in your belt along with an electronic signaling device. Keep your ability to fart deadly gas between you and me even when being briefed by the men in the outer office. You will use it of course, but lets' keep that our secret. Okay."

"Fine by me, I am not too proud of my 'Ability' as you have called it," said George. It seems to me; you have it backwards. The bad news is that I have to go on that dangerous mission—in harm's way—so to speak; the good news is that I won't have to do it again. Frankly, I never liked the stigma of what you call my 'Ability'. I have suffered all my life because of my ability. I really appreciate the purple pills you gave me to help control my ability; you don't know what it feels like to be normal. Not a day goes by that I don't pray to God for him to take away my 'Ability' permanently. Maybe this could be the answer to my prayer."

"Maybe", said the Colonel as he walked to the door and opened it, gesturing to three stern looking men seated in the outer office; all in their thirties and all dressed alike in grey suits.

After each one was seated, Benson introduced each one as Bill, John and Dick of the CIA.

Dick, who had a long narrow nose, a narrow jaw, beady eyes and long pointed fingers suitable for a pianist, looked George over before reaching into his brown leather, government issue brief case, pulling out a ten by eight black and white photo of a turbaned man with a heavy mustache but with a narrow beard neatly trimmed. He handed the photo to George and said, "This is Mehsud," as if George had heard of him. When he saw that George had no idea who this Mehsud person was, he continued with a forced half smile, "Hakimullah Mehsud. He is the most dangerous man in Pakistan, but just when we thought him dead after we blew up his house, he has now appeared. We think he was responsible for blowing up our CIA base killing seven of our best agents. Now in spite of numerous missile strikes by our forces from this very forward operating base and attacks by the Pakistani army, he is back in full force spreading the word that he is invincible; he cannot be killed.

Dick paused while Bill and John set up a monitor popping a DVD disk in a machine attached to it. Mehsud, in full vibrant color, was speaking publically stating in English, "Praise to God, I have good news to the Muslim world that I am alive and healthy and have been successful in helping to rid the world of the infidel invaders of our country and those who support them." He then showed his videos of explosions that took place in three different cities in Pakistan, one of which was the CIA base being utterly destroyed, depicting survivors funneling out of the burning building screaming in terror as they fell charred from having been caught on fire. He spoke in Urdu, the main Pakistani language which was translated into English. Behind him was a map of the United States, toward which he turned and with a pointer showed sections of the U.S. where his "Fighters" had penetrated the country and soon would give extremely painful blows to the terrorist America giving all Americans a humiliating defeat. He also took credit for suicide bombing at two other American bases: Camp Chapman and Camp Salerno in Afghanistan.

The spook called John walked over and hit a tiny button that froze the gruesome picture that George had seen so often resulting from suicide bombers exploding themselves as well as, in this case, what was once a check point entering an army base, all that was left of several soldiers guarding the entrance, was now charred remains of the building and an army helmet dented and battered laying in the middle of the tarmac road. "As you can see, Lieutenant Murfrey," said John gravely. "This man is a menace responsible for the lives of many people including our own CIA agents and must be stopped."

"What do you want me to do?"

"Glad you asked that question, Lieutenant," said John sarcastically. Bill will tell you briefly about your mission."

Bill, a short baldheaded black man with white teeth and pink gums, stood up; his innocent looking face smiled disarming George who was beginning to get apprehensive about what might be expected of him.

He said, "Lieutenant Murfrey, you are being loaned to us by the army. It just so happens that you have a Doppler ganger, someone who looks almost identical to you back in Detroit, Michigan, desiring to defect and join the Taliban in Pakistan. We have been monitoring his e-mails for months; now they are ready to recruit this individual; he has even sent a picture of himself to his recruiters in Canada and at this very minute arrangements are being made in which he will fly to Toronto, Canada to meet them and if approved, he will then be flown to Pakistan. We are pretty sure he will meet Mehsud, since in one of the e-mails intercepted, he praised Mehsud for his heroic efforts and in an effort to recruit this would be traitor, whose name is Peter Cooper, they have told him that Mehsud would, indeed, like to meet him and use him for propaganda purposes. Our boy, Cooper, replied that he wanted to be a fighter killing Americans for their cause." He paused, looked George over and continued: "We think they will accept him with open arms. Already we have our agents in Mr. Cooper's neighborhood who have reported Cooper being watched by certain foreign looking persons. They are checking him out and from all we have seen, they are definitely interested."

George was then shown a picture of Peter Cooper.

"I can't believe it. You are right; that man looks just like me except his hair is longer and he is growing a beard. How are you going to handle that?"

"We will pick up Mr. Cooper and put him away for safe keeping; he will be charged later. The Pakistanis will notify Mr. Cooper that they are going to arrange for his flight to Pakistan; send him airline tickets. You will be placed in his house and e-mail them that you are cutting your hair short and cutting your beard off so that the authorities will not become suspicious. You will send them a new picture of yourself and if they buy it, then in that case, you can count yourself in. So far they don't have Cooper's finger prints. When you meet with them, they will get yours which will reflect that you are Peter Cooper, if they go that far. Frankly, we believe if they fingerprint you, it will be solely to make sure you are the right person in Pakistan."

"You make it sound so simple," said George.

"It is simple," said Dick. "Those implants you will have imbedded in your body will let us know every moment just where you are. Colonel Benson has assured us that you will be able to escape without harm after meeting with Mehsud. Attached next to the GPS device is a button you can push and after that you will have thirty minutes to get out of their camp. How you do it is not our concern or responsibility, but after thirty minutes, the camp of Mehsud will be obliterated by rockets sent into it by drones. You may have read about them, but Mehsud is so slippery, this time we want a spotter before him to make sure he doesn't get away. Think you can handle that?"

Before George could answer, John added, "We think we have the perfect plan; you get in, where you will be greeted with open arms, and get out."

George looked to Colonel Benson who nodded approvingly.

"Okay, I am in. Now I know why I have been given a crash course learning to understand Urdu, but I cannot speak it very good. But what concerns me is that my cover in Iraq was blown. Won't they recognize me in Pakistan?"

Dick started to answer, but Bill waved him off. "Let me answer this, he said in his dry monotone voice, "All you have to do is to shave your head. Here is a composite of what you will look like completely bald. After you are on your way to Pakistan, you can start letting it all grow back." He handed George a photo that had been altered to show him with a shaved head.

This satisfied him; he really did look different; it was startling.

"Well what about it George; feel better?" said Colonel Benson who knew the answer.

"Much better. It gives me a whole new outlook on life; I may decide to keep the look, especially if it fools the bad guys."

The three agents were rolling their eyes at each other. George heard one whisper to another, "Is this guy for real?"

"I forgot to tell you men; George tends to be a smart ass. Isn't that right George?"

"Always have been; I don't ever plan to change."

Bill turned to look at George. "I don't care if you are a smart ass or not; all we want is for this mission to be successful and if you bring about the termination of Mehsud, to me that will be success. By way of advice, the Taliban don't have a sense of humor and if you smart-off with them, they won't hesitate to shoot your smart ass off."

"I will try to remember that," said George.

After that discussion, the three agents looked at each other and nodded. Bill said, looking at George. "Lets' get started. There is a military transport standing by to take you to the United States. Go like you are; don't even bother to pack. Colonel Benson will go with you and Kathy Brunson to Bagram to catch your flight. Good luck."

On the way to the airport, Benson asked, "You are not worried about the mission, are you George?"

"No of course not; it's just that throughout my training from the very beginning, you have been there guiding me. I trust you; you have always been honest with me. Now I am thrust with strangers, people I don't know and I am expected to trust them with my life. Frankly, I don't trust them; all they are interested in is for this Mehsud to be killed. I feel like I am expendable in their eyes. Also, what will happen to Mutt Hanson?"

"Just a change of plans, George. This mission is extremely important; look at it this way: It will probably be your last. If it is any consolation, I will be monitoring your progress throughout the ordeal and I will still act as your safety net. Here is my secret cell phone number; memorize it; call me any time if you get into difficulty and know this: I will move heaven and earth should you need help. Do you believe me?"

"Sure. Why not? You have always been straight with me. One way or the other it will be my last."

"Speaking of Hanson, I need you to sign this temporary waiver of the 'Army's buddy agreement'". He handed the paper for George to sign. "Mutt will be sent down to Southern Afghanistan to the Heavy Armament Division where he will again drive a Bradley tank; that should make him happy." The Colonel handed George a name tag that read, "Peter Cooper" and said, "Here. Wear this; you might as well get used to being Peter Cooper, Peter." Benson passed George a hand bag and said, "I took the privilege in rounding up some civilian clothes; you can change at the air field."

After changing at the air field rest room in a stall meant for bowel movements, George showed the Sergeant at Space Control his orders and was escorted to his airplane. The Sergeant politely told Colonel Broderick Nelson, who was sitting in the designated seat, that he had been bumped; that Mr. Cooper would occupy it. Colonel Nelson glared at George, loudly asking the Sergeant why he was being bumped. George did not hear the answer, but reading the irate Colonel's lips, he said something like: "I am going to get you Peter Cooper." George merely smiled; he was used to people out to get him. He turned to Colonel Nelson and mouthed, "You will have to stand in line."

Before going on to Detroit, George was met with waiting CIA agents who took him to their headquarters in Langley, Virginia. At Langley, he did not get a tour of the facilities but was put through a full body search, fingerprinted, his papers checked thoroughly and had his left eye scanned and recorded for future reference before being allowed to enter as Peter Cooper formerly George Cedric Murfrey. George had slept off and on during the fourteen hour flight, which was considered enough sleep, as immediately, he was escorted to a small room with no windows, paneled in light oak complete with a large panel monitor and one female instructor. He began another crash course on how to send e-mails by the real Peter Cooper's computer, a Dell; a litany of Cooper's life and friends; Cooper's mannerisms and personal data which upon seeing this man's life spread out before him, he wondered what kind of knowledge did the CIA have of his life. That afternoon, he was introduced to a new language spoken in Pakistan: Pashto.

His instructor explained, "This is the language spoken in the tribal areas of North and South Waziristan where we now are quite sure you will sent to meet Mehsud, if accepted, for training. This would be the area you would receive your training, but we believe that besides being trained to be one of the fighters, they would use you for propaganda purposes by videoing you and putting you on television around the world. Of course, your mission does not require you to go through all of that. Your job will be to get into the camp, verify that Mehsud is there; push your verifying button that was surgically implanted under your left arm pit; then get out before the rockets wipe out the camp; your presence pinpointing exactly where Mehsud is located. This will be tricky, but we have the greatest confidence that you can pull this off. We have studied your records and believe if they ever accept you as one of their recruits, you can easily complete your mission," he said repeating himself.

"How much do you know?" asked George.

"Everything and it will never leave the CIA."

"When do I begin living as Peter Cooper?"

"Tomorrow night you will be sneaked into Cooper's house where you will live as Peter Cooper and wait to hear from the Taliban."

Peter Cooper had lived in a two bedroom wood frame house on Siesta Street in Detroit rented from Mrs. Mable Strange, a widow who let it go for four hundred fifty a month. Cooper was a self-employed trader buying and selling on e-Bay plus visiting yard sales and garage sales frequently. His house was filled with relics from fishing rods, lawn mowers, clothing and TV's; it was junked up with very little space to move around. He drove an old model brown Ford Taurus which was parked in the closed garage.

When George Murfrey, the new Peter Cooper arrived during the next night, he was dropped off at the house behind Cooper's house, making his way into the house through the back door. He had been told that the CIA had its agents positioned in a rental house in the vicinity where they could keep an eye on Cooper's house as well as every vehicle that came down Siesta Street. They had spied one particular car, a silver Honda Civic, traveling slowly in front of the Cooper house at regular intervals, but as soon as a police patrol car entered the street, the Civic manned by a foreign looking man simply eased off without incident. The Civic had been present forty-five minutes before George moved into the Cooper residence; the CIA managing to have the Detroit Police send their patrol car down the street to flush him out. When George arrived there was no foreign man in a Civic to monitor his arrival.

George found some clean sheets after shoving aside all kinds of what was junk to him and after making the bed, went right to sleep.

The next morning after breakfast, he found a message on the Dell Computer. It stated that Cooper had been approved for a flight to Pakistan in two days and that the tickets could be picked up at the airport. His fake passport, which sported his recent shaved head, no mustache photo emailed to his new found friends, should be at the post office under general delivery where he could pick up his mail which also contained three hundred dollars for expenses on his trip. He was booked on Flight 1029 aboard Emirates Airlines leaving at 0600 arriving at Toronto and from Toronto he would fly into Dubai; his final leg would be to Peshawar, Pakistan. Upon his arrival in Peshawar, there would be someone who would pick him up; it was all very easy; maybe too easy.

CHAPTER THIRTY ONE

Infiltration in Pakistan

Although Murfrey had lost a considerable amount of weight, he was still considered heavy set for his five foot six inch height, his face still round and plump; not a face one would consider a potential foe; someone to fear. When his plane landed in Toronto, he had a two hour layover. To his surprise Arabian type men with turbans and flowing robes as well as women glancing nervously around hidden by Berkas leaving only a slit for their dark flashing eyes, were in large numbers. Canada, it seemed were more tolerant of those mid-easterners who walked around without concern. As George was examining a store inside the airport that had an abundance of cheap watches on sale, someone bumped into him, apologizing and upon examining his pocket, he discovered a pre-paid cell phone. His first impulse was to take it to the men's room and flush it down the toilet; he was so used to this instrument being one used to detonate road side bombs and suicide vests. But then he asked himself: "What would Peter Cooper do?" He kept it.

No sooner had he sat down to read a magazine he had purchased, his cell phone rang and when he flipped the cover open a foreign voice said, "Meester Cooper. Meester Peter Cooper?"

"Yes."

"How was your flight so far? Are you having any doubts?"

"No," George answered. "God is great!"

"God is great," said the foreign voice. "You will be met at the airport in Peshawar by a tall man wearing a blue robe and a blue and white striped skull hat. He will take you to your destination. God is great!"

"God is great!" answered George, but the phone had already gone dead. George now had a phone in which he could call Colonel Alan Benson on a number given him which he memorized --and it had been furnished by the enemy. God is truly great, thought George.

From Toronto, Canada George flew into Dubai where he spent the night at a designated hotel; not one of those used by oil magnates and billionaires, but a commercial hotel used by business men, hoping to get a piece of the action where big money was being passed around. His last leg of the flight would begin the next morning to Peshawar, Pakistan. After he had occupied his room, a package was delivered which contained a white skull cap a white loose fitting shirt and white baggy pants which he had seen worn in Iraq and Afghanistan. A note accompanied the clothes stating that he should wear these clothes prior to his flight to Peshawar as it would allow quick recognition by those who would meet him.

Sure enough, at the Peshawar Airport, George was met by a small dark skinned man, wearing a blue flowing robe and a blue and white skull cap who asked, "You, Peter Cooper?"

George nodded, "Yes, I am."

"Passport. Please."

George handed the bogus passport to the man who studied a fuzzy dark picture of George, being satisfied, stuck the passport in his trousers and said, "Come with me. Welcome to Pakistan, Peter Cooper." It was not a greeting of warmth, but one said perfunctorily from a face with cold dark eyes and a stern face, George thinking, "Don't these people ever smile?"

George was led to what used to be a blue Datsun four door sedan, now covered with dust; even the side windows were almost opaque; an apparent victim of old age and abuse; the little car had to be missing from someone's junk yard.

The interior was no better; the seats were thread bare, its springs compressed and the head liner had come loose in places, one portion touching George's head in the passenger's front seat, to which he found annoying.

Miraculously, the engine started when the little man, the designated driver who introduced himself as Rasheed, turned the ignition key, surprising George with its sewing machine hum, giving no doubt where the attention to the upkeep of the car had been focused.

"How are things in the United States?" asked Rasheed without any real interest; he could care less.

"Not good at all," replied George as the small Datsun pulled away from the curb. "You speak good English. Where did you learn it?"

"I studied two years in America as a foreign exchange student at Catholic University in Washington D.C. Kind of ironic," said Rasheed. "Then I was called back to Pakistan. Someday I will go back, but now I am needed here." He turned his head, eyes focusing on George waiting for an answer. "So you want to do something about the great Satan?"

"The great Satan? Oh, I get it; you mean America. Yeah, I am sick of it all; nothing will change from within. That is why I am here."

They were leaving the outskirts of Peshawar, which was like most cities in the world with its squalid area of slum shacks, the paved road narrowing when Rasheed pulled the car over in front of a busy market with dead chickens hanging from hooks attached to a timber overhead and bins of produce being picked over by Muslim women in their typical dress. No one paid any attention to them as two men brashly walked up to the car with their AK-47s' slung over their shoulders, which was a good sign to George; they were not going to shoot him in public. The market did become silent for a moment except for quaint tingling mid-eastern music coming from a boom box of Chinese descent. As the men climbed into the back seat of the little car, the noise of the market resumed as the women went back to grocery shopping.

George glanced at the two men who wore turbans, their faces covered with heavy black beards and hard cold black eyes that typically showed no expression. It was as if they all tried to look alike in contrast to his clean shaven face. Maybe it was too much trouble for them to shave or maybe they did not have a supply of razor blades.

Each man merely glared at George briefly then ignoring him and spoke to the driver. He could tell that they were speaking about him in Pashto, but he could only pick up a word or two as they spoke too fast for him to fully understand. George did understand one or two words which were "kill" and "infidel". He felt a shiver run down his spine realizing for the first time that he was all alone in a strange country with no one to turn to.

So he smiled and said to them, "Hi. I am Peter."

No response; they just sat there like tar baby.

"They don't speak English," announced Rasheed.

Along the highway, George noticed the few traffic signs he saw were in Urdu and English; Urdu being the main language in Pakistan, but as they left the urban area he noticed that the signs began to appear in squiggles which was Arabic. The paved roads ran out as they hit narrow goat paths throwing up gravel and dust which caused the Datsun to list and slide making it seem like the car was traveling faster than it was. No one else seemed to mind the pounding the Datsun was taking as it hit muddy potholes, splashing mud and rocks to the side. The trip had started an hour before the sun was setting, but now only rays of light managed to shine through at times; the sun being hidden by distant tall mountains. Meanwhile, George held on for dear life as he grabbed the piece of arm rest with the grip of death as the little car fishtailed, barely staying on the road. He had not ever seized anything so tightly; not even when he had been in the dentist's chair.

The long day which included his flight began to take its toll; only the occasional jolting of the car as it bottomed out and pointed questions by Rasheed kept him from going into a deep sleep. George glanced into the back seat and noticed his two silent escorts were both peacefully snoring away. Finally, he released his grip on the arm rest and joined them.

George did not realize when he fell asleep or how long he had dozed; he was suddenly awakened when Rasheed tapped him on his shoulder and announced, "We are almost there" and then in Pashto to the two bodyguards something similar. They came awake abruptly and for the first time, George noticed that they had a worried look on their faces. He turned his attention to the landscape which made him think he was back in Afghanistan with its level valleys, green trees and snow-capped majestic mountains. The air was thinner and cooler. As they climbed higher, the little Datsun crammed with four sizeable men, strained as Rasheed down shifted the gears, knocking George's left knee with the knob from the floor shift from time to time.

It was a wild country; it was a lonely country. They covered miles of broken rock on the side of the highway which had been broken due to water freezing between the crevices sending the separation dashing down the mountain as rubble. George wondered if nature would send a big boulder crashing down upon them as they swerved around mountains and into valleys with its greenery. Occasionally they would pass a single small tree that had somehow sprung out of the side of the mountain, then often passing miniature water falls with water cascading across the highway which had now grown smooth over the years of passage and then there would be snow flurries as they rounded along the narrow road that did not allow much room to pass if they met another vehicle coming from the opposite direction. George dared not look down the sheer drop off on the other side still clinging to his tattered armrest with all his strength.

One of the body guards leaned forward and asked in Pashto, "Where are we?" When Rasheed replied, the other man asked to stop, obviously for a nature break. George understood some of the simple words such as "stop" giving him some confidence in his crash course in Pashto.

Rasheed pulled the vehicle to a stop, everyone getting out, stretching and relieving themselves, George joining in. This human act became a bonding in spite of difference in language, looks, ideology and taught prejudices; everyone relaxed. Dogs could be heard barking; a tribal village ahead could not be far. It was black dark and very cold. The stars above seemed to jump out at them while a banana shaped moon added the Arabian touch.

He heard one of the guards remark about where they were and George picked up the words: "North Waziristan" and "camp". This meant that they were not far from the Afghanistan border and to George it meant he was not really that far from his own camp Sharana and Bagram Air Field; only a short distance and tall mountains separated them. He became amused when he thought that maybe they could hear him yodel as in the Swiss Alps over at Sharana, but suppressed a smile.

One of the guards produced a loaf of home cooked bread passing it around. George, realizing he was quite hungry, tore off a hunk chewing

390

it with delight. Next a goat skin filled with some indistinguishable liquid was handed to him to wash down the bread.

Still no one smiled; not even George, who wanted to, when he thought about his friend Mutt who, also habitually kept a dead pan face, was asked once if he ever smiled. Mutt answered with the straight face, "I am smiling right now." Then keeping the same dead pan look, he said, "Now I am laughing." Maybe the two bodyguards were silently laughing at him.

Although the tension had dropped several degrees between the men, there was the remaining air of distrust in this foreigner.

Rasheed must have tired of his interrogation for he now began to ask general questions about what was happening in the U.S. George, who had been out of the States quite a while, himself, answered generally repeating what he had heard on television and the brief time he had been on the streets. This seemed to satisfy Rasheed, who merely grunted in disgust.

An hour later as they drew close to the skyscraper-mountains bordering Afghanistan and Pakistan, George witnessing a magnificent view as the sun literally crawled up the mountain side from the East shooting out rays of splendid light into crevices, valleys and openings between the trees growing on slopes demonstrating to all the presence of God.

As if reading everyone's mind, Rasheed stopped the car to let everyone get a good view; it beat everything George had ever seen.

"Magnificent. Breathtaking," murmured George.

"God is good. God is great," said Rasheed in English and then in Pashto to the guards who acquiesced aloud. They got out of the vehicle each producing a cloth rug kneeling down chanting their prayers. Although George did not have a rug to kneel on, he fell to his knees and began to pray, picking up the chant, joining in with the group.

After about five minutes of praying and chanting, the group climbed back in to the car which now was slowly crawling over rough terrain, a make-shift road, and soon they were traveling downhill. Rasheed pulled out a black cell phone, flipped the lid, pushed several buttons and after several rings began to speak Pashto into the phone.

George concluded that their arrival was being announced; soon the camouflaged camp below could be seen, looming larger as they descended; he could see activity in the form of people going about their business some huddled over smoking camp fires, both men and women. It was quite a large camp with big and small tents along with some wooden houses spread out as far as the terrain permitted the eye to see. Camouflage netting protected portions of the area from air surveillance.

Rasheed hung up saying loudly, "God is good. Death to America." Taking the cue, George repeated this chant loudly which seemed to please everyone.

"Here is the drill, Peter Cooper," said Rasheed in colloquial English. They are expecting you, but first you will be allowed to shower and clean up. We have some new clothes for you; more in style here like the fighters wear. Otherwise, they might take you for a westerner and take a pot shot at you." He laughed for the first time. "They don't particularly like Americans; even those who take up their cause. Come join us in prayer again and then we eat. After you have dined on our cuisine and have filled your belly, the tribal leaders want to take a look at you and ask you a few questions. Not to worry, I have already told them that I have interrogated you and that you should make a good comrade in arms. Sound good to you?"

George nodded solemnly. "Sure."

"You are in luck today. I hear the great leader is here today and don't be surprised if he shows up. If he does, you will surely be impressed."

"And who might that be?" asked George meekly.

"Mehsud! Hakimullah Mehsud! The man responsible for wiping out seven CIA agents and blowing up many out posts and now is planning to target American cities. I am sure he will want to talk with you; pick your brain, so to speak." He looked George in the eye and said, "You are a very lucky man. God is great!"

CHAPTER THIRTY TWO

Wounded

George was led to a small wooden one room shack where he changed clothes after taking a shower. It had a cot and a couple of pegs to hang his clothes on, plus a small table with a glass pitcher for water, but no glass to drink from. He put on his new clothes which included a maroon and white turban and a white flowing cloth robe. When he stepped outside his two body guards were patiently waiting, directing him to breakfast, some strange tasting mush, which did not sit well in his stomach; it felt like he would explode prematurely.

About that time Rasheed showed up, seeing the apprehension George had that he might prematurely cut loose, letting some gas out before he could complete his mission. Holding it in was getting to be a problem as he had discontinued taking his purple pill, not bringing any with him; he started getting cramps, the pain contorting his face.

Thinking George's facial expression was his fear of meeting the great Mehsud, Rasheed said, "Calm down Mr. Cooper. I have already told them that you are alright; you are to be trusted. You will be welcomed with open arms!"

Then it was prayer time again and while the whole camp was dropping to their knees, George stepped into his living quarters and snatched a small rug off the floor and followed suit. While the rest were praying to Allah, George was praying silently to God for a successful mission; a prayer that asked for protection from all kinds of harm including gun shots, exploding bombs and even sickness from that strange tasting breakfast which now made his stomach rumble with a bloated feeling, insistently crying for relief. He knew he could not hold it in much longer and prayed he could control it until the mission was completed or at least give him the opportunity to squat down over one of the many camp fires in the area and burn off the blue flames that would blast out, knowing this would really go over big time.

393

Unaware that prayer time had ended; George was still on his knees praying when he heard Rasheed, standing over him along with the two body guards, say, "Show time, Peter Cooper. The tribunal is assembled and they want a look at you. Even the big man is there; so let's get with it."

George got up, adjusting his new turban and gown, marching to a long, unpainted wooden building that faced them. It had a porch that ran length ways on the front which had three steps at the entrance. Two guards with AK-47's stood on each side of the doorway. Inside was a long wooden table approximately twenty feet long and seated behind the table were eleven bearded men spread out the full length. There was a window at each end of the narrow building and amazingly thee was a skylight located overhead at the middle of the wooden table that allowed light to filter through the dimly lit room illuminating the table and the chieftains. There were masked guards at each end of the room heavily armed with their assault rifles. George had already been relieved of all his worldly good including his watch, the cell phone, Peter Cooper's wallet with his identification, handkerchief and earlier, his pass port. There was nothing to fear from Peter Cooper if he turned out to be an enemy.

George gave a faint smile as he recognized sitting in the middle of the turbaned chieftains, five on one side and five on the other, Hakimullah Mehsud. While the others had turbans which were blue, black, stripped and other mixed colors, Mehsud had a turban with a red band around a white one. Besides Mehsud, he recognized several other faces glaring at him, but could not remember their names.

No matter; this was it! He remembered Rasheed had said: "Show time!"

Since being assigned this mission, George wondered how he was going to accomplish it. Even now he had no plan. Dressed in Arab garb, how was he going to lift his gown that was like a small tent and deliver his noxious deadly gas without poisoning himself?

With twenty-two fierce eyes scrutinizing him from head to toe, Rasheed stood to the side delivering his favorable report. When

Rasheed finished, Mehsud lifted his hand in a sign of dismissal and Rasheed and his two body guards departed.

Now the man posing as Peter Cooper was left standing alone.

After an excruciating moment of silence, Mehsud spoke in English: "A few questions, Mr. Cooper. First, why are you here?"

George gasped, clutched his throat and as he faked a fainting spell, toppled to the wooden floor, belly first. The startled tribunal rose up and leaned over to see what the problem was, when George clutching his gown, pulled it up exposing his large hairy ass and with a mighty strain set off his best effort of a machine gun blaster that went rat-ta-tat-tat over and over until he was empty.

At first the surprised group of militants began to laugh at this ridiculous pitiful figure of a man who had fainted and farted in fear of them, but then the wave of the potent gaseous fog hit them causing them to sway one by one as they fell across the table retching heavily and delivering their breakfast mush onto the floor in loud gushes. The inside masked guards rushed to the table and were hit with the gas like an invisible wall; the last thing they remembered was that they had never smelled anything so odorous before they too crashed to the floor, their AK-47's clattering as they puked their guts out for the last time.

As the room quickly filled with the unbearable deadly stench, George held his breath as he gathered himself up and literally hit he door like a bowling ball. He stopped at the quizzical guards standing outside and using broken Pashto, told them they were wanted inside; they vanished inside and did not return. Rasheed and his two body guards were standing at the end of the steps looking surprised to see this fat man come barreling down the steps as if the house was on fire.

When George saw them, George hollered, "Rasheed! They want you back inside, now!"

Rasheed completely confused, said, "Why are you outside?"

"I am reporting to Akim Salim. (a name he made up.) That's what they told me. You had better hurry. They are impatient!"

Rasheed quickly ran up the steps and the two body guards obediently followed.

Now that he was outside and safe for the moment, he felt around under his left arm pit, finding his now itching implants, pushing the button that was supposed to alert the CIA that he had found Meshud so that they could send in the drones and finish the job. He had no sooner mashed the switch under his left arm when he heard a faint buzzing sound, looking up to see two flashes from a strange looking aircraft that had to be a drone. He instinctively threw himself to the ground as two rockets streamed overhead and crashed into the wooden building he had occupied just seconds before. At that time Rasheed and his two body guards were beginning to enter the building; what had once been a structure was now a huge orange fireball followed by billows of black and grey smoke.

Rasheed and one of the body guards disappeared, but one of the guards had lingered and was blown off his feet landing on his knees in the dirt and was grabbing his ears. George could not understand why that guard had not been vaporized also; perhaps he had delayed entering because he had doubts about being wanted inside.

Spotting the old Datsun that had brought them there, George got up and made for it as more rockets poured in obliterating everything where they hit; black and orange and red flashes similar to those he had seen when I.E.D.'s exploded in Iraq. He searched under the driver's seat, finding the keys where he had seen Rasheed put them; glad that those flowing gowns did not have pockets. The car engine started abruptly and George began to ease it out of the camp away from the pandemonium with survivors running for cover, in shock, hitting the ground after each explosion. Some were bleeding with loss of limbs while others sought cover. Tents were on fire and as were many of many of the former occupants. George hit his brakes to keep from running over a militant who lay in the road, his AK-47 a few feet from him. He had presence of mind to relieve the man of his automatic rifle. As he recovered the rifle, a voice shouted in Pashto, "Stop!"

It was that same bodyguard who had been with Rasheed, somehow surviving the blast, now lifting his rifle and pointing it at George when another series of explosions rocked the camp. George jumped back into the car, pushed in the clutch and shifted into first gear in an effort to pull away, when the body guard fired the rifle. The bullet tore through the back window and out the front just missing George's head, who now shifted into second gear picking up speed as shards of glass stung the back of his neck. The back wheels spun kicking up rocks causing the rear end to fishtail which worked in George's favor, as the body guard fired again missing the car. As more explosions hit the camp, George picked what looked like a goat trail for an exit and moved toward the mountains that were in the direction of Afghanistan. Frantically, he reached under his arm and pushed on a second button which was supposed to alert his team of Special Forces that he was heading home to Afghanistan whose border was only a few miles away. All he had to do was to take this path which wound around the mountain ahead, hope it was continuous without any gaps, maneuver around any Taliban militants who might be out head hunting and hope his call to Colonel Benson was received from his button pushing from under his left arm pit. So close, yet so far, with obstacles to overcome. As he was down shifting he heard the rat-ta-tat-tat from a real machine gun, bullets chipping rocks off the boulders imbedded in the mountain he was rounding. A glance in the rear view mirror told the story; a brown Toyota pickup was following him, the driver none other than the persistent body guard who had survived the recent holocaust destruction of the Taliban camp. He was alone driving with one hand on the steering wheel and the other on a machine pistol sticking outside his driver's window trying to stop George's escape.

The little Datsun straining to climb the mountain road was no match for the Toyota which was gaining on it. Above, the road took him into a cloud; the road became slippery with ice and below was a sheer drop off of a thousand feet. Several times the car veered to the edge of the road but George instinctively let off the gas and the little car coasted over the icy patch. It was cold and he could hear the gears of the Toyota grinding as if it was just behind him; only the numerous slippery curves kept the body guard from getting off a good shot.

Suddenly it dawned on George who now had the presence of mind that he was in serious danger of being killed. He could see the road several bends ahead and realized   all his pursuer had to do was to stop and blast away when he became into clear view. The driver must have seen the opportunity also; he stopped and got out of the Toyota waiting for George to come into full view as he rounded the curves ahead.

George had no choice but to chance it. As he came into view of the Toyota, the driver cut loose with a hailstorm of bullets which tore up the left back door, shattering the window, but miraculously missed George as he made it around that curve. Allah or God or both were good to him that time, but the driver of the Toyota got back into his truck and began his pursuit once again. He would not make the same mistake again; next time he would lead the Datsun with his pistol and carefully spray George with its deadly bullets.

Up ahead there was a sign indicating that he was approaching the Afghanistan border. George expected to see a border guard and a gate from which he could pass and maybe protection, but instead there was just a large rock that was too big for one person to move unless he was Samson.

End of the road; he would have to go on foot the rest of the way. He turned the Datsun half way around facing the sheer cliff, got out leaning his pilfered AK-47 up against the mountain side, putting the vehicle in neutral and easily pushing it over the sheer cliff thinking that maybe the relentless driver behind him would believe he had lost control, going off the road into the abyss below, bursting into flames, bounding off rocks and small trees, lighting up the area as it crashed downward.

Quickly George ran ahead hoping this ploy would work; hoping he would not run into militants, insurgents or terrorists, hoping the pursuer would give up, hoping his signal for help was received, hoping he was being tracked on Benson's GPS. He trotted on ahead and soon he was heading downward; his hopes increasing. Soon he would be out of harm's way.

Those hopes were shattered when once again bullets were zinging by him shattering the rocks to his left. Taking his weapon from his shoulder, George returned fire after ducking behind a sheer wall which provided little cover.

His tormentor had picked his spot with care; ahead for one hundred yards was an open road with no protection. He had full vision of George's meager hiding place while being able to hide behind a large boulder; all he had to do was to wait George out; to be patient.

George on the other hand was not sure how many bullets were left in his rifle, realizing that if other militants heard the shooting or if the ex-body guard had a cell phone, soon his help would arrive and George would be history. It was a no win situation. It would be even worse if the attacker had grenades.

A few minutes went by and then the attacker decided to end the stand-off; obviously an impatient man, he opened up with everything he had, bullets ricocheting everywhere, chips of rock gashed George's arms and face while George crouched closer to the mountain wall for safety. When he dared to peep out from behind the slender crevice, the body guard had stepped out from his barrier and was firing rapidly. Bullets flew everywhere again. George felt a sting in his lower side and was knocked backwards. Realizing that he had been hit he fired back emptying his rifle in the area of his attacker as blood was rapidly seeping through his gown. He shivered, suddenly realizing how cold it was up on the mountain, patches of snow everywhere; now he was worried. Taking a torn piece of his gown he plugged the bullet hole and with another torn pieced wrapped it around the wound the best he could. For a few minutes, his attacker was silent, figuring out his next move obviously not wanting to be tricked into exposing himself again in the line of fire.

The wind whistled and snow flurries whirled around the two men. Then the attacker began to fire again; maybe he had been reloading. George was out of bullets. Was this the end? Would just his head be shown on television around the world?

George shuddered at the thought. As he slowly eased down against the sheer wall of rock, he looked up to see a small tree growing out of the mountain. Then he was wracked with terrific pain as his vitals seized up.

For a few moments he lost consciousness, wondering just where he was when he came to.

The sound of gun fire shocked him back into reality, but as the firing sent more chips of stone and ricocheting bullets whizzing around him, George heard the thump, thump, thump that a helicopter makes. It was a Blackhawk gunship. He took off his turban in slow motion, exposing his shaved head, stretching it out, tying it to his rifle with an overhand knot, feebly waving it like a red flag, his heart racing; he might just make it. The answer came when the machine gun on the helicopter opened up and he could hear the hail of bullets destroying the defenseless area of his attacker as he was blown to bits.

Then there was only the thumping sound from the Blackhawk while he was being stared at by the pilot and co-pilot from a Plexiglas cockpit like welcome aliens from Mars, holding its place off the side of the mountain—a beautiful sight that would stick in his mind as long as he lived. George tried to rise, but being unable, sat down and pointed to the spot where he had taken a bullet which was now a bright red circle.

The pilot shook his head and the helicopter moved off out of sight. He lost track of time, but what seemed like a few minutes later he saw a U.S. Army soldier trotting down the pathway toward him. Was he dreaming? It was his friend, Sergeant Ziegfield who checked his bullet wound and said, "Pretty good patch job, George; now let me help you to your feet. There is a small convoy of pick-up trucks headed this way. They are bound to have surface to air missiles, so we need to get you out of here before they kill all of us."

Helped to his feet, the two staggered down the road until they reached a clearing with Ziggy supporting his friend. While George sat down, he saw the helicopter lowering a wire stretcher which landed next to him. He did not have to be told to crawl into it and lay still while Ziggy tied him down.

After that, he became unconscious and when he awoke he was in the hospital at Bagram Air Field; standing before him was Colonel Benson and Sergeant Ziegfield.

"How are you doing fella?" asked Benson. "You have lost a lot of blood, but is has been stopped for now. They don't have the facilities to handle your case, if you know what I mean, and I don't want a repeat of the one at Baltimore General; so George, you are being evacuated to where they have the medical facilities to operate. Here is one of your pills." He popped into George's mouth and gave him a glass of water to wash it down. "Maybe this will take care of the problem."

Two orderlies came and began pushing his bed on wheels out to an ambulance while Benson, walking alongside, continued talking. "I wanted to let you know the mission was a success, the camp was obliterated and it has been confirmed that Mehsud and his men died during the rocket attack. You did a good job; that threat to bomb American soil won't be carried out—at least, not by Mehsud."

"Thanks for coming to get me," said George weakly.

With a plasma bottle connected to his arm, George was carried to a transport plane complete with a medical team who stayed with him as he was flown out of Afghanistan, keeping him sedated. During the flight he came in and out of consciousness realizing that he was not the only wounded on board, but was accompanied by others missing their legs or arms, stumps being bandaged; the victims of I.E.D.s'.

CHAPTER THIRTY THREE

The Blessing

First taken to a combat hospital, the decision was made to fly Lieutenant George C. Murfrey to Walter Reed Hospital in Washington D.C. after his medical records were unsealed revealing his treatment for a stab wound at Gulfport Memorial Hospital deferring treatment to Baltimore General Hospital and later the devastation of the left wing at that hospital.

At Walter Reed they had a whole department designated to handle extremely contagious diseases and could quarantine safely even persons with unknown specified diseases. They had a team of specialists who were anxious to accommodate this unusual patient and eagerly awaited his arrival and if they could not solve his problem, they would find some specialist who could. George's secret was out.

While Lieutenant Murfrey was in flight, the doctors who would be treating this patient, boned up on all medical data of other known persons who had had similar diseases and this included the war hero buried at Arlington Cemetery, Private Fannie Mae McBride. It was decided that if they could not solve Lieutenant Murfrey's case, then they would petition to dig up McBride and perform an autopsy on her. Although Dr. Alphonse Aholie was up in age, and no longer head of the treatment of victims of dangerous gases, the specialists at Walter Reed notified Dr. Aholie that they were about to receive George Murfrey as their patient, picking his senile brain for any information he could give them which was mostly ranting and ravings about George being the "skunk man". Out of deference to their medical colleague Dr. Ahollie would be allowed to visit Lieutenant Murfrey and be present in the operating room when any surgery was performed with the wise proviso that he would not interfere or create a scene.

Dr. Aholie seemed to snap out of his senility after the news. No longer did he come to work at Baltimore General, just sitting in his chair, looking out his window over Chesapeake Bay, no longer walking around like a hunched over old man, but straightened up, greeting fellow doctors cordially and nurses with a gleam in his eye: His life was not over yet; inside he wanted to just bust out and holler. "Hooray!" Screw those so-called specialists at Walter Reed with their supercilious attitude toward him; how dare they tell him to keep quiet in the operating room or interfere with his lifelong findings which he intended to prove once and for all.

Aholie called downstairs where the medical records of George Cedric Murfrey were stored in archives, ordering every scrap of anything that dealt with his long standing nemesis, telling those nit wits in the basement he wanted those records immediately, if not sooner. Dr. Alphonse Krishna Aholie was not ready to die yet; no rocking chair for him and he had not better hear any of the employees call him, "the old man", either. He dialed a number at Walter Reed, talked to an ex-nurse of his, who remained loyal often remarking that the good doctor had been given a "bum rap", telling Nurse Brownlee to notify him as soon as they admitted a new patient, George C. Murfrey to their ward for which she sweetly agreed. "You can depend on me, Doctor," she said. "As soon as he comes in you will be notified."

On the long flight to the U.S., Lieutenant George Murfrey was in no danger of dying; as a matter of fact, the medical personnel were mildly amazed at the speed in which George's wound had ceased bleeding from the outside, now only minimal bleeding internally where the ricochet bullet had lodged in his colon. Pumped with antibiotics and filled with dripping plasma plus a sedative that knocked him out, George had an easy ride non-stop into Andrews Air Force Base, Maryland, doing so well, instead of being flown to Walter Reed by helicopter, he was transported to the hospital by ambulance.

At Walter Reed Hospital, George came out of his blissful sleep. He had been holding hands with a beautiful blonde angel; the stained glass windows of a cathedral formed the background when she smiled at him in an angelic way. He was smiling back squeezing her soft little hand, but something was not right: His eyes flew open as he surveyed the modern hospital room; overhead was a large panel TV, the bed had all kinds of controls including a button he could push to summon a nurse, on his right was a divan type couch where one could stretch out almost as comfortable as the patient, further to the left was a modern sink and faucet, a closet and a bathroom and across the room stood an old man dressed like a doctor!

As he tried to sit up suddenly, pain in his abdomen racked his body; the bliss of the pain pills suddenly vanishing. As he focused on the man he realized it was not a dream: It was an older version of Dr. Aholie, a man who had aged greatly in a short amount of time, standing there staring at him like some apparition. George croaked, "Help! Help me somebody!"

"Now boy, I am not going to hurt you; I just wanted to see if it was really you."

"Am I back in Baltimore General?"

"No. Boy. I wish you were; then we could see if you really are the "Skunk Man". Now quit your screaming; I am going now. It has been good to see you", said the old doctor whose face had wrinkled, his eyes had become bleary, his hair had turned white, thinning so much that only wisps of the white stuff hung in all directions, waving up and down from the breeze created by the air conditioner. But it was the high crackling voice that made George's hair rise up on the back of his neck, with cold sweat popping out on his brow.

As the doctor quietly left like a phantom in the night, George found the button to summons the nurse. He buzzed long and hard and within seconds came a middle aged brown haired nurse on the run swinging the door to his room open so hard it struck the door stop.

"I see you are awake, Lieutenant; what is the trouble?"

"That doctor, that doctor from Baltimore General was in here only he was old and decrepit. I thought I was seeing a ghost, but he really was here," said George in his high pitched voice always brought on by stress.

"Now calm down Lieutenant Murfrey. You just had a bad dream; there was no doctor here. Your doctor is Dr. Phillips who used to be over at the General, but he hasn't been in to see you yet. Now that you are awake, I will summon him if you like. He is in his office and asked to be notified as soon as you awakened."

The nurse picked up the telephone on the stand next to the bed and dialed a number. She said, "Doctor Phillips, you patient Lieutenant George Murfrey is awake and he would like to see you. I think he has either been dreaming or hallucinating. Okay, doctor, I will tell him."

After hanging up the nurse said, "Your doctor is on his way to see you."

While they waited for the doctor, George had his pulse taken, his temperature taken and was checked for other vital signs. When Dr. Phillips walked in, George recognized him immediately as one of the doctors in the operating room back at Baltimore General Hospital.

"I know you doctor; you were Dr. Aholie's partner at Baltimore General, I don't think I want you as my doctor. Can I get another doctor?"

"Calm down, Lieutenant Murfrey, I was the doctor who called off that operation. I am the only available specialist who has the expertise with the knowledge of you peculiar problem. You must be mistaken about Dr. Aholie being here."

George broke in, "Is he now white haired-- with lots of wrinkles and thinning messy hair and a crackly voice?"

"Sounds like him; I haven't seen him for quite a while." Dr. Phillips put his hand to his chin and said, "Maybe you are right; he may have been here—I wonder."

"Any way, Lieutenant, I see you have done quite well. The last I heard of you, you were in trouble with the law. Since then I see you have had an exemplary record in the Army. Congratulations!"

"I have viewed your x-rays and you have a bullet lodged in you colon which has received considerable damage. That bullet must come out immediately and the colon repaired. If you stomach has been punctured, you could be in a lot of trouble so we need to operate as soon as possible. Right now you are full of antibiotics, but you still are not safe from gangrene which could be fatal. I have scheduled you for surgery tomorrow morning. However, it appears you are a healthy specimen, no fever and all your vital signs are normal. The operation should go well."

"No exploratory surgery to see if I am a skunk?"

"No, of course not. This is Walter Reed Hospital, not Baltimore General. I am sorry Lieutenant but we cannot feed you before we operate, but I will see that you get some ice if you are thirsty."

"That's alright doctor. I don't feel hungry right now."

Back in his office, Dr. Rance Phillips got Dr. Aholie on the phone. "Against my better judgment, Doctor Aholie, I gave you permission to be present when we operate on Lieutenant George Murfrey, now I find that you were in his room scaring him. I am almost to the point of barring you from the operating room."

"Look Phillips, I did not scare the patient. I was told I had visitation rights; I merely slipped into his room to make sure he was the right person we once knew and after I verified that he was, I left. I did not cause a disturbance and if he had not awakened, he would have never known I was there. I gave you my word that I would be just a spectator and not cause any trouble. I have had all Murfrey's records sent up from Archives and could be of some help when the time comes. You never know what will happen during an operation and in case there is something unusual that you find, I might be able to add to your expertise; we are both medical doctors with the same goal."

"I hope so," said Dr. Phillips. "Just remember your word; stay quiet and keep out of the way."

"No problemo," said Dr. Aholie smiling as he put the phone gently back in its cradle.

Meanwhile, Dr. Phillips muttered out aloud, "That bastard is going to cause us trouble; I know him." He hit the button on his intercom to the outer office and said, "Shirley, would you please call Edwards, Head of Security and tell him I need to have a conference with him."

Bright and early the next morning, George was prepped and made ready for surgery, all tests had been completed in an expertise fashion; there was no joking around or forgotten procedures; George was treated with the greatest respect. This hospital would encounter none of the problems that plagued the Baltimore General Hospital at the time George Murfrey had been a reluctant patient. The wing of the hospital where the operation would take place was sealed with its own air system; patients with radiation sickness, highly communicable diseases and unknown causes like Murfrey's malady would be safely handled without fear of contaminating other parts of the hospital. The exhaust system was the finest money could buy being able to avoid clogging while filtering the smallest particles in a matter of seconds. Space suits and gas masks that covered the whole body with its' own breathing apparatus were available if needed; robotic arms reaching into a glass partitioned operating room could be used if the danger justified it.

Today, Dr. Rance Phillips saw no need for the use of the robotic arm, nor did he think that donning the "space suit" a necessity either. Instead, he ordered the gray charcoal filtered masks for all personnel in the operating room and had regular gas masks within reach for all. Dr. Alphonse Aholie, who had donned one of the gray masks that only covered the mouth and nose, voiced his objection and issued a dire warning to all that attended including the two security guards present: "Everyone had better beware! You don't know who you are dealing with; this man is not a normal human being, but a throw-back that baffles science. If he cuts loose with his gas, grab your gas masks and you had better have them near you; you won't get much time. He is the 'Skunk Man' you probably hers so much about. He is real!"

George Murfrey was wheeled into the operating room without ceremony catching a glimpse of that wild eyed old man glaring at him behind the gray surgical mask with a green cap covering most of his sparse white hair except that which stuck out billowing as he rocked from side to side. It was at this time that George began praying for God to send his angels for protection and that in the name of Jesus he would be healed. No sooner had he uttered his prayer, the antitheist slapped a plastic mask over his nose and mouth, turning on the gas and George was quickly put under losing all consciousness.

Dr. Phillips lost no time cutting through layers of fat and muscle to get to the damage colon. He quickly found the bullet and began to remove fragments of Afghanistan rock and then he said, "What is this?"

Dr. Alphonse Aholie who had been dozing while on his feet quickly came awake saying, "Huh, huh, huh. What is it? Did you find the skunk glands?"

He forcefully pushed a nurse out of the way and stuck his head over the opened abdomen and exclaimed in a high cracking voice, "You are operating in the wrong place; try the asshole, you fool.!"

Fortunately for George and all concerned, when Doctor Aholie grabbed a scalpel out of the pan containing instruments, one of the security guards had quickly come up behind Aholie and as Dr. Aholie said, "Here let me show you." The guard grabbed the doctor with one hand and with the other pulled him back.

Dr. Aholie was feebly struggling with guard saying in a tired crackly voice, "Let me go." But the guard took the scalpel from him easily, holding him—an anti-climax to the operation.

"I think I have found what made Murfrey's flatulence so different. Nurse hand me two large clamps." Dr. Phillips turned to the struggling Dr. Aholie and said, "Dr. Aholie, if you would stop struggling, I will show you the cause of Murfrey's unusual problem. It is not skunk glands, but this section of his colon."

Dr. Phillips held up a three foot section of George's colon that had been surgically removed placing it in a stainless steel pan while he joined the two ends of Murfrey's colon with self dissolving stitches. Dr. Aholie for once, kept quiet and stared at the removed section of colon. On it were three large black spots the size of a half dollar each. This section that lay on the table was hard and rigid as if petrified, smelling to high heaven.

"Nurse, put that piece of colon in a tight glass jar, and send it to the laboratory for testing. I don't see any more of those black spots, so I am going to sew him up. I think I may have just saved Lieutenant Murfrey's life. If that cancer had metastasized, it would have spread throughout his body. Best I can explain it Doctor Aholie is that when gas passed through that putrefied half rotten area of his colon, it took on that terrible smell that made whoever smelled it, sick. I don't think it was ever poisonous, but as it grew, the smell got worse. He turned to one of his assisting doctors and said, "Dr. Paul, close up the cavity and make your stitches as small as possible so that the Lieutenant won't have an ugly scar." Pulling his surgical gloves off over at the sink, he said,"

Come on Alphonse, let's go get a cup of coffee; I will explain it all to you. I don't think our boy will have any more gaseous problems."

Dr. Alphonse Krishna Aholie followed him meekly out the swinging door.

"So much for the theory of the man with skunk glands, but, then how do you explain Big Fannie Mae McBride? Perhaps she could be dug up! There had been some talk of doing just that before the operation." Dr. Aholie would look into that.

George, spending the night in Intensive Care with no complications, was brought back to his room. He hurt in spite of pain medicine, especially when two brutes from therapy got him out of bed, making him walk a few feet promising to return for two sessions the next day.

Dr. Phillips dropped by with x-rays and pictures of the removed colon proud and cheerful over his accomplishment. "Lieutenant Murfrey, I have got good news for you: No more will you have that bad gas problem, as you can see in this picture of the section of your colon we removed, these dark spots were what caused it all. You can consider yourself lucky; that bullet that lodged near this petrified mass was a miracle. Had it gone anywhere else, we might have never found these spots until it was too late. You probably had this problem before you were born, a birth defect if you will, and over the years it grew and grew and your situation got worse and worse."

"You mean doc that my gas was never deadly?"

"I mean in my opinion, that it was never poisonous, but it did cause extreme vomiting from any one in close contact with it as you may well know."

"Then I am not a murderer."

"No Lieutenant, I have read your medical history and as far as I can see, you never caused anyone's death; that is my medical opinion."

"Can I get that in writing?" asked George.

"It will be in your medical report and you can request a copy. It was a miracle that saved your life; you should live to a ripe old age; far as I could tell other the other sections of your colon are quite healthy.

"Doctor, it was an answer to my prayers. I give all the credit to God."

"Hey Lieutenant, I played a little part in it. I have a surprise for you; during the operation it became necessary to cut through your abdomen and that funny looking pig tail of a belly button was removed. I was not able to duplicate it so I did my best to construct a normal one. I hope you don't mind."

"No I don't mind; I always hated that belly button. I feel it was under God's direction, you did all those miracles, but I still thank you." laughed George.

The next day, George was visited by Colonel Alan Benson and Sergeant Ziegfield. "George, I heard about the successful operation. Congratulations!"

"God's work," said George. "It was the power of prayer; I owe it all to the Lord."

"That's good, George. That was some mission; from what the CIA boys tell me it was a complete success."

"Yeah, they dropped the ball. They were not supposed to attack until I pushed the button and sent the signal. I barely got out with my life. If I had not already done my business, I would have been blown up with the militants. What have they to say to that?"

"I discussed it with them and they told me that you must have accidently pushed the button that morning before you went in to meet the tribunal and Mehsud. He is confirmed dead, by the way."

"I never pushed any button until later and it was on purpose, but I am so overjoyed and happy that I will let it pass, but I will tell you this: I don't want to run anymore mission for those spooks--ever!" George grabbed a glass of water from the small side table and sipped it through his bent straw. "I have been told that I can eat red beans and rice, and don't forget the Andouille sausage, and I may still pass gas, but it will not injure any one, so I guess you can keep those purple pills; on second thought maybe you should give me a bottle of them to keep; you know; just in case." He looked up at the Colonel and said, "Alan and Ziggy, I am as normal as you two are!"

"That is not saying much," said Ziggy.

Colonel Benson, happy to see George so buoyant, said, "The CIA boys will be by later to debrief you; then they will be through with you. Remember, I told you that that may be your last mission? Well George it will probably be mine also; I am submitting my retirement papers while we are all in the clear. Any thoughts on what you would like to do in the future in the Army before I do retire?"

"Yes, I have given it much thought. I don't think I want to ride around as a machine gunner in convoys any more. They are withdrawing the troops from Iraq anyway, so there won't be much demand for those convoys. No, there will be suicide bombers as long as they can get those dummies to kill themselves for a promise of seventy virgins after death. I have that skill spotting suicide bombers before they can detonate. Perhaps I can be of some help there to the world or maybe I can become an instructor teaching how to also spot I.E.D.'s. I have had experience in that, also. What do you think?"

"George, I will see what I can do. They could certainly use your expertise."

The men from the CIA debriefed George on the Pakistan mission going away satisfied that the Taliban terrorist, Mehsud, would never get his chance to plant bombs in American cities. They swore that George had alerted them by pressing the alert button implanted under his left arm pit, assuring him that before he left Walter Reed Hospital, the apparatus would be removed as they wanted it back. They did not tell George that through their technology, they had been able to see images on their computers that showed exactly when he had reached the camp in North Waziristan, Pakistan and even when he entered the meeting with the Taliban tribunal which included Mehsud; George never saw them again.

While he was being walked up and down the corridor by the therapists from hell, twice a day, plus being put through all other kinds of devilish exercises with huge different colored wide strips of rubber, the honorific pain gradually subsided and George could tell his strength was coming back.

While he was watching "The Price Is Right" on the overhead television, Colonel Benson and Sergeant Ziegfield walked in the room.

"First, let me pin this on you; you earned it." He took out a Purple Heart Ribbon and pinned it on George's pajamas."

"Good," said George. "A Purple Heart-- instead of a purple pill. Dr. Phillips says I am definitely cured."

"George, I have good news: When you get out of here, you will become an instructor teaching how to spot suicide bombers and road side bombs. I am working it out for your two buddies who came into the Army with you so they will be within the agreed sixty miles from where you teach; speaking of your two buddies, I have a surprise for you— just outside the door is Major Maybellene Modine and Sergeant Iverson Hanson. Shall I send them in?"

"Just a second, Alan Benson, I know you too well; you have got something up your sleeve; you want something in return, so what is it?"

"George, I can't fool you can I. It is like this: The raid on the camp at North Waziristan will go down as being destroyed by rockets after you located it and we picked up your signal. The other mission was written up as death of the terrorists by Corporal Jacob Bannister who stabbed the insurgents in self-defense. That is the way it will go down should there be any inquiries or Congressional hearings on the matter. Dr. Rance Phillips has stated in your medical records, that you never had a problem with poisonous gas and in his expert opinion, he never found any indications of any deadly gas despite the misguided theories of Dr. Alphonse Aholie. On top of that your medical files once again will be sealed "Top Secret". Those, two missions must be kept secret by you; you are not to breathe a word about them to anyone else ever! How does that suit you?"

"Like a new suit," said George. "I have been given a new life and am thankful. Besides that I believe I have found a home in the Army."

Later after George had been forewarned that he would have two visitors, he was prepared. When they entered, he pretended sleeping and awakened slowly speaking with a very weak voice, "Is that you Mutt? Who is that foxy lady with you? Have you got a new girlfriend?'

"Cut out the crap," said Mutt. "I heard you got shot in the stomach, but it must have been your head that got the bullet. If you aren't up to this visit, we can come back."

412

"No wait a minute, Mutt; I believe I do faintly recognize that beautiful girl with you; she kind of resembles Maybelline Modine, except the Maybelline I knew once was a Captain and what happened to her? Gone is that figure, I used to hug and chalk. Come here you gorgeous creature and give me a kiss and a hug without the chalk," said George suddenly showing great recovery.

"Now look who is different," said May with a broad smile on her face as she bent over to give George a long kiss and a hug. "The George Murfrey I knew was not so bold; he was even a little shy. I think Mutt is right, that bullet must have made a turn into your brain, or maybe that doctor gave you a little too much pain medicine"

With Mutt on the left side of the bed and May on the right, George extended his hands to both and said, "I have good news for both of you. While I was in the lonely mountains of Afghanistan being shot at by this Taliban nut who would not give up, I thought it was the end, but I prayed for survival and I found out prayer works and here I am."

"I guess it wasn't your time yet, George," said Mutt.

"That is not all I prayed for, Mutt," said George. "I prayed that He would cure me of this malady, this embarrassing problem I have had since childhood and guess what!"

"This man is delirious," said Mutt. "We better call the doctor."

"No. Let him finish," said May as she squeezed his hand.

"They operated on me and took out part of my colon and the doctor says in that section was the reason I have had those gaseous problems and that now I am cured."

"You mean to tell me that no longer will you pass that foul smelling gas? I can't believe it," said Mutt.

"Believe it; I am not saying I won't react to my favorite, Red beans and rice with Andouille sausage, but it won't be as bad; no longer will people fall to the floor and start losing their cookies along with other bad things. It is the power of prayer—why don't you try it some time. The doctor says I never caused anyone's death; how about that and I have the medical records to prove it. Why I am as normal as you are Mutt; no I take that back, I am better than normal."

413

George went on telling how his life was going to be different from now on; how he had talked Colonel Benson into taking him off the firing line of combat duty and would be an instructor; that there was a place for May and Mutt to be with him. He rambled on and on; just could not stop talking; talking about the future; talking about the past. It was old home week; at one point, a nurse came in and told them that they had to hold it down; the other patients were being disturbed.

"Whatever you gave this fellow, please give me some of it," said Mutt to the nurse.

"It is called being cured," said George. "It called having a heavy load taken off you; it is called being blessed; it is called having your prayers being answered; it is called being saved. Hallelujah!

He looked at May and said, "You sure are beautiful. I fell in love with that sweet little dumpling girl with freckles around her nose—that's it! Its' your nose; the hump is gone!

"I took a leave and had plastic surgery or as you would say, I got a nose job."

"You sure did! Mutt, could you leave us for a moment or two, I have got something I need to say to May."

"They don't allow that kind of stuff in the hospital. Are you sure you are strong enough for that? I can stand outside the door as a guard and not let anybody in. while you say what you have to say," said Mutt grinning like the proverbial Cheshire Cat.

"Its' not that, Mutt; you are way off base. Okay, you can stay; you are my best friend and we are all family. Here is what I wanted to say to Maybelline in private: May, will you marry me?"

Before May could answer, Mutt said, "I knew it. I knew it! What did I tell you! I knew this was coming!"

"Quiet! Mutt! May how about it?"

She squeezed his hand softly and said sweetly, "George Murfrey, the answer is yes! I have loved you from the first time I laid eyes on you in that English class at JD when you were so hung over from being out on the town with this devil that you could hardly keep from falling out of your seat. The answer is yes. Yes. Yes. Yes! I will marry you, and don't you say another word, Mutt Hanson."

"Whew!" said George, "I am glad that is over. Now that is the power of prayer. You ought to try it sometime, Mutt."

Mutt said grinning from ear to ear, "I am real happy for you George. It is kind of sad that the old 'Fart's' Murfrey is gone. I liked that boob, but while you are on the subject, I will tell you this: I too, have started going to church. I even went last Sunday."

"You gotta be kidding. What was the sermon about?"

"The preacher did not say," said Mutt. "But it was a good one."

THE END

EPILOGUE

After several weeks of rehabilitation, George was pronounced fit for duty much to the puzzlement of the doctors; he was a fast healer. Part of his rehab consisted of Officer training wherein he learned table manners, little things such as using the right fork, keeping his left hand in his lap while eating, only cutting no more than three pieces of meat at meat a time and the size of the meat cut could be chewed in about three or four chews. He was given leadership courses and what to expect as an officer. May was a big help during this period having recently gone through Officer Candidate School.

George had been insistent that the army continue to honor the "buddy system", Mutt being transferred for duty in the area as well as May. The Army made Mutt an instructor, teaching the care and upkeep of armored vehicles, after he proved himself with the Bradley tank in northern Iraq that had been worthless until he saw to it that it was repaired and then taking it upon himself, to see that all the other tanks were inspected and repaired. It was a first for Mutt; at last he had found something in which he excelled.

First Lieutenant George C. Murfrey and Major Maybellene Modine were married by an Army Chaplin with all the pomp and circumstance befitting the marriage of two officers, both in full dress uniforms. George with his Purple Heart and Bronze Star along with his other ribbons hanging on his uniform made quite an impression; a copy of a picture taken with his bride being sent to The Sun Herald in his home town. It was a gala event with Colonel Alan Benson giving the bride away, Mutt Hanson acting as Best Man. Master Sergeant Alfred Ziegfield, his wife and three children attended along with Dr. Rance Phillips, Mrs. Agnes Murfrey giving her complete approval of this union.

Within a year of marriage, May conceived and nine months later had a normal little boy, named George Jr., who was followed by a little girl with a perfect nose two years later. She was named Florence for no reason at all except that the couple liked the name.

After being made an instructor teaching how to spot I.E.D.'s and suicide bombers, George became recognized as an expert, being loaned

416

to Israel, Great Britain and Russia, sharing his expertise with those countries who were having problems with fanatics blowing themselves up taking the lives of innocent citizens along with them.

Mutt, seeing the marital bliss between George and May, tried marriage on his own, resulting in divorce. The marriage never had a chance; the floozy blonde, Mutt betrothed, felt betrayed; the whirlwind romance that started in a barroom ran out of the hot steam; they never settled down. Mutt, who went for voluptuous heavily endowed women got back on the horse after being thrown, marrying a beautiful brunette this time. That marriage lasted five years. Neither had a clue why the marriage failed; they just did not get along or see eye to eye. During that turbulent interval of time, Mutt reconciled with his father, Dr. Peter Hanson; the only plus in Mutt's life during those tumultuous marriage years unless becoming a dutiful God father to George's son, George Jr. He never missed a birthday and sent gifts to the little boy for Christmas. Uncle Mutt as junior called him was a frequent visitor in the Murfrey household.

When little Florence was born, Master Sergeant Alfred Ziegfield was named as her God father. Although having a family of his own, he never forgot Florence's birthdays either.

The last time Alan Benson was seen or heard from was at George and May's wedding. Ziggy kept in touch reporting that Alan Benson had relocated in the upper peninsula of Michigan spending his time catching Northerns and Pike.

Agnes Murfrey would not leave her home on the Gulf Coast but made periodic trips to visit the happy couple and her grandchildren. She went on to become a grand Master at the game of Bridge having won many tournaments across the land.

As for Big Jake Bannister, who could not wait to get out of the Army after his four years of enlistment was up, went back to the Mississsppi Gulf Coast troubling law enforcement with his many bar fights, emerging the victor having whipped anyone dumb enough to take him on, talk back to him or even make eye contact while he was downing a cool one. Ironically it was an Air Force Captain who shot and killed Jake before Jake could inflict any harm on the Captain at

Beemer's Tavern, a raunchy redneck bar in D'Iberville, Mississippi; Jake had been about to use the wrong end of a twenty-one ounce pool stick on his quarry at the time.

On one occasion at George's home he and Mutt while reflecting on their past experiences, both agreed that even the bad times were good.

"You know George," said Mutt. "You were lucky to have been cured; most of us go through life carrying heavy baggage, we are unable to get rid of. In my case, my mother died when I was two; my father tried to literally whip me into line, but failed miserably. I guess he did the best he could, but from what I have learned over the years, that is why I was so aggressive always into fighting."

"You have that self-diagnosis down pretty pat," said George. "I have been asked how I was able to calmly shoot someone back in my convoy days in Iraq while I always seem to panic on other occasions. I think the fear of the unknown gets to me; especially when I have time to ponder over it, I tend to over imagine what is going to happen—too much imagination. When I fired my rifle or machine gun, there wasn't time; it was either do it or else. I just did it; that's all; it was like a sudden car wreck that seems like a dream while it is happening. Of course all those trials and tribulations I had gone through prior to joining the Army had an effect. Thank God I was wounded, almost dying; it was worth it in the end. Never a day goes by, I don't thank the good Lord and also, I might add, Doctor Rance Phillips for finding the cause of my life long misery".

"Glad you said that; God has been good to us worthless bums," said Mutt. "I wonder why."

"That is something, I guess we will never understand," commented Mrs. Agnes Murfrey who had just walked in to hear the profound discussion. I always saw some good in George, but I missed the boat on you Mutt. I will say this: You turned out to be a good friend, not only to George, but to May and the kids. Agnes reluctantly admitted to Mutt that she had been wrong about him. "I called you 'False Grits' once and I was wrong," said Agnes. "You have been a good loyal friend to my son and I take back what I said about you.

"That's alright, Mrs. Murfrey," laughed Mutt. "I never was one who liked grits; give me hash brown potatoes any day. And don't go getting mushy on me yet. I still have a long way to go."

"Amen on that!" said George.

FINIS

See Website at http://www.falsegrits.con